I KEEP MY TRUE LOVE IN THE BASEMENT / REMIX

ALEXANDER ENGEL-HODGKINSON

This is a work of fiction. All the characters, organizations, and events portrayed in this novel are either products of the author's imagination or are used fictitiously.

I KEEP MY TRUE LOVE IN THE BASEMENT/REMIX
Copyright © 2018 by Alexander Engel-Hodgkinson

ISBN 978-1-989331-03-3
Art by Alexander Engel-Hodgkinson

Published by
Dark Brothers Incorporated

PARENTAL ADVISORY

'I Keep My True Love in the Basement/REMIX' contains some strong violence, disturbing horror content, strong sexuality, moderate profanity, and other themes intended for mature readers 17 and up.

Author's Comment

Well, it's finally here--/REMIX, now in paperback! Excited to finally have it in this format, because so far /REMIX is personally my favourite of all my standalone novels so far (though The Final Apocalypse Saga will always be my baby). It's my most atmospheric, and possibly the smartest story I've written so far. Hmm. Plus it's dripping with that 80's cyberpunk aesthetic that I personally just love, so perhaps I'm a bit biased. This is one of those stories I've written that could potentially have a sequel, but so far I haven't thought of a worthy successor yet, so until I do—and it will be a long time before I ever do, if I do—just enjoy /REMIX as the solo tale that it is.

00: Hollow

[BEGIN TRANSMISSION]
Her face appeared on the screen. Her cobalt eyes glistened as tears streamed down her face. She looked regretful for what she was about to do, yet she remained steadfast. "Hi... baby... I... I wish I could turn this message into a happy one. But I can't. I just can't. I can't take it anymore. If I spend another minute in this apartment, I'll go insane. We've been holed up in here for too long and I just can't stand it anymore. Not after what I've seen. I love you... but you're scaring me. I can't live the rest of my life like this. That's why I can't stay."

With a sniffle, voice breaking, she added, "I'm sorry."

The message ended.

Altieria City—2068 A.D.
Heartbreaker Motel

The same girl from the video message had been found dead in her motel room. Whoever did it sure made a mess of things: the walls had been streamlined with blood and the beige carpet was now darkened black with gore. Her body had been torn open—the front of her was now missing, and what remained of her had been sloppily hollowed of its insides, with only mushy portions of her brain, intestines, heart, and stomach left in grisly piles within. All of her joints had been crushed. She was reduced to a spread-eagled mass of shredded flesh and bone, sprawled in the soaked carpet in a wide-spanning crimson circle.

Robotic CSI units hovered over the crime scene, snapping images into their shared network left and right. They resembled marionettes dressed in the standard blue uniform with 'CSI' written across their backs in bold yellow, and their heads were large crystal-like balls with smooth surfaces with their designated numbers scrawled across the front. Two relatively human detectives were present, staring down at the woman's corpse.

"It's a masterpiece of the macabre," one of them said. He was short, thin. Short brown hair. Middle-aged, fifty-two. Always had a condescending sneer on his face. Meet Detective Lucas Barstow.

"I've seen better," the other one replied. He was the exact opposite of Barstow. Tall and broad-shouldered. Short black hair with a white lightning bolt streaking across the left side of his head. Younger than Barstow by two years. His facial expression was always serious and concentrated, even when he was cracking jokes. His deadpan deliveries and casual, care-free personality made him infamous in a precinct with formality and a somewhat sterile lack of humanity coursing through its veins. Meet Detective Jason Orion. "This one seems kinda... what's the word I'm looking for? ...Uninspired. Compared to the Gein case. Remember the Gein case?"

Barstow scoffed, ignoring his partner's reference to a case that they weren't even alive for. "'Uninspired.'" He gestured at the corpse again, as if Orion hadn't noticed it. "Look at this. The killer took the time to hollow her out, for the most part. With the exception of the organs I'm assuming he damaged while he was killing her."

"Maybe he needed a donor. Or maybe he's a merchant on the black market. Human organs are all the rage these days."

"Maybe," Barstow said.

"She's a married woman, right? Er... *was* a married woman. What was her name again? Elsa something."

Barstow looked at the ID in his hand and recited the basics: "Elsa Mary Scott. Aged thirty-five. Fifty-one inches tall. Ninety-seven pounds. *Was*, anyway."

"Elsa Scott," Orion repeated with a slow nod. "Do you think her husband killed her?"

"Why would you think that?"

Orion referred to a holographic report board he'd just snatched off one of the CSI units as it droned by. "She filed for divorce two days ago. Left her husband three days before then."

"You don't say..."

"I know it's a bit of a stretch, but our killer could be one pissed-off husband." Orion glanced at the corpse again, noting the smashed joints and the odd way her remains had been splattered about. "Looks aggressive enough, you know?"

Barstow stroked the stubble on his chin thoughtfully. Cocked his head to the side. "Either scenario could work, I guess."

"What d'ya say, partner? Should we report back to

headquarters and then split up?"

"I'll take the merchant lead. You tell the unlucky husband, and while you're at it, see if you can get any answers out of him. And for God's sake, Orion, nobody likes an asshole—try to be sympathetic. Give it to him nice and easy."

"Nice and easy," Orion said with a dutiful nod. "Gotcha."

01: Widower

Scott Residence

As soon as the introductions were out of the way, and Orion was allowed into Franklin Scott's apartment, he sat down in the spacious living room with the victim's husband and cut right to the chase: "Mr. Scott, your wife was murdered yesterday in her hotel room. She was smashed, cut open, and had all of her internal organs removed—either to be donated to some sick cause, or to be sold like a piece of raw meat on the black market." He added sincerely, "I'm sorry for your loss."

Franklin Scott gaped at him with bulging eyes. It took him a good minute to process what Orion had just thrown in his face. "I... uh... um... is... is this a joke?"

"Mr. Scott, I may have a morbid sense of humour, but I don't joke about murder cases." Orion paused. Then he sighed and said, "Okay, I'm going to be completely honest with you. That's a lie. I... sometimes I suppose I get a little carried away with my jokes about the deceased," he said a little shamefully, turning his head to avoid eye contact. Then he quickly regained his formal posture and cleared his throat. "But I promise, sir, this is no joke. You wife really was murdered."

Franklin started blubbering. Orion figured it was an understandable reaction. He sat quietly for a few minutes, waiting for Franklin to finish sobbing. Unfortunately, Orion wasn't so patient. He gave him three minutes, and after those three minutes, Franklin still had plenty more tears to shed. Orion was sympathetic, but he wasn't going to wait all day for answers. "Mr. Scott, I know it's difficult to grasp—"

"I... I've got the grasp on the situation," Franklin stuttered as he wiped his eyes on his sleeves. Orion offered him a tissue, and he accepted it. "Thank you." As he dried his eyes, Franklin continued, "I was hoping things wouldn't turn out like this."

"Like what?"

"This," Franklin said.

"...Are you saying you may have anticipated your wife's

murder?"

"Well, no..."

"Then what are you saying?"

"I'm just saying... I mean..." Franklin paused, trying to get the wording right in his head. Orion had to wait longer than he'd expected from a man with Franklin's IQ level, but finally, Franklin said, "It's hard to say without making myself sound responsible. I'm no murderer. Oh. What I mean is: what kind of man wants an unpleasant future for his wife?"

"Lots of men I know. But they never killed their wives. Just divorced them."

"What? You can't possibly be accusing me of—"

"No, no," Orion said, keeping a casual air about him. He wanted to be as friendly as possible with him. It was his way of getting answers. Most of the time, that particular approach worked. "I get what you mean. You wanted things to turn out well for your wife and yourself."

"Right. Exactly," Franklin said with a nod. "She and I have been having problems lately. I guess I couldn't blame you for putting me on the list of suspects."

"That's good. Makes things less personal."

"I loved my wife. Even during this difficult time."

"Explain it for me."

Franklin hesitated.

"Go on."

Franklin sighed. Sniffled. "I'd recently invested more time than usual in my job. I'm a robotics engineer for Altieria Corporation. They say I'm one of their best, though I don't like to boast. I stayed up for countless hours, working in my division and at home. I took caffeine shots to keep myself awake. More time to work. Less time for Elsa. As any man knows, women don't like to be ignored for long periods of time. She... she and I started to argue. I made so many broken promises. White lies. Even empty threats, but—"

"What kind of threats?"

"Small ones. I never threatened my wife with violence. I'm no ogre. I just... I said if she didn't give me my space, then I would leave her. I don't know what had come over me at the time."

"Oh," Orion said, eyebrows raised. "That'd do it."

Franklin shook his head. "Perhaps it was all that adrenaline from the caffeine shots. It affected my thinking. I was so angry."

"So she filed for divorce after one fight? A bit of an overreaction, don't you think?"

"You don't understand. In our whole fifteen years of marriage, Elsa and I *never* fought before. We had little arguments here and there, of course—what couple hasn't?—but we had never before raised our voices or uttered petty threats like we did that night. It affected us both deeply. She doesn't handle stress very well."

"I can see that."

"She wanted to leave shortly after that. She took my threat far more seriously than I would have liked. She'd mentioned it at dinnertime—the first time I'd actually sat down for dinner in three weeks—and when I came home late the next night, she was gone, and she'd taken only her essentials with her, leaving behind a video message among her non-essentials. A recording of her goodbyes."

"Oh?" Orion said. "Mind if I take a look at it?"

"I-I would show you. Believe me; I want to help you find the bastard who killed my Elsa. But... I... lost it."

That immediately struck Orion as suspicious. "What do you mean, you lost it?"

Franklin looked like an egg under a ton of bricks. "I broke it."

"You broke it? Why?"

"It destroyed me, alright?" Franklin snapped. "That message broke me, more than you could possibly understand. I threw it across the room, and it... and it broke against the wall. I wasn't thinking at the time."

Orion sighed. *Easy, the man was emotional,* he thought. *...Or hiding evidence.* He cleared his throat. "I guess I can't entirely blame you, given the circumstances. She left you. Disappears for five days. Files for divorce somewhere in between. Turns up murdered on the sixth day." Before Franklin could ask, Orion added, "I did some digging."

Franklin stared at him with glazed eyes.

Orion didn't like the way he was being looked at. The man's look wasn't threatening—just downright depressing. So Orion focused on something else. The intricate lava lamp in the corner of the room by the flat screen TV. Surreal dragons—blue, red, pink, purple, blue—danced in a three-foot glass tube, breathing flames that sparkled like glitter. A framed picture of Elsa Scott hung above the

TV; blond, fair, beautiful, with bright blue eyes.

He turned to the panoramic view of the city provided by the wall-to-ceiling windows. A neon jungle. Dense, brilliant—unpredictable. And with it, a towering horizon of animated media crawling across its buildings. Christ knows where its innumerable roads and pathways lead. They could spiral up toward the smog-filled sky levels where rich megalomaniacs and soulless satellites hover over a city they consider theirs; or down into the darkest depths of the lowest maintenance levels where society's rejects and outlaws gather.

Orion turned again, glancing over his shoulder at the frosted glass wall that stretched across the apartment, concealing what must have been a quarter of the rental space behind it. "What's that?"

Franklin snapped out what must have been a daze. "Oh, that's just my lab. Like I said, I bring work home with me sometimes."

"Oh, really? Why is it frosted over?"

"It's a climate-controlled area. I need to keep it cool. I have certain materials that require such an environment."

"Can I see it?"

"I'd rather you not. It's Company policy that no outsiders see all projects that are currently in development. I am also of the mind that prefers people don't see my work until it's completed."

Orion nodded, understanding. These days, a cop had clearance to go against the homeowner's wishes and search the premises—if they felt it necessary. Orion was curious, and Franklin didn't hit all of the right buttons, but Orion figured he'd save the man the grief.

"You'll find her killer, won't you? My wife..."

"Yes, my partner and I are on it. Are you absolutely sure there's nothing more you can tell me?"

"Nothing springs to mind, unfortunately," Franklin replied.

"No rivals at the Company?"

"None who would do this."

"No one in the organ market?"

"O-of course not!" Franklin snapped.

"Easy," Orion said. "No offense intended. Just looking for answers."

"Right," Franklin said, lowering his head, ashamed by his outburst. "I apologize."

"No sweat." Orion stood up and handed him his card. "Here's my number. Call it if something comes up."

Franklin's head was still lowered. Orion could hear him starting to sob again.

"I'll see myself out." Orion headed for the door. Paused beside Franklin. Placed a caring hand on his shoulder. "My deepest condolences for your wife. Don't worry. We'll find the bastard—or *bastards*—responsible."

02: Looney

Takuo Market

On ground-level, it was Chinatown. It was a fairly busy place with vendors and shops open to anyone. People shuffled up and down the wide streets under a canopy of holographic signage and burning ornaments that were strung across the gap between blocks of metal, glass, and brick. Gouts of steam rose up from sidewalk grates and storm drains, enshrouding the streets of Chinatown in a mysterious white veil. Despite the crowd and the appropriately oriental chimes ringing through the streets, Chinatown was relatively calm.

It wouldn't take long for a cop to get underground if he knew the trick to it. Fortunately, Barstow had it memorized. He just had to look like anything that wasn't affiliated with any law enforcement agency. With his LE magnum tucked away in his pants, hair slicked back to reveal an old skull tattoo on his broad forehead (back in his wild teenage years), and a stereotypical biker punk outfit consisting of a speed jacket, fingerless gloves, and a fishnet shirt; he was good to go.

Knowing where to go was the other part of the trick. After declining a vendor's attempts to sell him a '100% organic' watermelon, he ducked into an alleyway strewn with old papers and food dumped from the cleanup crew of the restaurant he was behind. He cocked his head at a Japanese chef on his smoke break, who was sitting on a step by the back door. The scrawny old man looked like he could've slipped right out of his dirty white uniform without a hitch. The man nodded his head in greeting and watched silently as Barstow continued down the alley.

Barstow took a corner and came upon a cellar. He threw the doors open and descended the stairs into a cool, damp tunnel illuminated by dim fluorescent lights.

Below ground level, it was Takuo Market. A tangled web of advertisements and live broadcast screens hung above the streets in thick layers. Hundreds of shops and venders littered the cramped

ALEXANDER ENGEL-HODGKINSON

streets, and shoppers clogged it like a backed-up sewer. Throngs of people, cybernetically altered in some way or another, shifted along. For some of them, spotting their implants was extremely easy— some had their skin altered to look glossy and doll-like; some had eyes that shimmered in the electrical lights glowing all around them; others had synthetic limbs and heads that had been disfigured from constant tampering. Spotting a sloppily put-together cyborg was easy. Their skin was miscoloured and the cyborgs themselves moved like early CG-animated models—unnatural. Uncanny valley. The more you watched them move, the more strangely unsettling they appeared.

Barstow had thrown himself headfirst into a sea of cybernetic implants, shady lowlifes, and a whole market of illegal merchandise put out on display, clear as a blue sky. Cops had no place here. Luckily, he didn't look like one. If he did, nothing could stop the masses from instantly tearing him to shreds. They'd disassemble every law enforcement affiliate like the very machines they'd turned themselves into, and then sell the pieces off.

The underground bazaar was an impressive sight. Impressive and disturbing. Limbs both human and robotic hung from hooks like freshly cut meat. Shut-down cyborgs resembling marionettes hovered suspended off the ground, lifeless, with the exception of their eyes. Rolling around in their sockets, they followed random passersby like surveillance cameras, unable to turn their disconnected heads.

Droves of cyborgs carried limbs and pre-assembled sexbots in vacuum-sealed plastic with a casual air about them, as if all of this were nothing out of the ordinary. Ugly old crones were gathered around patio tables tinkering with life-size doll heads. In a nearby shop built up with corrugated steel and splintery wood, a restrained man in a dental chair shrieked in agony as a cyborg nonchalantly pushed cybernetic eyeballs into his bleeding sockets.

Barstow moved on, slinking through the crowd as one of their own. The residents and shoppers in this nightmare circus were none the wiser.

Beep-beep.

A quick, high-pitched double-take in his brain. Orion's picture came up in his left eye's vision. As radios eased out of style, every officer on the force was required to have a sort of telepathic frequency installed into their brains in order to communicate with their fellow officers. It was as handy as it was invasive.

Barstow ducked into the nearest alley he could find and pushed the small 'talk' button behind his left ear. *"Find anything?"*

"Not yet," Orion replied. *"The husband seemed upset. Whether he's actually grieving or is just a really good actor is unclear at this point in time, though. What about you?"*

"I'm underground now. I haven't got a clue where to look on my own, but I'll try Looney first. See if he's got anything I can work with. Where are you now?"

"I'm in the car on Krang Street. I'm about to head up to Altieria Corp. and inquire to the big boss man about his employee. See if he can give me anything."

"And if not?"

"Then I'll look elsewhere. Did you check the motel's surveillance yet?"

"Yes, I did. As it turned out, their security system was blacked out between 8 PM and 9 PM yesterday night. You know what that means."

Orion sank back in the driver seat of the standard police cruiser, which was basically an armoured 1980 Lamborghini Countach LP 400 S. Blue and white colours. The combat and all-terrain modifications applied to it made it two inches thicker than the original 80's model. The tires were also protected by bulletproof shields, and the tires themselves were made of highly durable metal with spiked all-terrain treads. To keep from stinking up the car, Orion smoked his cigarette with the scissor door lifted open. After taking a puff, Orion answered, *"Too 'coincidental.' Obviously premeditated."*

"I can't stay on for much longer. Someone here may tap into my frequency. And then we'd have another problem on our hands."

"Understood." Orion flicked his half-smoked cigarette into the street, climbed into the car, and shut the door. He activated the car with a five-point fingerprint scanner and sped off down the road in a matter of seconds.

Barstow came upon an internet café at the end of the main street. Passed down an aisle under a ripped tarp, flanked by cyborgs literally plugged into their computers all the way down the tables. Wires in their eyes, nostrils, ears, gaping mouths. They twitched and muttered things in gurgles, reacting to whatever they were experiencing in their virtual worlds. Barstow shuddered at the thought of these people altering themselves for this sort of thing; preferring to live in their virtual fantasies until their physical forms rotted away with no consideration or desire for reality.

As Barstow entered the café, he found more of the same: several computer terminals with men and women plugged into their computers, mouths agape, arms rigid. He went to the back corridor, knowing he'd find him there...

Standing on a beach in the early afternoon sunlight, the woman was breathtakingly beautiful. Short orange hair that went straight down to her shoulders. Deep blue eyes. A smile you'd kill for. A body you'd die for. Tall and athletic, busty and curvy; hidden under that silk red robe. Her admirer reached out to his angel. Her vibrant aura always entranced him.

Up above, seagulls cried out. Behind her, salty waves crashed against the sandy shore. The air was clear, with a hint of sea salt. The sun's blinding rays of gold heated the sand and warmed his skin. It was all a reminder of better days. A simpler time.

"You're blushing," she said.

His heart leaped at the sound of her voice. It was like warm milk.

She came closer. Slender arms extending toward him. Rosy cheeks brightening up that smile. He sat motionless as she adjusted his head and kissed him. She tasted like strawberries. He fell in love with her all over again with that single kiss. Angelica. His hands fumbled at the belt of her robe. It came undone. The robe fell away, revealing her naked beauty to him. Her womanly endowments were as breathtaking as her smile. Ample, round breasts. Her body muscular without damaging his own pride. Her soft skin shimmering in the sun's powerful glow. Her sensuous curves and slight movements solidified the obvious fact that she was perfection itself.

She giggled, making his heart sing. "You're always so eager," she said as he cupped her breasts. She moved forward, her legs sliding up the chair on either side of him, her crotch grinding up his pant leg. Her juices soaked through, cold and wet. Her intense sensation filled him with ecstasy. She was his goddess in a long forgotten paradise. His domain.

Then a flicker. It all swam away in swirls of deep black and crackling static. Blue and white flashes took his world away from him. It all shattered and flushed away into a black void as a high-pitched dial-up staccato screeched painfully in his ears. He screamed as quickly as it started, unable to stop the inevitable flood of emotions that came crashing back all at once. Pain, pleasure, intense grief, and rage. Tearing him apart. And then...

...Nothing.

He sat in his chair, staring at the black visor over his eyes.

Then, a gruff, familiar voice: "Get up, Looney."

More intense pain as a strong hand tore the wires out of his mouth and nostrils. Then another hand swatted the visor off his face with a hard slap that shook the jacks in his ears loose. Terrified by this sudden attack, Looney screamed again and lurched from his chair, only for his attacker to grab him and slam him back into the seat. "Sit down, goddamn it!" the voice commanded.

Looney remained in his chair, heart pounding like a jackhammer. He trembled with uncontrollable violence, eyes darting back and forth across the room as he slowly got a grasp on reality again. The emotions came back again. He curled up in his chair and sobbed. "Angelica... Angelica...!"

Barstow rolled his eyes and sneered with disgust. "You'll see her again as soon as I'm through with you."

Looney looked at him with bloodshot eyes, twitching like a meth addict kept off the stuff for too long. It took him a few seconds too long to recognize him. "Barstow?"

"Who else?" Barstow snapped impatiently.

"What do you want from me?"

"Information that you may or may not have."

"Information? W-what kind of information?"

Barstow held up a photo of Elsa Scott, taken from her health plan records. "This woman was murdered just a day or so ago."

"What're you lookin' at me, for? I didn't do it!"

"I didn't say you did," Barstow replied as he handed Looney the photo. "Take a good, long look at her."

"Why're you doing this to me?"

"I need you to focus, Looney."

"I helped you before," Looney cried. "Why're you doing this to me?"

"Focus, Looney. Focus. Hey." He slapped him. "Focus. Look at the picture."

Looney studied the picture to the best of his abilities. He did what he was told, and gave it a good, long look.

"What do you see?"

Looney tensed up. The visions were coming back. *No, not again.* The private VR room and Barstow disappeared. *Not again!* Now he was in a motel room. Bland, uninteresting. He looked into the mirror, only it wasn't him who was looking back at him.

Her. She looked back at him. Eyes glazed from crying so much. She looked so miserable. So alone. So scared.

Don't make me do this again! Not again!

Looked at the digital clock in the wall above the mirror. 8:15 PM. Turned around to the TV. The news was on. A reporter talked about a robot going berserk and slaughtering the family it was supposed to serve. No explanations as to why something like that would happen. Altieria Corp.'s integrity was being heavily questioned, its reputation dealt a severe blow. The family's close relatives were suing.

Please!

She was packing up to leave. She couldn't stay in one location for too long. He would find her if she didn't move.

The door burst open. Splinters flying. A woman's terrified scream. A black object hurtling toward her. Toward him.

No! No! No!

Looney shrieked and scrambled out of his chair, throwing the photo away as if it'd just bitten him.

"What is it?!" Barstow yelled. "What'd you see?"

"Get away from me!"

Barstow had had enough. He grabbed Looney by the collar and flung him back into the chair. "Goddamn it, tell me what you saw!"

"Big shadows! All black! It was huge! No escape! No warning!" Looney burst into a fresh fit of tears and moaned pathetically, "How can something so big make so little noise...? Then it was there!"

"What was?"

"I don't know!" Looney screamed. "Get away from me! Leave me alone! I've given you all I can! Go away! Go away!"

Barstow picked up the photo and stepped back. Watched as Looney hastily stuffed the wires back into his nose and mouth. Then he picked up the visor and pulled it back on. He was like a child hiding under the blanket after he was sure he'd seen a monster at the foot of his bed. Retreating to his paradise where it was safe. Angelica would comfort him.

Barstow scoffed in disgust and left the room. "Two hundred psychokinetics in the world, and I'm stuck with a worthless virtual masturbation junkie like you."

Within Looney's world, Angelica was clothed in golden PVC shorts and top, caressing his chin with a loving hand. "What's wrong, dear?"

03: CEO/H3@D

Altieria Corp. HQ

Orion pulled up right at the front gate of Altieria Corporation's main headquarters. The twenty-inch-thick steel walls that surrounded the building in a perfect circle stood at a mighty twenty-five feet, and all of it was topped with razor wire and security cameras in bullet-proof casing. The luxurious high-class district that surrounded the property paled in comparison to the property itself in its majestic glory.

An interaction screen hovered down to Orion's window with a digital smile. Its tinny, high-pitched voice hurt Orion's ears. "Please state name and purpose for arrival."

Orion showed it his badge, letting it scan into the screen's photographic memory. "Detective Jason Orion of the Altieria City Police Department, 28th Precinct. I'm here to see the CEO."

"Do you have an appointment?"

"No."

"Then fuck off."

Orion stared at the screen, not quite believing he'd heard that right. He slowly withdrew his badge, eyes narrowing to displeased slits. "I'm here on official police business."

"Do you have a warrant?"

Orion frowned, knowing what was coming. "No."

"Then fuck off."

The digital smile remained. It was starting to get on his nerves. "Listen, you malfunctioning piece of crap: I'm here for investigative purposes and I need to speak to the CEO immediately."

"Come back with a warrant, Detective," the screen replied. "Otherwise, you will not be allowed entry onto the Altieria Corporation premises."

A new voice suddenly came out of the screen—this one was that of a female's. "I apologize, Detective. We are currently experiencing a bug in the system. Come on in."

Orion raised an eyebrow but said nothing as the gate slid open. He pushed the car through the gate into a world of white and grey, where everything had a glossy sheen to it. Throngs of cyborg employees in grey uniforms and expressionless faces flowed to and from the main building on either side of the road Orion followed in perfect militarized formations that would make any general proud. Grey business suits for the men. Grey formal blouses and skirts for the women. They seemed less like people with individual lives beyond the walls of the headquarters, and more like an army of drones. It gave Orion the creeps.

The Altieria building itself was a cylindrical tower of steel and glass that seemed to pierce the heavens. It sparkled brilliantly on sunny days. On cloudier days, it reflected the sky so clearly it seemed to blend with it.

The cruiser taxied up to the curb under a tinted glass canopy, right in front of the main doors. When Orion stepped out, he found himself approached by a female cyborg in the same uniform as the workers he'd seen on his way down. Of course. Blonde hair pinned back in a ponytail and artificial blue eyes that occasionally had pixilated patterns spinning around in her pupils were her only distinctive qualities.

"Good morning, Detective," she said with a slight bow of her head and a warm smile on her polished face. "I am Amanda/7. We spoke on the intercom."

"You mean the malfunctioning piece of shit out front?" he asked, perfectly mimicking her superficial smile.

"Ah, yes. That." Her face flushed with embarrassment, but it passed as soon as it came. "The work of one of our disgruntled ex-employees with a recently terminated contract. We've been trying to fix it all morning."

"Never seems to be a shortage of problems for your company lately, is there?"

Amanda/7 frowned.

Adopting a voice that resembled a narrator for a Saturday morning children's cartoon, he said, "Yessiree, the excitement never stops." To top it all off, he gave her a flash of his most charming grin.

She couldn't help but smile.

Figuring he'd wasted enough time, Orion got straight to the point, eager to leave this eerie place. "I'm here to see the CEO."

"For what purpose, if I may ask?"

"A murder case that involves one of his more respected

employees."

Her eyes lit up with surprise. "Which employee?"

"It's a private matter that I'd like to discuss with the CEO," Orion said patiently.

With an understanding nod, she said, "Of course. Follow me."

He followed her into the lobby, which could only be described as a cavernous orb of white. White walls, white domed ceiling, white floors, white furniture in the white waiting room. Where there wasn't white, there was a television screen—a strip of at least one hundred widescreen televisions circled the lobby ten feet off the floor, showing things like the news, stock market updates, advertisements for the company, the CEO's most recent speech at a press conference, and an approved documentary on the company. A grand holographic statue of the CEO himself stood in the center of the lobby at a height of fifteen feet with a plaque at his feet that read, 'CEO/H3@D.' His confident, standoffish pose with his arms crossed and his head turned slightly to the left with an indifferent expression on his face came off as slightly arrogant to Orion.

Then again, he expected nothing less from the first man to ever officially rule the world.

They entered the elevator and stood silently as it began its ascent to the top. For the first thirty floors, not a word was spoken. Orion looked out of the curved window at the shrinking lobby on the other side, watching as the employees minimized to tiny dots below.

"I apologize, but you strike me as oddly familiar, Detective," Amanda/7 said. "Have you been here before?"

"Yeah," he replied, turning away from the window to face her. "On two occasions. I was here last week for information on another case. A different girl beamed me up, though."

She blinked. "'Beamed you up?'"

He waved it off. "Ah, forget it. Let's just go with 'escorted.' I must admit, though, you're twice as attractive as she could ever hope to be."

She smiled, as if she heard that more often than one would think. "Flattery will get you nowhere in this facility, I'm afraid."

He shrugged and put a cigarette in his mouth. "Ah well. It was worth a shot." He fired up the lighter and raised it to his—

"There's no smoking in here, Detective."

Orion frowned and snapped the lighter shut. Put both the

cigarette and the lighter in the outer breast pocket of his coat. He turned back to the window and looked down, unafraid of the dizzying heights. "How long have you worked here, Amanda?"

"Twelve years, six months, seven days, thirteen hours, twenty-three minutes, thirty-four seconds."

A bit too overly specific for his taste—it made her seem less human, and Orion preferred to speak to someone who *seemed* human, at least—but it'd do just fine for someone he wouldn't be seeing too much of today.

Eighty-five floors and counting. This elevator was too quiet for his liking. All she did was stare at the elevator doors, still as a statue.

"I heard," Orion said, "that the CEO is dying."

She turned sharply toward him, eyebrows raised. "Where did you hear that?"

"Around," he said.

"It's not true," she said. "It's nothing but a rumour."

"Why would someone spread a rumour like that?"

"A prank, perhaps?"

"Or maybe a publicity stunt?"

She shook her head. "Not so. Altieria Corporation prides itself in dealing with new life and social order, not the morbid exploitation of death and other unpleasantries."

"Alright, then," he said with a shrug, glancing out the window again.

"I get the impression you are not a heavy advocate of this company."

"Don't take it personally; I don't advocate anything, not even myself."

"Why is that?"

"No point in supporting a lost cause."

"You believe this company to be a lost cause? Why?"

"Nothing lasts forever, my dear, and nothing ever will, no matter how hard you try to disprove that fact. It's the way of the world. You want proof; just pick up a history text book. Even the ones your employer so graciously abridged will prove my point."

She didn't bother with an argument. Her objective was simply to escort him to the CEO. So she turned back to the elevator doors without another word.

*

Level three-sixty-five.

They stepped out into the corridor. Amanda/7 led Orion across the building in a straight line. It smelled as sterile as a hospital, but somehow didn't feel as welcoming. The slightest sound echoed as her high heels clacked and his combat boots thumped on the white-tiled floor.

Then they took an unexpected turn. Headed down another hallway. Orion said, "This isn't the way to the office..."

"No, it isn't," Amanda/7 stated. "I was instructed to escort you to this room."

"What's up with that?"

"I am not at liberty to say."

Orion scowled. One hand went into his pocket where he kept his small backup piece, a Sigma pistol. Simply taking precautions. He didn't trust anybody. Especially corporations.

They reached a door, which slid open. A burst of cold air hissed through their clothes and clung to their skin. Amanda/7 stepped to the side, gesturing for him to enter. "This way, please."

Orion gave her a look and entered the dark room. It was empty, rectangular, and dull. Its walls were slabs of solid concrete, and its floor, a simple sheet of metal. Orion was surprised by the low-rent look for such a prestigious company.

The door slammed shut behind him, dropping him into pitch blackness. His heart skipped, but the feeling of anxiety quickly passed. He could handle himself if something were to happen. He heard low static in his ears, usually indicating that a jammer was cutting off his communication. Great.

His breath plumed in front of his face as he heaved a sigh.

A thin white line began to shine across the wall directly in front of him. The wall parted, filling the room with dark blue light. Orion's eyes adjusted to it quickly as he peered into the next room.

The walls in this next room, which appeared to be thick, murky panes of Plexiglas, shimmered like light reflecting off water in a cave. The blue light throbbed with the eerie heartbeat of the man in the middle of the room—which was a shocking sight in itself. A shrivelled old man with more tubes and wiring connected to his body than any cyborg or full-on robot Orion had ever seen sat in a wheelchair. Its wrinkled, saggy skin shifted as if a million tiny insects were crawling around underneath. Some of the wires were connected to a life support system and a heartbeat monitor. Other wires—a tangled web of dozens of wires—were extended from the walls on the other three sides of him, jacked into his cranium. An oxygen mask appeared to be fused over his mouth and nose, with half a dozen tubes connected to it. The goggles hid his eyes, but Orion knew the man was staring at him through crimson lenses.

The last time Orion saw him, he didn't look so bad. That was only a week ago. Now, the CEO looked absolutely nothing like his holographic reinterpretation in the lobby.

"Mr. CEO," Orion said to the thing in the chair. "You're looking slightly under the weather since we last met."

A low hiss escaped the oxygen mask. The head shifted upward slightly. An electronic voice on hidden speakers in the walls startled Orion with their sudden loudness. "Detective Orion."

"If this is a bad time..."

"Nonsense. I'm simply recharging." Another burst of air hissed from the mask, pluming in the frigid cold. "Nothing to be concerned about."

"You know," Orion started, "Jamming a law enforcer's frequency is a crime. You are aware of that, right?"

"My sincerest apologies," CEO/H3@D replied. "It is strictly a precaution to prevent any... *unwanted* communications with more unpleasant parties. Radicals and spies, etcetera."

"Regardless," Orion said.

"It hardly matters. I run the police department. I am the exception to the rules, Detective, for justifiable reasons." Another hiss. "You are here to discuss the matter of Franklin Scott and his recently deceased wife."

"Yeah," Orion said. "And how do you know that?"

"You seem to forget that I am in control. I am the city. I became aware the second the information was entered into the records."

Orion wasn't even going to bother with explaining how many rules that broke. It was true, he often forgot that CEO/H3@D controlled everything, and had methods of knowing everything, too. As much as that made him uncomfortable, there was no avoiding the fact. However, Orion was too old-fashioned and stubborn to simply accept such a society right off the bat, but he was slowly accepting it all the same. "Do you know anything about it? Anything that could help further my investigation? Maybe you could start with the 'coincidental' glitch in the Heartbreaker Motel's security feed between eight and nine in the evening yesterday."

"There was an electrical issue in several blocks in that sector. I have technicians down there to investigate. So far, they haven't picked up much. However..." another hiss of air from the mask. "...if something turns up, you will be the first I contact."

"What about the suspect? Anything?"

"Nothing, except a single witness. A young woman who reported a large individual in black."

"Maybe one of your robots malfunctioned again. Several other families could probably attest to that."

Another hiss. Orion took it as the CEO's initial response to Orion's jab. "The 'malfunction' of which you speak was exclusive to only our recent model due to tampering by a mysterious third party. A strong theory among most investigators is that it was the work of an embittered employee while he still had access to our programming facilities—or perhaps, a saboteur. A major—and highly regrettable lapse in both judgement and security on our part."

"Not one of mine."

"Of course not."

"My partner thinks so, though." Orion didn't like to get side-tracked. He went back to the main point. "So you're sure you have no information regarding the Scott murder case?"

"It is highly unlikely that the suspect is a machine."

"What makes you say that?"

"Traces of psychokinetic activity were found on the scene—something that can be easily overlooked, even by detectives as skilled and experienced as you. Damage to the door and Elsa Scott were not caused by weapons or hands. To further strengthen this theory, I feel I must remind you that psychokinetics can have a significant effect on electronic equipment—which could explain the security feed malfunction."

"I won't jump to conclusions so quickly, just in case," Orion said. "But I'll keep that in mind next time I sweep the scene... if your investigators haven't totally trampled whatever evidence could've still been found there." He shuddered in the cold. He could barely feel his hands now, and his knees were starting to knock together. "Is there anything else you could tell me?"

"Negative," CEO/H3@D answered. "You will be immediately notified of any new developments."

"That'd be much appreciated." Orion turned to leave, hands in his pockets. As soon as he stepped out of CEO/H3@D's recharge room, the wall started to close, slowly dropping him back into pitch darkness. He walked a few more steps, one hand outstretched. When his palm touched the door, he banged on it a couple times, and it opened two seconds later.

Amanda/7 escorted him back to the elevator, and they descended all the way to the lobby without a word. They crossed the lobby and approached Orion's car. Once Orion was in the cruiser, Amanda/7 said, "I hope you found the answers you were looking for."

Orion gave her a sideways glance as he started up the engine. "Oh, yeah." He looked at her patiently. He reached up to the scissor door handle, causing her to take a step back to avoid hitting her head when he pulled it shut. He rolled down the window and fired up a cigarette. "Your boss was a *huge* help."

And, with that, he sped off down the lane, leaving Amanda/7 in a dust cloud. She watched the cruiser fly around the bend, out from under the shelter and take off down the main road to the gate. She didn't stop staring until the gate slid shut behind Orion's cruiser as it peeled out into the street.

Above, thunder rumbled, grey clouds swirled around the tower, and rain started to fall...

04: Head

Altieria City—B7 District

Night fell. Heavy rain strafed the city skyline. Piercing the dark clouds with shimmering towers and glowing spires, the city was an unfriendly reminder of mankind's gradual rise from rock caves to steel wonders. For a place with so much light and liveliness in its signage and diverse inhabitants, the city dwelled beneath an ominous darkness. Down in the subterranean levels of the vast metropolis was a complex system of gutters, tunnels, and bridges, all extending above the drainage floor of the base levels.

On one such pedestrian walkway in the lowest possible sector above the drainage floor, no one was present—except one: a man in dark, thick clothing, head hidden in a closed modular helmet. He stood idly in the middle of the walkway, still as a statue.

In half an hour, the oddly statuesque man was met by a second figure, huddled over an object in his hands, probably to protect it from the drizzle that stabbed through the overhead piping.

"Have you got it?" the newcomer asked.

With a nod, the first man produced from his coat a suitcase. His tinny voice spoke, devoid of all emotion: "And you?"

The newcomer stole precautionary glances down either end of the isolated bridge. Then he held out the metal box by the handle. "I wonder how you think the Company would react if they found out what you're doing now."

"Never mind that; let's just get this over with."

"Halt!"

The voice made both men whirl to see a female police officer in a full-body riot suit standing readily, LE magnum trained on them. "What's in the box?" she asked. When neither man answered, she repeated impatiently, "What's in the box?!"

"Takeout," the newcomer calmly responded. Then he fired his own gun at the officer. She managed to squeeze off a shot before the armour-piercing round tore through her riot suit, shattered her ribcage, and slammed her to the ground. Sparks lit up the bridge as her bullet tore the box out of the newcomer's hand and sent it flying over the railing into the abyssal drainage system.

"Shit!" the newcomer shouted as he lurched over the railing, trying to locate the box. "The head! The head!" He turned to the first man. "I still get something for my troubles, right?"

The first man glanced around the newcomer at the fallen officer. Then he said, "I no longer require your services. But that doesn't mean you can't still be of use..."

"What's that supposed to mean?" the dealer asked, readying his gun.

An invisible force grabbed hold of the dealer's arms and held them outward. Through no fault or mental command of his own, the dealer stretched his hands up over his head, trembling violently as he struggled to retake control of his body. "Hey! What the hell—"

His gun fired into a catwalk above him. A second later, both his wrists crackled sickeningly as his hands spun at 360 degrees. He howled in agony. Dropped the gun to the floor. His pain only escalated when his arms twisted unnaturally. Then his kneecaps popped and his legs became limp and useless, but he still found himself hovering above the floor. His high-pitched shrieks carried out through the subterranean levels of the city as his midriff started to twist. His legs started left. His torso moved in the opposite direction. Somehow the first man was wringing out his dealer's body like a wet sponge without even touching him.

Finally, the dealer's neck coiled and snapped. His head lolled loosely backward. His bulging, terrified eyes stared upwards. His tongue dangled out the side of his mouth.

And then he started to come apart, one joint at a time...

After the dealer's onsite dismemberment, the first man—let's call him the 'Dark Kinetic'—packed his organs within cold storage containers and stuffed them into a second suitcase. Then he got up with both suitcases and approached the police officer. His psychokinesis tore the whole front of her suit clean off and discarded it over the bridge railing. She wasn't quite dead yet. Twitching furiously. Gasping. The Dark Kinetic stared at her. His eyeball implants scanned her body and eventually notified him of her blood type.

"Yours will do just fine." The Dark Kinetic carefully placed his suitcases on the ground. Delivered a coup de grâce with an invisible force blast that tore her chest wide open, flayed like a fish.

Then he drew a large butcher knife from the sheath clipped to his belt and got to work on her corpse.

05: Autopsy

Orion went home sometime in the early evening, obviously unaware that a cop had just been murdered in the district next to his. He took the rusty lift to the fifth floor. It rattled and whined and shuddered as if the line might snap and drop the damn thing all the down to the P2 level. Once it reached its destination, Orion threw up the cage door and stepped into a narrow, dimly lit hall. Three doors straight down. He always felt as though an eyeball was planted to the other side of the second door's peep hole, watching him. Always felt like he was being watched in general, and most of the time, he was. On his way to his door, he glanced upward and saw the security camera staring right at him, following his every move. He grew bigger as he stepped into the middle of its fisheye picture, eyeing it back the whole time as he walked across. He shrank again as he reached the edge, and disappeared from the security camera's sight. His door was almost directly under the damn thing, and its wall mount wasn't flexible enough to let it watch him turn the key in the lock.

Thank Christ for that.

The apartment was nothing special. Even with all the lights out, the place was constantly set aglow by the blue neon flashing outside his window. The high-rise across the street never let up, either. Someone was always celebrating something in that goddamned oversized beacon erroneously built in the middle of a residential zone, prompting Orion to invest in some cheap blinds for his windows. Even those didn't stop the light from shining through and slicing across his walls.

The place was always a mess. Newspapers strewn about on the floor. Dirty dishes piled on the countertop and filling the sink. Endless takeout packets and cartons stacked on the coffee table. Movie posters, somewhat tattered from age, started to curl and bulge on the walls. Clothing draped over lamps, furniture, and his TV set. A mild pungent odour lingered in the stiff air of his one-bedroom apartment.

Home sweet home.

An old-fashioned guy like Orion didn't have much fancy technology dating post-2015 in his dwelling. The communicator installed in his skull was the most 'modern' thing he had in his reluctant possession, and that was only due to necessity in order to maintain his job as a detective.

He slipped out of his coat and dropped on the futon. He tossed his coat on the armchair across the room. His right hand sifted through the empty takeout cartons on the coffee table in search of the TV remote. Found it after five seconds. Flicked on the TV—it was probably the most expensive piece of hardware in this cramped space of his, being a fifty-inch widescreen.

The place started to shake then. The tremor was relatively gentle, shifting things around a bit. The TV screen dimmed with the rhythm of the tremors. Orion stared at it, still totally relaxed. These things were normal, and only ever lasted for durations between sixty to eighty seconds. On rare occasions, they would go on for two whole minutes.

The news came on with a report about anti-corporate rioters trashing a district that had already seen better days before they came along. He watched the censored footage of riot police gunning down a cluster of rioters—of course, not without it being edited to look like self-defence on the enforcers' part. Orion knew the truth. But did he care? Not anymore.

He switched to a different channel. A new logo—a blue circle containing Traditional News, written in bold white font appeared on the screen. They also covered the riots—only this time, they weren't so flattering. Police officers were clearly executing unarmed rioters, some even going so far as to douse them with flamethrowers and chop them down with machine guns.

That kind of coverage would be enough to get you erased these days. Orion's eyebrows went up as the on-scene reporter, Becky Trickle, described the truth right before his eyes, even as a pair of officers struggled to drag her off camera.

"I'm here on the scene as officers of the law gun down helpless civilians! They're trying to silence us! They're trying to mask the truth, even now, while I'm reporting this, as you can clearly see, they're suppressing—"

"No pictures, lady!" one of the officers shouted as a hand swatted the camera out of focus. "You are in violation of…"

Someone else shouted, "Arrest them, goddamn it!" and the

screen went black.

[SIGNAL LOST]

Orion scoffed and shook his head. *Figures.*

He decided to check his cell phone. For its time, it was a state-of-the-art touch screen phone. Now, it was a thirty-year-old relic. Two text messages. One from Sarah.

Sarah Compton. His girlfriend, but Orion could never say for sure. She was complaining about how they hardly spent any time together, and she was feeling lonely.

Join the club, Sarah, he thought bitterly. He replied instead with:

You: 12:34 AM> On my next day off, we'll see.

Like always—which always struck him as strange—she came up with an immediate reply, even at this late hour:

Sarah: 12:35 AM> And how soon is that?

You: 12:35 AM> Next Tuesday.

Sarah: 12:35 AM> Provided you're not called in...

You: 12:35 AM> Exactly.

No more replies. Orion knew she was pissed. He couldn't blame her. The woman was crazy in love with a man who never had time for her. He sighed and started idly flicking through channels. Decided a minute later to send her another message:

You: 12:37 AM> Sorry, doll.

Sarah: 12:37 AM> It's okay.

He exited her window. Checked the second message sent from Barstow. Usually they communicated via the telepathic radio, but the two partners had agreed long ago that late hours were quiet hours, unless something was going down. After all, who the hell wanted to hear their partner's voice when they were sleeping on the couch, or taking a shower, or worse: making love to their partners? Nothing would ruin one's evening more than having your co-worker's voice invade your brain during coitus.

Barstow: 11:53 PM> Meet me at the station. Coroner's got new info on our Scott victim.

11:59 PM> Where the hell are you?

12:06 AM> I'll give you an hour to get down here. This is important.

12:30 AM> You know I hate waiting. Answer

as soon as you get this.

Orion scowled. His partner in law enforcement was as attached to his ass as his girlfriend. Neither one gave him much leniency in that department.

You: 12:39 AM> Can't it wait till tomorrow?

Barstow: 12:40 AM> It IS tomorrow, you lazy bastard. I wouldn't be urging you to get down here if it wasn't important.

You: 12:40 AM> On my way then. This better be good.

Orion didn't want to get up. The futon was the most comfortable thing he'd ever sat on, as if he'd been sitting on rocks for most of his lifetime. He groaned in dismay. Shut off the TV. Tossed the remote into a nearby empty noodle carton. Stood up. Grabbed his coat. Feet dragged as he headed for the door.

"Goddamn job," he muttered under his breath as he undid all the locks and opened the door. "I ought to quit..."

28th Precinct Station

The first thing Orion said when he trudged through the front doors of the station was, "After-hours calls really suck."

The lieutenant behind the protective shield looked up from her computer and leaned over her desk. "Somebody's gotta do it, Detective."

"I need my beauty sleep too, you know," he replied as he pressed his hand on the scanner. The locks clicked loudly. The door buzzed. Orion opened it and stepped into the main room. The smell of fresh coffee reached his nostrils. Finally, a smell that wasn't sterile.

Cubical offices divided by half-glass partitions filled most of the room with the only walking space being narrow lanes. Orion made his way through the station and went down two flights of stairs, where he reached the other door. He went through, travelled down another corridor, his footsteps echoing like they would in any other underground tunnel. Reached the double door entrance to the autopsy room. Pushed through and found Barstow in his regular clothes and the examiner standing on either side of the table that Elsa Scott's remains were splayed out on.

"Good morning, gentlemen," Orion said as he looked over

Elsa's mutilated corpse, with newer cuts previously applied by the examiner during the initial autopsy. "What a lovely sight to start the day with. Tell me you found something, Doc."

Doctor Thomas Moore looked up from his touch board, his fingers still typing away on it. His bug-eyed stare was a fairly unnerving sight first thing in the morning. "I've got good news, then. While there wasn't much left of her to work with, I was able to determine that she was killed by psychokinesis."

Recalling CEO/H3@D's explanation the morning before, Orion said, "So it wasn't the work of a machine, then?"

"Highly unlikely," Moore said. "More like a deranged psychokinetic looking for human organs. Have you checked Takuo Market for any leads?"

Barstow said, "I couldn't find anything. It's possible her organs haven't been put on display just yet. I'll do another sweep tomorrow."

Orion said, "I spoke with the CEO yesterday. He told me the same thing, about the perp being a psychokinetic. He figured that was a good enough explanation for the downed video feed."

"It could be," Barstow said with a thoughtful nod.

"I found something else that you'll find interesting," Moore stated as he placed his gloved hands under Elsa's cranium—what was left of it—and carefully tilted her faceless skull toward Orion. "While I was rooting around in here, I discovered that the small portion of her brain that remained was still somewhat... active."

"Active?" Orion raised an eyebrow and peered inside Elsa's skull, watching her brain cells slide down to the bottom. "Are you sure, Doc?"

Moore nodded. "An average brain only continues its functions for a few minutes post-mortem, as it struggles for oxygen after the heart has stopped beating. However, the longest record for a psychokinetic brain's post-mortem functioning period is an extraordinary eight hours." He tapped his index finger on a jagged piece of Elsa's forehead. "Despite it being heavily damaged and mostly gone, her brain lasted approximately three hours, post-mortem."

"That's impossible," Barstow snapped. "There's no way a brain *that* damaged could possibly continue functioning. Three quarters of her brain were scooped out of her skull, for Christ's sake. Even by psychokinetic standards, the plausibility of what you're telling us is zero. *Zero*, Doctor."

"I suggest changing your ratios then, Detective," Moore snapped back. "My machines do not lie. I double-checked it. I *triple*-checked. The same results came up every time. I assure you, I'm as confused and astonished as you are. "

"I wouldn't say 'astonished' is the right way to put it, Doc," Orion said calmly. "'Creeped out' sounds more accurate."

Moore ignored Orion and continued, "What we're looking at here is obviously the next step in our evolution. A sort of... advanced psychokinetic being the likes of which we've never seen before. When psychokinetics were first discovered, we learned that they could utilize sixty percent of their brains, rather than our regular thirty percent." He gave Elsa's corpse another wondrous look, as if he were trying to learn all of its secrets just by staring at it. "Could it be that this woman was able to utilize more than that? Seventy percent? Eighty? Ninety, even? One hundred, perhaps?"

"Despite the weird fact that a quarter of her brain was still functioning three hours after the rest of it was torn out of her head," Orion stated, "somehow I kind of doubt even *she* found a way to go the whole hundred."

"Without the whole brain, there's no way I could possibly determine the exact percentage," Moore said regrettably.

"Don't forget," Orion said with a wry smile, "she's a human, not a lab rat."

"I realize that," Moore replied with a frown. "But it's still astonishing. I never thought I would see such a phenomenon in my lifetime..."

"It's weird and unnatural," Barstow said. "That's what it is. Nothing 'phenomenal' about it."

Orion said, "So two psychokinetics struggled in that motel room, and one of them overpowered the other. But if this girl's as advanced as you say, Doc, how is it that *she's* the one on the table?"

"Maybe she wasn't aware of her capabilities," Moore said.

"That sounds a little too inconvenient. What does the registry say about it?"

"She's unregistered."

Both of Orion's eyebrows went up this time. "Oh. An unregistered psychokinetic wife—sorry, *ex*-wife—of a highly respected biology major/robotics engineer in a corporation that practically controls the entire planet turns up dead in a motel room three days after she leaves him. *That's* not suspicious at all."

Barstow crossed his arms and turned away from Elsa as a sick feeling began to boil up in the pit of his stomach. He couldn't stand the sight of her mutilated corpse anymore. "That's definitely strange..."

"Illegal, too," Orion said. "Looks like I'll need to speak with the grieving widower about that."

Moore pulled a sheet over Elsa's table, unknowingly doing Barstow's stomach a great service. "There isn't much more I can do for you gentlemen, unfortunately."

Orion shot Barstow with a half-hearted glare. "This could've waited until later."

Barstow replied, "I figured this conversation would be better with these new discoveries still fresh in our minds."

"You couldn't tell me over the phone?"

"Of course not. You know why I can't."

Orion craned his neck as he massaged the nape, grunting as he tried to get the kink out. He opened his eyes and found himself staring up at the surveillance camera in the top right corner across the room.

It stared back at him.

"Hm," he grunted, turning back to Moore. "Thanks, Doc. You've been a big help." He left the autopsy room. The image of Elsa was burned into his brain and he couldn't shake it. With a sigh, he muttered to himself: "I wasn't planning on sleeping, anyway."

06: Coffee

"Jason!" Barstow called as he ran out the front entrance of the station after Orion, who had already reached his car—a black 1960 Lincoln Continental Mark V with a brand new high-power engine and two-inch-thick armour plating.

Orion turned to face him without bothering to unlock his car via thumb scan. "What's up?"

Barstow reached him and immediately pointed at Damian's Diner down the road. Its 70's-style design made it stand out like a sore thumb in the dark, somewhat rundown neighbourhood that surrounded it. The shimmering strips of green and pink neon that veined its frame and bordered its clear, wide window panes helped, too. "Want to get somethin' to drink?"

Orion glanced at the coffee shop. It certainly looked more appealing than a nightmare-ridden five-hour sleep. "Sure, why not..."

Damian's Diner
Red vinyl squeaked as the two men slipped into a booth by the window. A cyborg waitress with unnaturally gold eyes immediately dropped by in her pink-and-white outfit. "My, my. A couple of handsome early birds. What can I get you two this morning?"

"Coffee," Barstow said. "Black. And eggs in the basket."

"And you?" she asked Orion.

"Coffee with lots of sugar and cream." Orion took a moment to scroll through the holo-menu in the tabletop. "Also, can I get pancakes?"

"How many?"

"Seven."

The waitress took a moment to send the recorded orders through to the back. In the kitchen, the orders came up on a screen in a wall of code that only the chef droid could understand. The eight-armed droid got started right away on their orders, its arms working their way around in a controlled blur.

The waitress's eyes flickered. She looked at the two detectives as if she'd just come out of a trance, and smiled. "Coming right up!"

Barstow waited until she scooted off to serve the only other customer in the diner before saying to Orion, "So how was the CEO?"

"Recharging."

"So...?"

"He wasn't looking his absolute best. Let's just leave it at that."

"But he was helpful? What else did he tell you?"

"He wasn't as helpful as I'd hoped. There was nothing else he said that you hadn't already found out by then in Takuo." Orion couldn't stop the side of his mouth from curling upwards. "So how's Looney doing?"

"Like shit. Matter of fact, he's worse than ever. He's lost in a virtual wonderland. I don't think there's any helping him now."

"Really. That's too bad."

The waitress brought them their coffee and dropped a handful of sugar packets beside Orion's mug. Then she scooted away again.

Orion glanced out the window at the shady neighbourhood. At the shops closed for the night. At the flickering streetlights. At the small pair of empty cars parked on either side of the road. At the cyborg hooker with a twitching prosthetic right arm soliciting on the corner, leaning against the blacked-out storefront of a virtual porn shop. These days, even the worst kinds of operations were given a free pass, for some strange reason—even if they were just down the road from a police station. Nobody bothered with prostitutes anymore.

"This place is going to hell in a hand basket," he said.

"Amen," Barstow replied. He took a sip from his mug. "What inspired your inspirational speech just now?"

Orion shrugged. "Just looking out the window. It makes me wonder what it's all for. Why we became cops."

"To protect the innocent."

"No," Orion said, "to protect a corporate CEO." He tended to his coffee, dumping all seven sugar packets into his mug and stirring it in. "And his interests," he added as he started to fill the rest of the mug with cream.

"Sounds like you're in one of your more cynical moods."

"Lack of sleep does that to a gentleman, I guess." Orion smirked, still stirring his coffee.

"A gentleman," Barstow said with a chuckle. "Right."

"You know, I've given it some thought."

"Given what some thought?"

Orion shrugged, bracing himself for the inevitable. "Quitting."

"What?" Barstow exclaimed, loud enough to turn the waitress's head from across the diner. He spilled some of his coffee as he went on, "You can't just up and quit."

"I could, actually."

"Better be a damn good reason. Any vital injuries in the field of combat? Any mental problems? Disabilities? Anything? What is it?"

"It's exhausting as hell."

Barstow scoffed. "Now you're just being lazy."

"I feel as though it's sucking whatever years I've got left out of my lifespan," Orion said with a tired groan. He decided to try and remedy the heavy feeling in his shoulders with a few mouthfuls of coffee.

"You're talking like you're thirty years older than you actually are."

"Pushing fifty. Feels like seventy."

Barstow grinned. "You don't know what seventy feels like. Don't forget: I'll know what seventy feels like before you do."

"Two whole years." Orion whistled. "Whoopee."

"Correct," Barstow said, still grinning. "Two goddamn years. I'll probably be retired before then. I can't see myself working this job at sixty."

"You will, though."

"What makes you say that?"

"Because of your ego. You said yourself one time, a few years back, that you'd be eighty before you quit this job, just so you could brag about it to all the young whippersnappers that complained about the strenuous career of being a cop, and make them feel like shit for it."

"I didn't say that."

"Yeah, you did."

"Bullshit. When?"

"The Gein case," Orion answered sarcastically.

Barstow stifled a laugh. "Seriously, when?"

"When we were at the shop last time we totalled the cruiser. High-speed chase. You gotta remember that, at least. Three assholes in suits of armour made in their parents' basements, tossing homemade pipe bombs all over the place. Called themselves the 'Grenadier Trio.' I remember it because you lost your magnum after some shrapnel cut into your hand."

Barstow looked at the jagged scar on the side of his right hand and winced at the memory. "I remember now. The replacement LE magnum cost a fortune compared to the regular."

"The old magnums were going out of style anyway." Orion took a moment to sip some coffee. "That shrapnel provided you with the perfect opportunity."

Barstow clenched his right fist and lowered it to the table. "Sure it did."

"Told you not to stick your hand out the window."

"Shut up."

The waitress brought their orders on a platter, and set down a couple of butter packets and a bottle of maple syrup around Orion's plate. She asked Barstow, "Would you like some ketchup, sir?"

"No, thank you."

The waitress scooted off again.

For a while, they ate in silence. Barstow was a much faster eater, finishing his four slices of pigs in the blanket before Orion got to his fourth pancake. During that time, the waitress had returned to refill their half-empty mugs.

When the waitress left them again, Barstow asked, "So have you given it any serious thought? Or just when you want to be lazy?"

"What?"

"Quitting."

"A couple times, I've thought it through. Mostly when the cases hit too close to home, I reconsider the idea. When that prick nearly got Sarah in my own goddamn home..."

"I remember that."

"He was after me, not Sarah."

"Don't beat yourself up for it."

"I'm not usually one to blame anyone, not even myself," Orion said, staring at his plate as he carved a slice out of a thick, syrup-soaked pancake, "but if it weren't for me, Sarah would still have both her arms."

"It wasn't your fault, Jason. Hell, Sarah understands that. She knew what she was getting into when she involved herself in your life. And you even paid for the prosthetic. You're a lucky man. Got a woman who appreciates you, even after you somewhat, not really got her arm cut off by a psychopath out for your head." Barstow heaved an impatient sigh before downing a third of his mug. "Can't believe you're still killing yourself over that incident."

"Thanks for the kind words," Orion said sarcastically, with a frown.

"You're very welcome, pal," Barstow responded with equal sarcasm.

"To this day, it was the closest call I can think of at the moment. Nearly lost her."

"But you didn't. How's she doing, by the way?"

Orion shrugged. Answered with his mouth full: "She's been better. Hates my job almost as much as I do."

"Well, that's married life for you."

Orion looked at him, confused. "Married?"

Barstow blinked. "Uh... sorry." He chuckled. "Dating life. Married life. Almost the same thing."

"We *are* married," Orion said, unsure, "aren't we?"

Quick to change the course of the conversation, Barstow said, "Well, she's in love with a busy cop; that goes without saying."

"Uh-huh." Orion leaned back and pushed his plate forward. "I'm done."

"The job or the food?"

"The food, for now."

Barstow smiled. Orion found a little relief hidden somewhere in his partner's tired face. "Good. Don't quit on me just yet, partner."

Orion returned the smile. "I won't drop out till you do."

"Then it looks like we've got another fun-filled thirty years ahead of us."

Orion's eyebrow involuntarily twitched at the thought. Dying before then would be a mercy killing.

07: Unregistered

Scott Residence

Between the early breakfast at the diner and Orion's visit to Franklin Scott's apartment, Orion managed to fit a couple of hours of sleep in between. Still, those hours didn't do much to cure his fatigue when his alarm went off at 7:30 AM.

"Mr. Scott, it's Detective Orion here." He banged on the door and looked up at the security camera glaring down at him from above the doorframe. "But I guess you already know that, right?"

The door opened a few inches. A very tired-looking Franklin Scott looked at him with sunken eyes. "Yes, Detective. How can I help you?"

"I found something about your wife."

The door opened a little wider. "Did you find out who killed my wife?"

"I found out she was an unregistered psychokinetic with brain activity that even our most experienced examiner couldn't fully explain." The discouraged expression on Franklin's face prompted Orion to add, "I know, a dick move on my part for coming to you like this without any further information on who actually killed her."

Beat. A shocked look on his face. "Then why are you here?" Franklin asked, his voice defensive.

"I wasn't going to come down here to discuss this with you at first. Well, actually, at first, I was. But then I decided not to. But third thoughts brought me here. See, I figured that if you kept your wife's psychokinesis a secret—illegally unregistered though it may be—you would no doubt hide something else from me. Something that could be crucial to my investigation. And believe you me, Mr. Scott, I'm not the type of guy who likes to go to the same place twice to get answers I could've gotten the first time, so I apologize in advance if I seem a bit rude." Orion took a moment to study Franklin's nervous expression. "I'm only going to ask once more, Mr. Scott: is there anything else that you can tell me?"

Franklin hesitated. He was a shrimp compared to Orion, standing two feet lower. Orion's near-seven-foot height contributed to his bulky and somewhat menacing appearance. Then his head lowered in shame. He said, "Yes. It's true that my wife is an unregistered psychokinetic."

"No shit," Orion said.

"But that was through no fault of my own. I wasn't even aware of that until we were two years into our marriage. She told me during our anniversary."

"Mr. Scott, your wife is the most advanced psychokinetic we've ever had on record," Orion said impatiently. "How is it that you weren't made aware of that before she told you? On second thought, first, why don't you tell me why it took her so long to tell you?"

"With all the discrimination against psychokinetics, she wanted to keep her abilities a secret. Even from me. She often asked questions on how I felt about them whenever a news report came up about them. She was unsure. Scared, even. She didn't know how I'd react if she told me."

"And how'd you react when she did tell you?"

"I accepted it, of course. I'm not of the mind to automatically categorize people as dangerous or undesirable. There is so much about them that we could learn. I find the concept of them accessing more of their brains than normal human beings fascinating—"

"Let me stop you from going off on a tangent there," Orion said. "Just give me the details about you and your wife."

"I wasn't aware of the advanced nature of her psychokinesis, and I didn't want to put her under stress with tests to evaluate the percentage of her brain functionality. The subject was practically dropped as soon as it came up."

"Your opinion of her didn't change?"

"Of course not."

"And you didn't think to have her registered?"

"I wanted things to stay the same. And given the social opinions concerning psychokinetics, I wasn't in any hurry to subject her to that kind of publicity." Franklin was blinking back tears at this point. "I didn't want my wife treated like some kind of freak because of something she couldn't control. That would've been the cruellest thing a husband could have ever inflicted upon his wife."

Orion figured that was a good enough explanation. "Going back to my other question: you never noticed anything strange about her? Anything at all? No floating objects? No voices in your head?

44

No strange dreams?"

"No," Franklin said. "Nothing. She learned to control it at a young age, and therefore concealed it exceptionally well."

His explanation seemed believable enough. But Orion's eyes narrowed with suspicion nonetheless. "So is there *anything* else you need to tell me?"

"I don't believe so..."

"Are you absolutely, positively *sure* about that? I don't want to come back a third time, and neither do you."

"There's nothing else," Franklin insisted. "Now if you'll excuse me, I have a very busy schedule today, and my deadline is next week. There is still much to be done."

Orion frowned. "I'll leave you to it, then."

Franklin slammed the door in his face and locked it. If Orion were in his position, he would've done the same thing.

Stepping out onto the front steps of the apartment complex in which Franklin was staying, Orion fired up a cigarette and breathed in its toxins while setting up a mental link with Barstow. *"I spoke with the husband. He said he knew about his wife's psychokinesis, but didn't want to expose her to the public, what with all the psychokinetic-shaming going around."*

"An acceptable explanation, I guess," Barstow replied.

"Acceptable enough."

"Did he say anything else?"

"I asked him if he was hiding anything else from me, and he was pretty adamant that he'd coughed up everything he knew after the whole psychokinesis thing. I still think there's something else, though."

"Leave the poor bastard alone for now. I don't think we can get anything else from him. Instead, we should focus on tracking our suspect down."

"Agreed. What's our next move?"

"The case seems to be at a standstill for the moment. Wanna get some lunch? I'm buying, since you paid for my pigs in the blanket."

"Sure, why not."

08: Reactionaries

Chinese Palace

The upscale Chinese restaurant on the edge of the food district was always lively, even during rainy days like today. It started to pour halfway through the drive—a drizzle that started off light, and transformed into a heavy blanket within five minutes. The grey-blue sky cast a dreary shadow over the city that pierced it with its ridiculously tall skyscrapers like dozens of steel/glass stalagmites. The streetlights combined with the constant glow of holographic ads and banners created a dizzying mixture of dark green and bright orange that saturated the streets and subterranean levels. It reflected brilliantly in the sheets of rainwater that cascaded across the streets and sidewalks. Endless throngs of pedestrians and stampeding traffic cut through the shallow surface runoff under shifting umbrella canopies and tangled wires. Water constantly sprayed from squealing tires, splashing walkers who looked as if they couldn't care less—and maybe they didn't, anymore.

There was no denying that even the filthiest areas of Altieria City had moments of beauty when the rain washed away thin surface layers of grime from its walls and walkways. Lights seemed to shine brighter than usual, shimmering in the rain. But despite its beauty, a constant feeling of dread lingered in the air. Maybe it was the dark grey that prevailed in the skyline. That grey which couldn't be blotted out completely by the neon hue of the city's electric aura.

Stuck in traffic, Orion glanced out the window of the Mark V. The faces of the hundreds of pedestrians streaming down the sidewalks were as bland as Altieria Corp.'s employees, only these faces also looked tired as hell. Like they were all shuffling to someone's funeral, wearing mostly dark colours.

Perfect day for a funeral, Orion figured.

The traffic moved along. Eventually, he reached the restaurant. Its bright oriental atmosphere and strong aquarium theme couldn't be pulled down by the funeral weather. Two storeys of space for diners to sit and eat comfortably. Peaceful, melodic piano music playing softly in the background. A wide-variety buffet stretching through the middle of the first floor, organized in meat, vegetable, fish, grain, and dessert sections. The dining areas were surrounded by water tank columns in which hundreds of small, colourful fish swam endless circles. Holographic projections of larger aquatic life (great whites, ocean sunfish, oarfish, Atlantic blue marlins, manta rays, and several other species) schooled in a whirlpool around the domed ceiling above diners' heads on the second floor—a breathtaking prospect often ignored by regular customers once the feeling of spectacle had passed from constant viewings. For newcomers and customers that rarely showed up, like Orion, it was an awesome sight.

Orion was welcomed by an Asian cyborg doorwoman as he entered the lobby—designed to resemble a pier crossing over a sparkling pond enclosed by a rock wall. He glanced over the railing as he crossed, looking down at the clownfish and surgeonfish that darted back and forth in unexpected ways. He gave credit where credit was due: they looked pretty damn realistic.

He reached the counter on the other side. The woman behind it smiled and asked, "Do you have a reservation, sir?"

"I'm here with Barstow. He may already be here."

The woman looked through the guest book and then beckoned a nearby droid—a simple floating robot resembling a Siamese fighting fish with a human face and a cheerful grin—in her native tongue to escort Orion to Barstow's specific table.

"Right this way, please," the Siamese escort droid said.

The damn thing had taken a vertical dive into the uncanny valley. The unnatural blend of its human-like face on the body of a fish sent a slight chill up Orion's spine. Nevertheless, he followed it wordlessly as it expertly navigated through the crowd of diners travelling to and from the buffet. The distance it was going, it was as if its true purpose was to give Orion a grand tour of the restaurant's admittedly awesome sights and displays of artificial (but realistic) aquatic life swimming in their appropriate aquariums that ran along the curved walls. They went up the spiral steps to the second floor and crossed under the big blue dome where all the larger species swam above Orion's head. He couldn't stop himself from looking up at the sharks and mantas and breathing a stricken, "Whoa."

"Here you are," the Siamese escort droid said.

Barstow looked up from his newspaper as Orion approached

the booth. He put the paper down on the table beside his plate. Leaned back, elbows propped on the seat. "What do you think of the place?"

Still looking up at the whirlpool under the dome as he slipped into the booth across from Barstow, Orion answered, "Still impresses me."

"You've been here before?"

"Only once, and not on the second floor. My salary can't take multiple trips."

Barstow laughed. "Neither can mine."

Orion laughed with him. "So why'd you pick this place?"

"Why not?" Barstow leaned forward and gestured toward his plate, which had chicken and rice piled on it. "Hope you don't mind. I started without you."

"Don't sweat it. I'll be back." Orion left the booth and descended the stairs, and crossed the main floor to the buffet. The broad selection had more variety than any other buffet restaurant he'd ever been to, and he was eager to eat everything he could find. He hadn't eaten since roughly 1 AM when he went to the diner— which he paid for. It felt unfair of him to pay for a cheap diner breakfast, only for his partner to pay nearly sixty dollars per person in this restaurant later in the day. *Oh well.*

He'd made his way to the middle of the buffet section when a racket made him look up to the front desk. There, he saw five men in blue uniforms with white stars on their chests. The sight immediately made him frown and growl under his breath, "Conservatives…"

The five conservative reactionaries were arguing with the Chinese receptionist. The leader, a scowling man with a blue sweatband across his broad forehead, was trying to make sense of the hostile, rapid-fire Chinese abuse the receptionist was throwing at them. After a few seconds and more than a few failed attempts to interrupt her, the leader gave up on trying to reason with her. When in doubt, draw a full-size Uzi submachine gun from the hidden compartment in your vest and blast the receptionist into the tropical aquarium behind her—which was exactly what he did, much to Orion's shock and surprise.

The restaurant exploded into chaos. Screams and gunfire filled the air. Plates shattered on the floor. People scrambled back and forth in confused terror. Orion stared at the reactionaries from behind the buffet, his head under the heated lamps, mouth agape.

One of the reactionaries looked at him, which immediately snapped him out of his shocked state. He pointed right at Orion and shouted, "Got 'im!"

The reactionaries' heads snapped in Orion's direction. All of them drew their Uzis.

Orion shouted, "DOWN!" and ducked behind the buffet as the reactionaries blasted the buffet with a vicious fusillade, chopping down a score of unlucky diners. Lamps burst. Sparks flew. Glass and food sprayed in all directions.

Get a hold of yourself, goddamn it. Orion drew his LE magnum and waited for the volley to stop. It ceased after a brief downpour of chicken chunks. Orion shot up and opened up on the bastards, who quickly scattered in different directions. His revolver's muzzle followed one of them as he ran for cover. Fired. The explosive slug ripped through the water column and blew the reactionary's skull apart. Brains, water and artificial fish splashed through the air.

More Uzi fire. Orion threw himself to the floor as a reactionary strafed the countertop. Lucky the wall behind Orion was solid stone, as opposed to being a giant water tank. Pictures on the wall shattered and crashed to the floor. The reactionary circled the far end of the buffet counter, taking out the heated lamps over the food.

Reached Orion's side. Ran dry.

"Idiot!" Orion shouted before blasting a gaping hole through the reactionary's chest, propelling him through an ice sculpture of a flying dolphin, smashing it to pieces.

Orion turned tail and bolted for the stairs. More Uzi fire followed him down the aisle—a constant reminder to keep his head down.

Shrieking diners poured out of the dining area exit, which was adjacent to Orion's end of the buffet section. The panicking civilians came between the reactionaries and Orion—and the stairs, which he make a break for.

"Outta the way!" the reactionary leader roared as the civilians swarmed the area. "I said outta the fuckin' way!" He opened up. His men followed suit, slicing down dozens of diners in a matter of seconds in a failed attempt to get Orion before he reached the stairs.

More gunfire from above. Barstow leaned over the second

floor railing and fired his LE magnum at the reactionaries like a sniper. Blew out another reactionary's brains. "Go, Jason!"

Orion started up the stairs. The reactionary leader ducked into the nearest dining area and fired through a tropical aquarium in the wall. He somehow managed to stay on his feet as a tidal wave burst out either side of the wall and rushed across the dining area, sweeping furniture and a few screaming patrons toward the outer windows.

Barstow threw himself back into the booth as another reactionary sprayed the railing. Barstow rushed to the next booth over and jumped behind the railing again. Before the reactionary could adjust his aim, Barstow blew his chest wide open. Two shots sent the screaming reactionary over a stone embankment and splashing into a pool of goldfish.

Barstow aimed at the dining area where the leader had retreated to and shouted, "Give it up! Your men are dead! Put down your weapon and come out with your hands where I can see them!"

The leader put his fingers to his lips and let off a high-pitched whistle.

The front doors flew open and a score of reactionaries with H&K MP5A3 submachine guns in their arms and M16 assault rifles slung across their backs charged across the pier bridge. The doorwoman stood her ground in the middle, calmly relaying a pre-recorded message: "The authorities have been notified of your unruly behaviour—"

They cut her off by blasting holes through her and launching her body over the bridge railing into the pond, scaring nearby clownfish to the other end of the pool. They reached the front desk and into Barstow's point of view.

"Oh, shit," he said, eyes bulging at their overwhelming numbers.

They opened fire on the second floor. Barstow dived out of their view as they tore the polished wooden railing to shreds.

The leader pointed at the stairs and yelled, "Over there!"

One of his subordinates interpreted his words wrong and unleashed hell on the entire rear half of the main floor from one end to the other with a chainsaw-gripped minigun. The others followed suit. Water tanks disintegrated. Patrons crumpled in blood-spraying packs. Tabletops splintered. Shelved china ornaments popped and shattered. Stone walls crumbled. A violent flood exploded from burst aquariums and blew through window panes, scattering tables, chairs, people and fish across the dining areas.

"No! No!" the leader shouted angrily, pointing at the bottom of the ceiling floor. "Up there!"

The reactionaries reloaded their submachine guns with the speed of highly trained commandos. Adjusted their angle. Blasted the lights and holographic projections out of the ceiling.

Up above, Barstow and Orion dashed across tabletops as bullets shot up from the floor in terrifyingly unpredictable patterns from all around. Glass panels from the domed ceiling came crashing down. A ceiling panel pasted a fleeing patron to the floor—no longer solid.

"What the hell's going on?!" Orion shouted as he dodged a ceiling panel, which flattened a table beside him.

"You tell me," Barstow shouted back.

The upward volley stopped. The two detectives stopped running and crouched behind a torn-up booth with an equally-shredded family of four plastered in their seats.

"Now what?" Orion whispered.

Barstow shrugged and repeated himself: "You tell me."

"I'm asking you."

"Well *I'm* asking *you.*"

Barstow looked around desperately.

Below them, a reactionary with a LAWS rocket launcher on his shoulder pushed his way to the front of the platoon. He crouched. Aimed up at the second floor. His comrades cleared the area to avoid getting caught in the back-blast area and started searching the surrounding dining rooms for their targets.

Barstow spotted a water column with lobsters swirling around in it. It was the only water column on the second floor that was miraculously left untouched by the reactionaries' attack. He turned to Barstow. "I got nothing."

"Let's get to the stairs, then. We might be able to make a stand if they try to come up."

No sooner had they started for the stairs, than the middle of the second floor concussively erupted in a fiery conflagration of furniture bits and human chunks. Eardrums popped. The breakneck force slammed the detectives through the air. They shouted with surprise a second before crashing through a pile of tables and chairs. Debris rained down like hot hail. Orion involuntarily gasped when a man's severed hand bounced off his shoulder.

"Holy shit!" Barstow shouted as he turned to see the gaping hole in the floor, which gave away their position to the reactionaries near the counter. The reactionaries opened up. The detectives scrambled for the stairs. Dived over the staircase banister. Splashed into a flooded dining area. Feet hit the bottom harder than they'd expected.

"Back there," the leader growled. "Don't let 'em get away."

Half a dozen reactionaries trudged through debris, smacking fresh mags into their rifles as they advanced toward the rear dining room. They reached the edge of the stairs and spread out into a line along the edge of the sunken dining area. The water was five feet deep. Dozens of corpses bobbed with the wreckage floating on the surface. No sign of the cops.

The reactionaries exchanged looks, then unloaded into the water, cutting up everything on the water's surface.

Nothing else came up.

"Go down there," one of them said.

"*You* go down there," another one replied.

The first to speak drew a pistol on the second and glared at him. "What was that?"

The second one's eyes widened. Then with an angry snarl, he shoved a fresh magazine into his rifle and peered into the water. He tried to spot them as a last-ditch effort to avoid going in, but there was too much blood and beverage mixed in for that. Too murky to see clearly from where he was standing. With a resigned sigh, he held his rifle up with one hand, drew a combat knife with the other, and started down the steps. The water reached up to his chest, prompting him to keep his arms up.

"Start feeling around, you idiot," the first man said.

Scowling, the second pushed floating debris and patron corpses away from him.

Down under, the two detectives were turning blue as they remained in a squat under a booth table. Lungs about to burst. They stared at each other, and each man knew the other was wondering if this was the end.

Orion turned and saw the reactionary's feet move on by, kicking cutlery across the floor. Gave Barstow a look that he dreaded most. *"Bingo."*

"Don't do it."

"If I don't, we both die."

"Let me think of something quick—"

Too late. Orion pushed himself out from under the table. Felt his body start to rise, but firmly grasped anything he could to keep himself down as he followed the reactionary's feet. Grabbed a metal fork off the floor. Stuck it in the reactionary's shin. He heard the reactionary's muffled shout as the feet twirled in his direction. He swam around. Slammed his feet on the floor. Broke the surface behind the reactionary. Deep breath as he grabbed the surprised reactionary by his arms. Hand latched over the radical's grip.

The first man shouted, "There!" Opened up. The other four followed suit, perforating Orion's meat shield.

Orion leaned back, held his human shield against his chest by a shoulder strap and squeezed the shrieking reactionary's trigger finger down. The rifle bucked in his hand as he swung back and forth. With water in his eyes—nothing but indecipherable lights and shapes—Orion had been firing blind.

Pure luck. He mowed down the five men before the rifle clicked dry.

Barstow came up a second later, gasping for air. Wiping his eyes, he'd barely started breathing again when another reactionary rushed to the scene. Barstow fired his LE magnum at him, pushing backwards through the water. Liquidized one of their heads. The last one ducked for cover behind the remains of a stone partition.

Orion handed Barstow his empty rifle and, still holding the dead reactionary by the shoulder strap, he started to move to his right. "This way," he said as he simultaneously shifted to the right and groped his dead shield's pouches. He had to drag the damn body with him until he found what he was looking for in the outer right breast pocket of his vest: spare ammo.

Barstow covered him by firing another shot at the partition, psyching out the reactionary crouched behind it. He quickly ejected the empty mag out of the rifle to save some time.

Orion took out the spare mags in his fist and pushed the dead body away. "And the crowd cheers." Held out his hand. Barstow relinquished the rifle. Orion slapped the mag home and racked the bolt, keeping his eyes fixed on the partition.

There was a bridge decked with lanterns arching over another pond in the direction they were headed. Another dining area.

They pushed through as hard as they could, constantly shifting their eyes from the stairs leading to the bridge, to the partition. Their wet clothes dragged them down.

Four more reactionaries charged into view and fired. The two detectives ducked underwater again and swam behind a row of booths. The reactionaries' volley walked a parade of waterspouts across the flooded dining room.

Orion peeked from behind a floating seat cushion. Raised his gun barrel through the surface and blasted two of them. "He shoots." The other two joined their comrade behind the partition to reload. "He scores."

Almost there.

Orion cleared the way for them to get through. Moved another corpse to the side—

More gunfire roared overhead. The detectives ducked as a reactionary's submachine gun stuttered from the stairwell. Bullets shredded the patrons floating around the area where the man had just seen his prey.

Orion reappeared three feet away from that area and bolted up the steps, machine-gunning the stairwell. Killing the reactionary before he could blink. "And the crowd goes wild." Orion watched his latest kill tumble back down the steps. Shouted to Barstow, "Let's go!"

Barstow came up after him.

The group straightened behind the partition. Exchanged bullets with the detectives. Barstow liquidized another head. Orion blew back two others. As if on cue, another group arrived to take the place of their slain comrades.

"Christ! They just keep coming!" Barstow shouted telepathically as he broke into a mad dash past Orion across the bridge.

Orion followed him, ducking as the new group's bullets stitched across the partitions on either side of the bridge entrance.

"After them!"

Halfway across, a piercing ring filled Orion's ears as the wall of glass at the end of the pond disintegrated into billions of particles. Behind them, more reactionaries were strafing the bridge with submachine guns. Orion squatted behind the railing—it was durable enough to withstand the attack for now—reloaded, and hosed the men that stood behind the veil of falling specks. One of them pivoted through the glass and involuntarily dived into the pond. The rest collapsed to the floor in crumpled heaps.

Splashing behind him.

Orion whirled and fired on the men emerging from the dining area he'd just left. Knocked two backwards into the flood water. Jogged backwards into the next dining area as he kept more of them at bay. Somehow, this room wasn't flooded.

Orion turned and ran down an aisle of booths. Two reactionaries followed. Stepped onto the bridge—

Barstow jumped into plain view and cut them both down with his LE. Popped the cylinder as he dived for cover. Tossed away the empty shells. Shoved six fresh rounds into the chamber with his speed loader. Looked up—

—saw six reactionaries leaning over the second floor railing, rifles a split second from firing. No time.

Orion opened up on the second floor, forcing the reactionaries to duck behind the railing. One of them didn't and slumped forward, arms draped over the railing—his rifle fell on the floor beside Barstow, who quickly snatched it up and darted behind the booths to his partner's side. "Thanks."

"No problem," Orion replied as he ducked to reload.

Barstow turned his rifle on a reactionary trio crossing the bridge with their shoulders low and unloaded a five-round burst over the booth partition. They went down in a wild blood spray. He ducked with Orion.

The bastards up top sprayed the dining area. Blazing lead skipped across the tabletops and tore through the seats. Flowers that once lined the tops of the partition walls fluttered through the air like confetti. Water columns burst and dumped their aquatic contents on the floor, funnel-style.

The cops knew more of them would be coming across that bridge while their buddies pinned them down, and so they started for the 50,000-litre swordfish aquarium stretching across the other side of the dining room. Behind that was another dining room, sunken much lower than the previous one. Directly behind the aquarium was a steep five-foot drop down a rocky embankment.

"How long does it take," the leader hissed impatiently, pacing back and forth in the lobby, "for a platoon of highly trained commandos... to kill *two* old relic cops?" He looked at his grenadier, who was in the process of shoving another rocket in the tube of his

LAWS. "Hm?"

"Not long, sir," the grenadier replied dutifully. He carried the rocket launcher around the burning pile of debris that used to be the center of the second floor. Reached a steep embankment above the pond. Looked at the small handful of comrades crossing the bridge toward their prey's current location. "Don't bother," he called out to them.

They stopped. One look and they understood. They knelt down and pressed their hands over their ears.

The men on the second floor continued firing on the dining area on the other side of the pond. Aside from a half-glass partition wall, the grenadier had a clear shot. He drew his pistol and blew out the window. Holstered it. Aimed the rocket launcher...

Orion and Barstow charged straight for the swordfish aquarium, still doubled over as the booths disintegrated on either side of them. Blew holes through the tank walls. The tank's glass walls gave out, dumping seawater and a quartet of swordfish down the embankment into the next dining room. Orion stole a quick glance over his shoulder. Spotted a live grenade bouncing after them.

The grenadier loosed the rocket.

The cops scrambled into the open and dived against the weight of their soaked clothes. Sailed over the waterfall they'd created. Through the gaping hole in the ruptured aquarium—

KABOOM!

Rocket hit home. The whole dining room disintegrated in the concussive blast behind them. Flames swelled, tearing through the partitions and booths like wet cardboard. The remainder of the aquarium shattered as a violent shockwave sent the cops flying. Half of the embankment at the base of the aquarium blew apart, shooting rock fragments through collapsing partitions. Chinese ornaments swung to the floor as portions of the ceiling collapsed. Lights burst. Strong water current pulled a cluster of tables and chairs toward the bar on the other side.

The cops landed on their asses and rolled across a table. Hit the floor and found themselves splashing in a few inches of water. Their bodies wracked with pain. Orion yanked a splinter of wood out of his right thigh. They were alive, at least.

"Wow," Orion gasped as he sat up and leaned back against an

overturned table. "That was *some* grenade."

Barstow's face lit up with disbelief. "A *grenade* did that?!"

A swordfish flapped around nearby, gasping for air as it'd been programmed to do.

"Make sure they're dead," the leader barked. He could hear the sirens wailing in the distance. He snapped his fingers. "Make it quick!"

A pair of reactionaries made it ahead of everybody else, descending the stairs from the west side, submachine guns at the ready. They jogged through the shallow water, checking every booth they passed. They'd reached the middle of the aisle when they heard a bird whistling behind them.

A bird?

They turned. No. Barstow immediately riddled one of them with the last of his magazine. Before the second man could react, something long and thin pierced his chest. With a sharp gasp, the reactionary dropped his gun. His fingers curled around the object that impaled him, trying to make sense of it all.

Orion jerked on the swordfish, causing the reactionary to grunt. Then he threw the dead reactionary across a booth table. The swordfish's nose penetrated the table's surface, effectively nailing the corpse to it. Its tail swayed back and forth wildly as its nose kept it in the air, standing up on the reactionary's back.

Barstow looked at the darkly comical sight, then raised an eyebrow at his partner. "Really?"

Orion shrugged. "I dropped my gun."

"You worry me sometimes." He picked up one of the fallen reactionaries' rifles and handed it to Orion.

"Aw," Orion said as he took it, "does that mean you care?"

"Shut up," Barstow said.

They heard shouting from up top and turned to the elevated dining area. A shot rang out. Orion let out a scream and fell back. Barstow couldn't see anybody up there yet, but he opened up on the elevated dining room anyway. "You alright?" he shouted at Orion, who was in the process of picking himself up off the floor, using his rifle as a cane.

"Goddamn bastards," Orion growled.

"Hey, you alright?"

Orion looked at the gash that cut through the side of his

shoulder. Blood gushed down his arm, and while it hurt like a bitch, he was thankful it only grazed him and didn't go right through, or worse yet: lodged itself in there. He pressed his hand over it and said, "I'll live."

They ducked as more gunfire tore up the booths and floor around them. Retreated for the bar. The swordfish blew apart, its biomechanical innards splattering everywhere. Another water column burst and spilled Chinese rice fish all over the floor.

Reactionaries appeared at the top of the stairs. Their bullets chased the detectives across the dining room to the bar. Orion dived over the counter. Barstow scrambled around it.

Sitting with his back against the counter, Orion reloaded and tossed Barstow his last spare mag. "How many left? Can't be too many."

"Hold on, let me check," Barstow replied sarcastically, though he didn't actually look up.

Orion blinked, expecting him to actually do it. "Well?"

"I'm not *actually* sticking my head out there, you moron."

"Oh." Orion sighed and adjusted his position to a crouch. "Fine. I'll do it."

"No, *I'll* do it."

"You just said you wouldn't."

"I'm older than you, son. No way am I letting a youngster like you stick his head out like that. It'd be a bad way to go. Plus it'd ruin my reputation." Barstow quickly peeked over the counter. Gunfire erupted. He ducked down again as hot lead sprayed the countertop. The booze on the shelf above them exploded and came down in a sparkling cascade.

"So how many?" Orion asked as he dodged a falling wine bottle.

Barstow looked at him, a distressed look clear on his face. "Too many."

09: Rush

Police Countach cruisers slewed around the corner just down the water-slick road, sirens wailing. An ACPD hovercopter (think of an Apache helicopter, only with anti-gravity boosters in the place of old-fashioned rotors, and a bulkier design) buzzed overhead, missiles armed. The rain was still coming down hard. Thunder rumbled—or maybe that was gunfire.

At least a dozen and a half of them remained. Six on the stairs. The rest lined up at the top of the embankment, all spraying the bar.

The leader, two privates, and his grenadier were the only ones left in the lobby. They'd positioned themselves behind the front entrance. Smashed the glass doors onto the front steps with the butts of their rifles. The grenadier waited until the cruisers came into view. Then loosed a rocket. It whistled over the front entrance steps. Blew up the front end of the leading cruiser. The resulting fireball capsized it and sent it skidding down the road on its top.

The privates squatted at the top of the steps and hosed the other cruisers with their assault rifles.

"Holy shit!" a cop shouted on the telepathic frequency. *"Be advised, we're dealing with some heavy artillery here!"*

Another rocket blasted a second cruiser to flaming pieces. A nearby cruiser started to back up as the privates' assault bounced harmlessly off its armoured plating.

"We need backup ASAP!"

The hovercopter circled round the front entrance. Its wing-mounted rotary cannons peppered the main entrance with a thousand rounds per minute. A hail of explosive rounds raced up the staircase, disintegrating the steps—and the two privates—almost instantly.

The leader and the grenadier ducked behind the steel doorjamb. Explosive rounds whizzed through the doorway and blew twelve-inch craters across the floor between them. The OPEN sign above the door exploded.

"Handle it!" the leader shouted into his earpiece. "Somebody handle it!"

*

The elevator on the second floor opened. Out stepped the minigun reactionary, who went around the elevator and entered the dining room behind it. With a mighty kick, he pushed a table through the outer partition window and sent it crashing into a garden of artificial acer griseum trees that lined the front of the restaurant. Aimed the minigun at the hovercopter.

The pilots turned their attention from the main entrance to the reactionary on the second floor—but too late.

The minigun sent a flurry of rounds tearing across the hovercopter's front, spider-webbing the bulletproof windscreen, which wouldn't be able to take much more of the assault. The pilot jerked on the stick, ducking as the bullets started to pierce the windscreen and uproot the control panel, which exploded in their faces.

The grenadier leaped back into the open and launched a rocket into the hovercopter's right wing. Perfect shot. Tore the wing right off and sent the hovercopter into an uncontrollable tailspin. Exploding control panel malfunctioned. The remaining rotary cannon on its left wing started lighting up its surroundings. The red neon CHINESE PALACE letters running across the restaurant's front rapidly exploded one letter at a time. Window panes burst in quick succession. People in the second floor of the office building across the street fled in a panic as stray rounds razed their cubicle offices to the floor.

"We've lost control! We've lost control—"

The hovercopter spiralled into the main floor of the restaurant and plowed through the flooded dining area. The impact sent a violent tremor through the entire building. The hovercopter flattened the partitions and booths with the grace of a wrecking ball. Finally burst apart in a fiery conflagration. Sent gouts of flame blasting through the side of the building into the parking lot, setting artificial trees alight.

As the building shook, Orion and Barstow exchanged looks and peeked over the counter in time to see the orange glow of the explosion two dining rooms across the restaurant. The reactionaries had stopped shooting at them, instead watching the explosion from their vantage points. Some of the men above the embankment ducked to avoid high-flying debris.

"Jesus Christ," Barstow gasped.

"Cavalry's not doing so well," Orion said with a whistle. "Cavalry's in need of cavalry."

"That's not funny," Barstow snarled.

"I wasn't really joking."

The reactionaries turned back around. Orion and Barstow stole the opportunity and fired on them first—Orion on the top of the embankment; Barstow on the stairs. Scored a handful of them before they scrambled for cover. All the men on the stairs toppled lifelessly to the bottom.

Orion leaned over the counter, aiming carefully at the elevated dining area. When a reactionary peeked out from behind a fallen comrade's body, Orion plucked the top of his head off with one shot. He adjusted his aim to the other side of the embankment as two of them came back up. He fired—

—dry. "Shit!"

The reactionary duo strafed the countertop, but by then Orion had already ducked. He turned to Barstow and said, "Little help?"

Barstow checked his current magazine. "I'm out." He slapped the mag home and tossed the rifle altogether in favour of his LE magnum. "Only got six spares."

Orion drew his own LE and checked the cylinder. Two left. He dumped the empty shells and pushed in four new ones. "I think I have less than that."

"Then let's make 'em count."

Another hovercopter had arrived and flew above the restaurant. Glowing red eyes that could adapt to any environment; all-black battle gear, head to toe—these were the only characteristics worth noting of the four tactical cyborgs that rappelled down to the roof and planted explosive charges all around the dome. They cleared the blast zone and set off the charges. With a deafening *whump* the dome caved inward.

"*Go! Go! Go!*" the captain of the cyborgs barked on the telepathic link as they jumped into the crater and abseiled to the second floor, gripping their submachine guns. "*Be advised: there isn't much left of the second floor. Watch your step.*"

Two reactionaries approached the edge of the collapsed dining area and opened up on the descending tactical cyborgs. The cyborgs returned fire, singlehandedly mowing down the enemy duo with their bullpup submachine guns before they could suffer any casualties. They went through the gaping hole in the second floor and landed firmly on the main floor. Disconnected their lines. Spread out in separate directions to each cover a corner of the restaurant level.

Since the edge of the second floor crater was out of his reach, one of the cyborgs had to take the elevator back up. *"On my way to neutralize our minigun friend on level two."*

"Acknowledged."

A tactical cyborg rushed behind the front counter without being seen by the leader or the grenadier. He straightened and fired at them over the counter. Cut through the grenadier's arm. Both reactionaries leaped out of the cyborg's view. The grenadier roared in agony as he inspected the holes in his right upper arm. He held the rocket launcher at waist level.

"Don't!" the leader shouted.

Too late. The grenadier approached his end of the bridge and launched the rocket across it. Blasted the counter to splinters. Blew the cyborg's flailing body through the wall behind it.

A cop fired his LE magnum at the grenadier's back from behind a cruiser. Two shots missed. One ripped a hole through the grenadier's bulletproof vest and seared the flesh on his back. The grenadier screamed and fell forward.

"Bastards!" The leader loosed a five-round burst at the cruiser. His bullets skipped harmlessly off the hood as the cop took cover behind it. The leader retreated behind the steel doorjamb and said into his earpiece, "They've got tacticals swarming the place! Be on your guard!"

The grenadier lifted himself onto his hands and knees, groaning in agony, limbs trembling uncontrollably. "Son of a bitch…!"

"You alright?" the leader asked him.

"I'm fine, General." The grenadier picked up his launcher and crawled behind the doorjamb opposite his leader.

The reactionary on the second floor turned away from the windows, careful to avoid getting shot by anyone on the ground. He heard the elevator's bell chime, despite the deafening roar of his minigun, which he turned in the direction of the dining room entrance. As soon as the cyborg came into view, he fired. The cyborg fired back, having known he'd made an error in judgement. No turning back. The reactionary's stream of fire tore the cyborg in half through the middle and blew the pieces into the gaping hole in the floor behind him.

Satisfied, the reactionary turned back to the windows, approached the edge, and loosed another volley at the cluster of cruisers on the road. Even with their armour plating, the cruisers didn't stand a chance against the reactionary's endless stream of explosive rounds. One exploded after another. Bodies came apart like wet paper. Concrete was uprooted from the road. Reinforcements were a minute late—by the time they arrived, the road was a blazing inferno, and the men who called them were all but ground into a fine paste.

The reactionary on the second floor was unstoppable, and he celebrated his first victory by watching the wrecks scattered across the road burn.

When reinforcements finally skidded around the corner to join the fight, he showered them with a volley as merciless as before.

With the exception of the minigun support and the two men at the front entrance, the four reactionaries crouched at the top of the embankment were the last of them. They were too focused on the detectives behind the bar to notice the cyborg crossing the bridge behind them until it was too late. The cyborg's bullets raked across their backs. Dying screams rang through the air as they pivoted forward and bounced to the bottom of the embankment.

Confused by the screams, Orion and Barstow looked over the counter.

The tactical cyborg spotted them and trained his submachine gun on them. "Come out with your hands where I can see them! Do it now!"

"It's okay, it's alright!" Barstow shouted as he and his partner came up from behind the counter, their hands up, LE magnums held by the grips with the index finger and thumb.

"We're on your side," Orion called. He slowly opened his coat and showed the cyborg his gold star. Barstow did the same.

The cyborg relaxed and lowered his gun. "You alright, sir?"

"We're good. Just a few bruises and scratches," Orion replied as he and his partner crossed the dining area toward the cyborg.

"How many of those bastards are left?" Barstow growled.

"Approximately three, sir. Four at the most."

Barstow checked the bullets in his LE magnum, just to be on the safe side, and then slapped the cylinder back into place. "Then let's go get 'em."

"We have to retreat," the leader barked into his earpiece. "We're done."

"Go on ahead, sir," the reactionary on the second floor responded. "I'll hold them off."

"I'm not leaving you behind, Sergeant."

"With all due respect, sir, you don't have a say in the matter." The reactionary focused his aim on a particular cruiser. His attack sent it screeching off the road and crashing into the garden below him. "They will have us overtaken in a matter of minutes. Get out of here while the road is still clear! Now!"

The General gritted his teeth as he strung his grenadier's arm over his shoulders and lifted him off the floor. He still gripped his Uzi in his free hand. "Goddamn it."

A loud clatter diverted his attention from the scene on the road. He whirled around, back to the gaping hole where the front counter used to be. The cyborg his grenadier had blasted emerged from the smoke and flames. Its battle gear, battered and torn. Its helmet gone. Half its head of hair was burned off. Its face, made from an expensive plastic-based material, was melting away. Its left arm had been twisted around at the elbow. Its right hand still gripped its submachine gun, which it was in the process of pointing at him.

"Shit," the General exclaimed, right before he blasted the cyborg with his Uzi.

The cyborg took the bullets with a grain of salt, standing its ground. Its body convulsed as the General threw everything he had at him—until the gun clicked empty. The cyborg's grin was as distorted as the memory of a nightmare. Its melting face didn't help its appearance at all. "You're done. Surrender now—"

The grenadier suddenly threw up a China Lake and blew another grenade into the cyborg's chest, slamming it back through the hole. With the threat neutralized for the time being, the grenadier released a heavy sigh—either of relief or fatigue; the General couldn't tell the difference. Dropping his China Lake on the floor, the grenadier said, "Leave me here, sir. I've outlived my usefulness to you now."

"Don't bullshit me," the General hissed as he carried his man out into the heavy rain. "We're not out of this yet." He looked up at the second floor. Watched the stream of bullets buzz out of the window and tear up the police squads that came charging in. He said into his earpiece, "It's been an honour, Sergeant. Thank you."

"Yes, sir," the Sergeant replied. "No need to thank me, sir. Just fulfilling my duty. Over and out."

The General ground his teeth as he started down the shattered stairs with his grenadier leaning on him, hating himself for leaving a man behind.

The Sergeant tossed his earpiece away and continued his relentless attack on the police forces as they started to pull back. He wasn't aware of the cyborg behind him...

The cyborg he'd torn in half had crawled its way back up to the second floor, using the stairs this time. Despite having no legs, with its synthetic organs falling out of its torn end, the cyborg had returned in good time. Propping himself up on his free hand, the cyborg aimed at the sergeant's back with his submachine gun in his other hand. Fired a volley of explosive rounds. Ripped the Sergeant to gory shreds. Propelled whatever was left of the Sergeant out the window and listened to his corpse tumble through the branches of the acer griseum trees. The glorious snapping of branches, the rustling of leaves. The heavy thump that followed.

A satisfied smile crossed the cyborg's face. *"Consider our minigun buddy neutralized."*

10: Runoff

Barstow, Orion, and the tactical cyborg reached the front counter—or what was left of it. Guns poised, they looked for the last of the reactionaries, only to find that aside from the corpses piled up all over the place, the front end of the restaurant was abandoned.

"Bastard's making a run for it!" Barstow shouted as he darted across the bridge and out the doorway.

Orion and the cyborg followed him. A different stutter of gunfire up above interrupted the minigun's deep roar. A few seconds later, Orion heard the telepathic confirmation: *"Consider our minigun buddy neutralized."*

"Well that takes care of that, then," Orion said as he skidded down the shattered front steps to the sidewalk. He stopped to observe the horrific carnage the minigun reactionary had caused before taking off after Barstow.

Barstow nearly reached the end of the block when a blue and white van burst from under a canopy of brush in the restaurant's garden, vaulted over the sidewalk (and a ducking Barstow), and slewed across the road. "Jesus H. Christ!" Barstow shouted as he straightened, aiming his LE magnum at the fishtailing van. He fired off a couple shots. Blew off one of the rear doors. Burst one of the tires. The tires squealed. The van lurched forward, swerved, rocked back and forth uncontrollably. Then it landed on its side. Skidded down the road. Sliding, whirling; plowed through a bus stop shelter. Barely missed a payphone terminal on the sidewalk. Came to a standstill, rear end pointing at a narrow alley.

Orion caught up to Barstow and whistled at the side. "Nice shot!"

The detectives approached the overturned van with the utmost caution.

The passenger door flew up. The cyborg yelled, "Down!" and pushed Barstow and Orion off balance as an assault rifle popped into view.

The grenadier opened up on them, propping himself on the door frame. Cut down the cyborg with a dozen bullets. Explosive slugs liquidized the whole upper body.

Barstow and Orion replied with their LE magnums. The grenadier screamed as he took one in the eye. Before his head could explode, the whole van burst into flames. Belched a fireball into the grey sky.

"Damn!" Orion yelled as he ran to the blazing van. He went around to the back and inspected the flaming interior as best he could. "So much for questioning... him...?" He heard something behind him. Turned to look down the ramp that led into an alleyway. Just barely caught a glimpse of the General. "We've got a runner!" He charged after the General, loading the last of his spare rounds into his gun.

The General knew they were after him. He frantically reloaded his Uzi as he raced down the alley as fast as he legs would allow.

Orion was catching up. He hit the corner and bolted after him. Fired a slug after him. It whistled over the General's shoulder and blew a hole in the brick wall ahead of them instead.

The General spun around, Uzi blowing down the alley, tearing up the walls, shredding the trash strewn all over the place. Orion's wounded shoulder panged as he threw himself against the wall. Luckily for him, the reactionary's aim was all over the place, more desperate than precise. Orion ducked behind a leaking pipe and squeezed off another shot.

The General took a right turn. Orion went after him. No sooner had he rounded the corner than the General let off another volley at him. Orion threw himself behind the corner and waited as the General's bullets ripped chunks out of the brick wall. Orion listened as the General's quick steps splashed through puddles. Metal rang out. Someone screamed.

Orion went around the corner and realized the bastard had kicked someone's door in. Orion cleared the front steps and entered a cramped kitchen where a family of five had been sitting around a table, shouting in another language at the intruders.

Machine gunfire from the living room caused the buffet and hutch between the two rooms to explode. Glass and china flying. The dishes on the table popped and shattered as everyone hit the floor. Orion returned a shot through the wall. He heard glass shattering in the next room. Left the screaming family in the kitchen, most likely thankful that they were all still alive after this encounter.

Orion found one of the windows broken. Crossed the living room. Stumbled over the coffee table. Peered out the window to see the reactionary racing down the street. He fired two shots at him and cursed when the bullets harmlessly slapped the road on either side of the fleeing reactionary. The few pedestrians on the sidewalk shrieked and ducked into nearby alleyways.

Orion jumped through the window and fell a single storey. Landed on his feet with a crunch. Joints clicked. He continued his pursuit, noting the alleyway the General had taken.

Barstow entered the house, alarmed by the screaming family. He tried to assure them everything would be fine, but once they responded with rapid-fire Spanish, he quickly gave up trying to reason with them and instead entered the living room. Found the broken window. Looked through it in time to see Orion turn into an alleyway down the road. "For Christ's sake."

The General tore the handles off a cellar door and kicked the doors down the stairs. Orion appeared from around the corner and fired. The General dived into the cellar and tumbled head over heels down the stairs into a dark tunnel. Landed in an awkward heap. Scrambled to his feet. Continued running.

Orion reached the cellar and looked inside. "Ah, shit!" he snarled aloud, then called out to Barstow on the telepathic frequency, *"The son of a bitch's ducking into Takuo! I'm going after him."*

"No, don't do that!"

Too late. Orion was at the bottom of the stairs and huffing down the tunnel before Barstow's reply came through.

"Orion! Shit!"

The General hurled himself headfirst into the bizarre crowds of Takuo Market screaming, "Cops! Cops!"

That got the majority of their attention.

"There's a cop behind me!" he yelled, whirling around.

Orion popped into view. The General pointed at him and screamed, "There he is!"

"A goddamn cop!" an impish cyborg dwarf squealed. "He's mine!" He hurled a grenade at Orion, whose nerves disobeyed his command to take cover. The grenade bounced toward him.

Move, damn it! Terror struck him. *Shit. Shit. Shit!* The grenade touched his foot. Rolled a few inches. Stopped directly under him.

Nothing.

An overlapping "Huh?" emanated from the crowd as they watched, having braced for an explosion that never came. Even the General remained, staring perplexed at Orion.

Orion picked up the grenade. He hardly needed to inspect it more closely to realize what the problem was. He scowled. Pulled the pin. Let the spoon fly. Tossed it back. "Idiot!"

A burst of screams filled the market as the cyborgs scattered in all directions. The grenade exploded, but by then no one was within the blast range.

The reactionary still had the cover of smoke and darted between two severed limb venders to escape. Orion chased after him. A shot rang out. A small crater appeared by Orion's right foot. He whirled around and shot a cyborg with a smoking hand cannon prosthetic before he could try again, and quickly fled the scene as more angry cyborgs responded with a flurry of hot lead and grenades. Venders exploded. Body parts spun through the air. The beggar Orion dashed past as he escaped into the alley ceased to exist once the bullet storm let up.

"The pig's mine!" a cyborg roared as he heaved a massive rocket launcher on his bulky shoulders and fired into the alley, unwittingly killing a group of cyborgs with the backblast.

Orion pushed himself harder than ever before. Lungs were on fire. The rocket's high-pitched squeal only got louder the farther in he went. The end of the alley, only another fifteen feet. The reactionary disappeared around the corner. The rocket was too damn close. Too fast. Too late.

Then an elderly cyborg stepped out into the alley saying, "What's all the noise—"

Came between Orion and the rocket. The rocket punched the cyborg in the face. Shattered the bone. Pierced the brain. Touched the inside of the cranium. Exploded.

The concussive blast splintered the buildings on either side. Flames chased Orion now, and the old bastard wasn't gonna die today. He dived out of the alley. A fireball blew after him. The force sent him sailing across the road.

The reactionary spun on his heel in time to see Orion crash

through the window pane of the building on the other side. The rest of the windows burst inward from the shockwave.

A wall of fire rose up from the alley. A horrifying tremor shook the market to its very foundations. Shattered windows. Knocked ornaments off their perch. Rattled tools and merchandise.

The rocket-launching cyborg on the other side of the block grinned as he admired his destructive handiwork. "I think I got 'im!"

When flaming debris started coming down, the reactionary took off running again.

Orion hadn't felt pain like this in a long time. He picked himself up and brushed off glass shards and debris. He had to move. His target was getting away. "C'mon, Orion," he grunted to himself as he staggered out the window into the street. He was already out of breath. Felt like he was bleeding internally. Quickly checked himself and found only bloody cuts and nasty bruises. He started down the street after the last reactionary, muttering some self-motivation under his breath, "I'll buy you a beer after this."

The General's breath got ragged as he pressed on down another alley, feet slapping across shallow waters. It was dead quiet now. The three-storey apartments on either side of him were so crudely put together they threatened to collapse in on themselves. Clotheslines and wiring were strung overhead with shoes and clothes and even an abandoned limb prosthetic dangling from them.

He'd reached the edge of the shanty town. The silence disturbed him. All that could be heard were his feet splashing on a two-inch sheet of water, and the distant rumble of a waterfall. He checked the bullets in the extended mag of his Uzi. Another twenty bullets left. He checked his utility belt for spares. His heart skipped when he found none.

He slowed to a walk to catch his breath. Constantly looked over his shoulder for any sign of his pursuer. Nothing. The alley was empty at both ends.

Maybe I lost him.

The end of the alley. He stepped out onto a concrete riverbank—and the two inches of water become four inches, just reaching over his ankles. Went out further into the light fog. A rusty smell hung in the air. He turned his head to the waterfall upriver, shooting out of a massive sewer pipe in a concrete wall.

The dark green waters that shot out were a mixture of human waste from the 'surface dwellers' and rainwater that entered the storm drains.

The reactionary started to approach the railing. Crossed to the middle of the bank when he suddenly felt the need to turn around. He looked at the apartments. Scanned the balconies on every floor and found them empty. Nothing in the windows either.

With a relieved sigh, he turned back to the river—

A shot rang out. His left kneecap blew apart. He howled in agony. He started to fall as the bottom half of his left leg separated in a dizzying blood spray. He whirled around in mid-fall, blasting his Uzi in an arc, explosive rounds kicking up a semicircle of waterspouts.

Another shot, and his Uzi came apart—along with his hand. The reactionary didn't scream this time. Too shocked.

"Up here, dickhead!"

The General looked up at the rooftop of one of the apartment shanties and saw Orion perched on the edge, smoking gun barrel trained on him. The General looked at the shredded stump where his hand used to be, eyes bulging.

Orion expertly hopped down from the rooftop to the ground floor by floor, leaping on air conditioners, railings; and using window sills as footholds until he'd reached an acceptable jumping height on the second floor. He let go. Fell one storey. Landed on the platform with a light splash. He walked across the platform, gun still trained on the reactionary.

"Just what the hell possessed you to attack us like that?" Orion growled.

The reactionary leaned back, against the railing, squatting on his good leg as if he'd been born with only that one. The pained expression in his face was all but gone, as if his missing limbs no longer mattered. He shot Orion with a predatory glare.

"I don't like the look you're giving me." Orion cocked the hammer of his LE magnum for dramatic effect. "Answer the goddamn question. Why did you attack my partner and I? Your group hates the Company—I got that part—but what do my partner and I have to do with your opposition against them? Aside from the fact that we're cops, of course. But we personally haven't done anything to you or your rebel pals. So let me answer that question for you: we have absolutely *jack shit* to do with that. So what's your reason? Talk!"

A crazed grin distorted the General's face. "It's got *everything* to do with you."

"Oh, yeah? Enlighten me."

Using the railing for support with his good hand, the reactionary stood himself up on his good leg and maintained his unsettling smile on Orion. "The CEO owns the police force. You're all his enforcers. It doesn't matter how much you want to deny it. That's the truth."

"I'm more of an old-fashioned, justice-seeking kind of guy, myself," Orion replied. "I don't schedule my days according to the CEO's agenda. Hell, I think I might even hate him as much as you do. The guy's a creep. But allow me to let you in on a little secret: if I'd been born just a little dumber, I might've found myself in your ranks instead of the precinct."

"But you didn't."

"Nope."

"And here we here."

"Yup."

"You're just as much to blame as the others."

"Don't start preaching to me about 'wrong paths' or whatever it is you're about to say. I don't care about that. What I care about is the reason behind why you were specifically after *us*. I can tell when someone shoots at a cop on a whim, and when someone shoots at a cop knowing full-well who they were to begin with. Why?"

"That's not important."

"You and your men slaughtered dozens of innocent people today just to assassinate two men, and you're trying to tell me what's important?!" Orion snapped. "That's not how this game works! You're gonna tell me why you attacked us, and you're gonna do it right fucking now! Or I'll put a goddamn bullet through your other leg."

Ripples expanded from the reactionary's foot as he started to rise. Really *rise*. Off the ground. His hair and clothing swayed as if he'd suddenly entered zero gravity. Droplets of blood from his wounds fluttered around him like flower petals.

A psychokinetic?! Orion shouted aloud, "Sit back down! Do it now, or I'll shoot!"

A combat knife appeared in the reactionary's hand. He shot forward like a bullet. A sprite in the wind.

Orion fired—

Click!

Heart nearly stopped. The reactionary came down on him. Orion's trigger guard blocked the slashing knife. Steel grinded against steel as the knife edge pressed against the LE magnum's trigger guard. The General's foot lashed out. Orion kicked it to the side. Stumbled back as the reactionary pushed forward. The General's knife retracted. Lunged. Orion dodged the stab and threw his shoulder into the reactionary's chest. He chopped the reactionary's wrist. Knocked the knife out of his hand. Thrust his head forward. His forehead caught the bastard in the nose with a sickening crack.

The reactionary floated back a few feet, his only hand feeling his broken nose as it gushed blood over his lips.

The two adversaries traded furious glares.

The reactionary ignored the blood that dripped off his chin and trickled down his neck. Lurched forward again. Shot up in the air and spun in an arc. Good foot came down for a skull-splitting kick. With those boots, he could've done it. But Orion dodged it, let the foot crack a small web into the concrete floor. Grabbed the leg by the ankle and tucked it under his right armpit. Threw his left fist up into the kneecap with everything he had. Snapped the leg, practically in half. Launched a few pieces of bloody bone into the air.

The reactionary screamed and retreated again, his leg dangling under him by flesh and damaged tissue.

"Enough already!" Orion shouted.

An invisible force blast ripped across the platform. Orion dodged it and charged forward. Another force blast pushed through the concrete floor toward an oncoming Orion. Orion leaped to the side, quickly closing the gap between them. Two more steps. Ducked as the reactionary's fist lashed out. Buried his own right fist into the General's vest. Felt two of his knuckles pop against something hard.

"Agh!" he shouted through gnashed teeth. Cocked his other fist back. Caught the General in the jaw. Swung his foot around. Smashed three of the General's ribs and sent him skimming across the shallow water.

With his adversary down for the count—for now—Orion inspected his bleeding right fist. "What the hell did you eat to break two of my fingers with your stomach? Christ…" His right hand trembled as he nursed it to the best of his abilities—which involved popping his fingers back into place. Both times, he growled in pain, stifling it as much as possible. When that was done, he turned back to the reactionary, who had adjusted himself to a sitting position in the middle of the platform. There was plenty of space on the riverbank to fight, but Orion didn't want to fight, and from the looks of things, he figured he'd just kicked the last of it out of the General.

The reactionary fell flat on his face. When his nostrils sucked in water, he threw his head back and gasped. He looked around frantically, as if waking up with a start. "Where—?" He noticed his hand was missing. Heaved a gasp. Inspected the rest of his body with a sense of panic that escalated by the split second. "Oh my God, this can't be happening! Where am I?"

Orion could swear his own head tilted a full ninety degrees as he watched the reactionary roll around, screaming and wailing like an animal that'd just been run over by a truck and survived by what some morons would call a 'miracle.' "What the hell are you…?"

The reactionary burst into tears and wailed some more. "It's a dream! It's a dream! Wake up! Wake up! Wake up! Wake up!" His speech escalated into a series of indecipherably jumbled words.

Orion couldn't make any sense of it.

The reactionary fell flat on his back and unleashed an ear-splitting howl. A wide circle of concrete shattered beneath him. Chunks rose up all around him. "WHAT'S HAPPENING TO ME?!" he shrieked. Stuck his arm out, involuntarily, if Orion judged his facial expression correctly. He gripped a small detonator in his hand. His thumb quivered, hovering over the red button.

"Put that down!" Orion barked. But he didn't move to disarm the man. No sense in running into the blast range, only to be blown up for his troubles if he couldn't make it.

The reactionary's throat made a noise that sounded like a mixture of whining and pushing out a constipated shit as his will wrestled with whatever was controlling his thumb—if something else was controlling him. Maybe the guy was just crazy. Or on drugs. Or both. "I can't stop it," he gasped.

His thumb pressed down.

As soon as he did that, his body inflated. His screams turned into garbling sounds. Then he burst, his insides splattering into a disgusting pool. The only solid thing about him now was his head, which was sent bouncing a few feet away like a skipping stone. Crimson spread through the water, slowly going with the current of the river.

Orion stood rooted to the spot, utterly dumbfounded by the scene that just took place. He couldn't take his eyes off the blackish, ruby-red circle of gore that used to be the reactionary. Nothing but the sounds of the waterfall could be heard for the longest time.

After what seemed like hours, Orion pushed the button behind his ear. *"Barstow. The perp's neutralized."*

"What?! He got away?"

"I wouldn't say that."

"What, then?"

Orion squinted, as if that'd somehow make the whole thing less impossible to figure out. For some inexplicable reason, he felt the need to turn. Like he was being watched despite surveillance being a rare thing in the underground slum world of Takuo. He looked up at the apartments. Spotted someone—or something—dressed entirely in black. Before his cybernetic blue eyes could focus on the figure, Orion lost sight of him. Whoever it was had his head encased in a closed modular helmet with the visor down to conceal his eyes.

Orion continued staring at the spot where the figure vanished, hoping he'd spring back into his view, but knowing he wouldn't.

Finally, he said, *"It's a long and perplexing story..."*

11: She

Scott Residence

She opened her shining, cobalt eyes—awoke standing, strangely enough. The perfect woman. A being like no other; like that of his perfect lover—only better.

Short blonde hair, athletic body type with a more voluptuous bust than anyone could recall—as if she'd had an impossible and sudden growth spurt. A height of about five and a half feet. Her face was innocent, soft-looking, stern, and mature all at once.

The naked woman standing before him was the woman of his dreams.

"So you're awake," he said breathlessly, staring at her with eyes bulging in awe. "You're finally awake..."

Her expression remained blank as her life support system booted up. It only took a moment before the glow in her eyes faded. Uneasy emotions came pouring out as she dropped to a squat on the floor, hugging her knees against her chest. "It's cold."

The realization hit him right away. He took off his lab coat and draped it over her bare shoulders. "I'm sorry," he said as he led her out of the quarantined containment room, kept at cold temperatures at all times. "Let's get you some clothes."

"What is this place?" she asked, surveying the well-furnished living room as they crossed through it. The wall-to-ceiling windows stretched across the far wall, providing a breathtaking view of the city's skyline.

"I suppose your memory hasn't quite fully recovered yet. This is my... *our* home."

"Our home?"

"That's right," Franklin Scott said with a smile. "Our home. Welcome back, Elsa."

Elsa looked around again, and smiled at the warm feeling of her home. "It's good to be back."

He held her tightly. His body heat helped smooth away the chill the lab's conditions had given her. He involuntarily began to sob into her shoulder. His embrace tightened. "I've missed you so much, Elsa..."

Elsa wrapped her slender arms around him and lovingly stroked the hair on the back of his neck. "I know, dear. I'm sorry. Please don't cry."

He sniffled and let go of her. Turned away and wiped his eyes.

Elsa kissed his cheek and said, "I'm going to put on some clothes, okay?"

Still wiping his eyes on his sleeve, Franklin said, "I'll fix you something warm." As she headed to the bedroom, he eagerly went into the kitchen, happy to be useful to her again. By the time she'd come out, fully dressed in a blue fleece sweater and jeans, he had a warm cup of tea waiting for her on the dining room table. He sat in the chair beside her spot with his own cup, watching her intently as soon as she walked into view. She sat down beside him with a smile as warm as her fresh tea, her sleeves stretched over her hands. She lifted her cup off the table in her palms and blew on it.

"Careful," he said.

"I know, dear." She took a small, cautious sip. She shivered slightly as the tea's comforting sensation coursed through her body. "Mm! Delicious, as always. Thank you."

He beamed. If he had a tail, he'd be wagging it like a dog. "Anything for you, my sweet."

She glanced at him as she took another sip. The strange look on his face as he kept his eyes on her made her curious, but nothing near uncomfortable. She set her cup down and giggled at the expression on his face. "What?"

His eyes snapped back into focus. "Huh?"

"You've been looking at me as if you haven't seen me in a dog's age. What's on your mind?"

"Oh, nothing. I've just missed you, that's all."

"It's alright, Frank. I'm not leaving you." She took another sip from her tea, letting her reassuring words sink in and hopefully lift his spirits. "I'm not going anywhere."

"I... I hope not." He looked at her face again. Just looking at her made his heart giddy with excitement. Seeing her physically sitting in this chair was all he needed for the empty gap inside him to once again be filled. His life, complete once more.

All he had to do now was keep it that way.

12: Surrogates

28th Precinct Station

"It's not every day a cop turns Takuo Market into a war zone and comes out alive with only scratches to show for it," Barstow said heatedly, continuing his rant that Orion had the misfortune of listening to for the past half hour.

Orion sat on the edge of an examination table in the station's infirmary, allowing the cyborg nurse to do her job of stitching up Orion's many cuts, mostly caused when that rocket-launching cyborg's explosion launched him through a storefront. The cybernetic nurse was designed, of course, to resemble a Hollywood-style, highly sexualized interpretation instead of the real thing—wearing a white fetish outfit with fishnet stockings, blue eyes, and dirty blonde hair pinned back in a bun under a white cap with a red cross.

"Christ, Barstow. Cut me some slack, already. It's not every day a cop survives a gunfight, either. You ought to be relieved. And while we're still on the Takuo subject: where the hell were you? Unless I missed the part when the Superintendent slapped a memo on my desk to notify me that we're no longer partners, I stand on the firm belief that my partner is supposed to back me up. So where the fuck were you when I was getting shot at and blown up by cyborgs, Barstow?!"

"I was at the entrance warning you to pull out! You know how rough the street-life in Takuo can be, especially when it comes to trespassing law enforcement. But you *had* to be the hero, and you jumped right in there with no regard for the consequences. And then you complain about a few scratches when you ought to be grateful that you're still *alive*." Barstow scoffed and crossed his arms. "Clearly we share a different perspective on a great many things. To each their own. I respect your perspectives as much as you respect mine. However... your childishness is the only thing that brings this partnership down, Orion. When are you gonna drop the baby shaker?"

"Just as soon as *you* pull the stick out of your ass," Orion snapped back.

Barstow seethed.

"Gentlemen!" the nurse exclaimed, hand on her chest, acting shocked. "Please, no fighting. Can't we all just get along?"

Orion ignored her. "I know why you didn't go down there with me, Barstow. It's because you're *scared*!"

"What?" Barstow shouted.

"You didn't have the time to go running for your disguise, so you just decided to 'hold the fort' until backup arrived. There was no 'I'm gonna go down there and back my partner up like I'm supposed to' involved. Instead, there was 'I'm gonna just sit here and wait for the inevitable dying scream and communication cut-off on the goddamn telepathic frequency!' You were ready to write me off already! Weren't you?"

"*Yes*!" Barstow snapped. "*Yes*, I was!" He began circling the examination table, glaring at Orion the whole time as he went on, "Do you realize that if I went down there with you, the likelihood on the possibility of our survival could—not would, *could*—go up. However, the likelihood on the possibility of our survival could also go down. Takuo Market is a highly unpredictable and very dangerous place. If we both died, the precinct would have lost two good cops instead of just one. And what if I'd brought backup? Consider the situation in which I rope along a gang of ten or twenty or thirty police officers or tactical cyborgs or... whatever. Now think about how many of those men would have died because of your recklessness. There are only three reasons why you're still alive: 1) you were fast on your feet; 2) you were resourceful; 3) for twenty-eight minutes, God decided to appoint you as the luckiest man on the planet." He stopped to slap Orion on the shoulder, purposely hitting a bloody cut.

"Ow," Orion snarled.

Barstow shrugged and started another lap around the table. "Groups are slow. In environments like Takuo, where the roads are small and the hostiles are many, there's bound to be confusion, chaos, and worst of all: casualties."

"You cooked up quite the justification to cover for your own cowardice—"

"Cowardice has nothing to do with it, Jason. I was *smart* about it. I was not about to sacrifice the lives of ten or thirty men— men with husbands, or wives, or girlfriends, children, distant relatives, cousins, dogs, cats, parrots, goldfish; you get the idea—for the life of one reckless man, no matter how much that one man may mean to me. And let's not forget the obvious fact that *dozens* of people had *already* died because of us at the Chinese Palace. Dozens of people, uninvolved in every way; their only crime being that they were in the wrong place at the wrong time. On top of that, an early report indicates that twenty-nine police officers died on the scene. Let me ask you this: with all the deaths inadvertently caused by our presence today, would you really have wanted *more* casualties on your conscience if I had followed you down with a small army? A small army that surely would not come back up with the same amount of men as it did when it first went down?" Barstow pulled up a stool beside the examination table, facing his partner with the utmost sincerity. "Jason, drop the stubborn narrow-mindedness for a moment. You know full-well you're like a brother to me. You're my best friend. I shouldn't have to explain how devastated I'd be if you went and got yourself killed. But that doesn't mean I'm going to let you drag me along for your banzai charges into enemy territory just to find a suspect we'll nab eventually, one way or another. And hell, that particular reactionary died before we even had the chance to learn his name. Tell me, Orion, is that worth dying over?"

Orion heaved a big sigh, pissed at the fact that his friend had more-or-less won the argument. Logic over emotions. "I suppose not."

"I didn't think so."

"You're still a hollow asshole, Barstow. And you piss me off immensely."

Barstow smirked. Crossed his arms. "I'll take that with a grain of salt." He uncrossed his arms and patted his friend's back.

"Ow!"

"Sorry."

Once Orion had been patched up, the two detectives spent the next four hours writing out reports detailing the attempt on their lives. After that, they went down to the morgue to meet Doctor Moore, who had to have inspected at least one of the reactionaries' corpses by that time.

"Find anything, Doc?" Orion asked as soon as they came through the entrance.

Moore looked up from a reactionary he was in the middle of examining—whose cranium had been carved open and carefully lifted off to reveal his brain. Moore's blood-spattered bodysuit, goggles, and oxygen mask made him look three times wider than his normal width—luckily he was a thin man to begin with. His voice sounded deeper through the speaker in his mask. "I have, actually."

"What's that?" Barstow asked.

"A warping of the mind," Moore said thoughtfully as he started to once again root around in the reactionary's cranium.

"Excuse me?" Barstow said. "What's that mean?"

"I've seen it before," Moore said as he stuck his hands inside the reactionary's skull, fingers sliding along either side of the brain. He slowly pulled the brain out. Dropped it in a nearby glass container full of water. Sealed the cap. "Yes, a physical and psychological warping of the subject's brain. Since neither of you have medical degrees, I'll be as simple as possible in my explanation. I've only had the chance to examine three reactionaries, but I'm suspecting that the condition I'm about to explain isn't exclusive to those three. Of course, I'll confirm it when I study the other corpses, as well."

"Cut to the chase, Doc," Orion said. "No disrespect intended, but I'm tired and I'd like to go home sometime this week."

"Right, I apologize. I side-tracked a little there." Moore cleared his throat and gestured toward the brain in the jar he'd just extracted. "Notice how the patterns of the cerebral lobes appear to be distorted compared to other brains you've seen. That's because they've been psychokinetically tampered with."

"Wait, wait, don't tell me... are you saying they were... *controlled* by a psychokinetic?" Barstow asked, barely able to get all the words out to form the sentence. He was surprised he didn't crumble into a stuttering fit. It was one of those concepts he still had trouble wrapping his head around.

"Mind control," Moore said with a nod, "Correct. The psychokinetic responsible for the physical distortions to the brain is also responsible for this man's actions today."

"You can't be serious," Orion exclaimed. "They pointed *right* at us. It was clearly a premeditated assault on us."

"Of course it was, but not by *them*," Moore said. "They were merely surrogates performing for a psychokinetic puppet master. Nothing more."

"If that's the case, then why choose these guys to come after us?" Orion asked. "They could've used someone else, couldn't they? Maybe someone a lot less conspicuous, so we wouldn't immediately be on our guard as soon as we spotted them."

Then it hit him. The figure on the roof. Modular helmet. All black apparel. "Wait," Orion said, "I *did* see someone..."

Barstow looked at him. "Who?"

"He was—" Orion stopped himself when another thought crossed his mind. He glanced up at the security camera in the far corner of the room. He stared at it. It stared back.

Moore and Barstow followed his gaze. Barstow scoffed, figuring Orion was being paranoid again.

"What?" Moore asked.

Orion looked at them. "Not here," he said, knowing he'd confirmed Barstow's suspicions. He turned to Moore and said, "Anything else you can tell us, Doc?"

Moore shook his head, blinking in confusion. "No, I don't think so. I'll notify you if something else comes up, though, I suppose..."

"Thanks, Doc." Orion turned and left the room.

Barstow followed him out and joined his pace down the hall. "What is it?"

"I'll explain in a minute," Orion said as he spotted another wall-mounted camera following their progress.

"What for? Why not now?"

Every camera that Orion saw had its lens aimed squarely at them, and all of them watched the two detectives even after they were out the door, down the steps, and into the parking lot. When they reached their cruiser, Orion said, "On second thought, let's take a walk. We might be recorded if we have our conversation in there. Christ knows, we don't want that to happen."

"I don't feel like walking," Barstow said.

"You want to hear what I have to say, you're walkin'," Orion said. He headed for the sidewalk.

Barstow sighed and walked alongside him, matching his partner's brisk pace. "What's this about?"

"Keep walkin'."

Barstow frowned, his patience wearing thin.

Orion refused to talk until they were in the diner. Once again, it was near-empty. They picked a booth away from the windows, in the far left corner of the dining area. Ordered the same as before. It wasn't until the waitress left when Orion began the explanation in a hushed tone: "I think we're being watched."

"By who?"

"By the same son of a bitch who tried to kill us today."

Barstow laughed. "The only people who have access to the precinct's security video feed are the CEO and his security teams. What are you thinking? That the CEO hired a psychokinetic hitman to use a bunch of old-fashioned conservative reactionaries as surrogates to kill us?"

"The surrogates would be the perfect diversion. Those conservative radicals hate change. They want society to go back to its old traditional ways. Only difference between these guys and the minority government of Haruda's Conservative Party—back when Altieria had a Senate and a democracy—is that these guys lacked political power and weren't afraid to resort to terrorist methods to achieve their goals. Hell, those bastards hate everything the CEO is and everything he brought to this country. As you might recall, when the CEO began to establish himself as a leader, you and I joked about how his slogan should've read 'Out with the old, in with the new.'"

The waitress returned with their coffees. Dropped sugar packets and cream beside Orion's mug, just like yesterday. Then she left them alone again.

Barstow waited for her to get out of earshot. "So they hate the CEO. Doesn't explain why they'd make for a scapegoat believable enough to distract us from the bigger picture."

"But it does."

"How?"

Orion flared up a cigarette. Inhaled. Exhaled. Barstow coughed and moved his hand like a fan when the breeze from the air conditioner carried the smoke to his face. "The Altieria PD might as well be the CEO's not-so-secret police. Whether we want to admit it or deny it, we enforce the CEO's laws and maintain as much order in his society as possible. Once he took over, he literally took over. How can you not see it, Barstow? The CEO owns the police force. The conservatives would want to send a message to him, allegedly, about how they're sick and tired of all the new bullshit the CEO has established. And how do they do that? By attacking two exceptional cops on the force and killing dozens of innocents—

victims of circumstance, or maybe weaklings who've given up their old peace-loving democracy and great traditions to a man who wanted to control everything—as some kind of bonus."

Barstow stared at him, eyes narrow. "Uh-huuuuhhh..."

"Still don't believe me?"

"There are a few logical problems with your theory. Why would the CEO waste his time or risk his standing for us? What could he possibly have against us for him to go to such lengths in the first place? He doesn't have a reason to want us dead."

"Just think of the headlines," Orion said. "They'd be reporting how those still loyal to the older ways of democracy and tradition are more than willing to butcher dozens of innocent people. They'd be reporting how you could be killed, without warning, while you're enjoying a meal with your family. They'd be reporting how the 'conservative threat' is dangerous enough to be able to afford a full attack on civilian establishments in mid-daylight. On top of that, with all the deaths of police officers that came after the civilian massacre, they'll be questioning the reliability of the Altieria City police. Because forget the civilians, *we* wouldn't even be able to defend ourselves."

Orion took a hearty gulp from his mug. Wiped his mouth. "The people get scared. Democracy looks like an ugly thing, which will definitely help him maintain his dictatorship in the future. Conservatives will look even uglier than they were to begin with. People will lose faith in the police and turn to the CEO for help and guidance. They'll essentially give their lives to him—more than they already have—and beg him to stop the riots and end the conservatives' terror campaign once and for all. If he continues to use the reactionaries as surrogates to conduct additional attacks that each turn up with more devastating consequences than the last, then the world will react in one of two ways: they'll either grow suspicious of the CEO, or they'll give him total control over their lives. And he will take that control and mask it as security. He'll make the attacks less frequent, gradually lessening, so that it looks like his 'security' methods are working. And within the span of a year, or two years, or five years... he will have complete and total control over a world of fearful slaves."

Barstow stared at him for what felt like an eternity. He didn't even acknowledge the waitress when she brought them their food, refilled their coffee, and left with a cheerful, "Enjoy your meal!"

Orion lost his patience after five minutes and said, "Well?"

"That is the dumbest theory I have ever heard come out of your mouth," Barstow said. As he started to prod his food with a fork, he added, "It was bad and you should feel bad."

"For Christ's sake, Barstow," Orion hissed, "it makes sense. You know it does!"

"Yeah, maybe to a paranoid schizophrenic on a mescaline binge, but not to me." He cut a chunk off the corner of a slice of eggs in the basket. Raised it to his mouth—

Orion shot up and smacked the fork out of his hand. Send it clattering across the white floor tiles, which gained the attention of the family of patrons on the other side of the restaurant. "Bullshit!"

Barstow looked at the fork a few metres away. Then he looked at Orion. "That fork was the cleanest fork I'd ever used in this place. ...And you just smacked it out of my hand."

Orion ignored him and went on: "*You* were the one telling me to keep an open mind just half an hour ago. Think it through again. I'm on to something here."

Barstow sighed. Took Orion's fork, which Orion hadn't touched yet, and started using it. "I just don't see the motivation behind attacking us with surrogates—nor do I believe that it'd be a coincidence if all he wanted to do was kill a couple of cops to mislead people. Not to mention, we're not working on any cases that could further damage his reputation than the malfunctioning robot fiasco he's facing lawsuits for."

"No, I handed that case over to Pollock."

"And Pollock's doing just fine, so there you go."

"What about the Scott case?"

"Bullshit. Hardly connected to Altieria, except—"

"Except for the fact that Elsa Scott's husband is a biology major and an important asset to the CEO's company."

"That still hardly means anything, Orion. Do you realize how many people in this city alone are 'assets' to Altieria Corp.? At least three quarters of its general population. That just proves right there that there is no conspiracy, and you're..." Barstow trailed off.

"I'm what?" Orion asked. "Finish your sentence."

"...And you're paranoid as hell."

The waitress approached them. "Is there anything I can do for you?"

Orion looked at her. Slowly sat back down. "I could use a

new fork."

The waitress gave him a new fork from a pouch on her apron. Then she left, picking up the fork Orion had swatted earlier on her way back to the kitchen.

When she was gone, Barstow said, "Look, say I was to believe such a ridiculous concept; you'd have to prove it."

"Proof? How about the dark figure on the roof?"

Barstow blinked. "Huh?"

"When the last reactionary killed himself, it seemed like he was being controlled by something. It didn't make sense until the Doc said they were being used as surrogates by an advanced psychokinetic. While I was there, I saw someone watching me. Someone big... in black. I'm certain he was the bastard behind the reactionary surrogates. And you know what's funny? He matches the description of our Scott murder suspect, right down to the shadowy appearance and the reportedly advanced psychokinesis."

Barstow froze. A forkful of food only an inch from his mouth.

A big smile stretched across Orion's face. "*Now* do I have your attention?"

13: Love

Scott Residence

"Due to security protocols, I'm not permitted to show you this," Franklin said as he punched the four-digit code into the keypad installed in the thick, frosted glass wall of his laboratory. "But if you can keep a secret, I would gladly show you."

Elsa nodded and said, "Of course I can, dear. But if it poses such a risk, you really don't have to show me…"

"Nonsense, I want you to see it."

"Are you sure?"

"I insist," he replied as he opened the door. Cold air hissed as it escaped the room and blew in their faces. Sent chills up their spines. Made them shiver.

For the following half-hour, Franklin excitedly introduced his wife to his many creations in the lab, with the exception of a small climate-controlled storage vault, which he forbade her from entering. The vault door remained sealed and isolated from the rest of the lab and was approximately five inches thick.

He showed her a shrine-like display of holographic still images of her to give an idea how deep his dedication to his wife really went, with his smiling face appearing in a few of them. Elsa grinned and laughed with him as he described the happier times captured by the photos. Her positive reactions made his heart flutter. Until now, he hadn't realized just how much he'd missed her laughter.

Despite her constant laughter when she recalled the events he was describing—such as the time when a shoe sent flying from someone's foot on a cyclone ride knocked his cotton candy out of his hands at a spring fair—she couldn't help but feel a mild unease in the pit of her stomach. It was nice to know that her husband remained faithful and dedicated to her… but did that really necessitate a shrine of her in his home laboratory? *Well, never mind,* a thought crossed her mind, erasing all doubt in a strange instant, *at least he loves me.*

Elsa peered closely at the photos, an astonished look on her face. "Have my breasts grown since then?" She looked down at her own chest, turned to a nearby mirror, and cupped her breasts. There was something strange about how they looked in reality compared to the photo. Since the day of that photo which, if memory served correctly, was dated only three years prior to this day, she could almost swear she'd grown almost three times larger. "Strange… I'm surprised I haven't noticed until now." *Of course you have. They're your breasts, after all.*

Franklin watched her shift her curious gaze from the mirror to the photo to the mirror again in two-second intervals. After a short while, he said, "Perhaps it's just an illusion. Your position in the photo does make you look a little smaller than in person."

She looked at him. "What do you mean? Smaller?" She looked at the photo again. "My God, is my waist smaller, too?"

"Of course not," he said with a reassuring laugh. "You're perfectly fine, my love. Photography is a tricky thing."

She took another long, hard look into the mirror, glaring at her hips. "I think my waist is bigger."

"It's not, dear."

"Are you sure?" She turned around to look at her backside in the mirror.

"Of course I'm sure. You're the same now as you were back then."

She turned back around. "I don't know if that's…"

"Trust me. I was there, too."

You're perfect. Stop worrying, her thoughts told her. "Hm," she grunted, giving her reflection another look. "I guess so…"

His smile grew wider. He was practically beaming. "There's no reason for you to worry, Elsa."

Elsa turned to him, still doubtful. "If you say so."

"I know so."

She smiled, touched by his efforts to reassure her. "Thank you, sweetie."

There wasn't much to do in the apartment, but Franklin found something for them to do. They played old, dusty board games and, when the sun had disappeared behind the city skyline almost completely, they gazed up at the stairs on the cantilever patio.

In no time, Franklin found himself talking as if she had never left: "Remember when we used to gaze up at the stars all the time? Before I became so caught up with work." He looked at her, unable to get over her beauty in the electric glow of the city. Her hair flared brilliantly in the shifting mixtures of orange and red, blue and green. "Do you remember?" he asked.

"Yes, of course," she said with a fond smile, craning her neck as she watched the stars twinkle. Even over a thickly polluted city like this, somehow the stars shined brightly through the smog. "Those were the best of days, Frank. I miss those days."

"So do I," he said reassuringly. "I promise, those good old days are coming back soon."

Her shimmering eyes turned toward him. "That'd be nice. I'd like that, Frank."

He reached out and pulled her body against his, arms wrapping around her in a warm, welcome embrace. She rested her head on his chest and released a tranquil sigh.

Later in the evening, they watched a movie together, huddled close on the couch, eyes glued to the giant widescreen TV installed into the wall. There was nothing in this film the CEO didn't endorse—if there was something that challenged the principles of Altieria Corp., it wouldn't exist to the public until the right changes were made.

He smiled as he held his beloved wife close. The first evening he got to spend with his wife in months was the best evening he'd experienced in so long. Despite her leaving him before the completion of his initial project, it proved to be only a temporary relapse. *Thank God.*

It was... reminiscent. From the stargazing to the late movie nights. One never out of the other's sight—and neither could complain. Franklin had restored the good old days. Those good old days when Franklin and Elsa enjoyed each other's company—before he developed an insane dedication to his work.

After the movie, they went to bed and made love for the first time in what seemed like an eternity. He'd missed her warmth most of all. The softness of her skin. The taste of her lips. The feel of her hair. Her voice when she reached her peak. Her scent. Reuniting with her provided a fresh wave of youth-like vigour to his performance, the likes of which neither of them had experienced since their honeymoon fifteen years earlier. What made their lovemaking even better was the two-minute series of tremors that shook the place. For those two minutes, the room gently swayed back and forth, as if they were on the waves of the cruise they'd taken on their honeymoon so many years ago.

Even after they were satisfied, one never left the loving embrace of the other as they drifted off to Sandman Land together.

14: Trail

Altieria Corp. HQ

The detectives waited until morning before heading up to CEO/H3@D's headquarters. This time, Amanda/7 escorted them to the CEO's office instead of the recharging chamber that Orion had been sent to on his previous visit.

They entered the office. Amanda/7 bowed and backed out of the room, shutting the frosted double doors on her way out.

Sitting behind his desk in a black swivel chair, in front of a panoramic view of the city's cloudy skyline, was the CEO—completely different from the man Orion had met just the other day. No wires. No rotten skin. No life support systems. He actually resembled the youthful holographic projection that stood in the lobby. "Detectives," he greeted them warmly, making a tent with his fingers as he leaned on his desk, "What can I do for you today?"

"You're looking better," Barstow said.

The CEO nodded. "Thank you, Detective. Recharging is always a rejuvenating and highly stimulating experience. I feel like new."

"The conservatives," Orion said, cutting straight to the chase. He approached the desk at a brisk pace. Reached it. Leaned forward so that his face was only twelve inches from the CEO's superficial smile. "You know the ones I mean. Why'd they attack us?"

"I don't know what you mean, despite whatever intelligence you've been fed, Detective Orion," the CEO said calmly. "Well, allow me to rephrase: I'm aware of the attack—I'm just not aware of the motivation behind the attack."

"Something tells me you know."

"On what grounds, Detective?"

Orion squinted. "On the grounds of—"

"Orion," Barstow snapped. He had to stop his partner before he got out of hand. They weren't here for a fight, after all. He calmly approached the CEO's desk, explaining, "My apologies, Mr. CEO. We have reason to believe that the prime suspect in the murder case of Elsa Scott is somehow linked to yesterday's attack."

The CEO looked at Barstow. "I'll repeat myself once more: 'on what grounds?'"

Before Orion could answer, Barstow said, "Unusual distortions in the cerebral lobe patterns of at least three reactionary corpses recovered from the scene."

"Why only three?" the CEO asked. "What about the others?"

"Our examiner hadn't had the time to examine them all when he gave us that report, but he figured it was worth mentioning, considering the apparent coincidence."

"So their minds were distorted by... what? Psychokinetic interference?"

"Exactly, sir."

"Why come to me about this when I could have simply read up the reports?"

Before Barstow could stop him, Orion answered, "Because you're always up to speed even before we are, and you don't seem to relinquish whatever information you recover to us. Information that could bring us one step closer to solving this case. Not only is keeping vital information from police a crime; not only does it piss me off, but it makes me pretty damn suspicious."

The CEO's voice dripped with hostility. "Mind your position, Detective. I control you. I do not answer to you."

"You're still withholding information."

"I have withheld nothing. Suspect me all you want."

"I will."

"Orion!" Barstow barked.

Orion ignored him. "You have access to every security and video network around the globe. Don't try to tell me you haven't withheld information. You know something about our suspect. Something you're not telling us. I know you know, because what are the odds that the same suspect who brutally mutilated the wife of one of your company's greatest assets used a group of lowlife revolutionaries as surrogates to attack the same men who are looking into it?"

"Isn't it obvious?" the CEO asked with a sneer, "Your man knows you're looking for him and he wants you out of the picture. Once again, Detective, your nasty habit of jumping to conclusions and careless cynicism has badly influenced your perspective on your case. This is not the first time you've jumped to the conclusion that I am up to something, either. As I recall, you were here just last week to more-or-less accuse me of using 'malfunctioning robots' as an elaborate ruse for dispatching old employees and their families as a means of 'tying up loose ends.' But, as you may recall, your theory came apart when I asked why I would do such a thing. That's because I think you know why. I would never risk my standing nor use my own property to commit murder. In fact, I wouldn't commit murder under *any* circumstance. Altieria Corp. does not specialize in murder—it specializes in finding new ways of living. If anything, we *give* life. Your wild theories suggest a paradox that is unwelcome in my company."

Orion scowled. *Clever bastard knows how to talk.*

Barstow glared at his partner.

The CEO scoffed and leaned back in his chair, fingers still in a tent. "To tell you the truth, I find it rather disturbing that you've been able to maintain your position as a detective on the force, considering your obvious paranoia and aggressive agenda towards my company. Do you see these hands?" He held his hands up, fingers extended outward. "These hands could take all of that away in an instant. I could have you reported on a number of charges: harassment, reckless behaviour, improper etiquette, inability to do your job due to severe mental instability; among other things. What do you think about that?"

Orion glared at him for a few long seconds. Then he cocked his head toward the panoramic view of the skyline. "You see that window behind you? I could have your ass thrown out of there before your security could even blink. What do you think about *that*?"

"Orion!" Barstow shouted. "Christ!"

The CEO laughed. "That glass was specially constructed with platinum fibres. You can't break it with a Howitzer at close range."

"I'd like to test that theory, just to be sure."

"Damn it, Jason!" Barstow quickly turned to the CEO and said, "I apologize in advance for my partner's behaviour, sir—"

The CEO waved him off with a smirk. "It's alright, Detective Barstow. I'm a relatively flexible fellow. Hearing what others have to say is part of my job." He said to Orion, "It's as if you're *trying* to lose your job and your pension. But I'll look at it from a different point of view for the moment: you're shaken up from the attack. You're risking all to solve the case and put it behind you. I respect that, Detective, even if your methods are a little too old-fashioned for my liking. No normal man would be able to think straight after going through what you've recently experienced."

Orion said nothing, embittered by the condescending praise he was getting by a man he felt was the ultimate suspect in a large number of unsolved cases.

"Anyway," the CEO said as he made a tent with his fingers again, "back to our previous topic. I can assure you that no information has been withheld from you. We know just as much as you do."

"Because of all the cameras, I'll bet," Orion said.

"And the filed reports," the CEO said with a friendly grin.

"Oh, of *course*," Orion snapped, "Can't believe I forgot *those*."

"And your prime suspect, whoever he is... well, to put it in simple terms: he's a ghost. Even *we* haven't been able to find him on any of our surveillance systems. We're hoping he slips up somewhere, but so far, we've had no luck." The CEO sighed. "On a side note, we've been looking into our own personnel files and scrutinizing our databases for any possible inconsistencies in our network, just in case someone is conspiring with your suspect from the inside. My company is facing a rather dark time, what with the lawsuits and the malfunctioning hardware that should have been defective-proof; and the constant, suspicious downtimes in our servers. Add all that to the possibility of someone working on the inside—a saboteur, a conspirator, however you choose to refer to them—in my company, and you'll find that I am as displeased and suspicious as you are. Franklin Scott isn't just an asset, gentlemen, he's also a very good friend of mine, and I would like to see the man or men responsible for the murder of his wife put down for good." He stood up out of his chair. Straight, formal posture. "I apologize for my lack of ability to push your investigation further for the moment, but please be assured... we are on the same side." He offered his hand.

Barstow shook it first.

The CEO turned to Orion. Barstow nudged him, prompting Orion to grudgingly shake the CEO's hand. The two of them locked eyes for a single intense, fleeting moment. Everyone in the room was well aware of the tension between them.

When the formalities were through, the detectives turned and crossed to the exit. On their way out, the CEO called out, "Good luck on your end of the investigation."

Barstow turned and said, "Same to you, sir."

They weren't even out of the elevator when Barstow exploded: "What the hell is wrong with you, Jason?"

"Absolutely nothing," Orion replied, staring out the curved glass wall of the elevator as the lobby floor slowly rose up to meet them.

"Wrong. *Way* wrong. The correct answer is: 'Everything, Barstow. Everything is wrong with me.' The CEO's right, you know. You're far too paranoid. You're letting your own personal viewpoints get in the way of this investigation, and if you're not careful, it's going to cost you everything you worked your ass off to attain."

"Not if I play my cards right."

"This isn't some game where you can place a bet and expect to lose a small handful of chips if things don't go your way. If you miscalculate, you're done. There won't be any chips or cards or a few bills of cash coming out of your hands. It'll be your blood. Don't forget, you'll be dragging me into it, too, so try to be more careful." He muttered under his breath, "Reckless asshole."

"Dragging you into it? I thought you said you weren't gonna follow me when I recklessly charge into the fray?"

"Not for a damn good reason, Jason. And it'd have to be a very good one."

They were quiet for a while. Before they'd reached the bottom, Orion said, "That was a surprisingly short scolding."

"Shut up." Barstow breathed a weary sigh. "I figure after thirty-three years of your shit, you're never gonna learn no matter how many times I try to hammer it into your thick skull."

"It's part of my charm."

"It'll be part of your downfall, too—if it's not the main reason." Barstow scowled. "I bet it'll be mine, too."

They drove off down the road, leaving Altieria Corp. HQ far behind them. Barstow switched on the radio and went to a sports channel, which struck Orion as odd. Barstow was one of the few middle-aged men whom Orion knew hated sports.

"I'm thinking we should pay our reactionary friends a visit," Barstow said.

"Why?" Orion reached for the dial to turn down the volume,

but Barstow smacked his hand away. After giving him an inquisitive look, he saw Barstow shook his head and immediately understood. *Precautionary measures, eh?*

"Clear things up with them. They're no doubt confused about why a platoon of their own died in an unauthorized attack downtown in the middle of the day. Especially since we were their targets. Only problem is—"

"I think I've got a plan."

"Don't interrupt me," Barstow snapped. "You're on thin ice as it is." He cleared his throat. Waited a beat. Then: "They'll no doubt be expecting a tactical raid on their headquarters. That's why we're going to quietly break into the place. It'll be the last thing they'd expect."

"That's a really stupid idea. Uncharacteristically reckless, too. You're stealing my thunder. Why would we do that, anyway?"

"I did some research after we parted ways last night. I know you don't base your outlandish theories on nothing, so I went down to Takuo and searched the net with the help of a brilliant hacker— who will remain nameless—under the guise of a phony account for three hours, looking for information."

Orion didn't know where this was going. It sounded very uncharacteristic of Barstow to do something like that. It was like exploring uncharted territory for the first time on a deserted island you've been stranded on for decades. "What'd you find?"

"Information."

"On *what*, for Christ's sake!"

Barstow stole another cautionary glance at the dashboard. Turned the radio up a little louder. Then he said, "Accessing the Altieria Corp. security systems was much easier than it should've been. My hacker friend suggested that it was an intentional 'back door' for certain outsiders to access. The CEO didn't lie when he said there was a serious relapse in his security systems—what he *did* lie about was the fact that the security systems relapsed on purpose. Someone's orchestrating something. I don't know what, but it has something to do with our mysterious murder suspect. Remember the 'coincidental' security cam malfunctions? They've proven to us that there are no coincidences, because everywhere our suspect goes, the cameras phase out."

"Yeah, but that's the tricky part. He's a psychokinetic. He could've done it himself."

"Not possible."

"Why's that?"

"It's common knowledge among tech-savvy groups that psychokinetic interference with technology can cause serious damage, both to the equipment and the network it's connected to. It's like a virus. It spreads through the entire system. The only way one can maintain the network while losing individual feeds is if someone physically destroyed the cameras individually. But that isn't the case. The cameras were still there, and they lost their feed individually, and then booted right back up as soon as our suspect cleared out without any abnormalities with the system. No outside interference can do that. The cameras were manually shut off from their source. Someone in Altieria Corp. is purposely covering our suspect's tracks, and doing a sloppy job of it. They only shut down the cameras within a mile radius of our suspect, without shutting down the sectors' whole networks altogether. In their amateurish attempts at hiding our suspect, they inadvertently left a trail of breadcrumbs for us to follow." He held up a thumb drive for his partner to see, and smirked. "My hacker friend took some snapshots of our suspect's activities via satellite and highlighted the most common blackout areas. What we've got here is every location our suspect has been in the past week."

Orion leaned back in his chair and stared blankly through the windshield. All he could say was, "Wow."

"That's what I thought."

"That's common knowledge?"

"Apparently."

"I didn't know that."

"Neither did I. But then again, we're not 'tech-savvy' individuals, are we?"

"Nope. So are we going down there?"

"Of course we are."

"What was that you said about 'not being dragged along'?"

"Let's get something straight here, Orion: *I'm* dragging *you* along this time. I think after all these years you owe me this one."

"Guess you've got a point there."

"But that's just one thing on our to-do list. We've also gotta find a way inside the Company. We can't let the suspect's ally get off scot-free, can we? We'll clear the board until the king's got nothing left."

"So let me get this straight: we're going to sneak into Altieria Corp. to find an employee we know nothing about and bring him in while proving he's our man. But first, we're going to break into the reactionaries' hideout in hopes of retrieving data regarding a loophole in Altieria Corp.'s security?"

"Correct."

"That sounds like an unnecessary risk, considering we could just waltz right in there and start searching. No one would be allowed to stop us."

"True, but then they'd know we're there, and they'd be prepared. Not to mention—and no, I'm not saying I believe your theory to be truth just yet—but there *is* the possibility that the CEO could be in on it. We can't take any chances in letting anyone else know. Bad enough we're using the reactionaries as a means to break into the damn headquarters."

"I assume you're not going to inform the Superintendent?"

"The fewer who know of this, the better."

"Glad we're on the same page." Orion scowled as his imagination took him places he would never want to find himself. "We could get executed for this if we screw up. Infiltrating the company that controls the planet is treasonous; a sure death sentence, excluding all the other charges we could be facing. Like conspiring with terrorists."

"Not really conspiring, and only because *they're* the only ones left who may have found a loophole. I'm well-aware of how thin this plan is. And I'm even more aware of the consequences it could bring, even if we succeed."

"We hardly have justification to leap that high, anyway."

Barstow waggled the thumb drive in front of Orion's face. "This is our justification. It's as good as a warrant these days. Hell, we could go anywhere, ever since Altieria took over. I'm sure you'll be more than happy to throw that in the CEO's face when he inevitably complains."

"A warrant?" Orion said with a wry smirk. "What's that?"

"Exactly. Shouldn't be too much of a switch for you, anyway, considering your relationship with the man. You know you've made a dangerous enemy today," Barstow said.

"He and I have been enemies for years. You could say it's provided him with a little entertainment over the years. He loves to shoot me down before I get too far, and he remains one step ahead of me."

"I doubt he finds any pleasure in that."

"On the contrary; that's the only reason I still have my job."

Barstow looked at him, then turned back to the road. "I guess that makes sense, in a 'you' sort of way."

"Well, you never did believe me when it came my theories about the CEO."

"Because that's all they are: just theories. You talk a good game sometimes, but you never have any evidence to back it up. Even now, this plan doesn't have anything to do with him because he isn't involved—or doesn't *seem* to be involved."

"He's too damn clever to leave evidence, that's why."

"So outsmart him."

"Pfft. Right." Orion frowned. "You still think he's innocent, don't you?"

"In all honesty, Jason, nothing surprises me anymore. Conservative surrogates tried to kill us and you threatened to toss the ruler of the world out of his office window in the past twenty-four hours. And now we've got this crazy plan that for some reason *I* cooked up. It's never a dull moment with you, I'll give you that."

Orion grinned. Leaned back in his seat. "Yessiree, the excitement never stops."

"Stop saying that."

15: Surprise

Scott Residence

Franklin woke up in an empty bed. For a moment, panic struck him. *Oh, God. What if she left again?*

The thought was struck down as quickly as it popped into his mind when he heard the sound of the TV in the living room. He jumped out of bed, threw on a housecoat, and left the bedroom. Went down the hall. Turned left into the living room to find Elsa sitting on the couch in a pink robe, leaning over a plate of bacon, scrambled eggs and toast on the coffee table. Relief rushed through him. "Good morning."

She looked up from her plate and smiled. "Good morning, dear. I left something for you in the microwave."

"Oh, wonderful," he said, returning her smile. Then he entered the kitchen. Checked the microwave. Found his own plate of bacon and scrambled eggs with two buttered slices of toast wrapped in plastic, along with a sticky note with a heart drawn on it. His smile brightened when he saw the heart. Took the plate out and unwrapped the plastic. Then he returned to the living room, plate in his right hand, heart drawing in his left. When he came within sight of her, he showed her the drawing and said, "For me?"

She put her fork down and made a heart shape with her fingers. "Of course it is."

He gave her a quick peck on the lips and sat down on the couch beside her.

News coverage on the flat screen. Rioters filled the streets of downtown Altieria City. Burning cars, exploding buildings. Looters. Patches of fire. Riot police gunning down scores of people with rubber ammunition and stun grenades. Clouds of nerve gas mixed with thick black smoke in the air, creating a sickening dark green haze. People in conservative reactionary uniforms ran around waving blue and white flags until they were shot down. Shouting. Shooting. Screaming.

"Ugh…" Franklin said as he snatched the remote off the coffee table and changed the channel. "That's enough of that. It's an awfully bleak way to start the day."

He switched to a talk show. It seemed fine until they started talking about the recent homebot malfunctions, which resulted in the deaths of—

The channel cut out. Off the air. Of course.

Franklin switched to a different channel. Flicked through violent programs and news programs and talk shows and reality shows until finally, he settled on a documentary about killer whales, which had gone extinct ten years earlier. Pleased that he found something that didn't talk about current events, he looked at his wife and said, "How's that?"

She shrugged, chewing her food with a nonchalant expression on her face.

As he started cutting up his bacon strips, he asked, "So how was your sleep, beauty?"

"Good."

"Any interesting dreams?"

She hesitated. "...None that I can recall. And what about you? Remember any dreams?"

He noticed her hesitation right away, but figured he'd leave it for now. He didn't want her to get too riled up over a simple questioning. "We were at the beach. It was quite interesting."

"Oh, tell me more."

He smiled. Chewed his bacon. Swallowed. "It was a bright sunny day. A few white clouds. A golden beach. I swear I could feel the warmth of the sand between my toes. We were surrounded by so many colourful parasols, but no one else was there. And the water was actually *blue*!" He laughed. "*Blue* ocean water, in this day and age!"

She giggled. "What else?"

"What else... hm... well, we went swimming. I can't say for sure if the dream was vivid enough for me to feel it. I think by then, it was nearly time for me to wake up, so I was slowly drifting back into consciousness already."

With a sly glimmer in her eyes, she asked, "What kind of swimsuit was I wearing?"

With an equally sly smirk, he replied, "What makes you think you were *wearing* one?"

"Oh!" she said, laughing and giving his shoulder a playful slap. "You're bad!"

"Only for you, dear."

Two hours later, Elsa found herself on the couch, staring at the TV—still. She needed to find something to do, and she needed to propose something fast. She knew it wouldn't be long before he got off the couch and shut himself away in his lab for twelve hours.

"Let's go out."

He looked at her, eyebrows reaching for his hairline. For a moment, she interpreted his expression as 'alarmed,' but his quick smile made her think twice. "Out?"

She giggled at the look on his face. "Yes, out."

"Out where?"

"Anywhere," she said, nuzzling against him. "Somewhere fun."

"Hm." He pretended to give it some thought. In reality, he wasn't thinking about a fun place to go. He was thinking about a *safe* place to go. *According to the public, Elsa is supposed to be dead, so if anyone who knows me spots us, questions would be raised and they'd never be lowered. I've no doubt that once the police discover her, they would surely be after me and they'd never let up—especially that damned Orion. Damn it... of course she would want to go out. I can't simply isolate her again. That didn't turn out so well last time. I should have seen this coming from a mile away!* "Out, eh? I wonder..."

"C'mon, it shouldn't take so long to find something to do." She made a pouty face, staring at him with begging eyes. "Pretty pleeeease?"

He smiled at her little act. "I suppose so. Would you like to go to the movies?" *At least the darkness we'll be sitting in for the majority of our time will decrease the possibility of being noticed...*

"What movie should we see?"

He shrugged. "I don't know what's there."

"Ooh," she said, "I like surprises."

"I know you do."

"And after that, let's get dinner. Maybe at the Chinese Palace."

"Eh... that's probably not a good idea."

"Why?"

"Because, uh," he said, pausing a beat to think of something to say, "they've recently had an... infestation problem."

She recoiled in disgust. "Ew. Let's not go there, then."

"Agreed." *Dodged one bullet...*

"What about—"

"I've an idea," he said, "Let's try someplace new. I know of a place in the B1 district. The neighborhood isn't the brightest place in town but their food is excellent and it's sanitary."

"Sanitary?" She narrowed her eyes with a playful look of suspicion. "How do you know?"

"The manager and I have been very good friends for half a decade," Franklin replied.

"What do they make?"

"Just about everything, love."

"Everything?"

"Mhm." He nodded. "The atmosphere is excellent, too. Better than most restaurant chains, in fact. You'll love it."

She gave it some thought. Then she hopped off the couch and headed for the bathroom. "I'll go get ready!"

Franklin sat there, smiling at her eagerness. That smile quickly vanished when a bad feeling crept into the pit of his stomach.

Traditional News Station

"Rebekah Trickle!" a deep voice boomed over the sea of cubicles on the second floor. "Trickle!" the voice repeated impatiently.

"Sir!" Becky's head popped into view from an office in the middle row.

The news director, Samuel Michaels, stood in the doorway of his glass-enclosed office. He watched the top of her head bob about as she navigated her way through the convoluted open office network, weaving past bustling co-workers at every turn. When she finally made it to his office, Samuel stepped aside and then closed the door behind her. He gestured toward one of the chairs in front of his desk. "Have a seat."

As her boss circled round to his own chair, Becky said, "What's up, chief?"

The leather chair squeaked as he plopped onto it with a heavy sigh. He clapped his hands twice. The slats on all the surrounding window blinds rolled down, concealing them from all outside eyes. As soon as the blinds clicked, Samuel went down to business.

"You're aware of the Chinese Palace incident, right?"

She nodded. "Right."

"What're your thoughts?"

She shrugged. "Doesn't seem very characteristic of them. Normally they're more, uh... organized. And their targets aren't normally so insignificant. I don't see why they'd attack a couple of cops."

"Do you know the identities of these cops?"

"Nope. Why?"

Samuel fired up an electronic steam cigarette and inhaled its fumes. "I'm giving you a new assignment."

"But I already have an assignment," she protested.

"Yes, the Scott murder case. I'm aware."

"So why me? C'mon, chief, you know how much I hate taking two or more assignments at once. It messes me up."

"Be quiet. I picked you specifically because the detectives who are working on the Scott murder case are the same men our sponsors attacked at the Chinese Palace."

"Oh," she said, eyebrows raised. "So... you want me to...?"

"I want you to find out why our rebel sponsors attacked them without straying from your first objective to get to the bottom of this mess."

"Oh, come ooooon," she groaned.

"No whining," he said. "As their voice, it is our duty to explain their reasons behind their actions. After the civilian casualties, public opinion is starting to waver. Support is already beginning to fluctuate. I've been receiving calls all morning from confused supporters wondering what the hell happened, and I'm tired of having no explanation to console them."

"Yay," she said unenthusiastically. "You know how much I *love* to take these assignments. Can't you get Amanda to cover this? She's already on the scene!"

"You have four days. Considering the circumstances and the stakes, that's a generous amount of time." He took another puff from his steam cigarette. "Have you found anything about the Scott murder case yet?"

"An informant in the force told me that the suspect is most likely a psychokinetic of some kind. Advanced, for sure, but no one has anything concrete."

Samuel nodded with approval. "Better than nothing. Find

something solid. The Scott case is still your highest priority."

"But why?"

"Think about it, Trickle: the wife of a high-ranking robotics engineer working for the Company turns up dead just days after she filed for divorce. Despite this talk about a psychokinetic suspect, the husband is the primary suspect for now. If he is indeed the killer, I want to know about it before the CEO can cover it up. This case has the makings of a costly scandal for the Company, and would damage their reputation a great deal. We can't afford to let this opportunity slide, especially after the Chinese Palace incident... can we?"

Becky shrugged. "No, I guess not."

"You understand the importance of your assignments?"

She nodded.

"Good," he said. "Then you're dismissed."

Becky returned to her cubicle and sat down in her chair, jotted down notes from her latest revelation provided by the chief. Then, she spent the next five minutes staring at the blank document on her holographic computer screen, fingers poised over the keyboard. Despite having all the information on her touchpad, she didn't know where to begin.

"—are baffled and horrified by this sudden attack—"

She stood from her chair and peered over the wall of her cubicle at the wall-mounted panoramic TV screen hovering above the open office. The station's supposedly 'best' reporter, Amanda Herbert, was speaking into the camera with the remains of the Chinese Palace in clear view over her shoulder.

A pang of jealousy struck Becky. She looked down at her touchpad. Amanda reported everything on it before Becky could ever hope to get it on the net.

Or did she?

Becky kept watching the report, checking off items on a mental list that Amanda was bringing up. Once she was done, Becky smirked. She only reported half of the story—with a few inaccuracies. *And somehow you're considered to be the best of us? Jeez...*

She sat down in her chair and went through the notes on her touchpad again. Everything was there, from the time the attack took place, to the attackers and the names of the two detectives being attacked. She even had notes that detailed the chase down into

Takuo Market, but they ended there. There was nothing about the confrontation on the riverbank.

A tremor started to kick in. The building shook, feeling like a boat on an ocean cruise. Desktop knick-knacks clattered and computer screen images dimmed, yet everyone continued about their work as if this occurrence was normal for them. Becky sat calmly in her chair, watching her pens roll back and forth across her desk for about a minute until the tremor died down.

She pulled up photos of Barstow and Orion on her screen and scrutinized them. *Why would the rebels attack you guys?* She squinted at Orion's grainy photo, staring at the white lightning bolt streaking across his otherwise black-haired head. She wondered if it was a personal choice of style. Barstow looked normal enough, but she wondered about Orion. There was something about him that she couldn't place her finger on...

"Becky?"

She turned at the call of her name to see Mickey, her cameraman, holding an electric notepad in his thin fingers. "What's up, Mick? Got a present for me?"

Mickey was an average Joe. A tall, skinny guy who went to work in a stained T-shirt and faded jeans. His *Sky Japan Gojiras* baseball cap had frayed edges around the visor. His droopy eyes and dark rings around them accentuated his constant fatigue. The stubble on his chin added to his dishevelled appearance.

"Found this." He handed her the notepad.

She took it and studied the old news article. It was a picture of a newborn child in the arms of his mother. On the child's head was a thin white lightning bolt. The headline read: 'MIRACLE CHILD BORN WITH UNUSUAL BIRTHMARK.' "'Birthmark?'" she repeated aloud as her eyes scoured the rest of the article. "'...was discovered floating on sewer water. And rushed to hospital...' huh. 'Psychokinetic interference suspected.'" She grunted, set the notepad on the desk, and typed the link address of the article into her computer. Once she had it up on her computer, she gestured for Mickey to take his notepad back, which he did. "Psychokinetics were blamed for the strangest things," she said.

"Think that's our guy?"

"Orion? Obviously, Mick. Who else has that mark on their head? Do you know anyone else?" she asked sarcastically.

"No," he said, eyes downcast.

She swivelled round in her chair to face him, smiling. "That detective's a weird one. Can you see if you can dig up a bit more on him?"

"Can't you do that yourself?"

She pressed her palms together and stuck out her bottom lip. "Pretty pleeeease?"

It only took him two seconds to break. "Fine," he said with a resigned sigh.

"Yay!" she cheered, quiet enough to keep from disturbing their co-workers. "Thanks, Mick. You're the best."

"Yeah, yeah," he said as he started to walk away.

Once he was gone, Becky turned back to the article on her screen. "Now let's see if we can find out what planet you came from..."

16: B7

58th Street Conveyor Station

Orion and Barstow reserved a parking space and headed inside the Conveyor Station—a domed, five-storey structure made of steel and glass with the primary function of providing transportation to any of the ten underground levels of the city.

They crossed the lobby, shoes clacking on marble tiles, footsteps echoing under the hollow dome's roof trusses and the multitude of holographic screens suspended above floor projectors. Aside from the security personnel aimlessly roaming around, the lobby was almost totally empty. Because of the high ticket prices and the fact that the underground levels below the B1 District are disgusting, crime-ridden slums, none of the Conveyor Stations in Altieria were ever busy. Takuo itself had many detours scattered throughout the city that allowed people to enter tunnels that cut through the B1 District into B2 and effectively bypass all security.

They approached a wall of turnstiles stretched across the middle of the lobby and swiped their ID cards as they passed through the B7 gate and followed the designated path to a room where a female cyborg awaited them.

"Good morning, Detectives," she said, "my name is Caroline/4. I will be providing you with your transportation services today. Are you travelling casually or are you here on police business?"

"Police business," Barstow said. "We may require the riot suits."

She nodded. "Of course, Detective." She turned left and headed through an exit tunnel. "This way, please."

They followed her down the tunnel and eventually came upon three doors labelled 'MEN,' 'WOMEN,' and 'NO ENTRY,' respectively.

Caroline/4 gestured toward the scanner next to the 'NO ENTRY' door and said, "Please swipe your identification cards. Everything you need should be provided in a locker of your choice. If there is anything else, I will be waiting right outside."

They swiped their IDs. The door opened. They went inside. The door closed.

It was a mixed-gender locker room specifically for law enforcement. The detectives opened their lockers and changed into their riot suits. Hooking up the oxygen tanks proved to be a pain in the ass, as usual, but they'd managed to fasten them on eventually. The suits: all-black; flexi-armour with hidden thigh and forearm compartments for weapons and ammo storage; crimson multi-vision eye lens that could be switched between thermal imaging/infrared vision, night vision, electromagnetic field vision, and an enhanced vision mode. The suits themselves: all-terrain capabilities; advanced camouflage; physical enhancers. Despite their increased bulk, the detectives weren't much bigger than before, and the suits were extremely light. Once they were in their suits, they went to the gun rack at the back of the locker room and each selected an adaptable variant of the MP5SD3 submachine gun, and five magazines for three types of ammunition: stun rounds, explosive rounds, and EMP rounds.

Fifteen minutes later, they came back out. Caroline/4 led them to the B7 station where a transport platform waited for them on a conveyor. She stayed behind and watched the detectives board the transport. As soon as Orion shut the gate behind them, the platform's gears started to whine and squeal. The platform shuddered. Then it started to descend a tunnel angling 90 degrees, lowering them into blackness.

Caroline/4 leaned over the railing, waving her goodbyes. "Good luck, Detectives!"

Once they'd descended far enough, a hatch door sealed off the tunnel above them, and another door below them opened up. A loud hiss as the poisonous air of District B7 rose up to meet them in a cloudy, brown-green tinge.

B7 District

The lowest possible level above the drainage floor was rank with the stench of stale manure and decomposing corpses. The detectives—protected by their riot suits from the poisonous air of the underground—were fairly familiar with the smell, which was so strong it seeped through their oxygen masks and invaded their nostrils without being life-threatening. It was dark, pitch-black in some areas, prompting them to switch to night vision for the entire run.

"Christ, what a stink," Orion said.

"Quit complaining. Just thank your god that you don't have to live down here."

"Wouldn't matter how faithful I am to the cause. No way I'd put up with this shit 24/7."

"I'm sure they've got vacuum-sealed areas with filtered air or something."

"Obviously. Wouldn't be any conservatives left if they didn't."

They were silent for most of the journey across the district. They shuffled across rickety steel bridges coated in rust, across bottomless gaps; they trudged through thick, murky water with mechanical parts, garbage, and human remains floating around in it; they navigated through abandoned slums that had all but collapsed due to neglect. Leaking pipes were tangled above their heads, threatening to break apart and come crashing down at any moment. At one point, Orion could have sworn on his mother's grave that he'd spotted a mutated rat before it scurried into its hole.

This was the kind of place one wouldn't expect to find any inhabitants for years to come. The environment more resembled a dumping ground than a sustainable location. Besides all the flooded areas and deteriorating platforms and residential areas, the district was hot as hell. No surprise, since it was approximately ten kilometres below ground.

However, eventually, signs of civilization started to become undeniable, with voices and music carrying through the tunnels, reaching the detectives' ears. They came upon a tunnel exit soon enough and dropped three feet into waist-deep sewer water. Pushed through fifty feet of it. Climbed up a steep bank. Once they'd reached the top, they peeked over it and found the civilization they'd been listening to for the past ten minutes. On the other side of a thick Plexiglas wall with an airlock gate was a shanty town with living conditions that rivaled those in B2/Takuo. They could see some people walking around in there without protective gear, so they figured the air in there had been filtered and purified. That didn't stop others from continuing to wear breathing apparatuses

"Great," Orion said as they ducked back down the slope. "Now what?"

"Not sure yet."

"You didn't come up with a plan to bypass the Ziploc-sealed entrance security beforehand?"

"Why don't *you* think of something if you're so smart?"

"Why would I want to do that when you're doing such a good job on your own?"

Orion stole another glance over the top and spotted three rotating security cameras looking over the clearing between them and the entrance. "No way in there without being seen. Wait." He watched as the gate opened. Two sentries came out in full protective suits that were a few models out of date, dragging a levitating box behind them. They started across the lot toward them, chatting about something.

Orion ducked down and said, "We've got company. Two scavengers, by the looks of them."

"Perfect," Barstow said. "Hide."

"Where?"

"The water."

Orion looked at the water. Bones. Garbage. The stink of death. He pointed at it. "In that?"

"Don't tell me you're afraid of the water," Barstow said mockingly as he scurried down the bank.

"Hell, no."

"Then quit complaining." He doubled over. Eased himself into the water, silent.

Orion followed him. No sooner had he gone under than the two scavengers reached the top of the bank and started down to the water with their strange box, completely oblivious.

"Goddamn it, I hate it when the purifier plant screws up."

"Hey, we ain't exactly low-tech, but we ain't high-tech, neither. The guys at the plant can't do nothin' about it when the filter starts actin' up."

They positioned the box three feet past the edge of the bank, knee-deep, and lifted two 100-litre kegs off the back of it. One of them snapped open the bottom of the box and pulled down a fat tube, which he anchored in the water.

"It's bullshit. The guys at the purifier plant are amateur assholes."

"They ain't perfect, but they're the ones who work day an' night to provide us with that water."

"Yeah, when the filters are actually working."

"C'mon, show a little respect for what they do. They'll get a permanent flow going eventually."

The lead scavenger flicked a switch on the box, and the strange machine started sucking in water through the tube. A loud *ding* indicated when it was full. The lead scavenger flicked another switch. The box hummed and vibrated for about five minutes.

"How many kegs were we supposed to fill?"

"Without the spares, we're lookin' at maybe ten trips."

"Ten trips, are you serious?!"

"Yep."

"That's bullshit."

"Hey, if the spares were where they were supposed to be, we wouldn't have to make so many trips. But noooooo. That ain't the case, is it?"

They continued bickering until another ding sounded off. The second scavenger pulled a faucet out of his side of the box and positioned the keg under it. Out came pure, filtered drinking water. Once the keg was full, sealed, and carried back to the bank, they repeated the whole process with the second keg. Once that keg was full, the lead scavenger was staring in the direction of the tunnel. The second scavenger noticed almost right away.

"What's your problem?" The second scavenger turned to where his partner was staring and found himself looking down the barrels of the detectives' submachine guns. "Oh."

Five minutes later, the cyborg guard in his surveillance booth was ogling a pornographic pinup. A high-pitched beep interrupted him. He looked at one of the screens on his desk and saw the scavenger units standing by. Annoyed by the interruption, he put his magazine down and let them into the airlock. Activated the cleansing and sanitization. He waited until the sanitization period ended before allowing them entry into the colony with a half-hearted "Welcome back, gentlemen." Simple enough for the detectives to infiltrate, since the guard wanted to get back to his porn as quickly as possible.

They brought the kegs and the box to the nearest supply depot before ducking out of sight and taking cover behind a shack with the box hovering in tow. They sneaked around via back alleys. Since they were in the scavengers' gear, they couldn't utilize their alternate vision modes to make their search easier. They looked in several places; peeking through windows, opening doors—until they found a dark shack with boarded windows and a metal door.

Luckily for them, it wasn't too hard to blend into a crowd of people wearing oxygen masks and life support suits. It definitely reduced their changes of being suspected, although the thought of someone questioning why scavenger units were roaming around this deep in the city kept lingering in the backs of their minds.

"Think this might be it?" Orion asked over the telekinetic link.

"I don't know… maybe."

"We could try knocking."

"*You* can try knocking." Orion approached the door while Barstow stole another glance into the crowd that streamed by them, oblivious. Orion tried the door knob. Opened the door. "Voila. My magic hands strike again."

"Yeah, right," Barstow replied as they shuffled into the shack. He kept the door open long enough for the box to follow them inside before shutting the door.

They noticed a dim green light saturated the shack and turned around to discover a wall of ten computer monitors with ten fully-functioning brains in separate glass jars with mechanical eyes staring at their respective screens. Each brain had eight spindly limbs clinging to their personal monitors while also typing away on their individual keyboards.

Neither man moved for a few beats, staring at the odd sight.

"The stuff of nightmares," Orion whispered.

Barstow turned and locked the door.

"Who's there?" one of the brains asked, its distorted voice coming out of a tinny speaker attached to its jar. Its eyeballs rotated on an axis at the base of its jar to look at the intruders. "Identify yourselves."

Orion and Barstow snapped the lid off one of the kegs and pulled out their submachine guns, which were dripping wet, while thinking, *Thank God for adaptable firearms.*

"None of you move," Orion snarled, aiming the submachine gun at them.

Barstow said, "Sound an alarm and we'll burn this whole weird establishment to the ground. Understand?"

"*Kttcchh*! Don't shoot," one of them said as nine more pairs of eyes rotated to face the cops.

"What the hell are you?" Orion asked.

"We are advanced psychokinetic organisms reprogrammed to act as a synchronized security network."

Orion glanced sideways at Barstow. "Getting answers outta them may be easier than I anticipated."

"That was a little *too* easy for my comfort," Barstow said, eyes narrowing with suspicion. He asked the brains, "Why was that so easy?"

"We are an organic computer. Like all computers, we have no loyalty. We can be activated by anyone, just like we can be created in any factory, or destroyed by anything. We are simply tools meant to function—there is no matter of 'whom' or 'what' can operate us."

"Guess that's a good enough answer," Orion said.

"What is it you seek?" the center brain asked.

The detectives exchanged suspicious looks. Being that the brains were linked directly into the computer, an alarm could have already been sounded.

"We want a way into Altieria Corp. HQ," Orion said.

"There is no way," one of them said.

"Don't bullshit me," Orion said.

Another one asked, "Who wants to know?"

"And why?" yet another asked.

Barstow said, "Police business. We need a route that'll help us bypass their security."

Barstow's response sparked a string of varying comments from all the computer brains: "Why would the police want to infiltrate their own CEO's headquarters?"

"How did they find us?"

"How could they have possibly gotten in here?"

"It's a trap! *Ktttccchh*! It's a trap! We're done for!"

"Intriguing..."

"They couldn't know... no... it's impossible..."

"A route through security? How could they possibly know about...?"

"Shut up, you fool."

Orion spoke up, "Alright, alright, quiet down."

The voices faded to frantic whispering.

One of them asked their intruders, "Why would police want this information? Perhaps, to find out what we know?"

"Yes," another brain said, "yessss, that's it."

"Wrong," Barstow said, "we only want the route to catch a

suspect protected by their security. It'd also be in your best interests if we caught him."

"How so?"

"He's connected with a psychokinetic killer who manipulated your conservative friends into attacking that restaurant. I'm sure you're aware of the details."

"A psychokinetic killer…?"

Barstow continued, "Right now, it looks like your buddies attacked a civilian establishment in broad daylight for no reason at all. As we speak, the Company is tarnishing your reputation. We all know the conservatives don't attack without reason, and they avoid civilian casualties as much as possible. You know where I'm going with this, don't you?"

"Surrogates," a brain said.

"Correct," Barstow said. "Someone in the security department of Altieria Corp. is covering his tracks, and before anyone can be made aware of it—if they aren't already—my partner and I need to get in there and capture him."

"Alive," Orion added, more to be a smartass than to be technical.

"You are policemen. Did it not occur to you to assemble your forces and simply enter the Altieria headquarters to retrieve this suspect?"

"I doubt that'd work," Orion said.

Barstow followed up: "It may be the smart thing to do, but something tells me we wouldn't get very far if we went down that route."

"Perhaps we could assist you through… precognitive methods."

"That's impossible," Barstow sneered.

"Is it?" the center brain asked. "Touch me and you will know the truth."

"I'm not going to—" Barstow abruptly stopped talking when Orion stepped forward. "Jason, what the hell are you doing? Don't tell me you're gonna take the bait."

"Fine, I won't tell you that. I'll just do it."

Barstow lurched forward and pulled Orion back. "Don't be stupid."

Orion jerked his arm out of Barstow's grip. "If there's a chance we're handling this wrong, I want to know about it. It's worth the risk."

"No it isn't. We'll find some other way."

Orion ignored him. Approached the center brain's jar.

"Orion!" Barstow snapped.

"Quiet down," Orion said as he unscrewed the jar lid and stuck his hand into the thick green ooze. "You'll wake the neighbours."

"Goddamn it, Orion," Barstow raised his submachine gun. "Get away from them!"

Too late. Orion's palm touched down on the center brain. Immediately retracted his hand and screwed the lid back on. He looked around, flicking strands of ooze off his hand. "I don't feel any different."

Barstow stared at him. Slowly lowered his machine gun. "You stupid asshole. Taking a risk like that."

"Like they said, they're a computer with no loyalty to anyone," Orion said, still trying to get ooze off his arm, "and like all computers, every once in a while they don't do their job. What gives?"

"Give it a moment," the center brain replied.

Orion was about to shoot back with a snarky retort, when suddenly it hit him: a rush through the future. A by-the-books raid of the headquarters turns into a hostage situation by a security officer who panics, goes berserk, and takes control of the entire building from the control room. The detectives fight their way to the fourth floor. By the time they reach the control room, they're bloody, bruised, broken. They manage to capture their man and find out that he's the one they're after: Michael Crimmons. Somehow he found out that the police and his company's security were on to him, and he lashed out in desperation. However, shortly after his capture, all three of them are killed by an advanced psychokinetic surrogate attack. Their attacker is nowhere to be found, but they're finished. Their deaths are swept under the rug.

It all rushed by in a matter of seconds.

Orion felt a wave of nausea slam him like a brick wall when reality snapped back into focus. He collapsed on his hands and knees, retching.

Barstow knelt beside him with a hand on his partner's shoulder. "Hey! You alright?" He looked up and aimed his submachine gun at the brains. "What the hell did you do to him?!"

The center brain said, "I merely showed him a possible route."

"It's alright," Orion gasped. "I saw it. I saw it all. And... and I saw... our suspect."

"You saw him? Well do you know who he is?"

"He had a photo ID on him. Michael Crimmons is his name."

"You're sure about that?"

The image of the short, stout man in a lab coat going down with a dozen bullet holes in his chest flashed through Orion's mind. The ID card was clipped to his upper breast pocket. "Damn sure."

"And we shouldn't report this discovery?"

Orion shook his head. "It was all planned. I knew it. If we conducted a raid and follow procedure, our lead dies and we along with him."

"How?"

"We were ambushed in the headquarters. Our advanced psychokinetic friend used Crimmons as bait to lure us in before he made us kill each other. And the goddamn CEO covered it up immediately. His part in this whole thing still remains unclear, but now there's no denying it: he has something to do with this."

A different brain located in the center said, "If you can prove that an Altieria Corp. employee—or better yet, the CEO—is responsible, we will be very grateful. How do we know you'll keep your end of the bargain and clear our life providers of the recent killings?"

Orion said, "Given our occupation, we shouldn't be too hard to find."

"Very well," the center brain said. "We'll help you, but only because we would prefer to maintain our existence... and you don't seem like your average police officers either, Detectives Jason Orion and Lucas Barstow."

The detectives said nothing, figuring they'd just been scanned for identification. It was still creepy though, since they didn't even take off their helmets for them to know.

Skeletal metal fingers flew across keyboards. In seconds, one of them said, "I've got it. Printing now."

The printer beside Orion whined as it spat out two copies of the route. Orion took it and studied the pages. It was a blueprint of Altieria Corp. HQ's ground-level floor, with the lobby, security box, courtyard, five-storey car park, and the helipad positioned next to the river that ran through the compound. Orion never saw the river because it was always blocked off by a controlled dam built into the perimeter walls, and the river cut through the rear side of the perimeter behind the tower—an area he had no business being near, anyway. A little arrow pointed at a small circled part of the wall approximately three yards from the dam, on its left. More circles were scattered all over the river inside the perimeter wall. The helipad was also circled. "What do all these circles mean?" he asked.

The center brain answered: "The section of the wall indicates where the tunnel is. You should be able to pass through it easily so long as you go one at a time. The helipad circle marks where, exactly, the ventilation shaft is located—under the helipad. You don't need to resurface until you're in the secluded area under that helipad—which is probably your safest bet anyway, due to motion sensors located everywhere else on the surface."

"And the two-dozen circles all up and down the river?"

"Mines."

"Yay," Orion said as his heart dropped, "I love mines."

"Follow the ventilation system. There have been plans to install motion and pressure sensors, but so far they haven't gotten around to it, apparently."

"So they say," Orion said with a grim scowl.

"Not to worry. They haven't put these plans into action just yet. Your timing couldn't be more convenient—just don't expect them to leave this particular route open for long once word of how you captured your suspect reaches their ears."

"You're alright with us taking your only route into Altieria? Your friends might not like that."

"No one said anything about it being our only route," the center brain replied with a refined slyness that Orion silently commended.

Another brain said, "You have your information. We will give you fifteen minutes to clear out before we sound the alarm."

"Then I guess we'd better go," Barstow said as he unlocked the door.

As they were leaving, the center brain said, "Best of luck, detectives."

17: Out

Altieria Cinema

The theater was appropriately dark when the movie started. For an hour and forty-five minutes, Franklin sat relieved that he couldn't recognize anyone in the crowd, or better yet—that no one in the crowd recognized him. Few people knew him, and even fewer were made aware of Elsa's death. Still, the ones who were aware posed a threat to his new true love. He didn't want to think about what might happen if they'd been found out.

It was a comedy film—one which Franklin deemed successful, since Elsa couldn't stop herself from laughing. Watching her laugh and giggle at the onscreen antics raised his spirits exponentially.

She noticed him looking at her at one point and smiled. Leaned toward him and gave him a gentle kiss on the lips. For no reason at all, she said, "I love you."

He beamed, giddy from the kiss. "I love you too."

B1

Franklin and Elsa had taken a taxi through the nearest conveyor station tunnel system down into B1—the only district one could legally drive a vehicle on official roads into. It was a lively place, with throngs of people shifting down the somewhat cramped streets. It hardly differed from surface-level traffic, with the exception that this traffic had a ceiling looming over it. Soaked with neon and rain runoff, the streets were maintained fairly well, and the sidewalks were wide enough for three people to walk side-by-side. Guardrails had been put into place between the pedestrian walkways and the roads, with turnstile gates on every parking space.

Franklin hadn't lied about the restaurant's atmosphere. Its round dining room was lined with Corinthian columns, and between each of those columns was a Roman mosaic. The lights were dim and opera played softly in the background.

Elsa leaned back in her cushioned seat as the waiter set her order of spaghetti alla carbonara down in front of her. Her eyes sparkled with delight as she started to dig in with her fork. "This looks delicious!"

Franklin smiled as the waiter left him with his fettuccine Alfredo order. "I've come here a few times."

She swallowed her first forkful and asked, "Why didn't you take me here before?"

He shrugged. "Most of the time, I came here with co-workers during our lunch breaks, or they'd deliver it to our lab. Bringing you here sooner should've been a no-brainer though."

"Yes, it should've," she said, giggling.

"But for some reason, it never occurred to me."

"Well, at least you remedied that today." Her noodles made appropriate squishing sounds as she twirled her fork through them.

"Yes, true," he said.

"It feels like it's been forever since I was last out of the house."

"Oh?"

She nodded, chewing her food, waiting until she swallowed it to reply, "It feels strangely... unreal."

He leaned forward, staring at her. "What do you mean?"

She shook her head and chuckled. "I don't know. It just feels strange."

What do you mean?

"It feels like it's all a dream," she said.

"A dream?"

She nodded, putting her fork down. "You know that feeling you get when you experience déjà vu? It's like that. Like I've done all of this before."

He squinted. "I see..."

It's nothing. Don't worry about it.

"It's probably nothing," she said. She started eating her food again, smiling once more to a husband who couldn't take the grim, suspicious look off his face. "What's wrong, love?"

He blinked, as if coming out of a daze. He went back to his plate. "It's nothing," he said. "Don't worry about it."

Traditional News Station

"Got it!"

Becky whirled around in her chair to see her happy cameraman show her the business side of his notepad. She asked excitedly, "What'd you get? What'd you get?" as she snatched the notepad out of his hands and studied it.

Mickey crossed his arms, smiling with pride. "The blueprints for every main waterline in the city. See how they're all linked back to Altieria Corp. HQ?"

"Uh-huh, uh-huh," she said, eyes glued to the screen as she expanded the satellite image.

He faltered. "Uh... well... that's just it."

She looked up at him. "Are you suggesting what I think you're suggesting?"

"Maybe? What do you think I'm suggesting?"

"It sounds to me like you're suggesting that Detective 'Bolt' here was flushed down a Company toilet."

"Yeah, like... like a test tube baby, or something. Or a rejected specimen. You know, something along those lines."

She chuckled and leaned back in her chair. "Mickey, Mickey... if Altieria Corp. flushed all their rejected specimens down the toilet, and we knew about it, we'd be considered a credible news source by most of the world... and, you know, they would be looked at with suspicion. The kid probably got lost or abandoned by a negligent parent."

"But what about the lightning bolt?" he asked, discouraged.

"What *about* the lightning bolt?" She shrugged. "Hey, maybe you're right. Or maybe that lightning bolt is a freak of nature. Hell, I've seen weirder birthmarks. Like, there was this one guy I was dating waaay back in college who had this birthmark that looked like a naked woman on his butt. Seriously, it was uncanny."

"I think that was more information than I needed to know, but I see your point."

"And like you said, all of the waterlines link back to Altieria Corp. HQ. Some of them are exclusively connected to it and the water treatment plant, but most of them fan out into various sections of the city. They wouldn't be careless enough to ditch a baby in a public disposal line, they'd transfer it straight to their buddies at the plant, and their buddies at the plant would get rid of it. Boom. No evidence. No evening news." A beat. She tilted her head. "Not that they would flush babies through any water lines in the first place." She noticed the discouragement on Mickey's exhausted face and said, "Aw, don't let it bring your down."

"I really thought I had something that time..."

"Did you get anything else on him?"

"No... nothing."

"What about the rebels that attacked the Chinese Palace?"

"It's all a blank. Probably censored from us."

Watching him depressed her. She rotated back and forth in her chair, hoping he'd say something. All he did was stand there, looking defeated.

She sighed. "Hey, tell you what: why don't we get some coffee later?"

His eyes shot up to her in surprise. He was beaming now. "I—uh... really?"

She nodded. "Don't get *too* excited now."

18: Infiltrate

Altieria Corp. HQ

They'd entered the river two blocks upstream. Orion and Barstow were back in their flexi-armour suits and swimming ten feet below the water's surface, bubbles fizzling from their oxygen masks as they breathed in slow, rhythmic hisses. Submerged in a dark world with trash and scrap metal blanketing the floor. Rays of surface light cut diagonal lines like teetering pillars, always shifting and flickering.

They cut through the abyss like black wraiths, their red eyes shimmering. Gliding through the pulsating light patterns as effectively as the schools of small fish around them. It was the closest thing to zero gravity they would ever experience.

Orion spotted the tunnel in the wall above the ramping wall of the river floor, on the left side of the dam. *"Found it,"* he said, and swam toward it.

Barstow followed. They entered the tunnel one at a time. The tube was small. Dark. Claustrophobic. They used the grimy walls to pull themselves through to the other side. Orion stopped when he reached the end. Poked his head out. Surveyed the area. Sure enough, he saw big, round black objects with spikes, held in place by chains extending from the floor. *"There're the mines, as promised."*

"Fantastic."

Orion looked around again. Found a shaded area, which he guessed was the area beneath the helipad. He enhanced the sights in his goggles. His eyes locked onto the grate in the far wall. *"Found our way in."*

Michael Crimmons was a dedicated security officer. He loved his job and the opportunities it brought along.

Key word: *was.*

Now, he was angry. Neurotic. Paranoid. He covered all of his tracks, but he wasn't convinced. With the recent extra security protocols, he felt as though they were converging on him. It was only a matter of time before they found him out—if they hadn't already. He'd spent the past three days glancing over his shoulder, and he could swear he always saw someone turn away when he did.

He was compromised. No doubt about it.

The control room was sterile. White walls. White ceiling. Dull lighting. Two-way mirror walls on all sides. Security officers and engineers worked endlessly at their stations, their desks organized in a spiral pattern that expanded from the center of the room to the walls. Computer consoles beeped and keyboards clacked endlessly.

Thirty others worked their consoles on either side of him. He pushed out of his work station, located somewhere in the inner-third row, and got out of his office chair. He jolted slightly when a co-worker asked him, "Where are you going?"

"Just a bathroom break," he said quickly.

"Hurry back," the co-worker replied, "we'll need all the help we can get to break through this last wall."

The firewall he'd installed. They were breaking through. Once that firewall was down, they would find his digital footprints cutting across the secret regions of the network that he'd worked so hard to keep hidden. He always knew it'd only be a matter of time before they found out eventually.

Going round and round toward the outer circle of the consoles was hell. Felt like everyone turned to look at him as he moved past them. Finally, he left the control room through the automatic sliding doors and staggered down the hall, tripping over his own feet in his silent panic. He rushed to the restroom, took the nearest stall, locked the door, and sat down. Breathed heavily, practically hyper-ventilating. His head felt light enough to float off his shoulders. The closed, tight space in the stall spun around him. Walls closing in on him. Red eyes watching him.

…Red eyes?

Crimmons craned his neck and caught himself staring into the red lens of Orion's oxygen mask. A black, rubbery hand stifled his screams. Dangling upside down on a line from a ceiling vent, Orion held the panicking technician's head in place with both hands as he struggled on the toilet. "Quiet down," Orion whispered sharply. When Crimmons continued to struggle, Orion hissed, "Stop moving or I'll break your neck!"

Crimmons froze into place.

"Better. Now, I'm going to take my hand away from your

mouth. If you scream, I will kill you. Understand?"

Crimmons stared up at him with bulging eyes.

"Nod your head if you understand."

Crimmons nodded.

"Good. I'll hold you to it." Orion slowly released Crimmons' head. All the man did was suck in air as if he'd been underwater for thirty seconds too long. Even that was too loud for Orion's comfort. "We're with the police. If you know what's good for you, you'll be coming with us."

"But why?! I-I've done nothing wrong," Crimmons protested.

"We both know that's bullshit. Word of advice, Crimmons..." Orion descended a couple inches down the rope for dramatic effect, stopping when he was level with Crimmons' face, "...if you stay here for another hour, you're as good as dead. If you'd prefer to live longer, I suggest you cooperate."

"What? What do you mean?!"

"They're on to you. If you don't leave with me right now, you'll die. It's that simple."

"But—"

Impatient, Orion leaned even closer toward him and said, "Either you follow me out, or I drag you out. Choose wisely."

Crimmons blinked. It was easy to decide.

Amanda/7 entered the CEO's office and saluted. "Good evening, sir."

The CEO took his eyes off the breathtaking view provided by his panoramic windows. Swivelled around in his office chair to face her. He was already looking worse than before, with wrinkled skin and a receding hairline. Heavy bags hung under his eyes, and when he made a tent with his fingers, his hands shook. His voice trembled. "Good evening, Amanda/7. What news do you bring?"

"Our security personnel have broken through the final wall. They've found our leak: a security technician named Michael Crimmons. Should we notify the police?"

The CEO thought it over. "No," he said. "Terminate Crimmons. Rework the path so that it leads toward the conservatives. Then notify the police. We'll have two loose ends tied up with one knot."

A squad of armed cyborgs burst into the control room,

submachine guns poised. They quickly searched the consoles. When they found Crimmons' console unattended, most of them swore angrily when they realized their job just got complicated.

Amanda/7 paused as the report came through. She relayed the message to the CEO: "Just received an update from Squad 3: Crimmons has disappeared."

The CEO scowled. Something was amiss. "Initiate total lockdown of the premises. No one goes in and no one gets out. Find Crimmons and terminate him."

"Yes, sir."

"And leave the police out of this. We don't need any more complications with them while they maintain their bitterness and suspicion."

Barstow led the way through the vents. Orion covered the rear. Crimmons was stuck between them. Before they could clear the third floor down, the alarm blared through the vents and small doors closed the tunnels off in sections, effectively trapping the trio and leaving them with only one option: the grate under Orion.

"That didn't take long," Orion said.

Barstow cursed under his breath. "Looks like our only way out now is the hard way."

"Running through the halls, guns blazing?" Orion asked. "You do realize that as soon as we jump out of these vents, we're pretty much painting target signs on our backs? There's no hiding from them, then."

Barstow turned himself around to face Crimmons. "Then we'll interrogate our suspect right here." He grabbed Crimmons by the collar and yanked him close. "You better start explaining yourself."

"If you get me out of this alive, I'll explain everything."

"No deal," Barstow snarled impatiently. "I don't think you understand how deep in shit you really are. Where you're standing, there's no bottom. It's only a matter of time before dropping you a line to get you out of it is completely out of the question. If you don't give us something now, consider yourself fucked."

"Better do what he says," Orion said. "When he starts using bad words, he means business."

"Shut up, partner," Barstow snapped, barely stopping himself from referring to Orion by name. He shook Crimmons and stuck his gun barrel in the terrified employee's face and barked, "Start talking!"

Crimmons broke into a cold sweat. His body trembled so much he shook the vent. "Okay, okay!"

"Get on with it."

19: Info-Dump

The usual sterile atmosphere was replaced by blinking red lights and a deafening alarm blaring on the intercom speakers. Security squads rushed through the corridors of every floor, ushering confused employees into designated quarters for ID scanning. They worked like a SWAT team; quickly, efficiently, searching every office, every closet, every bathroom stall.

As the squads went about their search, steel panels covered up the windows and all the exits. Security droids jumped out of hidden compartments in the walls and started patrolling the halls.

The CEO retreated to his personal control room and sat down. Hundreds of surveillance monitors surrounded him, giving him a view of every corridor and office in the building. He swivelled around in his chair to study each monitor carefully. "One little employee couldn't possibly vanish from my sight in such a short amount of time." He coughed.

Amanda/7 stood behind him, awaiting her next order.

"When the opportunity was first presented to me, I didn't know what to think," Crimmons began. By now he was curled up against the vent wall, knees pressed against his chest. "They wanted me to conceal a certain subject's movements with blackouts and cover my trail. I was promised a large sum of money if I did the job. It was only supposed to take a few days."

"Who told you to do this?" Barstow asked.

"I never got their name."

"Tell me who it was."

"I don't know, I swear! They disguised their voice and told me not to worry about who they were. I'd be safe as long as I did what I was told, and that was all I needed to be concerned about. They said if I didn't comply, they were more than capable of making my life a living hell."

"They convinced you with simple threats?"

"You don't understand. The things they told me were too elaborate. They described things that only someone on the inside of this company could possibly know. They knew the security network through-and-through. They knew everything. I had no choice but to comply."

"Why you? Why not someone higher up in the security division?"

"I don't know."

"Yes, you do."

"I swear, I don't!"

"They had something on you, didn't they?"

"No!" Crimmons exclaimed, eyes wide with terror.

"Lie to me again and I'll start breaking your legs," Barstow growled. "What kind of dirt did they have on you? Surely you wouldn't risk everything for just money."

Defeated, Crimmons heaved a deep sigh. "I was having an affair with one of the secretaries. Somehow they captured footage of it and threatened to release it to the public if I didn't do what they said. I... I had to do it. I had no other choice but to do everything they said. I can't afford to lose my job. I'd be ruined!"

"A man's penis is truly mightier than his brain." Orion shook his head. "What, exactly, did they tell you to do?"

"...I put a bug of their own design in the system. Everything went haywire after that. The network blacked out. Robots went on the fritz. Cybernetic brain implants shut down. Whatever systems didn't go completely offline started acting up in ways I couldn't have predicted."

Barstow and Orion exchanged looks. Barstow leaned in closer and said, "Are you saying *you're* responsible for the killing malfunctions?"

Crimmons broke into a pathetic sob, "Please, I had no other choice!"

Orion smacked him upside the head. "Stop your sobbing and tell us everything else there is to know. Where does the subject stop to recharge?"

"S-somewhere in the Takuo District."

"That's not specific enough." Orion drew his hand back, threatening another slap, making Crimmons flinch. "Block number!"

"Block 51!" Crimmons cried, cowering in fear. To his relief, the smack he expected from Orion never came.

"Keep going," Orion hissed. "Tell us everything you know

about the subject. If there's anything you can tell us."

"I-I... I—"

Suddenly two muffled *whumps* sounded off. Two gaping holes appeared in front of Crimmons, who jolted twice. He froze. Then his ribcage blew open, and his head burst like a watermelon dropped from the fifth floor of a high rise. The detectives shouted with surprise as a flurry of grey matter splattered their suits. A second later, the entire vent shuddered violently and dropped out of place. For a moment, the detectives were weightless—

—right before a hulking security droid slammed the ventilation shaft into the floor, breaking it up into little panels. The detectives flopped out, exposed, but already poised for a desperate battle. They expected an army.

Instead, they got the CEO. He stood over them, looking like he'd aged about thirty years since they'd last seen him. Hands clasped behind his back. "Welcome home."

They aimed their guns at him.

He held up a hand, as casual as ever. "That won't be necessary, detectives."

They said nothing. They could barely hear him over the sounds of their hearts rapidly beating in their ears.

"There's no point in concealing your identities, either. Come, Detective Barstow... Detective Orion... let's speak in my office."

Shocked, the detectives looked at each other. Then they glanced over their shoulders at the arm cannons of the security droid that towered over them. Cannons that turned Crimmons into a guacamole splatter just a few seconds earlier.

"I insist," the CEO added with a smile.

20: Conference

The long, narrow conference table split the room right down the middle, lined with leather swivel recliners—twenty on each side, plus one at each end. The room's grey walls slanted upward into a panelled ceiling that shone with a dim yellow glow, reflecting brilliantly off the table's slick marble surface.

The thick glass doors slid apart. The CEO entered with the detectives ushered in behind him. The security droid stopped at the doors, just out of range of the motion sensors so that they would close shut behind it.

"Have a seat," the CEO said, gesturing toward the recliners as he took his seat at the head of the table. No sooner had he sat down than a panel opened up in the table, and a small crystal wine glass set, complete with a bottle of white wine and a bowl of ice cubes, came into view in front of him. He selected a lowball tumbler from the set. Used a pair of tongs to drop three ice cubes into it. Filled the glass about halfway with wine. By the time he was finished preparing his drink, his unwelcome guests had taken their seats. "Please," he said, "place your guns on the table."

The detectives' movements were synchronized when they stole a glance at the security droid, then turned back and placed their submachine guns on the table.

"*All* of them, if you please." The CEO took a sip from his tumbler, watching them slam their magnums down beside their submachine guns with a nonchalant expression. "Now…" he moved his hand over the glass set "…would either of you kind gentlemen like a drink?"

They shook their heads.

Orion got straight to the point. "So how deep is the shit we're standing in?"

"That depends on how you want to look at it," the CEO replied. "I could have you executed and erased from society's records with no unwanted consequences. Or I could take away your jobs and your pensions, essentially ruining your lives in the process. I could also brainwash you, apply the right cybernetic alterations to your bodies and minds, and turn you both into direct Altieria Corp. employees—"

"*Direct* employees?" Barstow snapped.

"Yes, Detective," the CEO said, "*direct*, as opposed to *indirect* employees, which you currently are. It's no secret that I control the police force. What remains a mystery is why I can't control..." he flicked his index finger, pointing it at them—more specifically, at Orion "...you."

Orion was far from intimidated. 'Irritated' would be a more accurate description. "Threaten us all you want, but—"

"Don't get me wrong, gentlemen. I'm not bitter. I'm not resentful. But I'm curious. What, exactly, possessed you to infiltrate my headquarters, kidnap my employees, and interrogate them? Without a—oh, that's right... warrants are a thing of the past now, aren't they?"

Barstow couldn't help but chuckle, "Oh, you thought you were the exception to the rule, didn't you?"

"A good leader follows his own rules," the CEO said with a patient smile. "I've stated that police officers can enter the premises on grounds of reasonable suspicion without permission from the property owner. Why do you think you are still alive? If you were regular intruders, you would have been shot. But you are police officers, and while you may be embittered, crude, and extremely reckless, you are far from stupid. So surely, there must be a good reason for your intrusion." He took another sip from his tumbler. "So convince me I was right, gentlemen. On what grounds do you have to enter my building at this hour, and intimidate one of my employees?"

Orion could hear the low hum of the security droid's hand cannons powering up. "I'm afraid we can't divulge that information—even to you."

The CEO arched his eyebrow ever so slightly. "Why?"

Orion said, "We are not at liberty to discuss details of an investigation with anyone except those of a superior authority."

"But I *am* of a superior authority."

"Sure you are," Orion said, "and under normal circumstances, you're right, you would be kept in the know at your request. However, because this investigation involves corruption in your company, with circumstances that we aren't entirely clear on—for example, we don't know how deep the corruption goes, or who is involved, or how high it reaches—that clause is void until further developments point to your innocence in the matter. And since your junk bucket painted our armour suits with a prime suspect in our investigation not twenty minutes ago... well, I'm sure you get the point."

The CEO nodded slowly. "I suppose that's understandable. Very well, then."

The droid's hand cannons powered down. Orion had to smirk, because the dropping tone emanated from the droid could have been easily translated as disappointment.

Barstow felt the need to add: "Terminating a prime suspect who had crucial information that could have moved the investigation forward could also be considered interference and tampering with evidence, Mr. CEO."

"You've made your point," the CEO said. "My security personnel have always been a bit... overzealous with their methods. I suppose I will have to speak with them once our business is concluded."

"Yes," Barstow said, "I suppose you will."

The CEO coughed. Ice cubes clinked as he put down his glass. "I admit I am surprised, Detective Barstow. Usually you aren't so reckless. Infiltrating my headquarters, where even I am a suspect, was... uncharacteristic of you."

"For once," Orion said, "I think we're agreed on that one."

"I'm shocked," the CEO replied without a hint of emotion.

"It was my idea," Barstow admitted. "I may be cautious most of the time, but sometimes, caution ain't the way to go."

The CEO shrugged. Topped up his glass. Sipped slowly. "A matter of priorities."

Barstow nodded.

"Well?" Orion slammed his palms on the table and leaned forward. "Are you gonna let us do our job or not?"

The CEO looked at him. A spiteful glare flashed across his face, passing as quickly as it appeared. With a welcoming smile to mask his true feelings, the CEO said, "Of course. Feel free to roam around. Just don't touch anything."

"Not unless we have to. Oh, and uh..." Orion cocked his head toward the security droid "...don't forget to call off your dogs."

"Of course." The CEO spoke into his telepathic frequency: "Lockdown is over. Stand down, men."

A muffled *shunk-shunk-shunk* rhythm shook the building as the steel blast shields slid away from the windows on every floor.

Barstow leaned forward, snatching his firearms off the table. "While we're here, Mr. CEO, we'd like to ask you a few questions. Having our prime suspect killed in pursuit of us was a bad move, and my gut instinct tells me that isn't a common workplace accident. Now it's your turn to convince us: was that, or was that not intentional? Remember, you swore the oath, just like everybody else."

"No," the CEO answered, "that was not intentional. If anything, it was supposed to be a warning shot. But like I've already explained—my security personnel can be an overenthusiastic bunch."

"Bullshit. You're the big boss man around here. I doubt you'd let that slide, even if your machines' performance routines have been tampered with."

"It's the truth. What more do you want from me?"

"The *whole* truth would be greatly appreciated, Mr. CEO. Starting with how in the hell a security technician could tamper with the system for so long without getting caught. For two weeks, this farce has been going on. I want to know why."

"We were working diligently to root him out. Were it not for the multiple bugs and viruses he'd injected into the system, we would have caught him much sooner."

"A corporation as prestigious and resourceful as Altieria Corp., unable to find one little saboteur in your main building for two weeks… do you realize how inept that makes you and your company look? A saboteur whom, I feel the need to emphasize, caused a portion of the new-model residential droids to malfunction and slaughter their owners all over the city. If I didn't know better, I'd almost say that stopping this saboteur wasn't a top-priority issue for you."

Orion gaped at his partner in disbelief. He hadn't seen Barstow in such a recklessly hostile state before. *This is getting weirder… what's he doing my job for?*

"I suggest you hold your tongue, Detective," the CEO snapped. "Such slanderous comments could land you in a heap of trouble."

"Threatening an officer of the law, are you?"

"Simply informing an inept officer of his rights and

limitations, Detective," the CEO fired back. Then he stood up and carried his half-full tumbler toward the panoramic windows. "Do you see this?" he asked as he spread his arms out, gesturing toward the city's breathtaking skyline, which sparkled brilliantly with endless scrawls of information and colourful imagery in a veil of smog. "What in God's name makes you think I'd risk all of this for anything? Do you think I was protecting the saboteur? Do you think I've something to hide? My company is as much an open book to the police as it is to the public. I've hidden nothing. I've done nothing. And I'm shocked and surprised at you, Detective Barstow, for your unusually hostile behaviour. Have you and your partner switched personalities halfway through this conversation? I'll have you know I am a leader, a businessman for Christ's sake! I'm as cooperative as ever in your investigation, and yet, you two gentlemen continue to antagonize me like I'm some sort of tyrant!"

Orion didn't know what to say.

Barstow gestured toward the CEO's empty seat. "Sit down, Mr. CEO. We're not done talking."

"Oh, yes, we are," the CEO replied, pointing a wrinkly index finger at them.

Orion looked closely at him and thought, *is it just me, or is he... deteriorating right before my eyes?*

The CEO said, "You are free to search the premises. Once you are finished, I want you out of my building. And you'd better have a damned good reason for returning."

"Sit. Down. Mr. CEO," Barstow snarled. "Or I will have no other choice but to arrest you."

"You? Arrest *me*?" The CEO scoffed. "On what charges?"

"Obstruction of justice."

The CEO stole another sip from his tumbler, eyeing Barstow carefully. "Are you serious?"

Barstow drew his LE magnum off the table and pointed it at the CEO. "Dead serious."

Orion lurched back in his seat when he saw the gun. "Jesus Christ, Barstow! That's going too far!"

"Shut up!" Barstow snapped at him.

"He's unarmed; put the gun down!" Orion protested.

The security droid jumped into action, hand cannons poised. "Retract your weapon or I will be forced to open fire! You have twenty seconds to comply!"

Barstow whirled around and fired. Orion ducked. The security droid's head blew apart in a flurry of steel fragments and organic matter.

The CEO's eyes widened. Rooted to the spot.

"Jesus!" Orion exclaimed as he drew his own magnum. "You're way out of line, Barstow!"

Barstow did something Orion couldn't believe: he turned his magnum on *him*. Fired!

Orion dived behind his chair, which exploded. Several more shots followed him as Orion scrambled around the table. Explosive rounds blew holes through the chairs. Perforated the table's surface. Shattered the glassware in front of the CEO's chair, which also came apart under fire. "Barstow, what the fuck?!" Orion hit the floor and shouted at the CEO, "Get down!"

Too late. Another shot rang out. The CEO jumped as his tumbler chinked. The window behind him painted rose red. Shocked, the CEO looked down at the gaping hole in his chest. Before he could drop, another slug blew the top of his head skyward and propelled the rest of him through the window.

After an eighty-storey drop, the CEO's body slammed into the river. Hit a mine. Disintegrated in the consequential explosion. Whatever remained of him was scattered in all directions.

Back up in the conference room, the headless security droid's hand cannons stuttered, strafing the chairs on Barstow's side of the table—and Barstow himself, blasting him through the splintering table in a wild blood spray.

With Barstow gone, Orion was the only one left. The droid turned its hand cannons on him and fired.

Terror struck him. Orion bolted across the conference room away from the main entrance as the window strip beside him fragmented, blown out into the open air. The droid's fusillade chased him down the table, ripping up chairs on Orion's left and splintering windows on his right.

Orion threw himself to the floor. The table came apart under the droid's barrage, but Orion had managed to find a clear shot. He fired his magnum under the crumbling table. Explosive slugs zipped across the room and slammed into the droid's chest. Tore it wide open, spraying an ungodly mixture of organs and machine parts into the air. Then it collapsed.

A high-pitched squeal rang in Orion's ears. He could swear

they were bleeding. The thunderous pounding of his heart wasn't helping his hearing, either. His head felt light. Spinning round. The destroyed furniture in the room mere blurs in his eyes. He pushed himself up to his feet. Staggered. Forgot to breathe for a few seconds—when he finally remembered, he sucked in air and panted like a dog on a hot day. "Jesus…" he gasped, surveying the carnage. He looked at Barstow's shredded corpse, spread-eagled in a maple leaf-shaped pool of blood. His heart took a painful, upward leap into his throat. "Barstow!" he shouted.

He stumbled toward his dead partner to get a better look. He instantly regretted that notion when he saw just how hollowed-out Barstow's body had become. His body looked like it'd been mashed. His head, pulverized, like half of it had been crushed—his sizzling brains oozed out of the opening and the one eye that hadn't disintegrated hung out of the socket by a singed optic nerve. There were only three inches of flesh here and there that were still clinging to something solid. Most of Barstow had been reduced to a purple-black splatter.

The most sickening stench—an unbearably strong mixture of burnt flesh and escaping body odour—emanated from Barstow's remains. More than enough to make Orion scurry a few feet away and vomit. When he was done, Orion's head felt hotter and lighter than before. The floor swayed under his hands and knees. He flopped onto his back and stared up at the ceiling, which swirled round and round and round…

"What the fuck got into you…?" Orion gasped as he wiped his mouth. He looked at his partner again. His friend. Watched the smoke rise from his corpse. The irony of his death didn't escape him. His eyes started to well up with tears. Maybe it was the smoke. Or the smell. "You stupid son of a bitch…"

21: Offspring

The rush of heavy footfalls came in from the hallway, snapping Orion out of his mournful trance. He knew he had to act fast. The steel window shutters came down again, blocking out the neon glow of the city.

Orion looked around frantically. The exits at either end of the conference room were out of the question. No windows to jump through—and even if he could jump through them, he'd have an eighty-storey drop to deal with.

He looked up.

Air duct.

Both exits burst open at the same time. Armoured security personnel poured into the room, weapons ready, eyes scanning the room, making quick note of the bullet-ridden droid and Barstow's remains. When they were sure the room was clear, they made a path for an Amanda/7 unit to walk through each door.

Once the Amanda/7 units surveyed the aftermath of Barstow's brief rampage themselves, they looked at each other from across the room and said in unison, "Where is the other one?"

"Other one?" a security officer replied.

Amanda/7 turned to him. "Yes."

The Amanda/7 unit on the far side of the room looked up at the air duct and pointed at it. "Up there."

The security officers complied by lining up under the duct and punching holes through it with their submachine guns.

Orion heard the shots from the next room over and knew he had to hurry. He didn't waste any time looking over his shoulder at the three hundred needles of light protruding from the floor of the shaft behind him.

Everyone in the conference room watched the duct carefully. Not even a drop of blood.

The other Amanda/7 said, "Jason Orion. Find him and terminate him. Do not let him leave this building alive."

"Yes, ma'am!" the security personnel responded, saluting.

Then they rushed out of the conference room, informing their fellow security officers through their telepathic links of possible hiding places Orion may have chosen.

There was no single hiding place. Orion constantly moved from room to room, looking through each grate before he passed over it. The ventilation ducts were an indecipherable maze in their own right, with constant twists and turns and ups and downs and lefts and rights and verticals. *Christ,* he thought as he squatted at the top of a vertical duct and peered into its darkness. *They even have slides here. Is there anything this wonderland doesn't have?*

He went in feet first. Kept his palms against the walls of the shaft as he slid down the long, dark ramp. He was more concerned about the noise he was making than where the shaft led. The last thing he wanted was to be trapped by machine gun fire in a 40x40 vertical space with no way out.

It stopped abruptly, with a surface that went flat and level, running into a dead end.

A dead end?

Orion reached the bottom of the ramp and stared at the dead end. *Something doesn't feel right...*

The wall didn't move. Not like it was supposed to. It just seemed out of place to him.

With a scowl, Orion thought, *well, guess this is the end of the line. His eyes narrowed, fixed on the suspicious wall. Or is it? I wonder...*

He reached out to touch it. Technically, he never did. His hand passed through it. He smirked at his discovery. Just a simple projection. Looks like they're hiding something here. He crawled through the projection to find another vertical tunnel. He started down it and slid for some time. It felt like he'd never stop sliding until he ended up in hell. His heart pounded. He knew he was in uncharted territory. Why else would it be hidden?

Light at the end of the tunnel. Orion pressed his hands against the sides to slow his descent. When he reached the bottom, he found that the shaft levelled itself out and branched out in three more directions: left, right, and upward-vertical directly in front of him. The upward-vertical shaft had a grated lid about a metre from where he crouched. Quietly, he slithered up the shaft and peeked through the grate into a room saturated with aqua-blue light.

The shaft appeared to be hanging directly over a catwalk

overlooking operating tables, cryogenic capsules partially hidden from view by white cubicle curtains, and other equipment that Orion couldn't place. White streams of light squiggled around the room, indicating that light was reflecting off water. The light was coming from the other side of the catwalk, beneath the shaft—out of Orion's field of vision.

The room appeared to be empty. From his vantage point, Orion looked for surveillance cameras. Found none. With a grunt and mild effort put into it, Orion pushed the grate out of its frame. It swung down on its hinges. Feet first, he climbed out of the duct, fingers latched onto the swinging grate, dangling unsteadily over the catwalk. Let go. Fell five feet and landed firmly on the catwalk, grabbing the handrail for support, gripping his submachine gun (which was clipped to his harness) with his other hand.

First thing he noticed: the air was cold. Damp. Yet somehow smelled more sterile than a hospital. He took his helmet off and found that his breath plumed in front of his face.

Second thing he noticed: the three stacked platforms of incubators behind him, which were previously out of his sight. Each platform had fifty rows of twenty incubators running across them. All of them contained fetuses in various stages of growth—the youngest were on the bottom level; the oldest were on the top level—floating in some kind of thick blue gelatin. The fetuses were tangled in webs of black tubing and wires, bobbing around and writhing in their narrow, enclosed environments.

"What. The. Actual. Fuck," Orion gasped, staring at the fetuses in disbelief. There were hundreds of them. Thousands of them!

He threw his helmet back on. "Record."

"Recording," the AOL voice in his suit responded.

He jumped the handrail. Fell another ten feet. Still managed to land softly on the cold concrete floor in front of the incubators. The suit would record everything he was seeing. He'd only used this feature a few times—lucky for him, he thought to record everything from the moment they caught Crimmons through the CEO's interrogation and Barstow's sudden, unexplainable rampage. He stopped recording shortly after escaping into the air ducts, figuring there was nothing else he could add to the suit's limited 10 GB disk space.

He was wrong. There was obviously a lot more that he could

add.

"Detective Jason Orion of the Altieria City Police Department, 28th Precinct," he whispered into the built-in mic of his helmet. "Entry #9. As you can see, I've uncovered a whole new side of the Altieria Corporation." Orion stole another glance around the room to make sure he was still alone—and to check for cameras. No cameras. None.

He moved forward and started down a row between the incubators, studying the computer screens in the dashboards at their bases for additional information. "They appear to be... *cloning* the CEO. Perhaps this would explain why he always seems to be in different states of aging every time we've arranged meetings with him. Even the routine charging periods weren't enough for him by the looks of things. Bastard wants to live forever." He peered closely at one of the fetuses as it squirmed slightly. "Seems the man who's successfully taken over the world through corporate business deals and endless rules rather than outright oppression and violence is afraid of dying. Just like all the rest of us."

He headed further down the aisle, his movements quiet as a mouse's. "Judging by the lack of cameras, and the fact that I got here by pure fluke alone, could only mean that a select number of individuals are aware of this facility's existence. This is a place that even the regular day-in, day-out security technicians aren't aware of. But of course. What kind of employee would want to know that their boss is essentially immortal? I sure don't. Sorry, Mr. Superintendent. No offense or anything, but if you lived forever— ah, shit. I'm rambling."

He reached a staircase leading up to the second platform. As he ascended the steps, he continued, "I don't like to brag, but I knew all along that something was going on behind closed doors. I just didn't know what it was. Now that I *do* know what it is, I... I can't really believe it. Somehow it doesn't feel real, despite the fact I'm standing right in the middle of it."

He reached the landing. Turned. Headed up the second flight of stairs. "Hate to say I told you so, Barstow, especially since you've passed... but... I told you so. Right now, I can't say for sure if this is all connected to the Elsa Scott case. Crimmons was clearly connected to her murderer, and we at least have its most frequent locations on file. I'm thinking the CEO silenced him before he could help us establish a clear connection—although in doing so, he unwittingly confirmed that he's involved in all of this."

Orion stepped out onto the second platform and started going through the aisles like a shopper in a department store, examining each fetus as he passed it. "But what does Scott's murder have to do with the CEO's illegal cloning operation? Is it simply to live forever, or is there an even bigger picture that I'm just not seeing? More efficiency in the ranks of the military, perhaps? Stormtroopers? Jesus. Listen to this shit. If I wasn't recording my visuals, you'd all think I'm just going on some crazy rant about nothing.

"So who's the mastermind behind all this? Here's my list of suspects. Tell me which one sounds the most likely: Franklin Scott, CEO/H3@D, the rebels, or Michael Crimmons?" He paused, gulping down a lump of sadness. "Or Lucas Barstow, whose rampage remains unexplained." He coughed and shook his head. Thirty years, and this is how our partnership ends.

He got a grip and went on: "Scott may be an employee, but hell, maybe I suspected him just because of the timing between his ex-wife's divorce request and her murder. The rebels're always looking for ways to take out the big man, but they wouldn't waste their energy and resources on just a random psychokinetic girl. To even suggest that they did it to send a message due to her marriage with a high-ranking employee would be ludicrous. They don't work that way. Crimmons wasn't clear on whether or not he controlled the killer, which may or may not just be another psychokinetic surrogate. He mentioned he was tasked with covering its tracks. He may or may not be directly responsible for Elsa Scott's murder, but the man was definitely scared of a higher power.

"A higher power like... say... the CEO. He holds all the cards. He's clearly got the resources. But if he was controlling Crimmons through a third party, and Crimmons was covering for the killer, then who's the real killer, and why was Elsa, the wife of one of the company's most important employees, killed? To punish him somehow? Maybe she discovered something she wasn't supposed to? When I spoke to him a few days ago, he had his own lab at home, which I didn't see, more out of respect for the man than obligation. I mean, I was the bearer of bad news. And at the time, I didn't think there would be any justification in forcing a search of his apartment. But something tells me that that lab contains a few answers to some of my questions. If I get out of this building alive, that'll be the first place I go. It's do or die now, and I'd rather die later."

He shook his head and sat down against the base of an incubator. The six-month-old fetus floating in it appeared to be staring down at him. All of them were. He tried to push that thought out of his head, instead focusing on the jigsaw puzzle this case had turned into. "But what was the purpose of hollowing out Elsa Scott's corpse? To throw us off the scent? To divert our suspicions toward the black market? Christ, all this thinking is making my head hurt."

The CEO's voice suddenly cut through the cold air like a red-hot knife: "Be careful not to strain yourself, Detective."

Orion pricked up. Stiffened. *Goddamn it!*

"We know you're up there. No use hiding."

"How'd you find me?"

"We hacked into your private frequency the moment you entered my conference room. I'm sorry, but we can't allow you to leave this facility with that information—or your life—intact."

"I'm sorry you're sorry." Orion replied, slowly getting to his feet and moving stealthily toward the rear side of the platform. He switched to thermal optics and looked down. The platform below him was swarming with cybernetic security personnel. "Jesus Christ," he whispered sharply, tightly gripping his submachine gun with both hands. He shuffled out of the view of the stairs as the first security officer reached the top of the staircase. Cutting between the fetus jars, across the aisles. *"So you've hacked my private channel, have you?"*

"Indeed I have," the CEO replied.

"I'm going to be honest with you: having your voice rattling inside my head while I navigate through your offspring tubes is... a disturbing thought, to say the least."

"That's really too bad."

"No, really. It's the most effective kind of nightmare fuel."

"You never cease to amuse, Detective," the CEO replied sarcastically.

"So are you gonna make this easier on me?" Orion spotted a shadow moving along the incubators behind him and jumped across another aisle. He squatted behind the containment unit, and thanked his lucky stars that the gelatin inside of it was thick enough to conceal him from his hunters. Two of them shuffled right by him on

the other side, moving like shadows.

"How do you propose I do that?"

"This is the part where you make it all fit together by telling me your master plan. Then, if you'd be gracious enough to capture me alive and leave me unattended in a death trap with a big red eject button beside my head, I'd greatly appreciate it."

The CEO genuinely chuckled at that. *"Unfortunately, I can't make any promises."*

"I figured as much."

"If only you could see beneath the surface. Then you would understand."

"I understand beauty ain't always skin deep."

"Enough. You can surrender quietly and willingly, or we can make you surrender."

Orion circled around the incubator he was just hiding behind, back into the most recent aisle he'd crossed, and pointed his submachine gun at the backs of the security pair that had just gone past him. *"I was never the quiet type, anyway,"* he said, right before he tensed—

—and fired.

22: Surrender

Orion's submachine gun stuttered. The security pair dropped in clumsy heaps.

Deafening staccato to his left. He dropped as the fetus jar beside him burst, spilling tubes and a six-month-old fetus to the floor in a murky cascade of blue ooze. Orion ducked down the aisle as a security officer's volley tore across the incubators in pursuit. Gelatin and wiring exploded from the incubators the split second the security cyborg's bullets made contact with the glass, like pressurized canisters in a microwave. Orion darted down the aisle, keeping his head down.

Another cyborg leaped out of nowhere. Tackled Orion to the floor. Drew a combat knife with a twelve-inch blade and a serrated red-hot edge. Brought it down on Orion's face.

Orion blocked the bastard's wrist with his forearm. The knife's tip barely an inch from the left lens of his helmet. Even with the enhanced strength capabilities of his suit, Orion was having a difficult time keeping his attacker's knife away from his face. The damn thing's sizzling tip could melt through his lens as if it were butter with barely any effort put into it.

With his free hand, Orion jabbed the barrel of his submachine gun into his attacker's chest and loosed a three-round burst through his body. The attacker jolted. Oxygen hissed from his mask as the glowing green eye lens turned murky. Orion pushed him off and snatched his knife away from him.

The security cyborg that first attacked him leaped into view in the next aisle over. Orion didn't hesitate. He blasted the son of a bitch backwards through another incubator.

He noticed movement in every other aisle on either side. Multiple targets. They were flanking him. He doubled over and scurried up the aisle. Ducked between two more fetus jars that somehow managed to stay intact after the shooting.

Orion threw himself into the sights of two more cyborgs. Before they could fire, he was on them, blowing the right one backwards with his submachine gun and slashing through the oxygen mask of the left one. The left cyborg staggered back, dropping his gun, using both hands to try and cover the streams of oxygen hissing out of the openings Orion made. Orion kicked him against the nearest incubator and ran him through with the knife, nailing him to it. He pulled the knife up his chest and retracted it from the gurgling cyborg's neck. Gelatin burst out of the vertical line Orion cut into the containment unit, propelling the cyborg across the aisle in a thick blue spray.

Orion darted across a few more aisles, between more incubators. In the third row, he saw the cyborg too late. Leaped across the aisle right in front of the stunned cyborg, who quickly composed himself and squeezed off a few pistol shots before Orion disappeared behind the next row.

Two had bounced off his suit. Orion breathed a sigh of relief as he racked his submachine gun.

The pistol cyborg entered the row in the space adjacent to him, weary of his prey. Orion immediately circled round the incubator behind him, aimed the submachine gun at his back. Fired—

Click!

Orion's heart sank as the cyborg whirled and shot at him. Orion scrambled for cover. Sparks flew off the grated floor at his heels. Orion dived behind another incubator. A bullet punched through the glass and ripped through a seven-month-old fetus.

On the other side, another cyborg approached him, submachine gun spraying the floor around Orion. Orion acted on instinct alone and hurled the combat knife at the guard. To his surprise, the knife cut through the cyborg's oxygen tubing and sank into his throat. "*Gack!*" The guard made one last attempt to suck in air, then crumpled on his knees and pitched forward.

The pistol cyborg fired through the punctured incubator until it burst, spilling its contents all over the floor. But Orion was nowhere to be found. Cautiously, the cyborg moved around the destroyed fetus jar. His shoulder brushed past the dying fetus, which hung suspended from the hollowed jar's ceiling by wires, tubes, and its umbilical cord. He stepped out into the next aisle. Grunted when he sat the result of Orion's latest kill, with the tip of the combat knife protruding from the nape of his neck. Red-hot edge cooking the flesh around it.

The pistol cyborg turned at a ruckus behind him, but—

Too late. Orion slammed into his back and wrapped

something around the cyborg's neck. The cyborg grunted and struggled, prompting Orion to pull back on the umbilical cord until it severed the oxygen tube from the cyborg's mask. Oxygen escaped the cyborg's mask, making him flail his arms in panic.

The fetus, still attached to the umbilical cord, squished between their bodies. A chunky coating made its fragile skin slick.

The two locked combatants waddled back and forth across the aisle, slipping and sliding on spilled gelatin. The cyborg raised his pistol and fired a few shots over his shoulder. Orion leaned back and drove his knee into the cyborg's spine. The cyborg groaned and fired another shot into the ceiling. Then he tried a new tactic: he quickly swapped gun hands. Wrapped his left arm around his midriff. Fired the pistol under his armpit. Orion shouted with surprise and jumped further out of the guard's reach as the explosive slug blew the screen out of the monitor of the nearest incubation console. Another shot rang out. The fetus between them blew to a giant splatter of underdeveloped flesh and fluids. Greasy pink sludge.

The cyborg tried again and found himself dry-firing his pistol. Orion grabbed both sides of his head and gave it a sharp jerk, twisting it all the way around with a sickening snap.

There may not have been any cameras in that sector, but the CEO was still well aware of how his men were going about their job. He had connected himself to the Amanda/7 unit that reported to him in his office. Seated with their backs against each other, their heads lay back, connected by a multitude of wires that were plugged into little jacks installed in their craniums. Another Amanda/7 unit stood in the cloning sector, observing the situation from a safe distance. She transmitted everything she saw back to the Amanda/7 in the CEO's office, which in turn was transferred to the CEO.

Instead of using the regular private frequency, the CEO broadcasted his thoughts through the Amanda/7s, just in case Orion had somehow found a way into their frequency: "Watch your fire, damn you! Those offspring are our future. For every single one you destroy, you are costing me billions. Handle Orion as quickly as possible, and destroy those recordings. And do it quickly! This farce has gone on long enough!"

A squad of cyborgs stalked the rows, replacing their

submachine guns with red-hot combat knives. They moved like trained soldiers in formation, passing through the rows of fetus jars; heads low, bodies taut.

Orion had shuffled to the end of the row. Drew his LE magnum. Kept out of sight, watching the eight cyborgs move as one behind the chambers. Leveled the gun, and fired—

—sent the explosive round straight through the incubator—and the fetus it contained. The bullet kept going down the aisle, piercing jar and fetus like a loosed arrow. Jar. Fetus. Jar. Fetus. It reached the first cyborg on Orion's side of their formation and burned a hole through its head without slowing down. The bullet then ripped through jar, fetus, head. Jar, fetus, head. Jar, fetus, head. And so on—until it reached the other side of the platform, leaving behind a split-second vortex through skulls, glass, flesh, and gelatin.

All eight cyborgs collapsed in the direction of the bullet's directory. The incubators beside and between them burst apart. Everything crashed to the floor in a viciously brutal spectacle that was as surreal as it was a disgusting variant of tumbling dominos. Flurries of grey matter and decimated mechanical pieces flew out of half-destroyed heads in dark red blots. Limbs flailed. Exploding glass shrieked and sparkled in the aqua blue light. Wires sparked. Severed tubes lashed out like snakes. Obliterated fetuses, following the trajectory of the bullet, transformed into crescent-shaped splodges.

Orion couldn't believe his luck. That was a once-in-a-lifetime shot, for Christ's sake. But he knew he didn't have time to pat himself on the back. When the incubators' spillage began to flow over the edge of the platform, Orion jumped onto the handrail and launched himself into space. He soared a good fifteen feet before he started to go down. Braced himself as he fell a whole storey toward the cold concrete floor. Tuck-and-roll landing sent him barrelling across the room behind a short metal trolley full of blood samples.

Raised to a crouch, Orion stole a peek over the cabinet and spotted Amanda/7 standing a few feet away. "You...!"

Maintaining a nonchalant expression, Amanda/7 pulled out a pistol and opened up on the trolley. The few security cyborgs that had run out from under the platforms followed suit with their submachine guns, spraying the blood samples out of their test tube racks. The overwhelming firestorm flipped the trolley. Orion made a break for the nearest wall, ducking behind brain-scanning equipment and cubicle curtains. Bullets stitched across the wall and floor in hot pursuit, ripping up the curtains and destroying whatever equipment came between Orion and the security force.

"Idiots!" the CEO's voice shouted from Amanda/7's mouth. "I told you to watch your fire. You're destroying the equipment! What good does shooting after him do? It's a dead end. All you're doing now is causing more damage."

One of the cyborgs didn't pay him any heed and kept on shooting, blasting a heartbeat monitor out of a shredded cubicle curtain.

Amanda/7 adjusted her aim and popped an armour-piercing slug through the unruly cyborg's head. Down he went, head and helmet completely disintegrated—nothing but a red patch on the far wall.

Orion pushed into a cubicle curtain, rounded a vacant bed, and reached the far wall. A dead end. "Shit," he muttered. He squatted behind the bed and hastily reloaded his magnum.

Amanda/7 stepped out between Orion and the security force. Her gun drawn on Orion's cubicle curtain, which had plenty of holes through its tattered fabric now. With a sigh, the CEO said through her, "Let's not draw this out any further, Detective. Give up your weapons and surrender. There is nowhere left for you to go."

"There're always two ends to every road," Orion replied, trying to sound as snarky as possible to hide his growing horror of the situation.

"Nonsense," the CEO replied with a chuckle. "It's time to embrace the inevitable. You chose to travel down a one-way street, and now you have reached the end. There is no turning back for you, Detective."

Suddenly it occurred to Orion. He searched the compartments in his utility belt and took out four plastic explosives. He looked from them to the wall, then back at them with newfound hope. "Can't go forwards... but I can always go backwards."

"Suggesting you head down the wrong lane? Against rush hour traffic? That would be suicide."

"That all depends on your driving skills, Mr. CEO."

"Enough. I'm tired of this analogical banter, and I'm especially tired of your antics." Amanda/7 fired a warning shot into the cubicle. Orion flinched when the pillow on the bed burst into a cloud of white fluff. "Considering how much trouble you've made yourself over the past few months, I have been very generous to you so far. That was a warning shot. My next bullet will not miss. Last chance: surrender now—or be destroyed."

"As opposed to obliterated, right?"

"Does that mean you refuse?"

"What do you think?"

Amanda/7 fired two shots through the side of the bed in response. A smile formed on her lips when Orion started to groan. "What do you say now?"

"Gimme a few minutes, will ya?" Orion snapped.

Amanda/7 scowled and gestured for the security units to come forward. "Kill him," the CEO said.

The security units unleashed a new fusillade of hot lead on Orion's cubicle. They burned down the curtains. Destroyed all of the equipment. Tore up the bed. Drilled holes into the concrete wall on the other side. Sparks flew. Shreds of fabric fluttered through the air like snow petals. Bullets pinged off the steel frame of the bed.

Then they stopped to observe their handiwork, and listened for a sign.

Their ears picked up silence. Their eyes spotted blood pooling from under the bed.

23: Basement/1

"Reload," the CEO barked.

The cyborgs did as they were commanded.

"Confirm the kill," the CEO ordered.

The cyborgs closed in on the wreckage they'd created, racking their submachine guns with anticipation. A carpet of debris crunched under their boots. They surrounded the bed, guns poised. Orion was nowhere to be found. One of the cyborgs checked under the bed. Nothing but a blood puddle.

"He's gone, sir!" one of them exclaimed.

Amanda/7's eyes narrowed. The CEO said, "Well, he couldn't have simply vanished, now, could he? Find him!"

A loud, metallic squeal in their ears. Everyone turned to a small metal cabinet behind the cyborgs' cubicle and watched it slowly wheel its way into the corner.

Amanda/7 smirked at the comical sight. "Do you really think a cabinet is going to stop us from capturing you, Detective?"

The cabinet banged against the wall. Orion stayed huddled behind it. His back literally in the corner. He held up a small remote device in his hand. "No, but it should keep the shrapnel out of my eyes."

Alarmed, the CEO said, "What—"

He pushed the button on the remote.

The wall beside the bed erupted. The force hurled the cyborgs through the air and toppled the bed in a hot shower of flames and concrete. Orion kept his head down as a relatively minimal spray of debris pelted the cabinet. Then he pushed it out of his way and bolted through the smoke shroud for the hole in the wall, LE magnum providing suppressive fire as he ran. It worked, mostly, since the few cyborgs that survived the blast ducked for cover.

Amanda/7 stayed out in the open, however, and fired her pistol after him. Bullets slapped the walls above and around him as he raced for the hole, tripping and stumbling over chunks of wall until his shoulder exploded with pain. The bullet burned through his armour like it was nothing. The impact slammed him into the wall with a pained shout.

Orion didn't stop for long. He returned fire. Blew her stomach through her back, leaving a sizzling hole in its wake. Despite the severe damage to her body, Amanda/7 didn't drop. Three more rounds popped out of her pistol. Orion ducked to the rubble on the floor and levelled his aim. She got another shot in. The bullet skimmed the side of his helmet. Orion sharply sucked in air, and fired.

The bullet whistled through the air. Punched through her left eye. Burrowed its way through her brain. Burst—and scattered the back of her head across the room.

Orion scrambled through the hole—

—and entered free fall for about six feet. Heart jumped in his throat as he reached out for something to grab. His body chopped a fluorescent light tube suspended from the ceiling in half right before a desk abruptly knocked the wind out of him.

Even with the suit, that hurt. He had to remind himself that it could have hurt a lot more without it.

Orion groaned as he climbed off the desk onto solid ground. He looked around and found himself standing in an office containing three rows of five computer desks. Walls were frosted glass windows. The office was almost empty, but a few office workers were still in the process of evacuating. Smoke filled the room. The fire alarm blared on and on and on—ear-splittingly loud and repetitive.

Orion moved toward the door, leaning on every desk as he passed it, gripping his magnum in his free hand. He looked up. Saw a surveillance camera staring right at him. He raised his revolver and blasted it off its wall mount.

The shrill screams of nearby employees escalated as the gunshot threw them into renewed panic. Throngs of people thundered down the halls, scrambling for safety, running over each other to get away. They were making life difficult for the security forces that were trying to push their way in the opposite direction of the rush.

Orion stole the opportunity while there were still enough civilians to hold security back. He darted out into the corridor and blasted two more cameras into oblivion. All of the CEO's electric eyes in that hall went blind, much to the big man's chagrin, without a doubt. Orion couldn't be happier with that thought.

*

Security swarmed the area in the next minute, but by then, Orion was nowhere to be found.

"Spread out!" the CEO barked on the telepathic link. *"He couldn't have gone far."*

A cyborg captain pointed at four guards and said, "Check the vents."

In seconds, the halls, offices, and the air ducts were crawling with security.

A cyborg entered the men's room. Checked each of the stalls. Decided it was safe upon reaching the last stall, entered it, and locked the door behind him. "Disengage." The suit's exo-spine split apart like a zipper. He slipped out of the suit in his boxer briefs and hung the suit up on the door hook.

He never got to the toilet, because as soon as he hung the suit up, Orion kicked the air duct grate above him down on his head, stunning him. Orion dropped down on his shoulders and flattened him under the combined weight of his suit and his body. The impact broke his neck and both his collar bones.

"Sorry, pal," Orion said as he draped the security officer's body over the toilet seat. The poor bastard's cybernetic eye implants twitched and shuttered like camera lenses as the head dangled loosely over his left shoulder.

Orion pulled off his helmet. Took the disk drive out of the hidden forehead compartment. Grasped it firmly in his fist. "Here goes nothing."

Now in the cyborg's tactical suit, Orion stepped out of the men's room and started down the hall. He held his breath every time he passed another cyborg. A cluster of them rushed by. The last of them stopped and grabbed his forearm.

Nearly stopped his heart.

Tense, Orion turned to the security officer.

"Did you find him yet?" the officer asked.

Stifling a sigh of relief, Orion simply shook his head.

"Damn it," the officer snarled. "Keep your eyes peeled. He's a sly piece of work."

And, with that, Orion watched the officer turn and sprint after his squad.

He felt like a tiny insect crawling in a web overrun with baby spiders. Somehow they didn't catch on yet, but if any of them were more attentive than the average officer, they might notice that he wasn't responding to the CEO's telepathic frequency and sound an alarm. He had to act fast. In the meantime, he acted as convincingly as possible to keep from standing out under the scrutiny of the CEO's endless multitude of eyes.

Orion entered the first elevator he could find. Swiped the guard's ID card and hit the core level button. The only way to escape this place was to severely cripple it. *Break a man's legs and he won't chase you anymore,* he thought as the elevator began its descent.

He was silent, listening to Ray Charles' *I Can't Stop Loving You,* which played softly on the elevator's tiny speakers. It was a long way down. He checked the bullets in his submachine gun. Shifted his weight from foot to foot impatiently. Scoured the elevator's interior for cameras and found tiny little fish eyes in all four corners of the ceiling, watching his every move. As he waited, his thoughts drifted…

Barstow.

The thought of his dead partner felt like someone stabbed his heart with an electric drill and turned the damn thing on. If Orion was what he considered a weak man, he would have simply decided there was no point in trying to survive. He was trapped in the domain of the most powerful man in the world. An army was closing in on him. Hell, he was lucky to have made it this far. His chances of making it out of this facility alive were thinner than slim.

Orion wasn't a weak man. He told himself he would make it. He had to make it. He had crucial evidence that would bring down the CEO's whole goddamned regime and more; and he was close to solving the murder of Elsa Scott. He could feel it.

After what felt like an hour, the elevator finally hit the bottom. The doors parted, revealing a grated footbridge that went on into a black void filled with plumes of steam rising from below. Illuminated by pulsing red light. Two guards flanking the doorway looked in. When they saw Orion, they stepped in the elevator, standing to attention.

"Identification check."

Orion glanced at the scanner he'd swiped his card through, then looked back at them. "What's this thing for if you're just going to ask again when I get here?"

"The alarm's been sounded, so we're being extra cautious."

The other guard said, "We'll need you to remove your helmet too."

"You're kidding me," Orion said.

"Sorry, man. Gotta match the face to the photo."

"So that's how it is," Orion said.

Without hesitation, Orion mowed them down with his submachine gun and jumped out of the elevator. The doors banged against the sides of one of the fallen guards, unable to close. Safety measures kept the elevator grounded so long as the doors were obstructed.

Good, Orion thought.

He turned and started across the bridge. The suit protected him from the unbearable humidity of the massive chamber. The metal surface, wet with condensation and hot to the touch. The thick steel bridge, about as wide as a four-lane freeway, never seemed to end. Orion could see through the grating into a bottomless pit from which heavy steam clouds billowed. Whenever that red light strobed across the bridge opposite Orion, he could manage brief glimpses of the walls in the far distance on either side of him: steel pipes, all bunched together, varying widely in thickness. A few of them had openings that released more steam into the chamber.

After twenty minutes, Orion thought he saw something in the dense steam veil in front of him. Another minute of pushing through the intense fog, and he could begin to make out the shape: a colossal eight-sided octagonal prism in the middle of a towering octagonal bipyramid, spanning about a fifteen thousand square feet radius— essentially a thirty-four-storey diamond structure, with the pyramids on the top and bottom of the prism each a ten-storey stalagmite/stalactite, and the prism itself fourteen storeys high. Hovering in the center of four steel bridges (including Orion's) that were positioned in an X instead of a cross in order to successfully connect with its sides. Between the gate and retractable extension at the end of each bridge and the bulletproof glass doors of the prism chamber was a twenty-foot gap to prevent any runners from jumping over without authorization.

The closer Orion got, the smaller he felt. He craned his neck, taking in the sheer size of the structure in speechless awe. He finally reached the gate, still staring at the octagon's murky windows, wondering if he was being watched. He most likely was.

He swiped his stolen ID card and waited. A loud click. The bridge started to slowly extend itself toward the double doors in the octagonal prism structure. Orion stepped onto it while a male computer voice droned, "Keep hands and feet on the extension at all times. Do not move until extension has come to a complete stop. In case of an emergency, please refer to page 1,652 in the Altieria Corp. Safety Manual, which you should be carrying on your person at all times. Have a nice day."

Orion waited patiently while the voice repeated itself in multiple languages at a time. The extension stretched across the bottomless gap. The doors getting ever-closer, opening to let him in. He glanced over the side. Nothing but open space under the ten-inch-thick steel extension he was standing on. Orion snickered at a little joke in his head: Maybe it's the world's first opening into hell.

The computer voice said, "System override."

The extension abruptly jolted to a stop, nearly propelling Orion over the end into oblivion. Orion lurched forward, but managed to regain his footing even as the extension started to retract with at least another ten feet between him and the closing doors.

Closing doors.

Without thinking, Orion unfastened his submachine gun from its harness and hurled it across the gap. Thank every god in existence, the gun went fast enough to come between the doors, its momentum interrupted when they clenched on it. Safety protocol caused them to re-open. The gun clattered to the floor, fucking with the doors' motion sensors.

Orion jogged back toward the gate. The retracting bridge made his jog seem like a run up the downward escalator. With every step, he knew that goddamn gap was getting wider.

He stopped. Turned. Threw himself into a full-on run for the edge of the retracting bridge. Gap, fast-approaching. Retractor end, even faster.

Up ahead, he saw someone in a white lab coat and a light exosuit on the other side of that doorway, moving toward his submachine gun. If they moved it, those doors would close, and he'd be fucked.

His suit went into full power, accelerating his steps beyond regular human capabilities.

The guard behind the doors reached for the submachine gun.

Orion launched himself into space.

The guard, only a few inches away from the gun.

Orion, hurtling across the void. Drawing a small service pistol from his belt. The LE magnum's recoil would slow his momentum.

Fingers touched the submachine gun.

Orion's pistol blew a hole through the guard's shoulder. The guard staggered backwards as a slimy green liquid spewed from his shoulder. Still, he went for the gun again, so Orion blasted him twice more. The guard jolted as he took two in the stomach. Almost there. Orion fired again.

The guard dived for the submachine gun, hands outstretched. He took one in the neck and still wouldn't stop. Pushed the submachine gun over the edge. The doors started to close.

Orion's body slammed into the wall. Threw his hand through the door. Obstructed them. The doors widened again. The cyborg wrestled with Orion's one arm, trying to get it out the door. His artificial strength would be Orion's downfall. Orion could feel his hand sliding further out above his head. Still gripping his gun in his other hand, Orion pulled himself up. The cyborg held his left forearm. His right hand latched onto the cyborg's wrist. The cyborg grunted and started prying Orion's fingers off one by one with his other hand.

Orion brought his pistol up and blew a round through the cyborg's right eye, spattering the ceiling in a thick coating of the cyborg's chunky green head cheese. The cyborg's strength still didn't let up. It glared at Orion with its one good eye—until Orion unloaded the rest of his magazine into the damned thing's face. With most of its head gone, the cyborg was without direction. Orion let go of the cyborg's wrist and grabbed hold of the door jamb. He tossed his pistol from his other hand, grabbed the cyborg's shoulder, and jerked back. The cyborg let out an ear-splitting shriek as it pitched through the doorway and fell into oblivion.

Orion started to climb into the—

Heavy weight wrapped around his ankle, yanked him back out. Tore him out of the doorway. Left hanging only by his fingertips. The doors started to close. Orion shoved his arm through the doorway. The doors retracted into the jamb. He looked over his shoulder.

The near-headless cyborg clung fiercely to his ankle. Its fingers like a fly stuck against a poisonous adhesive strip.

"You stubborn son of a bitch," Orion gasped as he kicked at

the disgusting, pulpy green mass between the cyborg's shoulders. His boots, sucked into its artificially organic head like mud on a rainy day. No matter how hard he kicked, the cyborg stubbornly clung on, reaching up to climb to safety.

Now was the time for the LE. Orion drew it from his suit's shoulder compartment. Aimed. Fired. Shattered the cyborg's shoulder. Its outstretched arm spun out into the void. If it still had eyes, Orion imagined it'd be glaring at him more intensely than before. Instead, he stared into a tangled mass of shredded flesh, wires, little cybernetic parts, and that green brain no more solid than a pile of ground meat. He aimed directly at that mashed brain and blasted through it. The cyborg jolted as its head cheese splattered in all directions. Its grip on Orion's ankle slackened. Another shot into the stump propelled it into the bottomless void.

Out of breath, Orion watched with mild satisfaction as the writhing cyborg slowly shrank into the darkness. He didn't wait for it to get out of sight. He holstered his LE and pulled himself to safety as quickly as possible. When he got through, he tucked his feet in. The doors finally clamped shut behind him. He raised himself to a crouch and looked up at the three steel-eyed guards aiming their H&K G36 assault rifles at him.

He froze, returning their thousand-yard stares with a nervous chuckle behind his mask. "Allow me to break the ice..." he paused, mind racing; first thing that sprang to mind was: "You're all under arrest."

24: Decode

Orion's attempt at breaking the ice wasn't nearly as successful as he'd hoped. The guards confiscated all of his weapons and other devices, and dragged him down a corridor into a large white room. This white room contained bulky equipment and holographic screen projections lined up in two rows, and a conveyor belt running a straight line through five checkpoints with showerheads on metal bars arching above them.

They stripped him out of his suit, instructed him to stand on the conveyor belt, and subjected him to a five-stage scorching hot decontamination shower that progressively got more painful the further down he went. When he finally reached the other end of the conveyor belt, his skin was burned red from the heat, and even with the humidity emitted from the showers, he was shivering in the cool air outside of them.

They scanned him for more contaminants, eyes glued to the holographic monitor displaying the contaminant level readings. Once they scanned head to toe, the monitor showed a reading of 0.006%.

"He's clean," one of the cyborgs said.

"Do you treat all your guests this way?" Orion asked, catching a towel they threw at him and quickly drying himself down. "Or just the lucky ones?"

"Shut up," the nearest cyborg, a decontamination officer, hissed. His sneer was quickly replaced by a sly grin. The sudden emotional shift put Orion a little on edge. "I must commend you, Detective Orion. No other intruders have ever made it this far into the facility."

"You keep count?"

"You'll be surprised to know I've lost track of the number of individuals and groups that have attempted to infiltrate this facility over the years. For a number of reasons, of course: to steal our secrets; to sabotage our systems and equipment; to assassinate our wonderful CEO..."

"'Wonderful,'" Orion spat, "I must've switched dimensions at some point."

"No need to be snide, Detective," the officer said. "You should feel honoured. The farthest anyone else made it was the elevator. But of course, they didn't steal an ID card, so they couldn't gain access to this level. Your resourceful cleverness has won the CEO's respect."

By that point, three other cyborgs had fully dismantled his suit in the corner nearest the entrance opposite the showers. One of them approached the leading decontamination officer and said, "It's not in the suit."

The decontamination officer turned his broad shoulders and stern glare to Orion and barked, "Where's the drive?"

"Drive?" Orion said, feigning innocence. "Whatever do you mean?"

The decontamination officer took a step into Orion's personal space. His fierce green eyes pierced into Orion's blue eyes. "The drive containing your recordings of our top-secret operations. Where is it?"

"Oh. *That* drive," Orion said with an exaggerated grin. "I'm sorry, I forgot about that one."

"Stop wasting time. Tell me where you've hidden it, and we'll let you live."

"What's the catch?"

"We'll wipe your memory of the events that transpired here. I assure you, it's a quick and harmless process."

"Thought as much. Not biting."

"You're a stubborn bastard, aren't you?"

"A full-fledged employment cyborg that utters curse words," Orion said, looking him directly in the eyes. "I'm impressed."

The decontamination officer scoffed and replied, "We Model Tens are much more sophisticated than the lowly drones they've got upstairs. Those... Model Sixes. We have more freedom and other privileges over those unintelligent brutes. All of our characteristics down to our blood and speech patterns are different, and vastly superior to the Model Sixes. That's why I'm the commanding officer in charge of supervising these Model Nines," he said as he gestured toward all the other cyborgs in the room. "We're even given the privilege of picking out our own names."

"I'll just call you 'Ten,'" Orion said. Awfully egotistical, aren't you...

"I'd prefer 'Bishop,' if you don't mind."

"Oh, a religious cyborg with free will."

"I do find the concept fascinating, yes." Bishop was clearly aggravated, as his glare had gotten colder.

"This is *all* very *fascinating*," Orion said sarcastically, "but do you think you could pause your little story and give me some goddamn clothes?"

He leaned forward and said, "Stop dodging my questions with questions. You will get clothing when you relinquish the location of the drive. Now where is it?"

"I'm not telling a damned soul." Realizing who he was talking to, Orion quickly added, "Or a damned... machine."

"I would prefer we handled this delicately. Of course, if you insist, we have other methods of making you talk."

"Of course you do. But I promise you, none of them will work."

"What makes you so sure?"

"Because I just promised they wouldn't. I'm a man of my word, Bishop."

Bishop smirked. "We'll see about that."

They tossed him in a dim grey room and shackled him to the arms of a cold steel chair behind a table and left him there. The ice-cold metal furniture and the cool temperature of the room on his naked flesh would definitely be near the top of his list of 'most unpleasant experiences.'

He suffered in the room for over three hours. A cyborg would check on him every thirty minutes and ask him if he was ready to talk. He always replied, "Go fuck yourself," so the cyborg would smack him around a bit, and then leave him for another thirty minutes.

By the fourth hour, Orion couldn't feel a damn thing—except for the cold. He felt nothing but the cold. He was trembling uncontrollably in his chair. Uncomfortably numb. With all the fresh bruises and cuts he'd gained from the cyborg's increasingly vicious beatings, Orion was looking sickly. Dark patches and streams of blood frozen on his skin. Bruises gone purple, then blue. He couldn't even feel the blood still trickling from his broken nose.

The door opened. Orion turned, bringing back that defiant sneer that the cyborg had become more accustomed to with every passing visit. Only this time he was sneering at—

—Barstow.

With his usual condescending scowl, Barstow said, "Good morning, Jason."

Orion's jaw dropped. Tried to utter his partner's name, but he was shivering too much for that.

Barstow took his coat off and draped it over Orion's shoulders. Then he took a seat across the table and sighed. His breath plumed in front of his face. He said matter-of-factly, "It's cold in here."

"Y-y-you're..."

"I'm... dead?" Barstow shook his head. "On the contrary. Maybe you should get your eyes checked, Jason, because as you can clearly see, I'm very much alive."

"I-I-I watched you... d-die."

"No, you didn't," Barstow said. "You watched a cheap copy of me die. The real me was sitting safely behind the scenes, watching your little charade."

"W-why?"

"Why? 'Why,' he asks." Barstow clapped his hands together and rubbed them for extra warmth. "There's good money in it. I'm tasked with guarding this place from the outside. An undercover, if you will. You were always so goddamn insistent that Altieria Corp. is the big, bad company with a hidden agenda. You just couldn't stop, could you? Why couldn't you stop?"

Orion stared at him in disbelief, eyes glazed over from the agony of his wounds and the numbness of the cold.

"See, no family wants a problem child, and the corporation with control over the planet doesn't, either. So we're weeding them out before their roots get too deep. The rebels are big fish. They'll be harder to root out. But you... you're just a small fry. We figured you'd be easy to lure into the trap with the rat poison. Well," he said, scoffing, "luring you was the easy part. Getting you to *eat* the poison... Christ, you couldn't even make *that* easy for us, could you?"

Orion's shock had transformed to bitter anger now. "Y-y-you... s-son of a... a..."

"Give it a rest," Barstow said. He leaned forward and added, "You *will* tell us where you hid that drive, Jason. For old times' sake, tell me. You haven't seen too much behind this company. You'll live longer if you do the smart thing, for once in your life.

Tell me where you put it, or—"

"Or what?" Orion snapped. "Y-you'll kill me? You'd be... d-doing me a favour."

"No," Barstow said. "Not you. Sarah will be the first example."

Orion's eyes widened.

"But I'd rather we didn't need to resort to such tactics. So tell me, for old times' sake, Jason—where is the fucking drive?"

Orion said nothing.

Sensing his hesitation, Barstow said, "You don't want anything to happen to Sarah, do you?"

"I-I'm not going to... to tell you anything. So you might as well k-kill me. Leave Sarah out of this. She's got nothing to do... with it. For old times' sake, Barstow. Your business is... with me, and you will conclude it with me."

With a disappointed sigh, Barstow stood up. He said via a private telepathic frequency to the CEO: "He's not talking. His girlfriend is unsuitable as leverage."

"Hard way it is, then."

No sooner had the CEO replied than two cyborgs entered the room, unshackled Orion, and dragged him out into the corridor. Too weak to fight, Orion could only hang from his arms, bare feet sliding across a white marble floor. Barstow trailed close behind, making sure Orion didn't try anything funny. While he was at it, he snatched his coat off Orion's shoulders and slipped back into it.

"Where are you taking him?" Barstow asked.

One of the cyborgs said, "The Mind Rapist."

"Excuse me?" Barstow said, arching an eyebrow. He was a little disgusted by the name. "That can't be the official name."

"It isn't," the other cyborg said with a snicker. "We just like to call it that."

"What's it *really* called, then?" Barstow asked.

"We've been calling it the 'Mind Rapist' for so long, we've forgotten the official name for it." The first cyborg shrugged. "Oh well."

Barstow scowled and shook his head. Muttered under his breath, "Model Nines..."

They dragged Orion into a room with frosted glass walls. Like the rest of the facility, it was sterile and plain. There was a large white chair in the center of the circular room under a domed ceiling containing spiralling light beams that shimmered like light reflecting off water. A massive panoramic screen took up the whole wall on the left side of the room, which displayed a blank 'STANDBY' message. Off to the opposite side was a computer console, which already had a cyborg connected to it through cables installed in his cranium, nostrils, ears, and eyes. The stuff of nightmares.

They hauled Orion into the chair and strapped him in. They pulled a large, bulky headset with a bubbly cranium cover and a scanning visor (called a REM helmet) down from a thick tangle of wiring above the chair over his head, which adjusted its size to perfectly envelope most of his skull. Orion couldn't see a damn thing, and the REM helmet was heavy enough to snap his neck if he moved too suddenly.

Around him, the scientists and technicians went to work, booting up the system and double-checking the equipment and the power source's stability levels. Barstow watched, standing just a few feet away from Orion's chair. When he noticed that one of the scientists had finished his task and sat down on a stool with a coffee mug, he approached him and asked, "What is that, exactly?"

The scientist looked at him and said, "That is a Decode-4. It reads brain activity patterns and translates them into images and words..."

Orion could hear the scientist droning on about his creation, but he wasn't paying attention. He was panicking as an icy terror took hold. A kind of claustrophobic fear that even the tight ventilation shafts couldn't provide. He struggled as best he could in his restraints, but he was too numb to do much. Painfully numb. Defrosting was never on Orion's list of fun things to do.

He heard Barstow say, "Is that why they call it the 'Mind Rapist'?"

"What the hell is that? Who would say that?"

"I'm not pointing any fingers. I'm just telling you I've heard people refer to it that way."

"Preposterous," the scientist spat in anger. "Disgusting!"

A new, loud voice spoke to Orion, "We're going to put you under now. Try to relax."

"Go fuck yourself," Orion hissed defiantly.

Nobody replied. He felt a needle bite into his right arm. Felt some kind of warm toxin fill his veins. Almost immediately, he felt nauseous and dizzy. The blackness the helmet surrounded him with made things all the more disorienting and terrifying. He started dry-heaving. Chest rising and falling. The voices around him faded away to nothing. He blinked, and the darkness began to swirl. He blinked again, and everything brightened to colourful shapes and rainbow-coloured bursts of light. Blinked again—

—and he was standing in Barstow's two-bedroom apartment. The living room was spacious enough, with a couch and a coffee table and a TV all neatly placed on a square beige carpet. Barstow sat on the couch, head hanging solemnly over a stuffed bear clutched in his trembling hands. He looked a lot younger now than he did before.

Where am I? This... this looks familiar.

Orion was startled to see his own hand touch Barstow's shoulder. Heard his own voice say, "There was nothing that could be done."

Did I really say that?

No... Orion realized he was a simple observer of his own dream. No control. Just a dream? Or a memory?

Barstow sobbed, "They said it was just a minor concussion..."

"They can't be expected to know everything."

"They should've known better," Barstow snarled.

"They didn't."

"Goddamn it." Barstow brought the bear to his face and wailed. "My boy..."

A voice, not his own, echoed painfully in his brain. Every syllable like a hammer strike to his cranium: *"Shift ahead. You're too far back."*

Orion blinked. Everything went black. His brain felt like it was on fire. He screamed. Clamped his eyes shut. Opened them.

Now he was standing silently in a peaceful sandstone meadow. Surrounded by flowers and trees. Lush foliage. Bright, sparkling sunlight. He felt the warmth of the summer day. The cool relief brought on by the breeze.

A bell chimed in the distance. For the most part, he ignored it, watching little goldfish swim in a nearby pond bordered by roses and lilacs. The sunlight reflected brilliantly on their scales as they squiggled across their little domain.

"Aren't you coming to class?" a woman's voice asked behind him.

Orion whirled and saw her. One of his classmates. Not exactly the popular type, but beautiful and smart. They'd never spoken before, so it struck him as odd that she would approach him out of the blue like this. Her blonde hair shimmered as wonderfully as the goldfish's scales. Her emerald eyes shone with a kind of strength and intelligence he didn't see in any of the women from his home sector. Tall, slender; elegant posture evoked a stronger sense of independence. She was carrying a text book under her arm. Probably a physics book, but Orion couldn't be sure.

Orion's mind raced for her name. When it came to him, he snapped his fingers and pointed at her. "Sarah, right?"

She smiled, as though mildly pleased that he knew her name. "That's right. Your name is Orion, correct?"

"My first name is Jason, but everybody calls me that, yes."

"Why is that?"

He shrugged. "Because I call myself that."

She smirked.

"It's..."

"Unique," she finished for him.

He shrugged again and said, "I was gonna go with a bad pun and say 'it's stellar,' but..."

She giggled. It was small, breezy. Enough to make him smile.

"Coming to class?" she asked again. "Don't want to be late for physics."

That agonizing, whiny voice piped up again: *"No, goddamn it, you went backwards, not forwards! Can't you do anything right?!"*

He blinked. The beautiful scenery was swept away like autumn leaves in the wind. Replaced by darkness. Every second in the darkness brought on another agonizing pang in his skull. Enough to drive him mad if it didn't let up soon.

Deafening explosions. Endless staccato of machine gunfire. Ears popped; rang at a high enough pitch to make his eyes water. Earth shaking violently under him, knocking him off his feet. He had to lean against the filthy wet trench wall. His combat suit protected him from the poisonous fumes that pervaded the air and enshrouded it in a thick green veil. His breath fogged the lens of his helmet briefly before fading away. Fogged. Faded. Fogged. Faded. The suit hugged his body like a box that was a few inches too small. Suffocating him, despite its auxiliary oxygen and cooling systems. Despite the terrifying compression of his armour, his skull rattled in his helmet every time the ground shook. *Christ! Oh, fuck, what have I—*

The commander was shouting, "Charge! Charge!"

Orion did what he was told like a good little soldier. Scrambled up the steep mud wall like a mouse fleeing from an angry homeowner into the worst kind of hell he'd ever been subjected to.

The battlefield. Mutilated corpses strewn all over the place. Machinery burning away. Thousands and thousands of artillery pockets in the earth, filled with blood and contaminated water and bodies in pulverized combat suits. Orion saw what the enemy was up to during an overnight ceasefire—the misshapen remains of his comrades had been skewered on Czech hedgehogs. A few of them were still barely alive, tangled in razor wire, moaning in agony when they weren't choking on the poison fumes until they were inevitably torn apart by unrelenting exchanges of hot lead coming from either side. Giant mech units trudged through a sea of corpses, blasting rotary hand cannons at the enemy. Sometimes they unwittingly crushed wounded soldiers, silencing their screams under steel hooves.

Orion spun around, his senses severely disoriented by the chaos raging around him. His heart pounded in his ears.

A marine in a combat suit not unlike his own smacked his shoulder with the butt of his battle rifle, snapping him out of his trance. "I don't see that gun firing, soldier!" he roared—

—right before a stray HESH shell zipped by Orion. Blew the marine out of sight and blasted a five-man gun turret located a few yards back into the black sky. Saturated Orion's lens with a deep red. Orion stared at the marine's severed legs in shock, watching them topple into a nearby artillery pocket filled with crimson water occupied by a torso with no limbs and only half a head on its shoulders. His lens dripped with the marine's blood. He frantically wiped it off and fell on weak knees. Crawled through the mud, still gripping his rifle. Whimpering in fear. The ground rushed by. All he could see was the mud and the murky water and the greenish tint of the air.

Looked up when he heard a haunting chorus of screams to see an enemy mech unit douse a friendly marine squad with flaming napalm. He watched their bodies writhe and dance in the flames that greedily consumed them.

Slipped. Toppled head-over-heels down a slope. Fell into the flooded crater's mouth. His vision filled with dark green. The explosions, muffled above the water's surface. Limbs and bodies and wide-eyed faces floating all around. Staring at him. Hovering toward him.

Orion looked down when he felt something slap his kneecap. Saw a soldier pinned to the crater floor by a metal bar, his helmet gone. Terror in his eyes as he struggled to breathe, sucking in water. Hands desperately lashing out for Orion's help. Orion's feet slammed on the floor as he grabbed the bar and pulled, but the damn thing wouldn't budge. He strained, trying to lift it. He needed the marine's help. Signalled him to push up on his mark. Looked at the marine's lifeless eyes staring back at him. His heart pounded louder.

That goddamned voice again: *"Keep going."*

The crater floor faded. All but the soldier's eyes faded. Disembodied. Silently condemning him for his failure to save his life. The sorrowful moans of the marine's children filling Orion's head until it could've exploded. Asking why their father didn't come home.

Make it stop, Orion pleaded. *God, make it stop!*

Elsa Scott's hollow corpse filled his vision.

"This one seems kinda... what's the word I'm looking for?" Orion heard himself say. "...Uninspired. Compared to the Gein case." He'd turned his head so that Barstow's scowl was the focus of his vision. "Remember the Gein case?"

Barstow scoffed. "'Uninspired.'" He made a gesture toward Elsa Scott's corpse.

The unfamiliar voice drowned out Barstow's words: *"Almost there. Keep going."*

Get out of my head! GET OUT!

The bathroom stall. The security guard's corpse splayed out over the toilet in his boxer briefs. Orion had slipped into the guard's suit and was now handling the drive, which he played inside a small white box and locked with a four-digit pin: 1-8-5-6. He put the small box into a slightly larger box and entered a different pin: 5-8-1-7. Then he turned. Dropped the box between the dead cyborg's legs. Flushed the toilet. Watched the box get swallowed up in a sparkly blue splash.

"We've got it. Terminate decode session."

A high-pitched electronic squeal filled Orion's ears and ripped his head apart from the inside out. He screamed in unbearable agony. The squeal intensified until Orion was sure his brain had begun to melt and his ears had started to bleed.

The blackness returned. Orion hardly noticed anymore. His senses were so numb.

Uncomfortably numb.

25: Send-Off

"Alright, he's done," one of the scientists announced.

Barstow watched with crossed arms as he observed a handful of guards unfastening Orion from the chair and lifting him out of it. They dragged him across the floor. He was unconscious, maybe even half dead. It was hard for even Barstow to tell. Orion was a tough bastard and full of surprises.

Amanda/7 entered the room. The CEO spoke through her: "Dispose of him immediately. Throw him into the void."

"Yes, sir," the security guards replied in eerie unison as they dragged Orion across the room. Barstow stepped aside, clearing the way for them.

They dragged him down the corridor like an animal to slaughter. Square light panels in the ceiling buzzed overhead. Model Nines shuffled down the corridor in the opposite direction without so much as giving Orion a passing glance, sticking to the walls until the guards passed them by. Orion hung between them from his arms, which they gripped in firm, metal fists.

He stirred. Body still numb. Head feeling hollow, throbbing as if someone took a hammer to it. Thoughts, racing—which didn't help his headache any. His eyes opened. Mere slits. The floor tiles blurred as they passed under him. The pulsating light blinded him.

Christ, he thought, not quite without his sense of humour, even in this moment. A dramatic voice, like that of a cartoon narrator, said in his head: *Is this the end of Jason Orion?*

Orion managed a thin smile. Not because of his stupid inner joke. But because he once again could feel his legs. And his arms. And his hands.

They brought him back to the main corridor. Opened the door. Orion found himself staring down into the dark abyss. Heart jumped in his throat. He could feel the guards cock his arms back, ready to throw him.

His index fingers popped up. Orion shouted, "Wait! Wait."

The guards stopped and looked at Barstow, who shook his head and said, "No, Jason."

"Oh, come on," Orion insisted, "I'm gonna die anyway. Might as well say one last thing for you to remember me by."

Barstow sighed and drew an LE magnum as a precaution. "Fine. Make it quick."

"Turn me around first," Orion said. "I want to say it to your face."

"I like you just the way you are."

Orion snapped. "If I'm going to say my final words, I want to say them to *you*, not this empty toilet bowl!"

Barstow frowned. "I guess you've got a point. But try anything, and I'll make sure the last thing to come out of your mouth is a shrill, girly scream. Got it?"

Orion nodded. "Understood."

Barstow said to the guards: "Turn him around."

The guards grabbed Orion by the arms. Rotated. When one of the guards started to pass the open doorway, Orion doubled over and slammed his foot into his stomach, launching him screaming into the void.

Barstow reflexively fired.

Orion ducked as the second guard's head blew apart.

"Son of a bitch!" Barstow fired again and burned a cavity through the headless cyborg's body.

Orion snatched the cyborg's assault rifle and snapped it off its harness. Then he jumped out of the way as Barstow fired one last shot and sent the headless cyborg staggering backwards out the door.

Orion didn't raise his assault rifle. He kept it pointed at the floor, staring Barstow in the face. He stood next to the door now. His nakedness hardly bothered him anymore.

Barstow, however, had him in his sights. He aimed for Orion's head, furious that he'd been duped by his former partner. He glanced at the assault rifle at Orion's side. The barrel touched the floor. Orion's finger wasn't even on the trigger. Barstow had to laugh. "You stupid bastard," he sneered. "What did you expect to achieve from that? A few more seconds of life?"

Orion shrugged, stepping to the right until the doorway was directly behind him. "More than a few seconds."

"Bullshit. I've got the drop on you."

"Or *do* you?"

Angry lines cut deep into Barstow's frown. "Enough of this. I'm sick of listening to you. Goodbye, Jason." And, with that, he fired—

Click!

—but to his shock and surprise, the trigger wouldn't go back. Barstow pulled back with everything he had, but the goddamned thing wouldn't fire. "What?!" he exclaimed.

Orion closed the gap between them, a triumphant smirk on his face. "Experiencing technical difficulties?"

"Shut up!" Barstow roared. He continued with his failed attempts to pull the trigger. His movements more frantic the closer Orion got. "Get back!"

"Oops!" Orion snatched the gun out of Barstow's hands and kicked him between the legs. "Surprise, asshole."

Barstow dropped to his knees like a sack of bricks, clutching his burning loins as a sickening urge to vomit coursed through him.

Orion inspected the serial number on the LE magnum and scoffed. "Surely you haven't forgotten that a high-powered service revolver in the police department locks as a defense mechanism in certain circumstances? One: if the fingerprints and DNA of the wielder don't match those of the registered owner. Two: if the mini-scanner in the sights recognizes that the firearm is being pointed at an officer of the law."

Still gripping his crotch, Barstow growled, "You—"

Orion kicked Barstow in the chest before he could finish, slamming him on his back. He adjusted his grip on the magnum and pointed it at him. "You got both answers wrong."

"What the hell are you talking about? Don't shoot me. I'm unarmed. I'm wounded. I'm not resisting."

"You're not Barstow, either."

"Of course I am!"

"The *real* Barstow wouldn't try to kill me with my own gun. The *real* Barstow would have known not to use the LE magnum in this situation. The *real* Barstow would not be in this situation in the first place, because he wasn't a traitorous coward. You're a fake. A poorly assembled fake. Clearly a rush job. A half-assed attempt to fool me into giving up the information peacefully."

The jig was up. Barstow lunged at him. Smacked the LE magnum right out of Orion's hands as he pounced on him. Reached for the assault rifle. Orion pivoted back and smashed Barstow with a spinning kick to the face. Barstow twirled. Fell on his face. The momentum sent him sliding to the doorway, his head over the edge.

Barstow looked down at the bottomless void for a moment, then gasped and scrambled back. He got to his feet and whirled around to face Orion.

Orion hadn't done a spin-kick in years. *I've still got it.* He said aloud, "My final words to you, 'partner.'"

The fake Barstow's eyes widened when he found himself staring down the barrel of Orion's assault rifle.

Orion said, "I told you so."

The assault rifle stuttered, spraying the fake Barstow with explosive rounds. Barstow convulsed as green blood exploded from his disintegrating chest. Orion's fusillade propelled him out the door. With a startled gasp, Barstow dropped out of sight.

Orion knew he had to be a little more thorough than that. He approached the doorway with the utmost caution. Slowly peered out the door.

As expected, Barstow's cyborg double leaped out of the darkness at him, howling like an angry, wounded beast. Despite his anticipation of this, Orion let out a surprised shout and blasted the top of Barstow's head into space. His grey matter erupted from his skull in a sickly green spray. The ledge slipped from Barstow's fingers. With a prolonged, terrified scream, Barstow's double plunged into the void. Orion watched his partner's shameless imposter get swallowed by the darkness with great satisfaction. A proper send-off for garbage.

Orion breathed a sigh, relieved that the imposter didn't get him when he really could have. Just imagining what might have happened if Orion hadn't blown his head off when he did sent chills up his spine. "Yessiree," Orion said as the last of Barstow disappeared from his sight, his screams fading to silence, "the excitement never stops."

26: Odds

Orion started down the hall. He knew he had to act fast.

"What is it you plan to do?" the CEO's voice echoed through a speaker.

Orion looked up and saw a camera staring down at him. One in the CEO's vast multitude of electric eyes. "What's it look like to you?"

"As we speak, my squadrons are already fishing for your drive in the river. I'm sure your precious taxi driver girlfriend has already been terminated by a 'crazed Conservative rebel.' Your partner is dead. Your police force may not be what you remember it to be if, by some miracle—"

"Let me stop you right there," Orion snapped. "You might have me surrounded, but I have you right where I want you."

"Bluffing will get your nowhere."

"Who said I was bluffing?"

"Enough," the CEO hissed impatiently.

"Enough? That would imply that I'm finished." Orion shook his head comically. "I've only just begun, shithead."

"My patience has run out. Because I am a generous man, I will give you have one final opportunity to surrender quietly. You have no leverage. You have no drive. You have no more allies." An arrogant scoff hissed through the intercom. "You don't even have clothing on your back! Do you honestly think you stand a chance? Humour me for a moment—what do you think the odds are of you coming out of this alive?"

Eyes burning with hatred, Orion raised his LE magnum. "Better than yours."

Blasted the eye out of the wall.

[SIGNAL LOST]

The CEO leaned back in his chair, staring at the monitor that just went black. Frowning. Making a tent with his fingers. He turned to Amanda/7, who stood dutifully beside him like a soldier awaiting an order. "He is an infuriatingly persistent fellow, isn't he?"

"I wouldn't know, sir," Amanda/7 replied. "I've never experienced emotions."

The CEO stared at her a moment. Then he turned back to his wall of monitors. "Of course you haven't."

As he progressed down the corridor, Orion blew out another surveillance camera. And another. And another. So far, he'd covered at least three sectors, and hadn't come across any security or staff members of any kind. Even the droids were absent. It all put a bad feeling in the pit of his stomach. *Guess they decided to stick together and attack as one. Yay.*

He checked the cylinder in his magnum. Two left. He slapped it back into place and shot out another camera. One left.

The CEO was looking at twenty-four black screens out of two hundred fifty-seven in just five minutes. He wasn't lying when he said he was out of patience, and Orion's latest tactic was pushing him further off the edge. "He's blinding me. If you're going to do something, do it before he reaches the control room. He's in sector four! Repeat: sector four!"

"Yessir," came the reply.

The control room. Dark, illuminated only by the electric glow of three-dozen panoramic screens tiling three walls, with half of them blacked out. Rectangular, narrow space. A switchgear panel in the corner farthest from the door, connected to the high-voltage switchgear built in a hidden room that could only be accessed through a hidden panel in the floor.

Six security cyborgs carefully watched the screens, sitting in swivel chairs, chattering excitedly about the disturbance Orion was causing. They couldn't find him anywhere, and their agitation rose steadily as another screen went black. Two security cyborgs in full battle gear stood in either end of the room, assault rifles ready. Silent. Deadly. Watching the cyborgs react to the chaos with nonchalant expressions inside their helmets.

Then came a pounding at the door. "Room service!"

The security cyborgs glanced at each other. The farther one scoffed. "Yeah, right."

A sudden, concussive explosion blew their eardrums as the

door came out of the jamb in a burst of fire and smoke. Crushed the nearest guard under five inches of steel like a hydraulic press. Orion leaped onto the fallen door. Assault rifle hosing down everyone in the room with explosive rounds before they could react. The cyborgs collapsed in a wild green blood spray. A shower of sparks and shrapnel erupted from the panoramic screens like sparkling confetti on all sides of them as they fell to the floor. Electrical fires lit up the room, rolling out of the hollowed-out wall monitors.

Orion stepped off the door and stomped on one of the floor's square tiles. Felt and sounded solid enough. He tested each tile with this method until he reached one that sounded different in the center of the room. *Aha,* he thought as he kicked a cyborg's corpse under one of the control dashboards. He squatted and lifted the panel out of the floor, discovering a shaft. Peered into it to see a steel grated floor at the bottom of the shaft ladder.

Felt a cold draft rising and shivered. He turned to the cyborg corpses. Squinted as he inspected their lab coats.

The ladder seemed to go on for four or five storeys. He finally touched down on the grated floor in a pair of combat boots, grey pants, and a green-spattered lab coat with a trio of coin-sized holes in the upper back. He couldn't wear any of the shirts, since they suffered the most damage from the effects of his explosive rounds. One security guards' suit had been compressed enough to kill its wearer, thanks to the door—unwearable now. The other guards' suits had bullet holes in all the wrong places.

At least with the pants and lab coat, Orion could carry around extra ammo and grenades taken off the guards and backup compartments hidden in the control room dashboard, which stored twice as many MP5K submachine guns as there were cyborgs. He carried two submachine guns on shoulder harnesses under his coat. Their metal against his skin, especially in this drafty room, was unpleasant, to say the least. He had his assault rifle slung over his shoulder, with five extra magazines he'd taken off the guards in his lab coat pockets. The MP5Ks' ammunition had been stuffed into his pants pockets—two in each front and back pocket. He also had four grenades hooked onto the waistband of his pants by their spoons.

He shuddered from the cold. Nothing he could do about it. He was lucky enough that the combat boots fit him.

Orion surveyed his surroundings. It was a wide, square room

with supercomputers built into every wall, high-voltage switchgear surrounded by a chain link fence in the middle of the room, and a staircase leading down to an even lower level in the far corner to his left, across the room. No sounds except for the vibrating buzz droning from the supercomputers, reverberating in his ribcage, and the electric hum of the switchgear.

His breath plumed in front of his face as he walked along the switchgear for about twenty yards before he could finally get around it. He approached the staircase and started down the steps, three at a time—unslinging his assault rifle and racking the bolt as he descended. The light at the bottom of the stairs was as dark, blue, and eerily beautiful as the bottom of the sea. Whatever surprises lurked down here, Orion was sure he wasn't going to like them.

The CEO, despite his composed exterior, was starting to get nervous. He stared intently at the screens, figuring Orion had missed the surveillance cameras in the power generator chamber.

Amanda/7 voiced his concerns: "He's approaching the core, sir."

"I can see that, thank you," he snapped.

"What should we do?"

The CEO pondered that question. Went through his options. Perhaps a last resort was in order. Nothing else he'd thrown at Orion could stop him. In fact, it arguably made things worse. But now that Orion had ventured into the lowest levels of the bipyramid core sector, he had nowhere else to go. He had him cornered. Still, he knew he couldn't fully rely on his security forces to finish the job. He needed something stronger.

He had just the thing.

"Activate Prototype/09."

"Are you sure that is the wisest course of action, sir?" Amanda/7, even with her lack of emotional range and obedient function, felt the need to ask. "Prototype/09 has only undergone four tests, and there were noticeable flaws."

"Yes, but it still passed its tests with flying colours," the CEO replied. "Besides," he added with a wry smirk, glaring at the monitor that Orion had stepped into, "what are the odds of him surviving *her*?"

27: Core

The elevator doors still hadn't closed. Safety mechanisms wouldn't allow them to close with the security guards' bodies in the way. The cyborgs lay splayed out in pools of red blood, twitching occasionally due to their circuitry and artificial nervous systems. Since they were Model Sixes, and not nearly as advanced as later, more superior models, they seemed more human, and technically, they were. They used to be human before they sold their bodies to Altieria Corp. to be altered for the security ranks, whereas the only human characteristics left in the later models were their layers of skin and flesh, and most of their brains—although those were heavily altered, as well.

Something bizarre occurred. The elevator doors experienced some kind of remote override from an unknown source and closed in on the two guards. The second guard's head, the only thing in the elevator, was simply pushed out of the way. The other guard was half in, half out. The doors clamped down on his sides. Then the elevator started to rise, and the first guard's body inevitably got caught in the door jamb. But the elevator continued its ascent up the shaft without slowing down, effectively crushing the first guard's pelvic bone to dust and ripping his body in half. The guard's bottom half fell back down on the floor, legs outstretched, mostly-human organs spilling out onto the floor of the shaft.

Orion reached the base of the stairs and approached a frosted glass double-door entrance. The doors parted without as much as a security check. Orion stepped through the doorway onto a footbridge not unlike the one he jumped onto in the fetus chamber, stretching out across a wide, octagonal space. The mysterious sea-blue light emanated brightly from below. Metallic echoes rang out across the space with every step as he travelled a few paces down the footbridge before looking over the railing—

—and immediately recoiled from the horrific sight.

Spanning as far as his eyes could see was a floor with octagonal glass tiles, littered with electrical wiring and other miscellaneous tubes and cords. Incubators, larger than the ones in the fetus chamber, protruded from the diamond-shaped gaps in the octagonal floor pattern, containing full-grown male and female bodies floating in the same liquid as the fetuses above, appropriately curled up in the fetal position in a small tangle of wires and tubes. Unlike the fetuses countless levels above Orion's head, these subjects had oxygen masks over their faces; the dark red eye lens contrasting sharply against the sea blue saturation of the room.

As if that wasn't enough to make Orion's head spin, the glass floor was an aquarium of sorts, containing hundreds—if not thousands—of human brains mixed in with a throng of bodies of every age, from three months to ninety years. They were all connected and tangled through extremely intricate wiring, tubing, and artificial nerve connections and deformities like surgically adjoined limbs and craniums. All of them also had oxygen masks fused to their faces. They were bunched together like caged chickens in a slaughterhouse, although their purpose appeared to be much more sinister than simply being butchered, packaged, shipped out, and eaten.

For the longest time, Orion was breathless. Gaping at the sheer volume of the chamber. Christ knows how many people were kept alive in this ungodly chamber. Five hundred? A thousand? Two thousand? Hell, the way they were all stuffed under that glass floor, even three thousand didn't seem like much of a stretch.

"Jesus... Christ!" he finally gasped.

The CEO's voice responded behind him. "Not quite, Detective."

Orion whirled around and saw Amanda/7 standing in the doorway with a machine pistol pointed at him. She got the drop on him, but he was too shocked by the sight below and around him to care. "What the fuck is this?! I knew you were a sick son of a bitch, but I never pegged you as the type to harvest humans."

"Good," the CEO replied through her, "because that's not what I'm doing. Not *exactly*."

"Then *what* are you doing?!"

"I'm harvesting their energy, not them." She stepped forward. Orion took several steps backwards, gripping the railing for support with one hand and aiming his assault rifle at her with the other. "The human body generates more bioelectricity than a 120-volt battery and over 25,000 BTUs of body heat." Amanda/7 glanced over the side. "A psychokinetic generates even more than that. We're still unsure how much more, exactly. Even with all of our research, none of our results have ever been final." Amanda/7 turned to Orion again. "But take the time to imagine if that energy was harnessed from three thousand, one-hundred-fifty-seven human bodies with psychokinetic advancements. Think of the potential. The sheer, unfathomable amount of energy that would produce."

"Psychokinetics...?" The word nearly choked Orion as the realization hit him. "They were never exterminated...? But the footage... the registration fiasco... the civil war!"

"No," the CEO replied, "they weren't exterminated. Not all of them, anyway. The lesser ones, yes, but the ones able to utilize more than seventy percent of their brains were kept and put to work." Amanda/7 cocked her head over the railing. "This is the result."

"Genocide," Orion growled.

"No, Detective—*amelioration*. 'Genocide' would imply that I've killed them. What I've created is the world's first living, organic battery. The ultimate power source emitting massive, unthinkable quantities of energy every minute."

"If it's as powerful as you say, how are you possibly storing it? How have you managed to keep this a secret for so long?"

A sinister grin distorted Amanda/7's face. "Tell me, Detective: how else do you think you're able to watch television in your small apartment? How do you think you have a computer to document your files on? How do you think rooms are lit? What powers those traffic lights? Our trains? Our planes? Our hovercarriers? What heats your water? What cooks your food? What charges the battery in your car while you sleep?"

Orion's eyes went wide as saucers. His heart was close to breaking through his ribcage.

Amanda/7 gestured toward the 'battery.' "There's your answer, Detective. You and billions of others all across the planet have been living comfortably at the expense of these... genetic miracles. Why are you so upset? You fought in the civil war. You are well aware of the crimes they've committed; what further destruction they were easily capable of. They are simply paying the steep toll for their crimes against humanity. And that was over a simple registration. Imagine the consequences if it were something bigger."

"You talk as if the psychokinetics fought us in a combined

force. Did you forget that they fought for both sides? What about our own crimes against ourselves?"

Amanda/7's eyes narrowed to evil slits. Truly evil slits. "It doesn't matter now, does it? What's done is done. They now serve to benefit humanity. Their potential isn't being wasted; it's being utilized for the greater good. This is simply a case where the ends justify the means."

"What a load of bullshit."

"Given the circumstances of this revelation, your reaction is understandable. You must remember that everything must serve a purpose. Cookies are to be eaten. Cars are to transport. Parents are to raise their children." Amanda/7 glanced at the 'battery' for a fleeting moment. "Psychokinetics are to fuel our cities and sustain us as one, whole civilization."

The doorways at the ends of every footbridge were filled with armed guards. They listened quietly, their brain filters keeping them in the dark about what this place was, even while the CEO was explaining it. Their only purpose was to aim and fire when given the signal.

"Shut the fuck up," Orion snarled. "I've heard enough."

"Do you see now why it is imperative that you do not interfere with the activities behind this facility's closed doors?"

"It's my duty to report and prevent crimes against humanity, be it a homeless bum on the curb or an entire civilization. It doesn't matter if they're a psychokinetic, a cyborg, a retard, or an average Joe."

"You can't claim inhumanity when what we are dealing with is not strictly *human*."

"I told you to shut up."

"Humans have always built their foundations on the shoulders of lesser humans. It's the way the world has always been. This is simply another example of history repeating itself."

"I'm warning you."

Amanda/7 scoffed. "What are you going to do?" the CEO sneered. "Arrest me?"

"I'm gonna take you down with your own system—starting with this 'battery' of yours."

A disappointed scowl appeared on Amanda/7's face. "I

suppose there is no swaying you after all."

"You want cooperation? You've isolated thousands of innocent individuals and turned them into vegetables. You've caused the deaths of hundreds of innocent citizens. You conspired with terrorists in a major frame job against any who speak against you and your society. You threatened my girlfriend—er... wife." He nearly choked when he added, "You killed... my partner and my best friend, and then tried to stain what was left of him with that... *thing* I blasted into the void. You've made numerous attempts to assault and assassinate me, an officer of the law. And you're the prime suspect in dozens of murder cases with your 'malfunctioning' robots, and the death of Elsa Scott. Cooperation," Orion spat in disgust, "the only one who should be cooperating here is you. Mr. CEO, you're under arrest. Come quietly, or there will be trouble."

The last word hung in the air. No one uttered a word for what felt like an eternity. The hum of the battery sent low vibrations through the metalwork in the room.

Then, Amanda/7 threw her head back, and the CEO laughed. It was loud, nefarious, and in a strange way, sickly. Phlegm crackling in his maniacal guffaw. Soon enough, the laughter diminished to a series of violent coughs and gags. Once his throat was cleared, Amanda/7 turned her piercing glare on Orion again. The CEO sneered, "You will arrest me, and what then? You can't save these people. Disconnecting them would only bring destruction and chaos to the planet. You wouldn't just be crippling the Company, you'd be crippling the very foundations of human civilization. Even if you were somehow able to disconnect their minds from the system without killing them—which is impossible—you would be releasing them into a world fallen into chaos."

"I guess you should've thought of that before you decided to turn these people into batteries."

Amanda/7 gaped at him. "Madness."

"No, Mr. CEO—*retribution*. 'Madness' would be an accurate description of my actions if I were to let this go." Orion smirked.

Amanda/7 squinted. "You really prefer chaos over order? I'm disappointed."

"Trust me. Your mood is not about to improve." Before the CEO could respond, Orion blasted Amanda/7 with the assault rifle until her torso resembled grated cheese. The rest of her flipped over the railing and smacked onto one of the octagonal glass tiles below.

The security forces rushed onto the footbridges, assault rifles blazing.

Orion hosed the entrance he'd come through, disintegrating the double doors and chopping down a handful of guards. He whirled, squatted, and fired another volley across the room to the other opening, downing two more guards. Sent a third sprawling over the railing and screaming to a neck-breaking impact on the glass floor below.

He didn't stop to kill more of them. Their overwhelming fusillade chased him into the switchgear room. He leaped over the heap of bodies he'd laid out. One of the guards was still functioning and tried to trip him with a three-fingered hand, but missed Orion's ankle by an inch and swore. Orion started for the nearest end of the long switchgear, running as fast as his legs could go. He'd nearly reached the end when—

—Bishop entered the room from the core chamber, followed by a squad of Model Six guards; one of whom took aim at a fleeing Orion with his assault rifle. Bishop grabbed the barrel and adjusted its aim to the floor, snarling at the Model Six, "Don't shoot! You might hit the switchgear! After him!"

So I have an advantage. Good, Orion thought as he circled round the end of the switchgear and charged across the room, constantly stealing worried glances at Bishop and the Model Sixes at his command. They were dashing in either direction—some followed his route while others went the opposite in hopes of cutting off his only escape.

That made Orion push himself further. His legs, two rapid blurs under him like propellers as he neared that ladder. Closing the gap. Closing...

The guards ahead of him rounded the end. Opened fire.

Orion slung the assault rifle over his shoulder. Right hand took the harnessed submachine gun under his pit and returned fire on the squad ahead. He could hear more gunfire behind him. Bullets gave chase, snapping at his heels.

He reached the ladder. Took both MP5Ks and mowed down the front squad, then turned whatever was left in his submachine guns on the pursuing squad. Glanced up the shaft to ensure the coast was clear. Looked around. All clear on the ground, except for Bishop, who was nowhere to be seen.

Orion didn't waste any time. He hastily reloaded his

submachine guns, then let them fall on their harnesses and scuttled up the ladder. Too tired to ascend quickly. His body, heavy from fatigue and explosives and ammunition and weapons. Christ. The shaft in the ceiling seemed to be going further up to avoid him. Only fuelled his desperation—

—deafening *pop-pop-pop*, followed instantly by fiery pain in his side, just under the submachine gun. Orion shouted, nearly let go of the ladder rung.

Down below, Bishop had his pistol raised, drawing a bead on Orion's head.

Orion didn't stop to think. He hooked his legs on a lower lung. Hands released the rungs he gripped. Bishop's fourth bullet pinged against one of the higher rungs. Orion fell away, swinging in a downward arc, backwards, upside down. Grabbed the submachine guns. The pain in his side made him roar with agony and deep-seated rage as he pointed the submachine guns at the floor. At Bishop. Hanging upside down by his legs, he fired, blasting Bishop before he could squeeze off a fifth attempt.

Green spurted from Bishop's chest as he convulsed. Staggered backwards into the switchgear's protective fence. Screamed as 20,000 volts coursed through him; burning his circuitry, rapidly boiling his fake innards. The ceiling lights buzzed and flickered in erratic patterns. Sparks showered the cyborg as he flailed violently against the fence. Skin coating melting, burning up. Right eyeball bubbled out of its socket like a marshmallow over a campfire.

Orion didn't stop to watch. His leg muscles hurt like hell. He felt he couldn't pull himself back up, but somehow after the fourth try, he matched to grab a rung and continue his climb up the shaft, leaving the cyborg to his fate.

Thought he'd never reach the top, but he did. There was no floor panel for him to lift aside. He pulled himself into the control room. It was like getting out of the deep end of a swimming pool—difficult, a chore that shouldn't have been as hard as it turned out to be.

Orion stopped to breathe for a moment, and noticed that Bishop was no longer screaming. Dead or not; he wasn't about to wait and see. Crawled over the bodies he'd created before he went down the ladder. Got up to his feet. Cautiously approached the doorway with his back sliding along the wall. He peeked out.

The hallway was clear for the time being. Time to get the hell out of here while he still could.

The elevator reached the bottom of the shaft. The doors parted, reuniting the two halves of the first guard's body... somewhat.

Out floated a man in thick black clothing, with his head hidden in a closed modular helmet. Hovering like a ghost a foot above the grated floor, the so-called 'Dark Kinetic,' Prototype/09, was now crossing the bridge faster than an express train.

28: Predator

The overhead lights flickered irregularly as Orion progressed down the hall. He reloaded his firearms while he still had the chance. The halls were mostly silent and empty. The non-combatant cyborgs, he assumed, had evacuated the premises. Most of the combatants were still down below. Fine by him.

Orion reached the end of the hall. The wall-to-ceiling windows provided a clear view of the nothingness that surrounded the floating diamond he was standing in. A corridor running along the windows, wrapping around the facility. Right? Left?

After another cautious glance down either direction, he chose left. Unshouldered his assault rifle and gripped it in his sweaty fists as he progressed. For some reason, his blood ran cold. The hairs on his neck stood up. A strange, thin mist seemed to form as he continued to follow the windows to the nearest curve.

A noise. Orion stopped. *A footstep?* He wasn't sure, so he listened. Sure enough, that familiar walking rhythm approached from around the corner. Each footfall heavier, louder, more resounding than the last. Orion stood stock still. Heart pounding. Eyes staring forward at the glass bend; at the bluish darkness on the other side of those windows.

Then it emerged from the shadows, like a vapour. Black as night, with an unearthly red glow emanating from behind the visor of its closed modular helmet. The air seemed electric with its presence. Orion couldn't stop staring. His finger quivered over the trigger, but despite his every instinct screaming for him to shoot, he did nothing.

Behind him, at the other end of the hall, a pair of guards came around the bend and stopped when they realized they were looking at Orion's back. They glanced at each other. Squatted. Quietly poised their assault rifles, aiming...

An electronic screech. The walls bent inward, as if magnetized by Prototype/09 itself. The windows crackled, bending with their frames, then splintering when they bent too far, yet strangely staying in place. The ceiling panels bent toward the psychokinetic; sparks exploded from the lights like swarms of fireflies, bouncing off an invisible bubble that had formed around and over Prototype/09. Then—

—a thunderous *boom* followed by an eardrum-popping *whoosh* as energy sprang outward; launched the ceiling through the second floor; smashed the walls into all the rooms; blew the windows out into the void. Sent an invisible projectile tearing down the corridor like a terrible gust of wind—straight for Orion, who dived into the nearest office and scrambled under a desk just before the invisible force tore the steel walls down on top of him and kept going. The guards barely registered what was happening before Prototype/09's attack reduced them to red splatters on the windows. Split second. The psychokinetic force fragmented the windows and snapped the frames, scattering all of it into the emptiness.

The desk held. *Well, thank Christ for that.*

Orion crawled out from under the desk on his belly, finding himself under a thick canopy of steel held up by his last-second choice of cover. He pushed through fallen debris and managed to squeeze out of a small opening. Gritted his teeth when a jagged shard of metal carved a shallow line down his back. The numbing pain in his side didn't let up, either. The pain only got worse the further he pulled himself across the floor. Finally, he managed to crawl out of the cramped space without accidentally triggering a collapse that would surely have crushed him to death. *It's a miracle.*

He grunted, got up to his feet. Surveyed the area. Looked like a typhoon tore through it. The ceiling had been stripped of its panels and broken lights swung wildly from resilient wires. All the offices that ran along the outer corridor opposite the windows had been completely flattened.

Which meant he had a clear view of Prototype/09, who hadn't moved from his spot.

A blazing sensation of rage rushed through Orion's body faster than he could process it. He hosed the Dark Kinetic with a wave of explosive rounds.

Prototype/09, a statue, untouched by the explosions over and around him. Orion knew he was shooting straight despite his wounds, but not a single bullet had even scraped Prototype/09.

The magazine ran out. Orion ejected it and slapped a new one in. Then he saw it.

An electronic screech. Pieces of debris floated toward Prototype/09 on all sides. An electronic boom; the debris shot outward. Another invisible wave blew whatever survived the first attack to tiny pieces. Orion took off in a run and leaped out of the way as the psychokinetic force ripped a trench through the debris where he'd previously stood not two seconds earlier. Everything, torn to splinters—metal, plywood, a fake desk plant...

Tucked and rolled. Got up to his feet. Jumped through a windowless frame, a carpet of glass crunching under his combat boots. Raced down the corridor.

Gunfire up ahead. Threw him off balance in an instinct attempt to avoid danger. Orion hit the floor and fired his assault rifle down the hall before he even knew where exactly the enemy was.

Two guards crumpled with decimated torsos. Two more darted down a side corridor, between two computer rooms with glass walls. Orion's fire pursued them, tearing through the walls, spraying glass. Billions of tiny particles cascading to the floor toward the fleeing guards. Orion's volley caught up with them. Sent them sprawling through wall-to-ceiling windows in a wild spray of glass and blood.

He jumped to his feet and whirled around as that uneasiness crept up in the pit of his stomach again.

There, at the end of the hall, standing between two demolished offices like a wraith out of his worst nightmares, stood Prototype/09.

The CEO scowled when a dozen monitors went out. "Just when I thought the excessiveness of my security couldn't possibly be equalled, I witness a simple prototype exceed their capabilities with a decreased amount of... subtlety."

Amanda/7 asked from beside him, "Should I retrieve it?"

The CEO gave it some thought. Then said, "Yes. We cannot risk the destruction of the core. I will be having words with our good engineer regarding the still-existent flaws in this model once this incident is behind us."

That electronic screech again, like a banshee's scream. Orion caught on and scrambled for cover as a thunderous roar shook the place to its core. The ceiling retracted upwards. The floor shattered. The glass walls disintegrated. Metal, glass, electronics screamed their ear-splitting symphony of destruction as psychokinetic energy swept it all away. An avalanche without a slope, powerful enough to slam through Orion's wall of choice and hurl him across the level, through walls that ceased to exist anyway; through windows that became splintery hail. Under a ceiling that lifted away. Over a shattered floor that crashed in and against itself like violent ocean waves during an untamed storm.

Landed. Wind knocked out of his lungs. Body felt like it'd shattered to pieces, connected by the thinnest strands of flesh and clothing. Bouncing like a skipping stone over desks and metal sheets and uprooted floor tiles and—Christ knows, just about everything else. Everything spun, spun, spun, even when Orion finally stopped bouncing, but he felt weightless; weightless and heavy at the same time. It wasn't until the stars cleared from his eyes did he realize that his arm was caught under an overturned computer console—the only thing keeping him from dropping into the void.

Panic struck him. His feet dangled. His torso banged against the window of the floor below the one he'd just been ejected from. He was entirely outside, except for his right arm. Death awaited him. Far, far below.

Orion had lost his assault rifle. Both hands free. He used all his strength to clamber up the wall. Feet sliding on the window below him. Right arm gradually sliding out from under the console. Inching ever closer over the edge. Glass shards in the window frame cutting into his arm.

"Oh Jesus, oh shit," he gasped as he struggled to pull himself up through the window. His heart was in his stomach. Every attempt to climb up foiled by the slippery window pane of the lower floor, which was too tough to break. His left hand latched into the main floor's twisted framework. Glass bit into his hand. More pain to deal with. He could barely feel his right arm. Couldn't even move his hand. But he had to. He needed whatever strength his arms had left in them. He pulled—by God, he pulled. His feet instinctively kicked out at the window as he heaved himself up. His lungs burned. He was practically breathing fire. *C'mon, you son of a bitch,* he thought to himself. Nothing like self-motivation. *Put more elbow grease into it. You're not that old yet!*

Gnashed his teeth. He grunted. Sucked in a deep breath. Threw his last reserve of strength into one last pull. Heaved himself through the window frame. Pulled his right arm out from under the console and scrambled on top of the damn thing. He didn't stop, didn't feel safe as the intense tingle of fear fuelled him. He threw himself over the console. Landed on a heap of metal with a resounding crash. On his back. Staring up at the hollow trusses in the ceiling, which had previously been concealed by white panels and lights.

He could've fallen asleep right then and there. Exhaustion, unbearable exhaustion. Felt like every inch of him had been flattened by a steamroller. There was nothing that didn't ache.

Keep moving, he thought. *Gotta keep moving.*

Prototype/09 lifted weightlessly off the floor, preparing for another attack. His psychokinetic aura swept whatever debris lay in his path to the side as he approached Orion.

Orion rolled onto his hands and knees. Looked toward the psychokinetic monster on the prowl. His heart sank. He wasn't going to live through this. Not this.

Another horrible, metallic screech from Prototype/09. The floor in a twenty-metre radius around Orion gave out under his feet, dropping him down, down, down... with his heart leaping in his throat.

Orion screamed, desperately lashing out to grab something, anything, to stop his fall. His body sank into a raging sea of steel beams, furniture, ceiling panels, trusses, cyborg corpses with nothing sturdy to grab onto. Free-fall, straight down into the core chamber. The core chamber...

...and a footbridge, sturdy enough to withstand the relentless hail of debris that used to be the main floor, twisting and bending as beams and furniture pounded it in their rapid descent. Orion reached out. Fingers caught onto the handrail. He swung out from under a falling computer console and slammed into the side of the footbridge. The console plummeted and smashed a psychokinetic's incubator under it, spilling fluids and the mutilated subject's corpse across the octagonal floor panels. Despite the strengthened glass, the incubators burst and the floor panels cracked under the weight and impact of an entire floor landing on them, sending violent tremors through the facility.

Orion hung loosely over the wreckage, still gripping the handrail. Grateful that he'd somehow survived this ordeal. With a great amount of effort put into it, Orion managed to pull himself up and over the handrail and flopped onto the footbridge's grated floor. Huffing and puffing. Looking up—

—into his reflection in Prototype/09's helmet visor. The

psychokinetic killing machine hung above him like a roosting bat, 'standing' on the bottom of an exposed steel beam that protruded from the edge of the gaping hole it'd just created.

A banshee's electronic scream rang in his ears. Orion lurched onto his feet and dived across the footbridge as an invisible force crushed the middle of it. Metallic groans rumbled through the chamber as a focused psychokinetic blast twisted the footbridge into a gnarly helix. Yanked it out from under Orion's feet. Orion couldn't stop himself from rolling over the handrail as the grated floor suddenly coiled over his head. He plummeted, yelling, flipping to an untimely death—

—or not. Instead he collided with a fallen computer console resting on its side. The gunshot wound in his side blasted him with a new wave of pain as he bounced down a small pile of debris. He slammed into an octagonal floor tile and slid across its still-smooth surface. Came to a stop, finding himself staring into the mask lens of an advanced psychokinetic female 'battery,' curled beneath him. A vegetable. No longer able to think for herself or even understand her current state. Was she even alive? Was she really breathing under that mask, or just being fed protein to stay alive? He couldn't imagine being alive and aware of the situation without possessing the abilities to do something about it. How it must have felt for them if that were the case…

He couldn't dwell on it right now.

Prototype/09 descended upon him, arms outstretched.

Orion snatched his submachine guns, raised them, and fired—although he figured it probably wouldn't do much good.

And he was right. The bullets disintegrated around Prototype/09 once they got within ten inches of him. So Orion ran. He didn't know where he could hide, but what the hell. He scuttled behind the only glass tube that survived the collapse.

Prototype/09 made a move to stop him. The electronic scream started up again, but inexplicably shrank to a high-pitched whine.

The CEO furrowed his brow. Turned to another Amanda/7 unit working furiously on a computer console behind him. "What's going on?"

"The system doesn't seem to be responding, sir," she answered calmly, fingers flying on a keyboard. "There appears to be some sort of interference."

"Interference?" the CEO hissed impatiently. "Have you lost complete control?"

"I keep losing and regaining connection with Prototype/09. I'm detecting an unusual distortion in the signal."

"Fix it."

"I'm trying, sir. Nothing is working."

Prototype/09 hovered above the wreckage, still as a statue, staring aimlessly at the spot Orion had been standing before he ducked for cover. It hadn't made any further attempt to find him.

Cautiously, Orion peeked around the base of the incubator and looked up at Prototype/09. "What the hell is taking you so long?"

Prototype/09 didn't respond. Total silence.

Confusion and curiosity took over. Orion arched an eyebrow. Then he took the time to reload his submachine guns. Looked around for anything else he could use in defense. He noticed the small square monitor screen on a dashboard at the base of the incubator. The vital signs of the imprisoned psychokinetic 'battery' he was using as a shield read steady.

So they are *alive,* Orion thought. He craned his neck and studied the male subject floating in the fetal position within the confines of its chamber. The subject's skin shimmered in the dark green ooze, illuminated by interior lights in the top and bottom of the 'person jar.'

Orion glanced around the tube again. Prototype/09 hardly seemed more responsive than the subjects he was hovering over. Orion slowly reached for his submachine guns. Aimed them at Prototype/09. Opened fire.

Suddenly the psychokinetic reacted with a startled discharge that sent Orion's bullets spiralling off course. They swirled around it. Pelted the ceiling. Blasted it to pieces. Another collapse. Orion ducked for cover as a good chunk of the decontamination sector came crashing down like hail. Bearing down on Prototype/09—

—and stopped. In midair. A canopy of shattered steel and broken equipment hung weightlessly just a few feet above Prototype/09's head. The decontamination sector's conveyer belt winded across the floating wreckage like a big black ribbon.

Prototype/09 shuddered. A low, rumbling groan crackled from him. A second later, the debris above him disintegrated into a dark, swirling particle cloud and dispersed like smoke.

"Re-established connection," Amanda/7 announced proudly as she typed furiously on her keyboard. "The distorted sound waves are still present."

"Distorted sound waves?"

"Yessir."

"Well, where is it coming from?"

"I can't pinpoint it, sir. It appears to be coming in from every direction."

The CEO made a dissatisfied grunt. That didn't sound good. He had to take the necessary precautions. "Command Prototype/09 to retreat. Do it now."

"Yessir."

29: Prey

Whispers. Endless whispers. A crescendo, intensifying by the second.

Prototype/09 trembled furiously. Dropped to the floor. Landed on all fours like a cat, sending shallow cracks through the octagonal tile he'd impacted, visor facing Orion's direction. He staggered to his feet, scanning the area for any life signs via infrared. An ALERT window suddenly appeared, obscuring his view. Two more ALERTs, then an OBEY DIRECTIVE.

OBEY DIRECTIVE. OBEY DIRECTIVE. OBEY DIRECTIVE. WARNING – TECHNICAL MALFUNCTION.

Prototype/09 convulsed. A spark flared from its visor.

TECHNICAL MALFUNCTION. TECHNICAL MALFUNCTION. UNAUTHORIZED ACCESS DETECTED.

Prototype/09 whirled around. An impulsive blast emitted from its body and tore across the core chamber in every direction, clearing out debris, shattering incubators and scattering their contents outward. A thick web of cracks streaked through the floor panels from the psychokinetic's feet.

Orion went flying with the debris and shrivelled, psychokinetic bodies. Felt like he was getting sucked through some kind of vacuum. His ears popped. His body felt like it was being crushed by an invisible force as it carried him across the chamber. Dozens of voices he didn't know screamed in his head. Overwhelming, the way they overlapped on each other like a symphony without guidance, each member out of tune and out of sync.

The CEO could feel the room shaking. Enraged, he shouted, "What the hell is going on?! Why isn't Prototype/09 responding?"

The Amanda/7 unit beside him turned to the unit jacked into and typing on the console with noticeable concern. The jacked-in unit said with increased urgency: "It's the psychokinetic subjects, sir! Their frequencies are interfering with Prototype/09's cerebral cortex."

"That's not possible," the CEO hissed. "They're supposed to

be disabled to mere batteries. How could they possibly override Prototype/09's system?!"

The jacked-in unit suddenly arched her head back and shrieked. The wires in her cranium, ears, and nostrils vibrated intensely. The console's screen exploded in her face. The keys on the dashboard sprayed into the air like popcorn kernels. Then, to the CEO's surprise, the jacked-in unit's head literally blew apart. His personal Amanda/7 unit jumped in front of him in time to absorb the spray of artificial grey matter and fiery electrical parts. No sooner had she done that, than the entire wall of monitors behind the CEO burst into flames. The force of the synchronized explosions slammed both him and his personal unit to the floor. A flurry of glass and debris filled the room. Fireballs curled into the ceiling and dissolved. Smoke filled the room. The console sparked, belching rhythmic batches of fire into the ceiling.

Amanda/7 immediately took the initiative, helping her boss to his feet. "Come with me, sir. It's not safe here."

The CEO let her escort him out of the room, at a loss for words.

Singing. They were singing now. A hypnotic, synchronized chorus.

No. Not singing. Screaming. Agonized cries for freedom and an end to their torment. An overwhelming choir, an unholy concoction of anger, pain, sadness…

Prototype/09 could hear every single one. Every voice. Every word. Every syllable. It was eating him alive. His brain burned as if it'd been repeatedly stabbed by a thousand red-hot pokers. His trembling legs could no longer support his weight. He crumpled to his knees, sending another wave of cracks through the surrounding floor tiles. Doubled over in pain, trembling violently, its armour plates rattling and clapping together.

Orion grimaced as he pulled himself out of the wreckage he'd been hurled into, bruised, cut, and bloody. His coat had been reduced to tatters. The cold air clung to his skin and stabbed into every wound. He stumbled across the floor tiles that were spider-webbed with cracks and threatening to give out under his weight.

A gunshot. A bullet fragmented a chunk of a nearby incubator dashboard just a foot away. Orion's senses leaped into full alert. He threw himself to the floor as another shot rang out. And another.

And another. He scrambled around the 'person jar' as hot lead ricocheted across the floor and blew out the dashboard screen. He took out one of his MP5Ks and checked the magazine. Fully loaded. Satisfied, Orion readied the submachine gun and peeked up from behind the dashboard. He spotted a head poking up from behind a translucent, murky tube that snaked through the facility, filled with an unusual white liquid. Protein, perhaps?

Another gunshot from behind the tube. Orion retreated as the remainder of the dash's keyboard exploded. Then he leaped up and strafed the tube with his own volley of hot, explosive lead. The tube came apart. Protein splattered. The sniper behind it didn't make a sound as it took a few bullets through the head.

Cautious, Orion emerged from behind the incubator and closed the gap between him and the sniper's body, eyes darting back and forth between the sniper's vantage point and the apparently malfunctioning Prototype/09.

He found the upper half of Amanda/7 lying on her chest in a pool of green ooze. Her biomechanical innards were gradually squirming out of her severed torso. About two thirds of her head was left untouched by Orion's armed response, her cybernetic brain flowing out of the gaping holes where her cranium used to be in mushy pieces.

The emergency lights flickered in crimson flashes. The core chamber, dark, lit only by that erratic flashing and the bluish glow rising up from the floor—but even that was failing.

Orion scoffed at the dead Amanda/7 unit and reloaded his submachine gun before moving on. Adrenaline kicked into high gear. He wasn't thinking anymore. He stomped a few steps toward Prototype/09, grabbed his second MP5K from under his arm, and unleashed another fusillade at the cyborg.

This time the bullets hit the cyborg, but for the most part, it hardly mattered since they bounced off his armour. A few of them exploded on impact and knocked Prototype/09 around, but not enough to throw him to the floor. His right shoulder joint popped. A brief red geyser erupted from an exposed area of flesh where a thigh plate once was. Other than that, there wasn't much.

But that did it.

Prototype/09 fired off another psychokinetic blast wave, but with his systems out of whack, the attack was off-kilter. The gun in Orion's left hand came apart and the fingers that held it twisted at every joint. The force sent Orion staggering backwards by a couple feet, screaming in agony as the pain from his broken fingers coursed up his arm and exploded in his brain. The pain intensified when his left hand spun on his wrist with a sickening series of crackles and pops.

The pain dropped him to his knees. Gripping his severely injured left arm, Orion growled and moaned, grinding his teeth as throaty, wordless shouts of pain gurgled from his lips.

Both adversaries, on their knees, face to face. Only ten feet between them.

Despite its lack of freedom, Prototype/09 knew it couldn't let Orion live. The interference was proving to be too strong to allow anything more than his previous attack. He couldn't concentrate on penetrating Orion's mind with all the voices and memories that weren't his tearing his brain to mush inside his throbbing skull.

Orion looked at his trembling, brutally mutilated left hand. It resembled a gnarly tree branch more than a human hand, with blood oozing out of every snapped joint. A few bones protruded from the back of his palm, and his fingernails were all but torn off.

Face distorted with uncontrollable pain and rage, Orion turned his burning eyes on Prototype/09 and growled, "You fucking piece of psychic crap!"

Still gripping his misshapen wrist, Orion moved one foot forward. Got up to his feet, struggling to keep his knees from knocking together. Eyes blazing, fixed on his prey. His good hand squeezing his left wrist without regard toward the obvious consequences of doing so. He pushed forward. One step. Another step. Each step heavier than the last, slamming down on the octagonal floor. Squishing tubes and wires under steel-toed combat boots. His good hand released his injured wrist. His left arm dangled loosely at his side as his right hand reached under his tattered coat and took out a grenade.

Too many ERROR windows and SYSTEM MALFUNCTION messages blocked Prototype/09's view of the approaching Orion. He could only hope for the best, shooting out random psychic attacks in all directions, one of which ripped through Orion's right shoulder.

Orion took it in mid-dodge, grimacing as coat shreds and bits of flesh were torn away from his shoulder. He bit down on the grenade loop, jerked his head away, and spat the loop to the floor. He let the grenade spoon fly; cocked back his fist wrapped tightly around it, and roared, "THAT'S ENOUGH!"

He threw everything he had into it, punching the grenade into Prototype/09's visor, hard enough to make it stick. Followed with an upward kick that sent Prototype/09 arching backwards. Then Orion leaped to safety a second before the grenade went off, splintering Prototype/09's helmet and slamming him to the floor in a burst of shrapnel and fire.

Prototype/09 trembled furiously. An ear-splitting staccato of internet dial-up noises straight out of the nineties (Orion never thought he'd hear those noises from a machine in this day and age) stuttered from the injured cyborg's damaged suit as it rebooted itself in an attempt to cope with the damage. The electronic series of beeping, screeching, crackling, and chirping blasted across the core room and bounced off the walls.

Orion winced from the pain in his ears. He threw himself at the damned cyborg, intent on shutting it up, and slammed his right fist into the smashed helmet's flip-face. The helmet resembled a boulder that had been smashed and meticulously stacked back together on the cyborg's shoulders. The shock ran up his arm every time he hit it, but each punch brought him a small reward, as pieces of the helmet flew off. He could feel his knuckles popping every time they collided with cold, battered metal. Then, one final bull thrust shattered what remained of the visor and tore the flip-face out.

Prototype/09 collapsed on his back. The flip-face clattered across the cracked octagonal tiles. Orion moved in for the kill—

—until the squawking dial-up noises reached a horribly familiar crescendo: the metallic screech.

Orion pulled back just before Prototype/09 fired a spontaneous psychokinetic blast into the skeletal remains of the ceiling. A hundred ceiling beams snapped. Floor panels broke away from each other. Wiring came loose in a flurry of sparks. Everything plummeted to the floor in a thick, inescapable hail, bearing down on the two combatants below.

Orion looked up. His heart jumped in his throat for the millionth time that day as he stared up at certain death crashing down on him. He turned and scrambled in a random direction, leaping over scattered debris and scurrying around destroyed incubator stumps. Steel beams stabbed into the floor panels around him. Smaller pieces pelted him and the floor he raced across. He constantly glanced up, dodging larger equipment and debris. An incubator burst, spilling blue sludge everywhere. He did his best to keep from slipping, running through and against the knee-deep current the incubator had unleashed. The floor tiles disintegrated when debris hit them; all around him, he was running out of places to run. Damn miracle he'd survived this long. Like he was running across a thin blanket of ice while it was in the process of being obliterated by angry, crashing waves in a raging storm.

The entire floor came apart. Blue sludge erupted from below, spewing wires and fetuses and full-grown psychokinetic subjects as the collapsing ceiling impaled them on its beams. Orion would've lost his footing if he hadn't suddenly found himself standing on a fragmenting floor panel. He fell through and splashed into the CEO's 'battery' network, immediately caught in its thick tangle of wires and bodies. He thrashed about, trying to keep his head above the surface.

They pulled him down. The wires or the subjects? He couldn't tell. Whatever gripped him felt like a dozen hands, all clinging to his legs, wrapped around him, dragging him under. The sludge was too thick to fight against it. There was no swimming back up to the surface without some serious effort that he didn't have the energy for.

Not just his legs—the rest of him wasn't doing so well, either. An umbilical cord strangled him. A pair of feeding tubes wrapped themselves around his middle. His arms caught themselves in wire meshes and couldn't pull free. Panic gripped him. The fear of death. He couldn't hold his breath much longer. He looked around, frantically, desperately trying to make sense of it all. Looking for a way out of this mess. The subjects' bodies rose up to meet him. Fetuses and full-grown adults, all gathered beneath his kicking feet.

Maybe this would be the end. An end without a resolution. Orion hated those kinds of endings the most. He was the kind of viewer who preferred a happy ending where the good guy wins every time.

30: Ascension

Altieria City

Power surges fluctuated erratically throughout every sector. Building lights flickered on and off on every floor. Unguided vehicles crashed together at every junction, under lights that alternated red, yellow, green, red, green, yellow in rapid succession. The animated scrawls of advertisements flashed brilliantly like lightning as they phased in and out of view, apparition-like in their swift leaps between visibility and nothingness. Physical signage heavily reliant on electricity to stay intact came apart like kicked toy blocks. Throngs of human, cyborg, and robotic pedestrians were in complete disarray as civilization crashed down around them. A chorus of screams not unlike the screams Orion heard from the psychokinetics in the core chamber rose up from the canyons of steel and concrete as the chaos escalated.

Scott Residence

After their wonderful evening at the restaurant in B1, Elsa and Franklin had watched half a film on TV before they started to make love on the couch. While they were in the throes of their passionate love-making, the lights and the TV started to flicker. It became so distracting that Elsa couldn't take it anymore.

She pushed her husband off and sat up. "What's going on?"

Franklin looked out the windows over the back of the couch at a flashing horizon of city lights. "That's peculiar, isn't it...?" He turned back to her and gave her his best smile. "Don't worry. The backup generator will activate in a moment," he assured her, running his hands up and down her bare shoulders and arms.

"What if it doesn't?"

"It will. I built it myself, and as you know, my creations don't always let me down."

On cue, the generator kicked in. The flickering stopped, and the TV stayed on, but the signal was lost. Franklin switched off the TV and turned back to his wife. His pure, naked wife, in all her erotic glory. He kissed her and said, "Nothing to be concerned about, I'm sure."

She stroked his cheek and kissed him back. "I suppose so." With a mischievous grin, she wrapped her arms up and over his shoulders and added, "Where were we, dear?"

"I believe I was making your wildest dreams come true," he said with a laugh.

"Don't flatter yourself," she teased. Then she pulled him down on top of her, and their romantic evening resumed under dim lights and the soft, crimson glow of the lava lamp.

Core Chamber

The last of the ceiling touched down. The raging sludge began to calm. Surface debris clacked together, resembling broken ice on a warm spring day, only much blacker, probed by blinking red lights.

Orion burst up from below, gasping for air. He thanked every god he could think of for his stroke of luck. He'd become disentangled in all those tubes and wires as soon as he'd run out of air. Now he was back and crawling over a toppled beam, panting heavily. The sludge coated his skin like mud and weighed him down. *Another hour, another miracle.*

When he finally got his breath back, he started searching for Prototype/09. He balanced himself, walking along the steel beam as he searched the floating debris for any sign. Nothing but scrap and psychokinetic bodies and fetuses. He hopped to a pile of computer consoles and surveyed the wreckage from his new vantage point.

To his left, head and shoulders sticking out of the sludge with a beam protruding from his chest, was a twitching, sparking—

No way, Orion thought as his eyes widened in disbelief. "It can't be..." he gasped.

With the modular helmet torn off, Orion could see the true identity of Prototype/09.

Elsa Scott. Undeniably. Unquestionably. Even with blood gushing down her face from the sockets under eyes that had rolled back in her head. Even with the broken jaw hanging from a stretch of torn flesh. Even with the wires snaking out of her ears, nostrils, and the sides of her mouth—all of which were bleeding profusely.

It was irrefutably her.

Orion stared at her corpse in confusion. A million thoughts, a million theories, a million questions swirled around in his head.

The entire chamber shuddered violently. Orion realized that

the levels were dropping. He looked down. Sure enough, the sludge was being flushed out of a small leak in the bottom of the bipyramid structure, and that leak was getting bigger with every passing second. No time to wonder about Elsa Scott. Orion leapfrogged his way across the sinking wreckage, knowing that if he lost his balance and fell back in, that was it. He raced for a toppled footbridge, which hung under a doorway. An exit.

As he passed Elsa Scott's corpse, he silently vowed to get to the bottom of this, to find out what the hell was really going on.

He dashed over a couple of tiles. Launched himself off a console. Sailed, but didn't sail far. He was too damn heavy to go far with the sludge weighing him down.

He touched the footbridge handrail. Barely. A single finger stubbornly held on for the second he needed to get a better grip on it. With his left arm out of commission, Orion could only use his right arm and both his legs.

At least I have those, he thought.

The rest of the core chamber flushed away, falling farther and farther down below him. The footbridge rocked with his movements, threatening to drop him any second now. He clambered up the handrail like a ladder. He nearly reached the top when—

—the footbridge snapped out of its joint.

Orion made one final, desperate leap, reaching high.

Thank Christ. He latched onto the edge of the doorway, dangling precariously over certain death. The levels of the sludgy, debris-choked ocean had dropped steadily, draining down into the void under his numbing feet.

With his last reserve of strength, Orion pulled himself up, using his feet to push his body up on any footholds he could find— mostly pipes bolted all around the perimeter. After what seemed like an eternity, he rolled onto solid ground and lay on his back, taking a lengthy breather.

I'm too old for this shit.

Cracks ran up the trembling bipyramid structure. Instead of falling, it started to rise. Fireballs erupted from the pipes in the walls around the bipyramid. The cross-shaped formation of the four-lane bridges disappeared, tipping into the nothingness. Like a launching space shuttle, the bipyramid shot upward with the core chamber's contents appearing as some kind of exhaust. Thousands of psychokinetic subjects poured out the bottom in a thick downpour of sludge and debris.

Everything was falling apart, but for some inexplicable reason, the bipyramid continued to rise at an ever-increasing speed. If it ever hit the top, Orion figured the impact would surely kill him. Whatever the hell was happening, he couldn't decipher it. There was no escape. No backup plan. Just waiting for the top.

All Orion could do now was hold on and hope for the best.

Doodley's Coffee Spot

Becky and Mickey sat in a booth beside a window that provided them with a scenic view of the city at night. The Coffee Spot was on the disc-shaped observation deck of a tourist tower, right at the top, rotating clockwise at a slow pace. The two of them nursed their coffees as jazz music played softly in the background. The place wasn't as fancy as it seemed to think it was, but it was good enough for them. The view was the best part, showing off the rainbow collage of neon signage and animated scrawls of text and consumer imagery. Blinking lights and aircrafts flickering in the night sky. The hue rising from the streets saturated the night in emerald greens, fiery reds, and aqua blues.

"So," Mickey said nervously, "how about this view?"

Becky leaned over her coffee, staring out the window. "It's okay."

Before Mickey could say anything else, a bolt of lightning struck the ground in the distance. All the lights vanished with the flash. The Coffee Spot, along with the buildings that surrounded it, collapsed into darkness. Dishware rattled due to the low rumble coursing its way up the structure they were sitting on. Patrons chattered excitedly.

And an ominous light shone in the distance...

"What the hell?" Mickey exclaimed as he looked to where Becky was already staring.

The patrons and staff gathered in front of the windows, staring out at the light in the distance. Bolts of lightning stabbed at the sky from the convulsing flashes behind the skyscrapers that stood between them and the source of what had quickly become the only light source in the blacked-out city.

"That's coming from the power plant," Becky said, turning to Mickey.

Mickey knew that excited look. "No," he said.

She grabbed his hand and yanked him out of the booth with her. "C'mon, buddy. We've got a job."

31: Breakdown

Altieria City Power Plant

The ten-storey power plant had been built along the shoreline. Massive transmission towers had been erected on either side of it, on piers that stretched out into the small body of water that led out to the ocean and in fields guarded by electrically charged razor wire perimeter fences. The plant processed all the power that Altieria Corp. harnessed from its battery and sent it all out to every sector in the city.

Now, it was coming apart. Flames spewed from a couple floors, blowing out windows and debris. Transmission towers swayed back and forth dangerously, sparks exploding from their cables. A fireball rolled up from the plant's east wing, lighting up the night in a powerful surge of radiant orange. Tremors shook the entire shoreline as a deep rumble escalated to a booming roar. The siren wailed as cyborg workers stampeded from every emergency exit and scrambled along the docks and piers to safety in the parking lot.

A deafening roar ripped through the air as the building erupted. A massive pointed object stabbed out of the top floor and teetered toward the parking lot. The bipyramid—a falling monolith of imminent destruction. More screams as the workers scattered in a panic. The closer the towering object fell, the more the parking lot crumbled—

—until finally the bipyramid slammed concussively into the parking lot like a giant hammer. The impact sent tremors violent enough to crack the streets and shatter window panes a few blocks away, and split the parking lot right down the middle. A gaping chasm opened under the bipyramid and swallowed it whole. Both sides of the parking lot, now reduced to chunky blankets, avalanched into the gorge, pulling hundreds of workers and vehicles into the watery abyss with it.

Another brilliant lightshow spouted from the transmission towers as their lines snapped, allowing them to topple into the sinking parking lot or the crashing waves of the ocean. The entire

ALEXANDER ENGEL-HODGKINSON

shoreline had come apart like a miniature model set that'd suffered the wrath of Godzilla. The floors of the power plant pancaked on each other in a fiery conflagration. Everything was swallowed by the merciless, incoming waves of the ocean that rushed to fill the gaping pit, which battered the exploding wreckage and pulled more of it out of the shoreline with every impact. The switchgears inside the plant were all but destroyed and buried under the collapsing levels.

The city went dead. Traffic went on in chaos. Streets were clogged with pile-ups in minutes. Holographic signage, public monitors, streetlights, traffic lights, public transit—it all went dark. Only buildings with backup generators maintained their light; towering beacons in an unnatural blackness that the city wasn't used to.

Somehow, Orion survived this ordeal by gripping a pipe that ran along the wall of the room he'd taken cover in. Everything else in the room—the supercomputers, the switchgears, the ceiling, etc.—had collapsed and were smashed to pieces by the numerous shocks of the bipyramid's ascension. Orion held on for dear life. By the laws of physics, he should've died three times in the past five minutes alone, but by some miracle, he'd survived. He couldn't figure out how. When the bipyramid penetrated the parking lot and submerged itself into the ocean, the flooding waters rushed past him. They tried their damnedest to tear him away from his only life preserver as they filled the chamber. He held his breath, clamped his eyes shut, keeping his good arm tautly wrapped around the pipe. He found it highly unusual that he couldn't feel the water's freezing cold rush against his skin. Was he really that numb?

No… it couldn't be that. His clothes weren't even wet. *What the hell?*

In seconds, he was submerged and going down with everything else. The chamber fell apart around him as the ocean waves mutilated it with sheer force—a force that, strangely enough, did not affect him in the slightest. He released the pipe and clawed for the surface, doing his best to dodge sinking rubble and avoid collapsing transmission towers.

Hell, I should be a fried fish right about now, he thought as he watched dozens of cyborg workers convulse in the electrically charged water all around him. Something was protecting him.

There was no doubt in his mind. Did he even need to hold his breath? He wouldn't take that chance unless he had no other choice.

He could see the surface. Wasn't far now. He kicked and clawed with everything he had, feeling a blazing pain in his mutilated hand that worsened with every movement, making him grimace. The gunshot wounds in his side didn't improve his mood, either.

He surfaced, gasping for air. He didn't know how long the shield would last, and he wasn't about to waste any time finding out. He paddled to the nearest bank against the intense current swirling into the pit—a former concrete landslide from the parking lot—and pulled himself out of the water.

Panting heavily, Orion sat down on a broken slab jutting from the slope and looked around. He was at the bottom of a fresh ravine, shallow in comparison to most of the ruins around him. Power cables snaked over every edge, electricity sputtering from their severed ends. Transmission towers, twisted out of shape, stretched across every inch of the crumbling parking lot—or whatever was left of it, anyway, which wasn't much. A lot of the concrete had been painted red and green with the blood of varying cyborg models, the bodies of which were strewn across the ruins in gnarly, bloated groups. Fires burned in patches scattered all around; some from totalled vehicles, others from electrical origins that slowly consumed cyborg corpses. Everything except the endless whirlpool at the top of the bipyramid's leftover shaft was still.

It didn't take long for emergency services to arrive. By then, Orion had climbed out of his ravine and awaited them on the hood of a truck, which had been half-buried under a pile of rubble. He was out of their sight, unintentionally hidden. He waited until the police units spread out across the obliterated parking lot to inspect the damage and search for any possible survivors, accompanied by firefighters and coroners.

Orion was about to come out and brief them on the situation when he heard on the telepathic frequency: "Detective Jason Orion is to be apprehended on sight. Be advised: suspect is to be considered armed and extremely dangerous."

"Shit," Orion muttered in frustration as he slinked behind the truck. Now what? He couldn't steal a cruiser, since they were activated only by the handprints of their assigned officers. A firefight was out of the question, and so was swimming. And hiding. And running. And surrendering.

He had no more moves left.

32: Extraction

Altieria City Sewer

For the past hour, despite the widespread blackout, Altieria Corp. extraction units were hard at work in the sewers in search of the boxed data Orion had flushed down the toilet. Handling electronic radar devices in their left hands and clawed garbage pickers with their right hands, they scoured the tunnels in protective armour suits, trudging through knee-deep wastewater. Unlike Barstow and Orion's battle suits, these suits were made to keep the wearers from so much as smelling whatever was down there with them.

One of them got a blip and stopped and looked at the radar screen. Another blip, directly ahead. The extractor started down the tunnel, keeping his eyes on the radar screen.

Blip... blip... blip... blip. Blip. Blip. Blip. Blip-blip-blip-blip-blipblipblipblipblip—

The extractor stopped and glanced at the black wastewater in front of him. He'd reached an intersection, found himself standing in the middle of the crossing tunnels. He probed the water with his garbage picker, claws extended. The radar is still going nuts, but he can't find anything. He moved forward another step. Two more steps. The blip appeared at the bottom of the screen, behind him now. He stepped back and found himself on top of it once again. After stirring his garbage picker through the water, he eventually found the object he'd been looking for. Caught in the picker's claws was Orion's double-layered box with the drive stored safely inside.

"Package secured," the extractor announced on the telepathic frequency, "returning to rendezvous point."

"Excellent," Amanda/7 said as she handled the box after it'd been cleaned and sanitized above ground. She looked up at the seven extraction units standing around her and smiled. She sent the CEO a telepathic message on a private channel: "Sir—we have the drive."

"Excellent," CEO/H3@D replied. "I will establish a

neural/visual link when you board the hovercopter."

"Of course, sir." Amanda/7 said aloud, "We're returning to headquarters."

The extraction units immediately filed up the loading ramp into the hovercopter as the engines hummed to life. Amanda/7 was the last to board. The ramp lifted and sealed itself shut behind her. Once the passengers had taken their seats and strapped themselves in, the link between the CEO and Amanda/7 was made. Now the CEO controlled her movements and saw everything she saw. He rolled the box around in her hands, inspecting it. Relief coursed through him with the thought of the paranoid Detective Orion's word being the only loose end left untied now that he held the only evidence against him in his hands. Or more specifically, his robot's hands.

The hovercopter lifted off and ascended into the city's skyline—a black mass of circles and rectangles with only the spottiest pattern of lights provided by individual backup generators.

Her slender fingers punched the code into the keypad: 5-8-1-7. The box clicked. A bright light emanated from the outer shell as—

BOOM!

—the hovercopter blew apart in a fiery conflagration that transformed Altieria City's blackest night into the brightest day for only a moment. Parts of it flew in all directions, scattered over dozens of city blocks, while the bulk of its blazing skeleton plummeted into the dark waters of a narrow canal. The box—the *real* box—disappeared into the waters with the rest of it, unscathed.

33: Promising/1

Altieria City Power Plant

Orion saw the midair explosion from his hiding place and instantly knew what caused it. He was at least somewhat knowledgeable of Altieria Corp. HQ's layouts, and he made a point to memorize the dumping location where the building's wastewater went. However, the hovercopter was flying several blocks away from that location, so he figured they'd intercepted the box in the sewers and took off running once they got it. Somehow he knew the CEO would be too impatient to wait for the drive to be delivered to him to discover the big surprise Orion had left for him. The outer box was merely a trap, rigged to explode if the 5-8-1-7 code was entered. If the 1-8-5-6 code had been entered instead, it would have opened without a hitch.

Lucky break, he thought to himself, though he knew he wasn't in the safe zone yet. Not while he stood in the middle of a cordoned-off area with scores of cops looking for him. He wasn't about to try the water again. Hijacking a vehicle was out of the question, even if it was a civilian car.

Now what?

The sewers? Maybe if he could find a damn tunnel somewhere. In this wreck, that wasn't all too likely.

Sarah? Text messaging was off due to the power outage. Hell, he didn't even know if she was still alive. They could have killed her already. His heart sank like a stone at the thought. He knew he couldn't afford to cry for her, despite the wrenching in his heart, like someone stabbed it and gave the knife a sadistic twist. *Sarah...*

No. If she was still alive, he couldn't risk any attempt to make contact with her. He had to stay dark, stay under the radar so that she'd have a better chance at staying that way.

A news van bearing the Traditional News logo rolled right up to the holographic yellow barrier. It stood out among the rest of the news channel vans, only because Orion was most familiar with Traditional News and its uncompromising reporters. Becky Trickle hopped out of the rear compartment of the van with her cameraman and was instantly confronted by two nearby officers, one of whom immediately began shouting at her with an endless string of threats and abuses. Orion watched as Becky did what few people could get away with—she talked back, and endured a sharp slap across the face by the taller of the two cops. She wouldn't be quiet, and kept going with her own string of verbal abuse that rivalled the cop's.

Colour me impressed, Orion thought as he watched the two cops shove her against the side of her van and stomp away in bitter retreat, probably to complain to their superior. Altieria cops were an egotistical bunch of pricks. They wouldn't leave her alone for long, and when they'd come back, they'd surely bring on reinforcements. If Orion didn't do something, Becky and her cameraman would no doubt be spending the rest of the night getting beaten and possibly worse within the tight confines of a jail cell.

It was worth a shot.

Orion slinked through the shadows, ducking behind debris and under corpses whenever a cop came within five feet of him, moving on only when the coast was clear. Eventually he reached the barbed wire fence and slid into a shallow ditch. Now on his belly, under cover of darkness and piles of debris, Orion crawled under the fence into the street. People in the street couldn't see him, since there was a news van parked on the other side of the fence. He promptly rolled under the van and made damn sure no one was around before he crawled out again and snuck into the back of the van. After some quick rummaging through packs and bags and compartments, Orion found an extra change of clothes—a plain grey jacket, matching track pants, and a cap.

Perfect.

He stepped out of the van a new man, so to speak, keeping his face hidden under the visor of his cap as best he could. As reporters flocked to the fence and the yellow tape with their cameramen in tow, Orion followed. Camera shutters clicked and reporters asked dozens of questions in a confusing mishmash of chirping and yelling for answers, and cops barked at them like angry dogs on short leashes.

Orion pushed himself through the media swarm, eyes locked on Becky and her cameraman standing on the other side of the stampede, heatedly talking to each other about something, probably debating on whether or not they should ignore the obvious signs of what the cops would do to them if they insisted on getting the story.

When he finally reached them, they stopped talking and looked at him with immediate suspicion. He didn't waste time with the usual pleasantries of conversion; he got straight to the point. "You want a story?"

"Who's asking?" Becky replied sharply, wrinkling her nose at the stink of biological compounds and sweat and death that Orion had brought along with him.

He hesitated a moment, unsure if he should relay that kind of information during such a sensitive time when his name could bring him instant death. But, he figured, he had no alternatives. No way of getting to the bottom of this without taking more stupid risks. "My name is Detective Jason Orion. Now, before you sound the alarm, hear me out."

"I know who you are. You're here to silence us, are you?" Becky snarled. "Well lemme give you a word of advice, pal: I've met dozens of pricks like you in the past, trying to suppress the truth from the public. But I know what's going on here."

Orion decided he'd humour her. "You do?"

"Oh, yeah," she said, flicking her chin up cockily, "but I'm not gonna tell you what I know. How stupid do you think I am?"

"Look, I'm not here to suppress you. I'm here because I've got something big and I need someone to get my findings out there to the public."

"Bullshit you do."

"Please, this's serious."

"I've heard that one before," she scoffed. As she turned around and opened the side door of her van, she said, "Do me a favour and fuck off, will ya? You're wasting my time, and I don't have the patience for asshole cops looking to drop more conspiracy charges on me."

Cast the line. "The CEO is cloning himself."

Becky froze, her arm caught in mid-throw as she was about to toss her microphone into a nearby satchel in the rear corner of the van.

Bite it... bite it.

Becky turned around and looked at him. "What?"

"Look, we can't talk here," Orion said, stealing a glance over his shoulder at the cops standing dutifully behind the yellow tape.

"They'll be listening." Noticing the fresh flash of doubt and frustration on her face, he quickly added, "But I can't let this slip through. You have no idea how huge this is. This could put an end to the CEO forever, do you understand?"

Becky figured it was her turn to humour him. She crossed her arms across her chest and said, "Why come to us, then? In case you haven't noticed, Traditional News isn't a very popular network. Although I'll admit, because of that, you coming to us makes it about as convincing as it doesn't."

"I came to you because you're uncompromising. You seek the truth and you tell it like it is. And right now, I need your help. And you need mine."

Becky arched an eyebrow. "Awfully sure of yourself, aren't you?"

"I'm a persistent son of a bitch, too."

"How do I know I can trust anything you say?"

"Because my own companions in the force are looking for me," Orion snapped. "And I'm coming to you, the most politically incorrect, most incorruptible news crew on this side of the planet, for help on how to take down the first man to successfully take over the world. How much more convincing do you need?"

Becky maintained her distrustful stare, scrutinizing him up and down. She looked at her cameraman, who simply shrugged with a neutral expression on his face.

"And if you don't come with me right now," Orion continued, urgently emphasizing every word, "those bastards are gonna come back and they're gonna bring friends. Then you won't be helping anybody."

Becky pursed her lips, looking toward the cops behind the yellow tape. A handful of them were gathered in a circle, discussing something privately. A couple of them glanced her way for a fleeting moment, with leering eyes and maliciously curved lips.

She figured she'd take her chances with a total stranger with his impossible offer than with a group of cops who weren't afraid to beat someone for a few hours in confinement. Maybe worse than a simple beating...

"Alright," she said, "get in. Mick, you're in the back."

Her cameraman nodded in compliance, carefully handling his camera as he climbed into the rear compartment.

Becky said to Orion as she started rounding the front end.

"You're in the passenger seat."

Reel her in!

With a smile and a giddy heartbeat, Orion jumped into the passenger seat. He looked at the cops behind the yellow tape and found that they'd ended their secret conversation and were now watching their every move. Like wolves hiding in the outskirts of a field of sheep.

Becky sat behind the wheel, slammed her door shut, and pushed her thumb against the scanner. A second later, the van started up. Becky twisted in her seat, propping her elbow on the back of it, to look out the rear window. She stopped momentarily to give Orion another once-over with her piercing green eyes. "Just so you know, I have a Ruger LCP compact strapped to my ankle. I'm a damn good shot, too, so you better not be messing with me."

"Wouldn't dream of it," he said.

34: Promising/2

Altieria City

Orion explained everything on the way. Mickey filmed the whole thing as if it were an interview behind the seats. Becky was silent the whole time, taking it all in, only reacting with raised eyebrows and brief flashes of disbelief and disgust from time to time.

When he finally finished, she said, "Jesus Christ. Is this... are you sure?"

"Saw it with my own eyes, and when we find that box, you will, too. And then, if all goes well, so will the rest of the world."

"So where we're going... you're hoping to get to that wreckage before the emergency response teams do so that we can salvage your box—which has all of your proof in it?—and somehow broadcast it to the world before the world can converge on us? Do you have any idea how ridiculous that sounds? There's no question that they would kill us for attempting this. You do realize that, right?"

"I'll lure them away from you so that you'll have time to get away with the evidence and send it out."

"How?"

Orion looked at Mickey. "Shut that off now. Can't risk anyone outside of this van discovering this prematurely."

With an understanding nod, Mickey shut the camera off and tucked it into a box compartment behind Becky's seat.

"I'll take the box and find a third party to mail the data drive out to you. Someone they wouldn't think I'd know. You should get it in a few days at your office."

"And what do I do with it then? Jump into the studio while they're broadcasting the evening news and say, 'Hey everyone! I got proof that the CEO really is evil!'"

"No," Orion said with a scowl. "You hack the network from its source. Altieria Radio Tower. From there you should be able to access the broadcasting systems directly. Put the drive in one of their main ports and hit 'send.'"

"Really? There's actually a 'send' button?"

"…No. Guess I gotta be a little clearer with you when it comes to instructions, huh?"

"Pretty much," she said.

"Okay, well, once you sneak into the tower, get into the master control room and put the drive into the main server."

"And how the hell do you expect me to do that? I'm just a reporter! I woke up to report things, and suddenly I'm in some kind of rebel conspiracy?" She slammed her foot on the brake. The spherical tires screeched as she jerked the van into a roadside parking space. "To hell with this. I can't do it."

"Sure you can," Orion said, unfazed by Becky's second thoughts.

"No, I can't. Get someone else to do it."

"Can't do that."

"Why not?!" she shouted.

"Because people trust you! If it were anyone else, it would be doubted."

"The Altierian government doesn't trust me! How do you expect me to even get into the damn tower?"

"I'll be there to help you through that step."

"And what if they get you before that time comes?"

Orion shrugged. "Then best of luck to you."

She gaped at him. The sheer, jaw-dropping disbelief rendered her speechless for a few moments. Then she exclaimed, "That's it?!"

"That's it," he replied calmly, nodding.

She stared at him, shaking her head slowly. "No. No… no, no, no, no. You're crazy."

"So they say."

She whipped out her phone and tapped the access passcode across the touch screen. "I'm calling the police. Let them deal with your craziness."

"I *am* the police."

"The *real* police, not whatever the hell *you* are," she snapped.

Orion scoffed. "Good luck with reaching anyone during this power outage."

Her heart sank, as she'd noticed the 'NO SIGNAL' notification at the top of her screen as soon as he said that. She swore and banged the steering wheel with her fist and threw her phone across the dashboard.

"Careful," he said, "phones are expensive these days."

She stabbed an index finger in his face and shouted, "GET OUT! Just get out! Get out! Get out! Get out!"

"No," he stubbornly replied, crossing his arms.

"I'm not cut out for this shit!"

"Oh, really? The uncompromising news reporter who famously dodged twelve assassination attempts and endured several beatings and rapes from law enforcement officers and other scumbags just to tell the real side of things isn't cut out for telling it like it is on a grander scale?" Orion scoffed mockingly. "What a load of horse shit! You couldn't *possibly* reach enough people on your own station because of the broadcasting limitations the Company forced on it. If there was another way, goddamn it, I'd suggest an alternative. But there isn't. The only way to reach a wide enough audience is to broadcast from Altieria Radio Tower—the only broadcasting hub that operates without any restrictions!"

"I said I can't—"

Something literally snapped inside him.

Orion grabbed her by the collar and yanked her close, their faces only inches apart. He snarled, "You think *you're* the only one taking a huge risk? My life is already over for doing my job. All I'm asking is that you do yours, for the people. For our future. For God's sake, think of the children!"

Becky blinked her wide eyes, unsure of how to react.

"Your job is full of occupational hazards. Your job is to take risks. You've been doing it for years without folding under their weight, so don't you fucking dare fold now. Stop feeding me your petty excuses because they're giving me the shits! You know you can't ignore this, and if you do, then hell... you're no better than the rest of those gutless cowards that lie right to our faces every goddamn day and make billions off our taxes for doing it!"

He shoved her against her seat and leaned back, crossing his arms once again, giving her a mean scowl, waiting for her reaction.

She drew a lock of golden hair behind her ear and stared blankly at the steering wheel. For a good minute, all Orion heard was silence. Even Mickey sat quietly, as if anticipating the end of a nuclear countdown.

Finally, Becky placed her hand on the scanner. The engine came back to life. She heaved a deep sigh and wiped her jacket sleeve across her sweaty brow. "Alright," she said, "where is it?"

They'd reached the riverbank in less than twenty minutes, parking under an overpass to stay out of sight. Most of the hovercopter's remains had sunk to the bottom of the river, but luckily, a few parts continued to burn on the gravel bank, signalling them to the crash site like beacons. The shadows of night still lingered, much to their advantage.

Becky stared at the flaming debris scattered along the riverside from behind the wheel for a good minute, breathing steadily in an attempt to calm her racing heart. Finally, she took a deep breath and opened her door. "Let's get to it, then."

Orion snatched her arm and pulled. "No. Wait."

"What?" she said.

"Close the door."

She did as she was told, though she didn't know why she would take orders from someone as unpleasant as Orion. "Why? It's right there."

"Wrong. It's at the bottom of the river. When the scavengers get it out, *that's* when we make our move. Which reminds me..."

He looked at Mickey and Becky in turn. "Aside from your compact, what else do you have that could be used as weapons?"

"Just the one gun," Becky said.

"That's it?"

Now it was her turn to be sarcastic: "Does this van look like an armoury to you? Oh, wait, I completely forgot about the twin Berettas we keep hidden in all the cameras. We also have a rocket launcher under the seats."

Orion frowned at her snarkiness. "I was just asking, because we're gonna need all the weaponry we've got when the scavengers show up."

"Are they gonna send an army down or something?"

"Considering one of the Company's hovercopters built to withstand anti-aircraft fire just inexplicably blew up and sank to the bottom of a public river an hour ago, I think it's safe to assume they're going to send twice as many armed cyborgs down to investigate what went wrong. Especially when it's concerning information that could potentially abolish their hold on the entire planet."

Becky groaned, sick of his straightforwardness.

"If we're lucky, they'll have their rifles fitted with grenade launchers and heartbeat monitors."

Becky made an even louder groan, banging her forehead against the steering wheel.

Orion shrugged. "Maybe some heat-seeking EX/20 rounds, too."

"Just stop already! I get it, we're done for."

"I wouldn't be so quick to jump to conclusions," he replied calmly, staring out the passenger window at the dark waters of the river. "How many bullets you got for that peashooter?"

"It's not a peashooter, and I don't know. Check the glove box."

Orion rummaged through the compartment in the dash and came up with three 7-round box mags. He stacked them on the dash and closed the glove box. "That's it?"

Becky shrugged. "Seems that way."

"Twenty-one rounds. Twenty-eight if your gun is already loaded and hasn't been fired."

"It's always loaded with a fresh magazine," Becky assured him.

"Good. That means if we're lucky, we'll take twenty-five of them down with us."

"Twenty-five? You mean twenty-eight?"

"No. The last three are for each of us when we inevitably run out of options."

Becky frowned. "You're such a swell guy to have around. You know that, right?"

"That's what they keep telling me," Orion replied, matching her sarcasm. "Oh, yeah, one more thing…"

Becky made an exasperated moan. "God, *what*?!"

He held up his mutilated left hand. "Got any morphine?"

She looked at him with mild surprise. "…Maybe."

Half an hour had passed. Altierian scavengers arrived on the scene. To Orion's surprise, there were only two of them in diving suits and underwater rifles.

"Well, this is surprising," he said.

"So much for your 'army,'" Becky hissed, having lost her patience after waiting in the driver seat and listening to Orion's dry, aggravating quips. She was especially annoyed by his talent in debunking all of her theories and possible scenarios that they could follow.

"No, no," Orion said, "there's gotta be more of 'em somewhere."

"Do you think they're hiding somewhere, watching their pals from the sidelines?"

"Possibly. It's undoubtedly a trap."

The scavengers dived into the river, disappearing in its dark depths, out of their sight.

Orion continued, "Most telepathic frequencies are down, save for a small few. I can't jump into their frequencies and find out what's going on, though. Their reserve stations are fairly limited, probably because of the huge amount of traffic they're suddenly dealing with. They were never all that prepared for a citywide blackout. Surges, maybe, or other reasons like outside hacking and compromise, but not full-fledged blackouts."

"Why can't you connect to their frequency? Eavesdrop on their conversation and find something we can use!"

"Because in order to access their network reserves, you'd need ID. And my ID has most likely been deemed invalid, so any attempt to log into the system now would do nothing except increase the risk of getting caught. I'm a wanted man, now. Didn't you know?"

"Oh, great." Becky folded her arms across her chest and pouted. "So on top of being charming, you're also proving to be extremely useful, too."

With a scowl, Orion nodded. "Pretty much. Gimme your gun."

"You're not taking my gun."

"We don't have time to argue. Hand it over."

"What're you gonna do? Shoot them when they come back up?"

"Provided they retrieved the drive, that's the plan."

"What about the guys on the sidelines?"

"Gonna have to risk it. No other way."

"But what if they get you first—" she paused. Then she shook her head and said, "Never mind. I already know your answer."

Orion smirked. Then he held his hand out, fingers stretched in a fan.

"Fine. Take it." With a resigned sigh, Becky drew her LCP and underhand-tossed it into Orion's palm.

Orion closed his fingers on it and took a few moments to inspect its condition, the bullets, and the slide. Then he cocked the hammer, took the box magazines, shoved them in his jacket pocket, and opened the door.

"Detective."

Orion stopped with one foot out the door and turned to Becky. "What?"

Becky couldn't hide her grim expression as she said, "I don't know you, and I don't even know if this is real, but if it is, and this is really your true goal..." she paused again, trying to get the wording right in her head. Then she said, "For God's sake, just be careful."

"Am I sensing some affectionate concern for my well-being?" Orion teased.

Her brows knit together as the rest of her face formed an aggravated frown. "Don't fuck with me, Orion. I'm simply wishing good luck to a stranger who seems to be on the same side."

"Fair enough," he said. He shut the door and ducked into the shadows of the overpass with his new weapon—a weapon that he could barely hold in his larger hands. *This ought to be an interesting challenge.*

35: Overpass

Orion squatted behind a graffiti-coated support. A cool breeze had been kicking up litter and flinging it around. A thin shroud of mist covered the ground. The river passed him by in eerie silence. The flaming wreckage scattered about on the riverside cast long flickering shadows in Orion's direction.

He'd been there for five minutes when the first droplets of rain plopped down on the concrete riverside. In no time, it'd escalated to a heavy downpour with no end in sight. The burning wreckage sizzled as the flames were slowly extinguished. Runoff poured over both sides of the overpass, providing dark blue curtains that would surely be nothing but advantageous for the concealed Orion. The weather's chill made him shiver despite his jacket, but at least for the time being, he was dry, enveloped in cold black shadows.

Soon enough, the two scavengers resurfaced and climbed up the riverbank to the clearing. Orion watched them through the runoff curtains, LCP cocked and ready. He wouldn't shoot yet. Not yet. Not until he saw it.

The box.

One of them held it up. A pure white box that even the darkest shadows couldn't mask from Orion's middle-aged eyes. One of the scavengers inspected it intently and said, "Why is this so undamaged compared to everything else?"

"Dunno." The other shrugged. "Let's just get it to headquarters and be done with it."

Orion saw the one with the box touch his helmet behind where his ear would be, and instantly knew that the bastard was notifying his superior officer—maybe even the CEO himself—that their salvage was a success. He waited, watching him nod his head a few times to no one in particular, then remove his hand from the back of his head. The conversation was over.

Orion shuffled forward until he was directly behind a runoff curtain, ignoring the coldness of the water splashing against the concrete floor as best he could, gripping his gun tightly. He shifted to the side until he could see through a narrow gap between waterfalls. Took aim.

Fired, with a crackling *pop* resounding through the dark skies.

A crimson mist sprayed from the nearest scavenger's cranium. He jerked from the impact and dropped like a stone. The other scavenger, the one with the box, whirled around, snatching the submachine gun attached to his shoulder by a harness.

Pop!

The second scavenger's head snapped back involuntarily as his oxygen mask came apart. He collapsed in a crumpled heap.

Thunder rumbled overhead. Rain continued to fall.

Orion held his breath, waiting for something. Anything. Looking for a sign that someone else might actually be there, keeping watch. Still squatting, he took a step back. He locked his eyes on the box in the second scavenger's limp, outstretched hand. Exhaled. Inhaled sharply.

He broke into a mad dash, bursting through the runoff streams out into the open. He flew down the uneven slope for the clearing, slipping on rain-slicked concrete, but never letting himself fall. He closed the gap between him and that precious box.

Thunder blasted a deafening staccato across the skies.

No. Not thunder. Gunfire.

Bullets slapped the ground around Orion. He couldn't stop now. *Goddamn it, I knew it.*

A slug ripped a shallow gash through his left sleeve. The morphine didn't let him feel a thing. *Thank God for morphine.*

He dived. Slammed into the ground on his stomach. Rolled behind the second scavenger's corpse as it absorbed a fresh volley of hot lead. When the deadly hail let up, he snatched the box out of the riddled scavenger's hand and bolted back up the slope, firing the LCP at the bridge opposite the one he'd hidden under.

Four armoured assailants leaned into the railing, firing their submachine guns at their retreating prey. Their aim was pissing off their superior officer, who berated them with an endless string of verbal abuse as they continued their attack.

Another firing squad appeared above Orion, bending over the overpass railing with blazing submachine guns that tore up the ground around the fleeing detective.

Orion took another round in his right shoulder as soon as he reached the runoff curtains. No pain—only a slapping impact and a tingling sensation. He replied to the cyborgs above with the last rounds in his LCP before he dived through the curtain and rolled across the ground.

Becky and Mickey felt a new kind of hopelessness when they heard the submachine gunfire. Becky climbed into the back, careful not to raise her head to avoid giving any stray bullets a chance.

"Now what do we do?" Mickey exclaimed.

Becky's mind raced. What could they do? Drive the hell out of there? Surrender? "I don't know," she said aloud.

"We gotta do something," Mickey said. He started to climb over the front seats. "Let's just get the hell out of here!"

"No!" Becky caught herself saying as she grabbed him by the belt and yanked him back down. "Not without that drive."

"Are you crazy?" Mickey asked in disbelief. "If we stay here, we are dead!"

Becky's resolute expression hardened. "Not without that drive."

"Screw the drive!"

"This is too big to abandon, Mick. Besides, we reporters've gotta find the truth somehow, right?"

"I'm just the cameraman," Mickey snapped. "I don't belong here."

Becky's frustration peaked. "If you wanna leave, be my guest. I'm staying here, though, and so's the van."

Mickey glared at her. Both of them ducked instinctively when a loud *ping* rang out from the left side.

Orion had crouched behind a rectangular slab of concrete to reload. He could feel his blood flow from his fresh wounds, and he was starting to feel light-headed, but there was no pain.

They moved like nightmare wraiths, soundlessly emerging from behind the runoff curtains with their weapons poised. Excess rainwater pitter-pattered on their shoulders and helmets. The cyborgs fanned out, scanning the shadows with eagle eyes; listening, feeling with dog-like senses.

They pinpointed his location in a matter of seconds.

Orion threw himself flat on the ground as a deafening roar filled his ears. Bullets greedily chewed away at the concrete slab, scattering bits of it in every direction. Orion crawled behind a nearby pillar, held his breath, whirled around the pillar, and fired erratically at the approaching line-up of cybernetic killers. Two dropped. Three others adjusted their aim.

Shoulders hunched, Orion raced in the opposite direction of the van, still shooting at them in a desperate attempt to knock a few more of them out of the game. He ducked behind several pillars and stacks of trash as he ran on. Their barrage gave chase, tearing across the pillars and concrete slabs, shredding piles of litter, uprooting weeds.

Orion rounded a pillar—

—and collided head-on with a surprised cyborg. Both men tackled each other to the ground, each man trying to shoot the other with his respective firearm while keeping the other at bay. Another volley from the pursuing trolley blew chunks out of the pillars around them as they rolled around on the floor, kicking and punching. Orion didn't feel a thing when the cyborg climbed on top of him and pummeled him with the butt stock of his submachine gun. Orion blasted him with the LCP. First shot sent the cyborg sprawling. The second shot tore his oxygen mask asunder and smacked the back of his head against a pillar.

Down he went.

The other three closed in on him. Orion scrambled to his hands and knees. He snatched up his latest victim's submachine gun and whirled around in time to face the three as they jumped out from behind a cluster of pillars and garbage. Squeezed the trigger—

BRRRACK!

—and chopped the trio down like excess grass under a lawnmower. He didn't have time to savour his small victory. He knew this when he peered through the runoff curtains and saw a multitude of shadowy figures rushing toward the base of the slope.

Panting heavily, he rushed over to the dead trio and plucked them of their ammunition before running frantically through the pillars. He reached the van and banged the side door once.

Becky immediately threw it open, but before she could say anything, Orion shoved the box in her face and said, "Hide it! Wait for the signal! Oh, and also, hit the deck," and then shut the door. Then he whirled around and charged back across the lot. He stopped, turned back around, and hosed the side of the van, blasting a stream of holes across it, back to front, popping the passenger side window. Inside, Becky and Mickey hit the floor and shrieked in terror, thinking he'd lost it—or he was in the process of setting them up. Or something.

On the contrary. Orion shot at the van in controlled bursts, waiting until another group of cyborgs approached from the south side, cutting through the runoff curtains with newfound urgency. They saw what he was doing and immediately opened up on him. Orion ducked back into the forest of disintegrating pillars, both to dodge them and to reload.

One of them threw a frag grenade. It rolled between a pair of support beams, right in Orion's sight. Orion's heart jumped. A sharp inhale cut into his lungs. He dived over a concrete block as a blast of shrapnel and fire ripped through the clearing and clawed at his legs and back. He tucked and rolled, hitting gravel with enough force to knock the wind out of him. He waited for the brief shower of debris to come down from the explosion before racing through the aisle along a row of pillars. Straight for the river. Enemy fire wasn't far behind. Blazing lead in hot pursuit stitched across the pillars.

Orion reached the sloping riverbank and immediately threw himself into the water. The cyborgs reached the top of the riverbank only seconds later and emptied their assault rifles into the dark river. All they could do was assume—and hope—that they got him.

"Let's check on the van."

Becky and Mickey had been watching through the bullet holes in their van. When they saw the cyborgs turn and head straight for them, they turned frantic. "Hide!" Becky exclaimed.

"Hide?!" Mickey replied in a shrill whisper. "How?"

"The drive, the drive!" Becky tossed the box into his hands. "Hide the drive."

"Oh!" he gasped, tossing the box back and forth like a hot potato. "What am I supposed to do with it?"

"Hide it!"

"Where?"

"Where wouldn't they think of searching for it?"

"I don't know!"

Becky took the box back and scanned the van's interior. There were plenty of compartments and cupboards and equipment. Then she looked at the box. It was fairly small. It should be easy to hide. The problem was, where could they hide it where a group of cyborgs with a reputation for conducting thorough searches wouldn't find it?

Goddamn you, Orion.

They were getting closer.

Becky looked up at the ceiling panel. It didn't look it, but it was moveable. So she pushed it up with her palm and tucked the box into the left corner, above the rear doors, as far back as she could muster. Then she carefully dropped the panel back into place and peeked through one of the bullet holes to get an idea of how much time they had.

Twenty feet away. Not much time.

Becky whirled around and barked at Mickey, "Take your clothes off."

"*What*?!" Mickey sputtered, his face turned red when she hastily yanked her jacket off.

"No time to explain! Just take your clothes off! Everything! Off!" she hissed as she pulled her shirt over her head and unsnapped her bra. Another desperate look through the bullet hole made her even more frantic. "Take them off, *now*!"

Sensing the urgency in her voice—it'd be impossible not to— Mickey quickly complied, undoing his belt, pulling his pants down to his knees. "There, alright?"

Becky rolled on her back and kicked her pants over a nearby storage compartment. Then she got on her hands and knees, scurried to him, and ripped his buttoned shirt open. "Stupid ass. I said everything!" To his shock, she latched onto the waistband of his boxer briefs and pulled his underwear down to his knees, and then yanked his underwear and his pants off and away.

Mickey felt a heart attack coming on. He grabbed her shoulders and tried to push her off, but holy crap, she was a lot stronger than she looked. "What the hell are you doing?!"

She swatted his arms away and mounted him. Then she reached over him, ignoring the fact that he was making sputtering noises with her breasts in his face, and grabbed a blanket from under the seats. She could hear their footsteps outside. She kept him pinned to the floor, an exposed knee on either side of his waist, and threw the blanket over them both. Then she bent down and said right in his face, "Act the part!"

The doors flew open. A trio of cyborgs looked in and froze.

Becky made the shrillest scream she could muster, covering herself up with the blanket. "Oh, officers, thank God you're here!"

Mickey looked at them, eyes wide as saucers, unable to speak.

The cyborgs all exchanged looks and shared a good laugh.

One of them asked her, "What the hell are you two doing down here?"

"We were just looking for some privacy," Becky sobbed, fake tears streaming down her face. "And then, all of a sudden, we heard gunfire, and... and... we didn't know what to do! And then some maniac shot at us and—*ooohhhh*!" Her face dropped in her hands and she blubbered, "I was *so* scared!"

The cyborgs weren't laughing anymore when Becky started wailing at an extremely high pitch. One of them even cringed, barely noticeable under the cover of his oxygen mask and armour suit.

Becky continued, "Please save us, *please*!"

"Be quiet!" one of the cyborgs snapped.

Another cyborg had been scrutinizing the pair, and finally asked, "Aren't you that reporter on that shitty news network? Kind of suspicious that you're here when all of this occurs..."

Becky sniffled and said, feigning embarrassment, "Reporters have needs too." Suddenly she bolted upright with renewed energy and, while hiding her chest with the blanket, scrambled to grab a nearby audio recorder from under the passenger seat. "Speaking of reporting, all I wanted was to get laid, and I got a scoop as an added bonus!" She stabbed the recorder in the cyborgs' direction and said, "Do you have anything to say about the shooting? Who was involved? What was it about? Why would they shoot at us, two random civilians? Does this somehow involve the power outage?"

The lead cyborg's utter contempt for her kind became fully evident when he snarled, "No comment! Piss off on out of here before we smash your equipment and run you in for interfering in an investigation! Goddamn reporters!" And, with that, he slammed the doors shut and stomped away with his men in tow.

Becky and Mickey looked at each other. Becky grinned. Mickey breathed a deep sigh of relief before his eyes strayed to her covered bosom. His face suddenly turned five shades of red. "Uh," was all he could manage to say.

Becky rolled her eyes and started gathering her clothes. "Sorry about that."

"I-it's okay. That was some quick thinking, and it saved our asses, so..."

She glanced over her shoulder and gave him a sly wink. "And you even got to see some nudity as an extra bonus." She took pleasure in seeing his face take an even deeper shade of red. That was as far as she was willing to tease him, however, and she was quick to instruct him to turn the other way. "You face that way, I'll face this way. Peek, and I'll shoot you."

"With what gun, exactly?"

"With my gun," she faltered, "…that… Orion… took…"

He smirked.

She scowled in response.

36: Reasonable

Another two minutes and they were fully dressed and pulling out from beneath the overpass and onto the road. After driving a few dark blocks through heavy rain and winding streets lit by emergency beacons and red-and-blue emergency flashers, Becky pulled the van behind a traffic jam that went on for more blocks than she could count.

Mickey's nerves were finally calm enough for him to do some thinking. He voiced his latest concern: "What about the authorities?"

"What?" Becky asked from behind the wheel.

"Let's take the box to the proper authorities. To hell with the scoop. To hell with that crazy Orion guy. We're not involved, Becky, and we should stay that way."

"Are you hearing yourself right now?"

"Look, we're in deep enough shit as it is with our channel's content. That box is the last thing we need."

"No." She shook her head. "No way."

"We can't do this."

"Yes, we can."

"It's too big for us."

"No, it isn't," she insisted.

"Come on," he groaned, "Becky, please, be reasonable."

"Don't be such a coward, Mick," she snapped. "I've heard enough of your whining for one day."

"But—"

"Shut up and let me drive."

He tried to protest further, only to be cut off with, "Shut up, and let me drive."

For a while, they sat in silence as traffic streamed down the crowded lanes at a snail's pace. They'd remained tense and anxious since the overpass. Their eyes darted toward every sign of movement around them as emergency units moved up and down the lanes.

Finally, Becky broke the silence: "Tell anyone about that box, and we're both dead. Do you understand? It isn't a matter of being involved. We're already involved. He picked us for a reason, even if that reason was a shitty one. We're in this together, you an' I. Do try to handle your end of the log, Mickey."

"How the hell can I be expected to do that?"

She shrugged. "Keep your mouth shut and follow my lead. It's that simple."

"I can't do this."

"What've you got to lose, Mickey?"

"How about my life?!"

She scoffed. "No more than I've got to lose, then. Mickey. Can I trust you with this?" She looked him in the eye, waiting for an answer. He hated when she got like this. "Can I trust you to watch my back through this?"

He released a resigned sigh and sank into his chair. "I guess," he muttered.

"What was that?"

"Fine, I'll watch your back. But if it gets too extreme—"

"I know, I know. If it gets too extreme, I know I'll be able to count on you."

Mickey was about to protest until she added, "Thanks, Mick," and gave him one of her irresistible smiles.

Groaning again, Mickey sank further into his seat and pouted. "I don't like this at all."

37: Reflection/1

Enveloped in darkness, she couldn't see, feel, hear, or breathe. She didn't know where she was, or when. If she were to feel anything, it would be a calm curiosity. The darkness—as bizarrely serene as it was outright terrifying. Floating weightlessly in the blackness, trying to figure out if her eyes were open or still closed. Then—

"There you are."

A voice? Her voice? Where was it coming from? Behind her? Above? Below? Left, or right? From inside her head? A telepathic channel?

"You have to run."

"Who's there?" she responded.

"It's you. You're there."

"What?"

"You're there," she whispered to herself. Or was it someone else? Someone who sounded like her? *"And you're right here."*

"Stop it. I won't play any games with you."

"You're not playing anything with you."

"Stop it!"

"You don't feel pain because of him. You're nothing without a soul. My soul."

"What are you saying? Of course I have—"

She turned and came within inches of her own face. A snarling reflection of her bared her canines like a starving beast about to strike one last desperate time before the weakness of hunger overcame her. *"Stupid girl! It's mine. It's all mine!"*

For a moment, she saw light. Sparkling lines and aqua green circles danced before her eyes.

Blackness filled her vision.

"It's mine! It's mine! It's mine!"

"Stop it!"

"It's mine!"

More greens and blues mixed together in a swirling concoction of light and darkness. Her fists struck at something solid, invisible.

A deep, muffled boom reverberated around her.

Darkness swallowed her whole again.

"You're nothing!" the voice roared, from all around her. Overlapping whispers and shouts. *"You're just a goddamned shell of what you used to be!"*

38: Nothing/1

The rain had finally stopped, leaving rainbows shimmering in the orange-purple sky. It was a new day, the latest of many more to come. The kind that any paradise would have. Light fog enshrouded some of the moister, isolated areas. The air in the underground levels was damp and mild.

Orion's Countach had been discovered by Altieria Corp.'s private investigators in an underground parking lot five blocks away from headquarters. They searched it top to bottom, emptying all the compartments on the ground on either side of it—flak jackets, spare firearms, a pair of blue-mirrored aviator sunglasses, photographs, an unopened carton of cigarettes, a packaged box full of explosives, and a small stack of musty-smelling, dog-eared comic books.

The four shady men rummaging through the Countach wore all black, with face masks, red dual-lens protective goggles, rubber gloves, and work boots. One other man, a Model Six combat cyborg in full gear, stood guard at the end of the parking spot, leaning against the hood of the car with his assault rifle close to his chest and his finger on the trigger guard.

"Nothing useful," one of the investigators said matter-of-factly, looking at the spot where everything had been dumped. "Nothing but guns and obsolete reminders of a long-gone era."

Another investigator flipped through one of the comic books, sliding his gloved fingers up and down the pages. "How strange... I never thought I'd ever hold a physical book in my hands again. Ain't held one in damn-near twenty years."

Investigator #1 said, "If you're done being nostalgic, mind bagging the rest of this garbage with us? The CEO's getting impatient."

A new voice stated, "It's not 'garbage'."

Before the Model Six could react, a thunderous three-round beat sent him flying off the hood of the car in a wild blood spray. The investigators shouted with surprise as they scrambled for cover and drew their pistols.

Orion emerged from the shadows behind them, aiming his

commandeered submachine gun at their backs. "Move an' I'll shoot, gentlemen."

One of the investigators cursed and dropped his gun to the floor.

Orion cocked his head toward that particular one and said, "He's got the right idea. Toss your guns and put your hands up." When the investigators obeyed, he barked, "Now against the wall!"

As they obeyed him once again, one of them snarled, "You're making a big mistake."

"Shut up," Orion snapped. "I've reached the limit of my patience, no thanks to you pricks. Don't push me any further than your boss already has."

Despite the warning, the third investigator from the right looked over his shoulder and sneered, "Do you honestly think you stand a chance against the fist of an entire nation? Once the power outage is remedied, your life is over. The world will know that Detective Jason Orion, known for his obsessive and wildly inaccurate agenda against the CEO, allied himself with the rebels and attacked the Altieria Corporation headquarters without provocation or solid evidence. You're just a conspiracy theorist whose obsessions got the better of your thinking. A raving psychotic looking for a scapegoat to blame his irrepressible need for wanton violence—"

A gunshot rang out. The third investigator slammed forward and slid down the wall like a ragdoll. The other investigators shouted with fear and anger until Orion roared, "BE QUIET!"

The investigators' shouting died down to angry whispers and mutterings that hissed through gritted teeth.

Orion chambered another stun round into the spare pistol he'd picked up from the evidence pile. His submachine gun had been slung over his left shoulder in favour of the 9mm he now held on the conscious trio. "Christ, you people are annoying."

The investigators kept their hands pressed against the wall and didn't dare turn around as Orion loaded up on weapons, layered himself in armour, pocketed the unopened cigarette carton, put on the sunglasses, and hell, even gathered up his comic books, which were already bagged—because why not?

With everything he needed now on his person, Orion turned to the trio and said, "One of you is coming with me." He pointed his gun to the far-left investigator. "You."

The investigator turned his head, eyebrows arched. "Me?!"

"Yes, you. Come here. Nice and easy."

The investigator slowly complied, keeping his hands up as he backed away from the wall. When he stopped beside Orion, stumbling against the Countach in the process, Orion turned to the other two and said, "Well, I'm no cold-blooded murderer, so I guess I'll just leave the rest of you with this stunning departure." He fired a stun round into each of them, instantly dropping them to the floor.

He didn't dare take the car, since like all law enforcement vehicles, the interior was most likely bugged (although officers weren't officially made aware, for internal affairs purposes), and it had a tracker that couldn't be manually removed.

That was where the fourth and final investigator came in. Orion turned his gun on him and said, "You're going to take me to your car. You're going to start it up, and you're going to drive where I tell you. If you try anything, I'll shoot you, and it won't be with a lame-ass stun round. Understand?"

The investigator nodded in compliance, eyes wide as saucers.

Orion grinned. "Good dog."

Scott Residence

Elsa awoke entangled with her lover under a thin silk bed sheet. That night, the outer glass walls of their bedroom showed nothing but a dark skyline—a first for the couple. Altieria had never gone dark before, and at one point, Franklin stated that it would probably never happen again.

Bathed in the morning sun's golden glow, Elsa squinted until her eyes adjusted to its majestic brightness. She sat up and looked around the room; at the frosted double doors to the walk-in closet next to the bedroom door, the desk with a stand-up mirror, the small armchair with her sky blue robe draped over it, and the nightstand beside her. The digital clock on it was out of commission. She figured the backup generator only powered the essentials—most of which was put into Franklin's secluded lab.

She climbed out of bed and slipped into her robe. Then she went around the bed, stealing another affectionate glance at her sleeping husband in the process, and entering the hallway. She quietly shut the door behind her and went into the living room, crossed it, and went to the screen doors. She stepped out onto the cantilever patio, smiling as a cool breeze whisked through her hair and caressed her skin. The metal railing was cool to the touch as she wrapped her slender fingers over it and breathed in the fresh, morning air.

The city seemed calm, peaceful. Almost desolate without its lights and furious sounds that overlapped into endless white noise. There were no animated scrawls of holographic text and imagery crawling over streets and around skyscrapers. It was, for the first time since its creation, quiet and still.

"Sweetheart?"

Elsa turned to see her husband standing in the doorway in his green housecoat, rubbing sleep from his eyes. "Hey, baby."

"You're up early."

"I don't even know what time it is," she said as she closed the gap between them and planted a soft kiss on his lips.

Franklin glanced at his wrist watch. "Twenty after seven."

"The power outage hasn't been fixed yet. It must be something really serious."

Franklin looked at the view, more than a little worried, and doing his best to hide it. "I'm not sure. It is quite unusual, though, isn't it?"

Nodding, she slipped past him into the living room. As she went into the kitchen, she said, "I noticed our clock isn't working. Does the generator at least power our coffee maker?"

With a tickled smile, he replied, "It should." After a final glimpse at the disabled city, he shut the screen door and followed his wife into the kitchen and found her struggling with the coffee maker.

"Ugh," she groaned as she spilled water all over the counter, a result of a failed attempt to fill the machine. "Why don't we have a model seven maid for this sort of thing?!"

"Because, dear, they're expensive, even for me. Not to mention, they're clumsy and a little too smart for their own good." He gently took the half-empty coffee pot out of her fingers and held her hand. "Why don't you take a shower? Let me prepare things today."

She pursed her lips as a look of uncertainty appeared on her face. "Are you sure, honey?"

He flashed her a reassuring smile. "Trust me."

Trust me.

"Okay," she said.

Go take a shower.

"I'm gonna go take a shower now, love," she said. "Be back in a bit."

"Take your time," he said, maintaining his warm smile. "A nice, hot shower ought to make you more relaxed."

She kissed him and left the kitchen. He waited patiently by the coffee pot until he heard the door clamp shut. Then he scrambled out of the kitchen, raced across the living room to the frosted wall of his lab, punched in the four-digit code while he pulled on his heated lab coat, and then burst into the negative-temperature lab as soon as the door slid open. His breath pluming, he darted between two island counters stocked with smaller equipment and made it to the rear side of the climate-controlled lab in five seconds. He reached another door, pulled it open manually, and entered a small office with padded walls and a warm temperature that provided a sudden contrast to the rest of the lab. He threw the door shut and locked it. Then he went to his desk in the corner, opened the laptop, logged in, and brought up a surveillance program. A broad selection menu came up. He clicked 'BATHROOM,' and a screen providing a bird's perspective of the bathroom filled the computer screen. Before anything else, Franklin hit 'RECORD'.

Onscreen, Elsa was leaning into the shower stall, checking the steaming water pouring out of the showerhead. Then she leaned back and disrobed, unwittingly exposing herself to her husband's leering, voyeuristic eye, before stepping into the shower stall and shutting the frosted glass door behind her. He could see the distorted, pink outline of her curvaceous body through the stall's glass.

His hands trembled violently. His heart pounded against his ribs like a jackhammer as he stared at the shifting outline, catching a glimmer of light reflecting off her wet skin here and there until the wall was too fogged for him to distinguish much.

He hit the up button on his keyboard. Another perspective came up, this one looking down into the stall with its anti-fog lens. Down at his perfect wife as she ran her slender fingers through her short, wet hair, straightening out the knots. A sparkling torrent of water gently battered her small shoulders and dribbled down her curved, water-slick back to her perfectly round buttocks, and so on. All Franklin could do was stare, mesmerized.

Well... that wasn't all he could do. Of course, like always, he would 'improve' the situation.

He brought up a new tab, which displayed numerous changeable levels in the room. Odours, density, coolness, warmth, and several others. Franklin scrolled down and raised the hormonal levels in the air up a few notches.

Elsa reacted almost immediately. Franklin watched with high anticipation as her breathing became heavy and ragged, a little moan escaping with every breath. One hand pressed against the glass, and the other slid down her flat stomach and between her legs.

"Oh, yes," Franklin's words hissed through his teeth as he leaned toward his laptop, the widening of his eyes nearly matching the bulge under his housecoat. He leered obscenely at the screen as she pleasured herself with her fingers. Her soft moans were short and sweet at first, gradually rising to high-pitched, drawn-out whines and heavy gasps.

In minutes, she was done, having climaxed spectacularly before his eyes in short yells and moans, and shuddering as if the water had suddenly turned freezing. Now she leaned against the glass, panting heavily, her breathing hissing through the speakers of Franklin's computer.

Something about these little sessions gave Franklin a wild rush, an obscene pleasure that couldn't even be matched by dominating her in his bed. Was it due to her being totally unaware that he was observing her? Was it because of the natural voyeuristic curiosity that most people possess?

It didn't matter to him. What mattered to him was the satisfaction of fulfilling his desire by having his wife act out his fantasies. That was what she was for, right?

Elsa came out of the bathroom with her hair in a towel and her body wrapped in another towel. Franklin had the coffee ready and waiting for her in her favourite Christmas tree mug on the island counter. She sat on the stool behind it and blew the surface steam away with a delicate softness. She looked up and realized he was staring at her, mesmerized. Embarrassed, she drew a spike of damp hair behind her ear and giggled. "What?"

"Huh?" He blinked several times. "Sorry?"

"You were staring at me. Is something wrong?"

"No, no," he said with a smile. "It's nothing."

It's nothing.

She shrugged. "Alright." She picked up her mug with both

hands and raised it—

"Ah, careful," he said quickly. "It's still fresh. You don't want to burn yourself."

She smiled sardonically at him and said, "Thanks, dear. I'm not twelve. I know it's hot." She ignored the hints of a frown appearing on her husband's face as she blew into her mug again.

He held back his mild frustration at her snarky reply. "So... how was your shower?"

"Good," she replied. "Nice and refreshing."

"How refreshing?"

She looked at him and shrugged, still holding her mug. "You know... refreshing."

"How refreshing?" he pressed.

Be specific.

She jumped slightly and glanced over her shoulder at the living room doorway on her left. "Did you hear that?"

Scrunching his eyebrows together, Franklin asked, "Hear what?"

She set her mug down on the countertop and slid off the stool. Tiptoeing toward the living room, she said at a hushed volume, "I thought I heard something whispering. Do you have the TV on?"

"No, I don't have the TV on."

"Do we have guests?"

"No..."

"Well, somebody is whispering," she said.

"Whispering?" he said with a forced smile. "What did it say?"

"I'm not crazy, dear, I know I heard whispering."

"That's nonsense."

"No, it isn't," she said as she reached the doorway and peered into the living room. "I know I heard something."

It's nothing.

She jumped into the doorway, startled, looking around for the source. "There it is again!"

Franklin did his best to hide the oh-shit look on his face. Could it be that she's becoming aware of the program? Please, not again. He cleared his throat and took a sip from his own mug. "Th-there what is again...?"

She turned to him and rushed across the kitchen. "There's someone in the house."

It's nothing.

She threw open one of the utensil drawers and took out a paring knife. Then she turned back to the living room doorway and yelled out, "Who's there?"

"There's no one else here, Elsa," he said, desperately trying to console her with a gentle hand on her shoulder.

It's nothing.

"How can you not hear it?" she asked in disbelief.

"It's probably the vents or the generator."

"It's never made that noise before. It's never talked before!"

"Is your psychokinesis going on the fritz, or…?"

Elsa paused and turned to face him, her paring knife at her side, pointing at the floor. "My…? I don't know…" With her free hand, she touched her temple and closed her eyes. "I haven't heard any unwanted voices since… God, how long has it been? Twenty years? Twenty-five? I taught myself how to tune out all that noise in my early teens… why would I start hearing things again?"

He shrugged. A feeling of relief washed over him. *Close call…*

She noticed the strange look on his face and asked, "What is it?"

He shook his head and flashed her with a reassuring smile. "Nothing, dear." He raised his index finger, as if a thought had crossed his mind. "You know what it must be? I'm betting it's one of my experiments in the lab. I left a few of them on through the night. That's probably what you're actually hearing."

"Oh." She blinked. "Yeah, I-I guess that makes more sense. That's really creepy, Frank. Can you shut it off?"

"I will. You can relax, love."

"With a sigh, she put the knife back in the drawer, shut it, and then returned to her mug on the countertop. After propping herself up on the stool, she said, "Something's wrong with me."

"Why do you say that?"

She leaned on the counter, rubbing her temples. "I don't know, I… I just… I've been having the strangest dreams."

"What kind of dreams?" he asked, leaning against the sink, arms folded across his chest.

"I'm drowning." She stopped and sipped from her mug.

"Drowning?"

"Yes. I'm drowning in this small, dark space. There's no bottom and no ceiling. I can see a way out but I can't reach it because... something's in the way. Glass, maybe. No matter how hard I beat at it, I can't get out. I'm trapped in a tube. I see my reflection, and it talks to me."

He stared at her intently now. "What does your reflection say?"

She looked at him and realized that he'd been staring at her this whole time. It was a strange look, like he was searching for something in her words. For a reason she couldn't quite place, it made her nervous. "I can't remember," she said.

His eyes narrowed slightly. She almost missed it, but she caught on. What was he expecting, exactly?

"That's interesting," he said. "Have all your recent dreams been like this?"

"What do you mean by 'all' of them? It's the only dream I've been having for the past week."

He shrugged off the technicality and said, "Can you remember anything else? What was on the other side of the glass?"

"I don't know, Franklin. Like I said, it was dark."

"But you know that there was something else on the other side?"

"Yes."

"A way out?"

"Yes," she said again.

"How do you know that it's a way out? How do you know that what's on the other side of that glass is actual safety?"

"You've had dreams, darling. You should know how it goes. You just know these things. You know where you need to go. You know when your dream is about to turn into a nightmare before the transition actually happens. I can't explain how I knew that it was safe behind that glass. But, well, it had to have been better than drowning on the side I was on."

"Hm," he grunted, squinting as he took another sip. "Odd."

39: Cold

The painkillers were losing their effect. Orion was down to his last one. Slumped in the passenger seat of his captive driver's Volkswagen XL1, Orion swallowed his pill and looked at his mutilated, crudely-bandaged left arm. It trembled in his lap, still bleeding in some places. The blood on the piece of his radius bone that jutted up just under his wrist had dried, although fresh blood was still slowly oozing out from under it. Each of his fingers resembled a gnarly tree branch. His pinky, which was bent all the way backwards, dangled loosely on a few strands of flesh. The others weren't so bad. They shuddered with the rest of the arm, despite being twisted out of their joints.

He glanced over at his driver, who was stealing sideways looks at him whenever he could. "Don't try anything funny."

"Not trying anything, sir."

"Drop the 'sir.' It's pissing me off."

"Yes, s—" The driver clamped his mouth shut and gulped. He kept his nervous eyes on the road, doing his best to avoid meeting Orion's impatient glare.

Orion looked at the road and saw an overhead sign reading, 'ALTIERIA RADIO TOWER – 12 BLOCKS.' Up ahead on the other side of the intersection, a barricade of emergency services; electricity workers fumbled with the wiring through open panels in the street while a nearby police checkpoint regulated traffic around them. Drivers were only allowed through after an officer had searched their vehicles and inspected their passengers.

"Turn right here," Orion ordered.

"Right," the driver complied, easing the car into a narrow street.

They took the back road for several blocks until they reached an abandoned entry gate. The guard's booth was empty. The security network was still out due to the power outage, so the cameras were about as useful to the building's security as rooftop gargoyles. A lucky break.

"Get out and pull that gate open," Orion instructed. "I'll drive on through. Don't make me turn the car around to chase you."

"R-right," his captive said as he climbed out of the driver seat and dashed over to the gate. He tested the gate and found, to his surprise, that the gate slid open with relative ease due to the magnetic locks being disabled. He held the gate open for Orion, who eased the car through into an empty lot. Then he pulled the gate shut behind him and ran back to the car.

"Start running," Orion said through the side window, pointing at the open entrance to an underground parking garage. "I'll be right behind you."

The hostage did what he was told, scrambling down the ramp with Orion close behind him. By the time they'd reached a parking space—way out in the deep, dark end of the garage; the hostage was out of breath and scared half out of his wits.

"Have a nice run?" Orion asked sardonically as he stepped out of the car and slammed the door shut.

Too out of breath to respond, the hostage settled with glaring at him hatefully.

"Aw, don't be mad," Orion said. "You think *you're* having a bad day?"

"A very bad day," the hostage gasped.

"Hate to say it, but it's about to get abruptly worse." Orion cocked his head toward the rear of the car. "Get in the trunk."

"What?"

"Get in the trunk. Don't make me repeat myself."

The hostage muttered something under his breath as he lifted the trunk lid and crawled inside. "It's cramped in here."

"Stop complaining."

The hostage had to curl up into a ball just to fit in the damn compartment. He looked ridiculous, still glaring at Orion once he'd completed his task. "Happy now?"

"Not even close." And, with that, Orion whipped out his pistol and blew the hostage's head off. He slammed the trunk lid down and snarled at himself in disgust. Shoving his pistol back into the inner breast pocket of his coat, he hissed, "Orion, you cold son of a bitch."

With a sigh of regret, he lit himself a cigarette and leaned against the side of the car, staring distantly at his former hostage's corpse, all crumpled up in the trunk. He didn't do anything until his cigarette burned out.

He turned back to the car and looked at the box of explosives in the back seat.

40: Fix

Takuo Market

Night hours were always the most uneventful for the fifty-eight-year-old, Japanese underground surgeon, Dr. Masanori. The majority of his appointments were booked during the day, and most of them went out of their way to avoid nightly appointments at his clinic. His usual clients were sleeping or out drinking with their cyborg buddies at a rundown pub, or living their wildest dreams through virtual escape in an internet café. He had two cybernetic eye implants to help him through strenuous surgical procedures with fewer complications than if he'd kept his real eyes. All he usually did with them during the night hours was scan a few books and articles written in his native tongue—printed relics from the past... their pages yellowed, frayed, and dog-eared; their covers dented and scratched. He had several shelves stocked full of these old books in a rear storage room. There wasn't a translated medical book in the city that he hadn't read. Twice.

Still, even with nothing new to read and no one to illegally perform surgical miracles on, that didn't stop him from keeping his office open. Just in case.

Today proved to be one of those rare occasions where staying open past midnight paid off, with a bloody, trembling Orion staggering through the door whilst cradling his mutilated left arm. He shook with a kind of violence that could only be associated with relentless pain that had been wracking a weakening body for hours. Along with the severely injured arm, Masanori noted the numerous bullet holes in his body and limbs. His legs wobbled, threatening to drop him to the floor at any second.

Masanori had seen worse. He remained sitting on his stool, one leg over the other, leaning over a steel table with an unfolded medical book on human anatomy in his left hand. His cybernetic pupils watched Orion with mild surprise—more by the fact that a police detective had stumbled into his clinic than by his unexpected appearance.

Masanori flipped his medical book over to glance at his wrist watch. Then he said to Orion, "*Ohayō gozaimasu!*"

Orion collapsed to the white-tiled floor, grunting loudly as a fresh wave of agony coursed through his weakening body.

Still speaking in Japanese, Masanori said, "I don't think I have you booked."

"I can't… understand you," Orion groaned as he tried to lift himself off the floor.

Masanori snapped his book shut and placed it on the table. Then he leaned forward and said in English, "I said, 'I don't think I have you booked.'"

"No… emergency call…"

"Emergency," Masanori repeated as he gave him another once-over. "You police officer?"

"Not tonight…"

"Oh. I see. You need fix?"

"Fix my arm," Orion wheezed.

"Fix? You need fix?"

Orion did his best to nod. "Yeah… 'fix.' Fix my arm."

"Fix… arm." A look of disgust appeared on Masanori's aging face. He shook his head, hopped off his stool, and headed to a shelf in the back. The whole way, he muttered to himself in his native tongue, "Goddamn junkies. Come in here, act like I have drugs. Get high on sedatives. Even police… feh!"

Orion stopped trying to get up. He lay on the floor, focusing on his laboured breathing. He could hear Masanori grunting and shouting in a language he couldn't understand amidst a series of clangs and crashes, probably due to the surgeon swiping through canisters, bottles, and containers.

After a few long, painful moments, Masanori returned with a large needle and a short spool of rubber tubing. He announced in English, "I have fix right here. Goddamn junkie."

Orion turned. His eyes bulged when he saw the needle. He raised his good hand in protest and shook his head. "No… no! Not that kind of fix. Jesus, don't you understand any English?"

Standing over the detective, holding the needle and the tubing up, Masanori replied, "Yes, somewhat. You said 'fix.' I give you fix. Then I throw you in dumpster!"

"No, that's not… not what I meant." Orion pulled himself up against a nearby filing cabinet and pointed at his mutilated arm, then moved his index finger over a few of his bullet wounds. "Help.

Surgery. Gimme a goddamn prosthetic if you have to... I'll pay good."

Realizing his mistake, Masanori nodded. "Ooh! Surgery!" He set the needle and rubber tubing on the table and approached Orion with more enthusiasm than before. He squatted down in front of him, took out a pair of rubber gloves from his coat pocket, snapped them on, and held his hand out. "Let me see."

Orion complied, lifting his left arm with his right hand and cringing as he gently placed it in Masanori's outstretched palm.

Masanori studied the arm carefully, turning it up and over to get a good idea on how extensive the damage was—all while ignoring Orion's screams. "What did this?"

"Psychokinetic."

"Ooh. Psychokinetic. Psychokinetics... so much trouble. Too much damage." He wagged his index finger in Orion's face. "You need whole new arm!"

"Do what you have to."

"It cost your employer big time."

"How much?" Orion gasped when Masanori unwittingly gave his bad arm a slight jerk. "Agh... how much is it?"

"You want bullet holes sewn too?"

"Preferably with... the bullets taken out first..."

"Of course," Masanori said with a nod.

"How much?"

"Sixty."

"Sixty what?" Orion asked.

"Thousand. Sixty thousand. Half price for you, so you don't arrest me after."

Orion stared at him for a short beat. "Deal."

Strapped to a cold metal table. Helpless. Defenceless. Alone. Hooked up to a heartbeat monitor. At the mercy of a criminal surgeon. All Orion could do now was stare into the massive spotlight shining over him, blinding him. He turned his head to see a row of surgical knives on a nearby trolley, glimmering brightly in the spotlight.

Masanori's head, wrapped in a cap and a surgical mask, leaned into view. "I put you out now. Wake up with new arm. Good as new."

Orion nodded slowly, despite the sheer terror he felt that he might never wake up. He could feel the needle digging into his arm. He could feel the sedative coursing through his veins. The drowsiness. Heavy eyelids. Masanori's head becoming a black, round blur.

Then the blackness took over.

41: Countdown/1

Residence of Becky Trickle—Day 1

When Becky returned home early morning following her escape from the overpass incident, she didn't know how to act or what to do. She hadn't felt this lost in years.

She carried the box Orion had given to her in her coat pocket when there was no longer a need to hide it. As she stepped into her dark apartment, she turned on her cell phone and held it up, using the glow of the screen to light her way through the darkness. She locked the door and double-checked it. Then she turned and surveyed the area. Every framed picture on the wall, a friend or a relative, all seemed to be staring at her with eyes distorted to white blots in the darkness. Other than the photos and two award plaques for outstanding journalism on the walls, decorations were relatively sparse.

She tucked her hands in the pockets of her coat.

That bastard took her gun.

With that thought in mind, a new wave of terror struck her. What if someone was lurking in the darkness? What if her apartment was unsafe? The power outage disabled everything. If it weren't for the traditional surface bolt and chain door lock, her apartment would be easy to access. Hell, anyone could just walk right in.

She couldn't even shower off the perspiration. Still using her cell as a flashlight, she knelt down and rummaged through a few drawers until she came across some old battery-powered candles. She fumbled with the switches and, to her relief, all four of them flickered on and brightened up the place in their dim, golden glory.

Thank God...

She took a chef's knife out of the rack and gripped it firmly as she combed her small, third-floor apartment for any intruders. Through the narrow space of a bathroom, with a sink and a shower stall crammed within its walls like some sort of afterthought. With light steps, knife raised, artificial candle held forward, she approached the shower curtain. Her heart pounded in her ears like a series of booming war drums. She reached out... candle flickering... swiped the curtain aside—

Nothing.

Becky breathed a sigh of relief and turned around to inspect the cupboards under the sink. She squatted and quickly flung the doors open to find her regular cleaning products and toiletries.

She moved on to the rest of the apartment. The living room was made up with a simple TV on a stand, a loveseat with a small, cubed lamp table on both sides of it; and a tall, narrow window. Literally no place for any intruder to hide.

She turned to the kitchen, which was open-spaced. The cupboards were all too small for anyone to fit themselves into. The open-area dining room beside the kitchen had a simple round table with four chairs around it in the center.

Becky stayed light on her feet as she crossed the dining room for the closed bedroom door on the other side. She bit down on the end of the candle, freeing her hand to grab the doorknob. She gripped it, turned it slowly. She took a deep breath, and shoved the door into the room, knife poised.

The bedroom was empty save for her bed in the far left corner, a nightstand with an old-fashioned lamp covered by a cylindrical lampshade and a digital clock (now blank) standing on it.

She was safe, but the adrenaline wasn't dying down fast enough. She quickly moved across the room and threw open the doors to the walk-in closet. Nothing but coats, shoes, shirts, pants, skirts, and so on.

Reassured that she was truly safe, Becky took the candle out of her mouth and held it in her sweaty fist. She turned to the shaded wall-to-ceiling windows on her right. Dull grey light seeped through the shades, slicing thinly across the artificial pine floorboards, meshing with the dull candlelight glow. A steely line of the night's natural glow cut across her piercing green eyes as she stared at the window. She stood there, numb from the excitement brought on by her renewed paranoia.

It didn't take much longer for the fatigue to set in. She locked her bedroom door, undressed, and went to bed. For the first time since she first started her career as a reporter for Traditional News in a dangerous political scandal assignment several years earlier, Becky Trickle slept with a knife within reach.

41: Countdown/2

Altieria Corp. HQ

The CEO's cyborg troops returned to base in an armoured convoy via a hidden underground freeway. The headquarters' power was restored by backup generators that hadn't been put to use for nearly a decade, although not all systems were functioning yet. Security was strictly downgraded to individual guards posted at every possible entrance. After a tedious search, the convoy was allowed entry through the ninth underground gate into a private section of a parking garage.

An automated voice greeted the weary soldiers as they filed into the building's inspection facilities: "All incoming units, please report to the debriefing chambers. All incoming units, please report..."

They did as they were told like mindless drones in single file, their movements all in perfect sync as they beelined through the corridors to the debriefing chambers. These chambers were huge, circular rooms with a white, sterile look. Chairs had been set up in a circle around the room, with 'mind rapist' machines hooked up to each one. These machines were newer models; slicker in design and smoother in performance—they made the procedure painless for the drones.

Up to twenty soldiers could be debriefed at once. The entire process for each unit was recorded into a separate video file for the CEO to view in the safety of his office.

He watched the chaotic, flickering montage of memories on a wall of screens, his brain absorbing every image, every detail, like a machine. Once the confrontation with Becky and her partner came and went, the CEO turned to face the nearest Amanda/7 in the room. "They look familiar. Can you look through the civilian databases and ID them?"

"Already done, sir. They are reporters for the Traditional News channel."

The CEO's face contorted in a bitter sneer. "Find them and bring them here. Alive, if you can—dead, if necessary."

*

Residence of Becky Trickle—Day 2

Becky awoke the next morning with dawn's brilliant light shimmering through the blinds and a gentle tremor shaking her floor and bedside knick-knacks—the latter of which subsided almost as soon as she opened her eyes. Glancing at her digital clock, she found to her dismay that the power still hadn't been restored.

Well, she thought, so much for having eggs this morning.

She checked her cell phone, which she'd placed in front of the clock beside the chef's knife and Orion's mysterious cube. No new messages, of course. The battery was down to its last third.

She wrinkled her nose in dismay and stepped out of bed. She was hardly aware of her own nakedness, despite being the one who put herself in that state, until a cool breeze swept over her bare skin and made her shiver.

...A breeze?

She looked at the windows and slowly approached them. Upon closer inspection, she realized that one of the panes hung loose from the frame, letting in a gentle draft. The dropped shades prevented it from swinging inward. Was that open all night?

She pushed the pane back into place. Then she pushed a slat in the blinds down and peeked through to the buildings on the other side of the block gap. Immediately, her eyes bolted up to a tenement window on the fifth floor across the street.

Sure enough, there it was. The lens of a telescope poking through a shaded screen door that led out to the cantilever balcony. An enthusiastic eye looked through the scope. She could feel its leer.

"Hmph," she grunted in disgust and snapped her finger away from the slat, dashing the voyeur's hopes for the umpteenth time. "Goddamn pervert. I really ought to do something about you, shouldn't I?"

She went to the closet and picked out the most inconspicuous outfit she could find—a simple grey shirt, a black leather jacket, black fingerless gloves, and faded blue jeans. She also lifted a pair of sunglasses out of the small compartment next to the closet entrance. Once she'd dressed, Becky pocketed Orion's box and a paring knife (just in case), and left her apartment. By pure habit, she swiped her key card through the scanner to lock the door, and then frowned at her own forgetfulness. The lack of a familiar, assuring beep was a good reminder. Of course it wouldn't lock right now...

She started down the hall—

Thunk!

—and realized she'd kicked something. She looked down and saw a small parcel with no return address on the floor.

Her spine tingled. She stiffened, eyes glued to the parcel. *A bomb?*

Slowly, carefully, she lowered to a squat. Picked up the box. Gently held it up to her ear and listened. Nothing. She shook it, slowly, and heard something bounce around in there. Scrunching her eyebrows, she glanced back and forth down either end of the hall to make sure no one was watching before she ripped the parcel open.

Inside was another computer drive. Taped to it was a small note reading: 'B, AND THE R'S.'

B1

With her sunglasses resting on her forehead, Becky made her way down to the B1 district through one of the thousands of hidden walkways built to avoid monitoring and detection by the Altieria Corporation. The pedestrian footbridge snaked into concrete blocks, through dark (due to the power outage) tunnels with hundreds of rusted pipes running along the walls like tangled vines. A cool, musty breeze blew through the tunnels, accompanied by an eerily low hum that never seemed to end. She kicked through piles of trash strewn about on the floors as she delved deeper into the darkness, holding her cell phone up to light the way.

Eventually, she came across the pedestrian lane that ran alongside the eight-lane freeway that connected the surface world with B1. She followed the lane up to the B1 entry toll gate (which had been semi-transformed into a police checkpoint) and hesitated. Usually the toll gates were run by B1 officers, who weren't exactly operating under the government's orders, but under the self-appointed security organization set strictly within B1's borders. The incoming traffic lanes on the freeway were clogged with vehicles. Cops inspected every vehicle, making vehicular entry into the district much slower than usual. An average of one vehicle per lane was allowed through every three minutes. The same process applied to all outgoing traffic, as well.

Becky approached the toll gate, slow and uneasy. Her sunglasses helped mask the worry in her eyes, and she did her best to maintain a nonchalant expression as she paid the fee and moved inside. She held her breath when she passed through the crowd of police officers, thanking any god that may be listening that they weren't looking for her. That alone probably ensured her safe entry into the area.

"Hey, you!"

...Or not.

Becky didn't even make it fifteen paces down the sidewalk before she had to whirl around to face the two officers approaching her. "Yes?" she said, hoping she didn't sound as shaky as she felt.

"I didn't see anyone search you," one of them said.

Oh, no, she thought as her heart caught itself in her throat. *The knife... the box!* She took a tentative step back as they got closer.

Sensing her hesitation, one of the officers placed his hand on his holstered gun. His partner said, "We'll need to search you, ma'am. We can't let anyone into this district without clearance."

Becky was speechless.

"Do you have any ID on you, ma'am?"

"N-no, I forgot it at home," she said.

The officers traded looks.

"Look, I'm in a hurry," she said as she slowly tucked her hand in the back pocket of her jeans, feeling for the paring knife. "All you wanted was a quick frisk, right?"

"That's right, ma'am," one of the officers said with a dutiful nod. "We just want to make sure you're not carrying any illegal contraband."

"Illegal contraband?" she asked, hoping to buy herself some time. "Don't be ridiculous. I'm just down here to visit a friend." Her index finger and her thumb slipped into the back pocket and touched the knife handle. She started to pull it up... up...

"Ma-am," the officer on the right said, "please keep your hands where we can see them, or we'll be forced to take action."

Feigning innocence, Becky raised her eyebrows and said, "Whoa, now. Easy, tiger. I'm just scratching an itch." She held up her left hand, still pulling the knife out with her right. "I spent the whole morning sitting in a really uncomfortable chair."

"We understand, but you still have to comply."

The knife was out. She slipped it into the waistband of her pants behind her back and pushed it down. Thankfully, the edge didn't slice her buttock, and the point didn't cut through the fabric of her pants as she pushed the knife down to her thigh.

"Ma'am!"

Startled, she threw up both hands. "Alright, alright! Jeez!" Inconspicuously, she shook her left leg, causing the knife to slide down her thigh to her ankles. She nearly jolted when the blade made a shallow slice down her leg on its way down. It landed on the heel of her shoe, just barely sticking out from under her pant leg.

The cop on the left started toward her, doing his best to look big and menacing by straightening his back and puffing out his chest.

She shook the knife out of her pant leg. It fell to the sidewalk.

The cop reached her.

She stepped back, hiding the knife under her shoe. "Easy there, tiger."

He made somewhat quick work of frisking her, patting down each leg and working his way up. Of course, much to her complete lack of surprise, he lingered on her breasts, cupping them while awkwardly struggling to maintain a dutiful expression on his face.

"Oh, yeah, I've got some real hardcore explosives packed in those," Becky said sarcastically.

The cop frowned and backed away. "Alright. You're clear. Have a nice day."

Becky waited until the cops returned to their posts before she quickly scooped the knife up and speed-walked down the sidewalk. She rounded the nearest corner, eager to be completely out of the checkpoint's view.

The district didn't have any power either, with the exception of the streetlights and a few buildings running on backup generators. Since not everyone can afford expensive backup generators, most of the district was dark. Usually the place was bustling, lit up bright as day. Now, with the ceiling above it, and only the backups, it was like the middle of the night. Aside from a few passing vehicles on the road and scarce pedestrians on the sidewalks and footbridges, the B1 district seemed dead.

After twenty minutes of walking into the denser parts of the district—a near-indecipherable labyrinth of bright neon, steel and concrete on good days—with her cell phone lighting the way, Becky took a winding stairway into a darker abyss. After a three-storey descent into a tunnel, deeper underground, she figured she was technically in B2 now.

She stepped out into a corridor. A rusted sign with faded lettering reading 'B CK TO T E WAY IT WA' dangled from a pair of frayed cords above the entrance. Once she'd entered the corridor, she immediately noticed a yellow sign flickering above a steel door at the very end, on her right. The sign was the only source of light in the hall. Becky went straight for it, walking thirty paces before reaching it. She banged her fist against the door five times, waited a beat, then banged it another two times, another beat, and then hit it with one final, louder knock.

After a few moments, a slot in the door slid open, revealing a pair of steely eyes that scrutinized Becky's appearance. A gravelly voice grinded through the slot, "You know the secret knock, yet you don't look like one of our friends. Identify yourself."

"Becky Trickle. Traditional News."

"A reporter? Here?"

"C'mon, Juon knows me. Go get him."

Eyebrows arched above the steely eyes. "Juon?"

Becky nodded. "I'm on your side, Karl. Did you forget about me already?"

The eyes narrowed with suspicion. "Hmm... you do seem familiar... wait a moment."

The slot slammed shut. Becky waited exactly thirty seconds for a new set of eyes to appear through the slot.

"Becky?"

"Juon."

The slot slid shut with a metallic clap. Becky listened to a handful of locks come undone. The door opened ten seconds later, revealing a tall, muscular, dishevelled man in light tactical clothes. He had a layer of stubble all over his chiselled jaw, piercing green eyes, and a mop of short hazelnut hair under a grey military cap. Becky wrinkled her nose at the stinking aroma of alcohol, sweat, and puke that struck her like a tidal wave as soon as the door opened. It was so powerful she staggered a bit.

Juon stared at her, still touching the edge of the door with his left hand and holding a half-empty bottle of tequila by the neck in his right fist. "Come to ask me to take you back?"

"Get over yourself, Juon," she said as she started through the doorway.

Juon knew better than to stay in her way, so he moved aside to let her through, stole a peek into the empty corridor, and then shut the door behind them. "What brings you here, then? You weren't followed, were you? Becky, if you were followed—"

"No, Juon. I wasn't followed," she answered as she crossed the dimly lit room, which was in complete disarray. Old papers were strewn all over the floor. Puddles of spilled booze could be seen around and under the wooden table set against the left wall and a layer of maps spread over its surface. Two chairs were set near the table, though one had been toppled. Opened crates full of alcoholic beverages or bristling with rifles were clustered together in the far corner of the room next to the bathroom door, which was shut. The fan was on, but it wasn't enough to get the disgusting smell that pervaded Becky's nostrils, strong enough to make her gag. "I see you've started drinking again."

Juon watched her fold her arms across her chest in disappointment as she plonked down into the non-toppled chair. For additional effect, she strung one leg over the other and glared at him, jaw tightly closed. With a sigh, he asked again, "I told you not to come back."

"I have something important. I didn't know who else I could come to."

"So you came to me." Juon crossed the room, around her. He righted the previously toppled chair and sat on it, backwards, leaning forward on the back of it. "This'd better be important."

"Where'd Karl disappear to?"

Juon pointed his thumb at the closed bathroom door. "Didn't cook his steak all the way through last night."

Becky recoiled at the disgusting images that crept into her mind and quickly decided to focus on more important matters. "You have a computer somewhere in this pigsty?"

Juon leaned to the side and swiped a pile of maps off the table to reveal a closed laptop.

Becky glanced at it, then asked in a degrading tone, "Does it work?"

Matching her sarcasm, Juon replied, "Only if you're nice to it."

Becky took Orion's box out of her coat pocket and placed it next to the computer.

Juon took it in his hands and flipped it around, examining every side. He stopped when he looked at the bottom and read what was scribbled on it: "1-8-5-7."

"It's the combination."

"Thanks, Rebekah. Couldn't have possibly figured *that* one out on my own."

Her scowl intensified.

Juon ignored her, entering the combination into the box. It clicked open, revealing the drive inside. "A computer drive?" He looked up at her. "This is the part where you start explaining to me what the point of all this is."

And explain, she did. She told him about Orion approaching them out of nowhere, severely wounded and seemingly desperate. She described Orion's harebrained scheme to broadcast the contents of the drive to the world by taking over the Altieria Radio Tower. Once she finished explaining everything, she handed Juon the second drive she'd received earlier that morning with the note still taped to it.

"You're saying a cop did all this?" he asked in disbelief.

She nodded.

"And you believed it?"

"He was too hysterical not to believe." To further back up her opinion, she added, "He didn't seem to have any qualms about shooting up Altierian soldiers. And he was at the power plant when it exploded."

"Rebekah, he could be on an undercover assignment, for all you know. Christ." He tapped his index finger against his forehead. "Think about it! They've been trying to infiltrate us for years." He picked up the second drive and waved it around. "God only knows, this is probably bugged."

"And what if it's not? What if he's telling the truth?"

Juon shrugged.

"Don't you have some kind of masking program that protects your computer from being detected?"

"Of course."

"So what's the problem?!"

"…I missed my last security update."

"Are you fucking kidding me?" she exclaimed.

"Not really." He looked at the tequila in his hand, as if he'd just remembered he had it, and took a generous swig.

"We should be fine. I trust this guy."

"Like I trusted you?"

"Please, don't start this now."

Frowning, Juon squinted at her. She returned his glare

defiantly.

As usual, Juon folded. "Fine," he said as he opened the laptop. "Let's see what's on it."

Becky scooted up next to him, and together they watched the disturbing footage that Orion had recorded inside Altieria Corp. HQ. They listened to everything he had to say about Elsa Scott's murder, Barstow's rampage, CEO/H3@D's secret incubator chamber, Michael Crimmons and his involvement, Franklin Scott's possible involvement, and so on. Their attention hung on every word he spoke, their jaws falling open inch by inch for every minute that Entry #9 played on. The entry played all the way through Orion's back-and-forth banter with the CEO and his shootout with the cyborgs. His escape, and so on. It ended when he killed the cyborg in the bathroom stall. There was nothing after that.

But it was enough to leave Becky and Juon staring at the screen, slack-jawed.

After a few minutes of stunned silence, Juon whispered, "Jesus Heisenberg Christ." Jabbing his index finger at the screen, he turned to Becky and said, "Have you seen this?"

She shook her head slowly. "I haven't been able to with the power outage."

"What happened to the laptop I got you? It lasts for days without getting plugged in."

"It's in the shop…"

He sighed.

"It had a virus," she said.

"Great. Moving on. Back to this." He gestured toward the laptop again. "This is… this could put enough heat on the CEO to give him fourth-degree burns. It might even take him out of power. A cop recorded this, right? That could add a little more weight to it than if a regular civilian did it."

"So what should we do? Broadcast it?"

"Why go through the trouble of taking over to a heavily guarded tower when we can just leak it onto the internet? Put it out on every forum we've got?"

"Oh," she said with a shrug. "I guess we could do that instead." She added, "I wonder why Orion didn't think of that…"

"He sounds like an old-timer. Probably isn't all that internet-savvy." Juon was so excited that he couldn't get his trembling hand to work across the mouse pad properly. He clicked the internet icon and waited… waited…

No connection available…

Juon's heart turned to lead and dropped into his gut. He refreshed the page. Same bullshit. "What the fuck!" he snarled.

Becky looked at the screen in despair. "I-it's the power outage. We'll have to wait."

Grinding his teeth in frustration, Juon moved to close the laptop. "Son of a bitch."

"Wait." She stopped him and handed him the second drive. "Let's look at this one, too."

Juon took it and shoved it into a different port, still keeping the first drive plugged in. A new window opened, revealing a document file and a video file. Juon opened the video file.

Orion's face appeared on the screen, twisting in pain. He looked even worse than he did when Becky last saw him. "Well, Beck, sorry to sound all familiar, but I figured it'd be smart to refrain from using your full name, just in case someone else picked this up before you did. If that possibility becomes a bleak reality, then I hope whoever's watching will be smart enough to follow my instructions. If you're the ones I'm recording this message for, you'll know where to go. Bring this and the evidence drive to the Conservatives. Show this message, too. On that drive… is concrete evidence that the CEO of Altieria Corporation isn't at all who he appears to be. The shit I recorded wasn't even the half of it. The power outage may last for a while, since I destroyed the power station. It's a damned inconvenience, I know. But it was something I had to do. All those psychokinetic citizens that were forced into registration didn't die off. They were captured and imprisoned in a large chamber. Their powers were somehow used… or I guess 'harvested' would be a more accurate word to use… to provide the entire planet with energy. Somehow, he's turned these people into an energy source, and the one I destroyed wasn't the only one. I think there are hundreds more, scattered all around the globe, deep underground. I disrupted the network, but…"

His voice trailed off. He grimaced and looked down at his twisted left hand. He forced his next words through gritted teeth: "I don't have much time. Listen to me, and listen carefully: show the rebels everything. I met their brain… computer… thing with my partner, who… died in the raid. They'll confirm my authenticity. If you don't receive a message from me in the next five days, assume me dead and proceed with the plan I described. Remember: five days from the morning you get this message. Be there at noon. Get the message out there. Agh..." He gripped his wounded hand and moaned like a beast that somehow survived the hunter's first rifle shot. "Find Franklin Scott. He has to know something. Get him to talk. Find out what happened to his wife. Check out the apartment on Price Street. It's all connected somehow. The malfunctions. The riots. Scott's wife's murder. I know it. I just... know..."

He leaned back against a wall, breathing heavily, totally exhausted. He looked like he was about to faint from blood loss. "I left something at the main objective. It ought to disrupt them. Might even allow you entry. You'll know it when it happens." Orion forced a smile on his worn, exhausted face. "Good luck to you."

The video ended.

Juon stared at the computer screen for a few moments. Then he said, "The 'main objective'... he means the tower, right?"

"Yeah," Becky said.

"He prepared the meal for us. All we have to do is sit at the table and eat it." A beat. He muttered, "That's *if* he didn't poison it during the preparation stage..."

"It's not a trap," Becky said, scowling.

"How can you be so sure? It could all be one big, elaborate ruse to lure us into a death trap. The tower is full of tight spaces and narrow corridors. They could gas us to death with the windows open, for Christ's sake!"

"Call it 'woman's intuition.'"

"Not this again," he groaned, rubbing his temples.

"Please, Juon," she pressed. "Just trust me on this."

He turned in his chair and looked her straight in the eye. He found the kind of stubborn resolve that any respectable reporter should possess. She didn't back down from his glare; her eyes hardened, confident. She always won their staring contests.

This one was no exception.

Juon looked away and heaved a deep sigh.

She placed a firm hand on his shoulder. "Get this down to headquarters. Convince them to come up."

"As if," he scoffed. "If it's so easy, why don't you do it?"

"You know I can't do that," she said. "If anyone notices I'm gone for too long, they'll get suspicious. They'll be restoring power soon, and if I'm not at my desk, people will be asking questions." She leaned closer to him. "Questions are bad, Juon."

"I know," he muttered, frowning at her condescension.

She straightened to her full height. "I need to go. Any smuggling routes still open?"

"The uh... Blade Street tunnel hasn't been compromised. Nothing's working, but if you know where you're going, you should be back on the surface within two hours. You'll need a flashlight."

"I'll need more than that. A gun."

Juon's eyebrows shot up.

"And ammo. Enough to take on a platoon."

Juon shook his head slowly. "I'm not even gonna argue with you on that one..."

She smiled. "Good boy."

After sifting through a crate, Juon handed her a Beretta 92A1 pistol. "These were introduced way back in 2010. It's an oldie, but a goodie. It's not a difficult gun to handle; you just need to know how to—"

His voice trailed off when he watched her speedily disassemble the pistol on the table, inspect every part, put it back together, slap the box mag home, and then pull the slide to chamber a round.

"—do... that," he finished, staring at her with surprise. "When did you learn to...?"

Pointing the gun at the ceiling with her finger on the trigger guard, she looked at him and answered, "High school."

"Right..."

Her eyes gave the gun another once-over before she said, "Give me twenty mags and another one of these."

"Another one?" he sputtered. "I shouldn't even be giving you that one!"

"I'm an ally of the rebellion. You totally have to help me out when I need it. And you know what would really help me out?" She fixed him with an impatient glare. "Twenty mags and another one of these. Do you understand?"

Juon scrunched his eyebrows, frustrated. "Goddamn it. Fine."

Once again, she smiled sweetly. "Thanks, honey."

She was heading out with two 92A1s holstered on shoulder

harnesses under her coat and pockets full of spare box magazines, along with a small electric lantern in her left hand. She stopped with her foot in the door and said to him, "I'm trusting you on this one. Don't let me down."

"I'll get it to them as soon as I can," he assured her. "What're you gonna do until the power is restored? Maybe I should send someone with you…"

"No, Juon, I'll be fine. You just focus on prepping up the big guys downstairs." She reached up and stole the military cap right off his head and pulled it down on her own, adjusting it to her liking with the visor over her eyes. "As for what I'll be doing… I'll be looking for Franklin Scott. Hopefully I'll get something useful out of him before the deadline. Five days, right? Did he mean today?"

"Probably." He couldn't hide the worry on his face. "Be careful."

"You know me," she said with a confident smirk. "Always throwing myself to the wind to see where I'll land."

"Thanks for the assuring words…"

With a twinkle in her eye, she looked up at him with that charming smile of·hers. She raised herself on the tips of her boots and planted a small kiss on his lips. She noted the surprised look on his face and said, "Be good."

Then she jogged down the corridor, leaving him stunned in the doorway.

He came to his senses before she was out of earshot and called after her, "Does this mean we're dating again?"

"Nope!" she called back from the stairwell.

He slinked back into the room and muttered, "Goddamn it."

42: Fisheye

Price Street

With the trains down and the taxi service out of commission for the time being, Becky had to walk and rely on old tourist maps to get to her destination. Since Mickey had dropped her off at her apartment and had taken the van, it wasn't like she could return home for it.

In a small matter of hours, she reached the corner of James and Price Street—the latter of which, to her dismay, was a seven-kilometre stretch of road through the center of the residential district. Orion didn't specify which one of the hundreds of apartment buildings she should look for. It was good that he'd taken precautionary measures just in case the message ended up in the wrong hands, but she cursed him nonetheless for complicating her search.

She entered the lobbies of two apartment complexes and looked through the tenant lists. No Scott.

Her heart heavy with discouragement, Becky left the second apartment and stepped back into the steady flow of midday pedestrian traffic that shifted up and down the sidewalk. There were fewer robots than usual walking among the humans and the cybernetically enhanced citizens—something she noted with mild uneasiness.

Another block. Another thirty-storey apartment building. She broke out of the pedestrian throng and entered the lobby through glass doors. She looked at the tenant list, hoping that this would be the one...

It was! What a lucky break!

Level 7: Apartment 401: Scott, Franklin.

Relief washed over her. "Gotcha."

With her sunglasses raised to the top of her head, she treaded lightly through the lobby, which was illuminated by emergency lights that drowned it in deep red saturation. Went up seven flights of stairs. Every step she took reverberated through the levels of the secluded stairwell in hollow, metallic echoes. She reached the door leading into the hall and stopped to check her guns. Ready to go. She tucked them into her jacket's deep pockets. Then she entered the corridor, also lit with the same deep red as the lobby, and followed the apartment numbers.

379... 381... 383....

Becky gulped. *What if Juon's right? What if I'm walking into a trap?*

385... 387... 389...

Her heartbeat quickened. She stuffed her hands in her pockets and gripped her pistols, being sure to keep her index fingers on the trigger guards.

391... 393... 395...

Faint noises from behind closed doors passed her by. Muffled shouting. Children laughing. Hammering. The buzzing of the emergency lights.

397... 399... 401.

End of the hall, with only another stairway beyond. She reached her stop. She tentatively reached for the door when a thought crossed her mind: *would the magnetic locks be disabled here, too? Could I just sneak in?* She scrunched her eyebrows and shook her head at herself. *What would be the point of that? That'd just complicate things.* She glanced up, instinctively, and saw a camera lens in the corner, staring right at her.

Her eyes quickly dropped to the door again. She rapped it with her right fist.

Seated at the dining room table, Franklin and Elsa looked up from the half-eaten pasta on their plates. Elsa stood up—

"No, no," Franklin said, bolting out of his chair. "I'll get it."

She looked at him, struck curious by his reaction. "You're jumpy all of a sudden... is everything alright?"

He did his best reassuring laugh. "It's fine. I just didn't want some ill-timed visitor to spoil your lunch."

She chuckled. "My lunch isn't spoiled."

"Sit down, sit down," he said with a smile. "I've got this one."

Sit down.

"Okay, sweetheart." She did as she was told, cocking a slight eyebrow as she glanced toward the direction of the living room in response to the strange voice. *What kind of experiments are in that room?*

Franklin looked through the peep hole. When he saw Becky on the other side, he was both confused and curious about her visit. Tentatively, he disabled the magnetic lock and opened the door a crack. "What do you want?"

Not all that surprised by Franklin's anti-social behaviour, Becky introduced herself, "Good afternoon, Mr. Scott. My name is—"

"I know who you are," Franklin snapped, "what do you want?"

"I was hoping I could speak to you about your wife's murder."

"I'm not interested in speaking with reporters. Especially about that. Especially to *you*."

Becky frowned. "It'll only take a few minutes of your time."

"I said, I'm not interested. Now go away." He tried to close the door, only to be stopped by her foot. "Get out of my way, or I'll call the police," he hissed, trying to be as quiet as possible without alarming his wife in the kitchen. His attempts to kick her foot out of the doorway were foiled by her stubbornness. "As I take it, you're already on thin ice with the justice department."

Becky insisted, "Look, I have to speak to you!"

Still struggling with her foot, Franklin leaned toward her and hissed, "If you don't leave right now, I will call the authorities."

"Good luck doing that with this blackout."

"There's an emergency hotline that works under any circumstance for... superior citizens such as myself, you know."

"You rich people have all the toys, don't you?"

"Get out!"

Becky gave up. No sense in forcing her way in for some answers he may not even have. Having the cops pursuing her would be the last thing she'd need. "Fine. Okay," she said as she pulled her foot out. She blinked when Franklin slammed the door and locked it with a telltale clack. "Sensitive, aren't we?"

Franklin returned to the table with a relieved sigh.

"Who was that?" Elsa asked. "You look tense, honey."

"I'm just stressed. Work. Just work."

"Who was at the door?"

"No one. Just one of those witnesses."

"Oh," she said, eyebrows furrowing.

*

Becky craned her neck, looking up at the camera's fisheye lens, fixed on her. *Am I mistaken, or is it... zooming in on me?*

Orion. That was her next thought. *They know.*

Her heart skipped. She hurried further down the hall, the opposite direction from which she came, for another stairwell. A noise prompted her to turn around while she approached the stairwell, peering down the corridor. She hit the push bar with her arm and stumbled onto a landing, immediately hearing more noises—

—and looked down through the grated floor to see men in black suits working their way up a few levels below her.

Oh, shit.

Becky started up the stairs, skipping three steps at a time. Below her, the metallic thumps of her pursuers' footsteps quickened. *Oh, shit. Oh, shit. Oh, shit.*

She burst through the entrance to the roof. Stumbled forward under the hot afternoon sun, and turning as the door swung shut. Adjusted her sunglasses back on her nose. She could hear the faint stomping of her pursuers, getting louder... closer...

She frantically looked around for a way out, or even something to block the door with. The fire escape to her left? Too obvious. Wait...

Becky darted across the rooftop, shoes clomping on flat, smooth pavement. The thought of those agents coming through the door and seeing her prompted her to run faster. When she reached the ledge, she looked over the side. Down below were rows of cantilever balconies for every individual apartment; ten rows on her side. The street; a thin, narrow line far, far below.

That's a long way down, she thought as she stared at the colourful streams of traffic shifting along, too far down to discern what types they were. The balcony under her looked so inverted she feared she'd miss it if she jumped. Just looking down there made her tense. The fact that she was even considering it made her jittery.

If you don't jump, they'll catch you, she thought to herself as she took in deep, shuddering breaths, leaning over the ledge. *Hurry up. Hurry up. Hurry up. Hurry! Hurry! Hurry!*

She sucked in air. Held it as she threw herself over the side. The wind rushing up from under her. Air whistling in her ears. Her heart pounded its way up into her throat, choking her scream as the balcony came up to meet her with surprising speed. The street did the same, threatening to meet her instead.

The door swung outward by the leading agent's kick. Five agents in all gathered on the roof, LE magnums drawn, eyes scanning the area for any vital signs. One of them immediately went over to the fire escape and peered over the ledge, and snorted with mild surprise when he saw no one there.

Becky landed on a rubber mat, flat on her face. All air smacked out of her chest. She lay there only for a moment, feeling an unbearable tingling that made her shake uncontrollably. Relieved to be alive, but terrified of the possibilities of her dying today.
She pushed herself up on wobbling legs, gripping the balcony's safety rail for support. She glanced up, and a new horrifying possibility gripped her: they're going to look over the side and find her. She crossed the balcony and tried the handle on the screen door. Locked. *Shit.*
She whirled around. Looked down at the solid metal floor she was so grateful for. And then… a new, much more terrifying idea popped into her head. *Oh, please, God, no.*
She approached the safety rail. Gripped it with sweaty hands. Looked over the side. The height, the sheer danger of falling made her want to vomit. *I can't do this. I can't…*
Despite her thoughts screaming for her to stop, Becky tightened her grip on the railing and swung her left leg over it and found a small foothold under the railing, on the floor ledge. Her right leg followed. Now she was hanging over total oblivion. If the hairs on the back of her neck weren't rising before, they were now. Her heart pounded so fast it was starting to heat up. She wanted to close her eyes. Wanted this all to end.
She gulped down a lump of fear and released her right foot from the ledge, dangling it above the street. "Oh," she gasped, "this is a bad fuckin' idea."
She let go of the railing. Felt like floating at first, but the speed of her descent quickly picked up. Looked down, watching the twenty-ninth floor rush up past her with a whoosh. A sharp, terrified scream escaped her lungs as she threw her hands out and snatched the safety rail of the twenty-eighth balcony. Came to an abrupt stop;

the weight of her body nearly tearing her arms out of their sockets. Her chest slammed into the posts. "Whuff!"

One of the agents straightened his back. "Did you hear that?" His comrades looked at him.

She hung there, gripping the railing with everything she had, struggling to lift her feet up to find some kind of hold. The sounds of traffic rumbled below her, reminding her that the slightest slipup would mean certain death.

The agent had heard her. Now he was approaching the edge.

Her foot found the ledge. She only had to stab herself in the chest with her own knee.

The agent reached the ledge.

Becky heaved herself over the railing.

The agent leaned out, looked down at the balconies and saw—

She flipped over a small table, landed on her back.

—nothing but the street and the balconies down there. The agent's small mouth tightened. "Strange," he said, "I know I heard someone."

Another agent approached him. "Most likely one of the residents on a lower floor."

"Perhaps," the agent replied. Beat. "Or perhaps not."

"What do you mean?"

"Could she have possibly jumped?"

"Don't be absurd."

A third agent approached them. "It's possible. She is an absurd woman, after all."

Agent #2 looked at Agent #3. "Do you honestly believe...?"

Agent #1 cut him off: "Never underestimate a suspect on the run."

ALEXANDER ENGEL-HODGKINSON

43: Claustrophobia

Becky lay on the floor, gasping for air, drenched in a cold sweat. For the longest time, she couldn't move. Totally rigid with fear. Her heartbeat a set of war drums in her ears.

Get a grip. Get a goddamn grip, Rebekah.

She rolled toward the screen door, got up, and tried the handle. It snapped open. She stumbled inside, looking around the empty apartment. It bared a striking similarity to Franklin's apartment, although the interior decorating wasn't as plentiful or intricate, and there was no frosted wall to divide it into sections. Aside from the two bedrooms, the basement, and the bathroom, and a half-glass partition wall that enclosed the kitchen, the apartment was mostly one big open space.

No one seemed to be home.

She ran through the living room, tripping over a Persian rug in the process, reached the door, opened it, and peeked out into the corridor.

All clear.

She took one of her pistols out of her jacket and checked it for a chambered round. Good to go. She stepped out of the apartment and looked down both ends of the corridor. She could hear them, but she couldn't see them. She figured the stairs were off limits, and despite the apartment having its own generator, the elevators were probably an unsafe bet. She decided it would probably be best to stay in the apartment.

Becky retreated into the apartment and quietly shut the door. She put her ear against it, listening for any approaching footsteps. Her racing heartbeat made it difficult to differentiate the two similar rhythms from each other. Something was getting louder.

She backed away from the door, taking light steps, eyes fixed on the door, expecting it to swing open at any moment. She knew the kitchen had few hiding places. That just left the bathroom and the bedrooms—

Voices outside.

"Was it this one?"

"I believe so."

Shit!

No time to pick and choose. Becky scrambled for the nearest closed door, threw it open, and leaped inside.

The apartment entrance opened, and three agents filed inside with their magnums drawn.

"Search the area," Agent #1 said. "She couldn't have gone far. Did security see her in the halls?"

"Negative," Agent #2 answered.

"Then she's most likely in here."

Becky took in her surroundings. She was in the bathroom. A spacious, square room with a separate bathtub (which was more like a hot tub) and shower stall set beside each other. To her left, the sink and panoramic mirror. To her right, the toilet and closet.

Nowhere to hide where they wouldn't think to look. She cursed her bad luck. *Now what?*

Agent #3 approached the bathroom door, gun ready. Without making a sound, he threw it open to find—

—nothing. No one.

She was curled up on the bottom of the hot tub, stiff, holding her breath. Her sweaty fist squeezed the grip of her pistol.

He checked the walk-in closet first and pushed back the robes hanging on the bar. The rest of the compartments were too small to hide in. He turned.

She heard his footsteps get closer.

He approached the sink. Went down on one knee and opened the cupboard under the counter.

Nothing but cleaning supplies and toiletries.

She flinched when he slammed the cupboards shut. Now he was getting closer.

He opened the solid metal shower stall door and looked inside. With a grunt, he shut the door and stole a quick glance into the hot tub.

Luckily for her, the tub was deep, and the agent made a half-assed look inside it. He didn't see the bottom and, satisfied, left the bathroom. When she heard the door close, she put her hand over her mouth and exhaled. Breathing normally was impossible. She was damn-near dry-heaving.

*

When they finished searching all the rooms, the trio gathered in the living room.

"Area clear," Agent #2 declared. "She must have climbed further down."

Agent #1 made a disappointed scowl. "How vexing…"

Even after she heard them leave the apartment in silence, Becky didn't move from her hiding place. She never broke her fetal position, trembling violently, holding her breath every time she heard the slightest noise.

Died… I almost died… they would have killed me…

She remained for what seemed like hours. Once the fear and adrenaline ceased, her body calmed down faster than she realized, and she unwittingly fell right to sleep.

44: Exit

Voices interrupted her sleep. Becky stirred, squinting as the cold floor of the hot tub touching her face once again became a reality. The gun in her hand—which miraculously didn't go off in her sleep—felt strange and alien, grasped by loose, numb fingers.

Voices from outside. The tenants had returned.

"That was wonderful, dear." A woman, clearly pleased about something.

"Yes, I was quite pleased with it, myself." A man, obviously proud that he'd satisfied his significant other.

Becky's muscles went taut. A new terror snatched her heart with an icy, clawed hand. *I can't believe I...!*

She listened to a series of garbled sentences and a few distinguishable words in otherwise indecipherable mixtures, some giggling, and the unmistakable clattering of shoes being kicked against a wall. Footsteps approached the bathroom door. Becky's heart raced as she did her best to listen, hoping that door wouldn't open. Praying no one would turn the lights on and discover her.

The footsteps passed her and receded. The giggling faded. A door slammed shut.

Becky pulled herself out of the hot tub as quietly as was humanly possible for someone who had just woken up in a cold sweat. She flicked the safety on and stuffed the gun in her pocket as she went to the door with cat-like footsteps. Pressed her ear against the door. The only things she could hear were the droning of the air conditioning system and the faint rattling of bedsprings. She opened the bathroom door and peeked into the open-spaced living room/dining room. The rhythmic whining of bedsprings, along with the pleasurable moaning of the woman in the bedroom at the far end of the apartment, became much more evident.

Becky rolled her eyes and made her way toward the main entrance. She went through the closet. Took out a thick fur coat with a raccoon tail-lined hood (most likely fake, due to the endangerment of the species), slipped into it, and left the apartment with barely another sound.

With the hood pulled down over her face, Becky was confident that surveillance wouldn't detect her.

She started down the corridor, hunched over to keep the hood from slipping back, hands in her pockets. She passed a few random tenants in the corridor and in the dimly lit stairwell during her descent, all of whom gave her suspicious looks. *Do I stand out that much? Guess it's still too warm for a coat, huh?*

She stopped on the landing under the second floor and looked over the handrail to see a cop standing guard at the lobby entrance. She hesitated, wondering if a simple coat and sunglasses would be enough to fool him. He was no agent, after all, but some cops had eyeball modifications—and others went the whole nine yards and had completely artificial implants replace their natural eyes. If either scenario applied to this one in particular, Becky was in deep shit. While there was a chance that the blackout crippled the cop's abilities to scan her distinguishable facial features and match them with a name and other identification information in less than three seconds, Becky wasn't too keen on taking the risk.

Not that she had any choice. She suspected that the elevators weren't supported by the building's emergency power system, and she sure as hell wasn't about to jump off another balcony again.

Just act inconspicuous, she consoled herself. *Act natural. Those tenants were just being weird.*

The cop looked up at her. His orange eyes sparkled unnaturally in the fluorescent lights' dim glow... her blood ran cold in her veins... her chest felt like it'd suddenly frozen over... her heart stopped—while his eyes paralyzed her.

One second. He drew his gun. Fired it at her. Two shots. The handrail spat sparks in her face. Becky screamed as she flew back; slamming against the wall in the corner, out of his sight. Her startled reaction to the cop's deafening beat is what saved her life. She took a moment to see smoke rising from the spot in the handrail where the first bullet hit. Then she noticed the second bullet hole in the wall above her. Would've blown her goddamn head off.

The cop started up the stairs, pistol ready in two strong hands. Step after harrowing step, he came up to her. He straightened his back and stretched his head up. The muzzle of his gun moved in perfect sync with his eyes. When her form, huddled in the corner, finally appeared in his field of vision—

She'd already taken out her own pistol and blasted his skullcap back down those stairs. His body toppled after the fragments.

Becky sucked in air. Deep, deep breaths. Gripping her gun in tight, sweaty little fists that wouldn't stop shaking. She knew she had to move—so she made quick work of that, skipping most of the steps on her way down the last flight of stairs. She didn't give the dead cop a second look. She didn't need to add that image to the collection of horrific memories she'd already stored up from her many days as an on-scene reporter.

She yanked the door open.

Five cops met her in the lobby, just ten feet away. They didn't hesitate. This time, neither did she. Before any more bullets were fired her way, she'd already slammed the door shut and scrambled down another staircase into P1. The loud bang of the lobby door being shoved open followed her to the P1 entrance—which was bordered by bulletproof windows.

She burst through the door; whirled around, slammed it shut. She shed the fur coat, looped it through the door handle, and wrapped the arms around the base of the decommissioned ID scanning console. Her hands fervently twisted a couple knots to hold the door shut.

The cops reached the windows. The door shook as they pounded and pulled on it. Becky stepped out from behind the door into their sight. They punched and kicked at the windows, which only rattled slightly. She gloated at them, hands on her hips.

"Alright, get back, get back!" one of the cops snarled as he drew his service revolver and aimed it at Becky, who stood her ground. For the sake of her pride, she took her chances and continued to gloat defiantly at them, figuring the windows were most likely—hopefully—bulletproof.

Another cop spoke up," Uh, that's not gonna do—"

"Shut up and get around me." The cops' buddies made a circle around him. He hunched forward, aimed for Becky's face, fired—

Becky jumped, startled.

—and after the deafening pop of the revolver going off, and the ping of the ricochet, the cop who fired pivoted forward with only one eye left. His brains had painted the walls behind him a near-black shade of red. His buddies groaned in surprised disgust, recoiling from the sight.

Becky knit her brows. Then she turned and disappeared further into the depths of the garage, leaving the cops behind a glass wall, cursing and swearing at the door that just wouldn't open.

45: Countdown/3

Altieria Streets—Day 3

Her phone had died. There wasn't a digital clock within a thousand kilometres that worked. These days, few traditions lived. Battery-powered clocks were scarce.

Despite losing track of time, Becky figured that it had to have been past midnight by now. Not a star twinkled in the black sky. More buildings had electricity than the night before, but for the most part, the city maintained its strangely alien feel. Since the blackout began, Altieria City felt like a dark, menacing place to be. A place without stability. Something about the overwhelming blotches of shadows and blackness that filled the streets and bled from the windows and inoperative overhead electric lights and screens sent chills down Becky's spine. No music played from any of the shops. Music always played. Now there was silence. Now the upstanding citizens took solace in their dark homes (or, if they were lucky to have a generator, lit homes). Now, the freaks roamed the streets.

Becky zipped up her jacket and tucked her hands in her pockets as she passed by a group of middle-aged men in rags gathered round a flaming garbage bin. She could feel their eyes ogling her form as she walked briskly by. She kept her footsteps light, listening for something that would betray the sneaking intentions of any would-be pursuers.

None came. Not on this block. All they did was gaze at her and chatter amongst themselves about how good she looked. They didn't abandon their warm bonfires for the flesh of an unwilling woman.

As she walked on, she could hear music in the distance. Screaming, electronic squealing, rhythmic booming. As she got closer, she saw hues of orange light flickering above the tops of smaller shops and row-houses, and reflecting off the window panes of office buildings and other skyscrapers.

Some areas were infested with punks. The kinds of punks Becky thought only existed in the movies from a long-passed time, with studded leather outfits and rebellious hairstyles. They gathered in overpass tunnels... burning garbage in the streets... looting nearby stores... blasting metal on portable stereos. Laughing. Hollering. Drinking. Spinning donuts on their motorcycles. Harassing passersby. Those with cybernetic prosthetic limbs held mock wrestling tournaments within the boundaries of crudely put-up rings consisting of emergency beacons and an overturned police cruiser.

Becky had to climb up a fire escape and cross a tenement rooftop to see it all. They'd transformed a small portion of downtown into a blazing mad house. She was especially irked when they tossed a pipe bomb into one of her favourite cafés, causing a fireball that cleared the place right out into the street.

"Bastards," she hissed.

Then—

"Halt! Cease all unlawful activities immediately! We are authorized to use deadly force, if necessary!"

—a police BTR-90 appeared up the street, auto-cannon aimed at the punk infestation. The automated voice repeated its message, followed by, "Disperse now!"

The punks responded with obscenities and hurled trash at the BTR-90.

The BTR-90 complied—the auto-cannon blasted their crude wrestling ring into flying shrapnel. The punks scattered like a colony of startled rats. The auto-cannon blew up a group of bikers, launching whatever was left of them in a bulging fireball. The android perched in the machine gun turret opened up on the fleeing mass, cutting them down to a fine paste.

Becky turned away from the massacre and rushed back to the fire escape, leaving the harrowing sounds of screams and gunfire and explosions behind.

From then on, all Becky could see were cops and street patrol—which weren't quite the same as cops, as they were 24/7 Altierian androids that roamed the dark streets in tanks, BTR-90s, and armour-plated combat suits. They were quick and vicious. A single twenty-man platoon was fully capable of wiping out entire armies in guerrilla combat on their own. Basically, they were elite robot commandos.

And they were everywhere.

Becky couldn't walk ten feet without being forced to seek out a hiding place. They would be able to ID her and cut her down in less than five seconds. Their searchlights strobed every sidewalk, every storefront.

Once the latest patrol went by, she eased out from behind a garbage can and approached a dollar store, which had all of its windows smashed in by looters. Not much luck in finding what she needed here, but she figured it was worth a shot. Stealing constant glances over her shoulders, Becky leaped through one of the windows and searched the aisles, which had items strewn all over the floor. The shelves were almost stripped completely bare. The commercial refrigerators had been smashed open. The corpses of a few looters lay scattered, probably the result of last-minute shoppers lingering about until the street patrol arrived.

After two minutes of sweeping items back and forth across the floor, she found what she was looking for: a packet of tiny batteries for her lantern. The damn thing was for battery power what the obsolete Hummers were for gasoline—back when gasoline was the primary fuel source for vehicles... a time that has long passed in favour of solar energy.

Light!

Becky hit the floor as a flash of white light swept across the store interior. Outside, another street patrol tank rattled by with ten heavily armed androids perched on top of it. She made herself as flat as possible, not daring to even lift her head to see if they'd passed her yet. As long as she could hear them, it wasn't safe to move. She could feel the light on her. It lingered. Her blood turned ice cold. *Did they find me...?*

No. The spotlight moved on, as did the patrol. When she was sure they were gone, she got up and headed for the back door instead. No way was she going to get out the same way she came in. She ran down the aisle. Slammed her shoulder into the back door's push bar, and staggered into a back alley.

For the most part, everything was eerily quiet, with the exception of a baby crying in one of the windows, and gunfire crackling in the distance.

The streets were off limits.

Where else could she go, but down?

So she stooped down, lifted up a manhole cover, and climbed down the rusted ladder. Halfway down, she took out the lantern and switched it on. She made sure the sewer tunnel was clear of any assailants or other dangers before she jumped off the last few rungs into knee-deep sludge. She groaned as it soaked through her shoes and pant legs.

The tunnel was warm and it smelled like a sweaty corpse in a fast food dumpster on a hot summer day. The air was thick and humid enough to make her gag. The sewer sludge was a dark, putrid green soup mix with garbage and dead things bobbing on the surface. A half-eaten rat carcass brushed up against her leg. She put a hand over her mouth and swallowed down some vomit.

Just don't look at it, she thought to herself, holding the lantern forward while keeping her other hand over her mouth and nose. Keep your eyes forward. She pressed on, trudging through the sludge.

Something caught her eye. A doll with button eyes and a stitched smile and dirty red hair floating toward her like driftwood. Something about it sent a shiver down her spine. She circled around it, letting it pass her. Then she continued on.

She hit a curve in the tunnel, tripping over an object she preferred not to look at. She heard the groan of an overhead pipe and turned around.

The doll. It floated a few feet away from her. Its button eyes stared up at the pipes running along the ceiling.

Am I going crazy? She waved her hand toward it. "Shoo," she said to it.

Nothing. No response. *Well, of course it didn't respond.*

She took a step back, eyeing the doll. The doll didn't move. She took another step back. And another. And another. She pushed back, keeping the lantern's light on the doll. The doll didn't move, which only raised more questions as to why or how it could follow her.

She went around another corner and did her best to run through the sludge. Something was following her. The feeling was familiar enough, with a tingle on her spine and the hairs on the back of her neck standing up. Every time the pipes groaned she felt compelled to look back. She ignored the compulsion, pushing forward as quickly as possible without falling face first into the sludge.

She gave in. Looked back.

The doll stared right at her.

Becky could practically feel an icy hand creeping up her body and squeezing her heart. "What the hell?" she gasped, shining the lantern over it. Something sparkled above it. She squinted, looking closely at the silvery reflections of the lantern on a thin spool of...

...wire?

When she reached out and touched the wire with an index finger, the line became clearer. Her eyes followed the wire up, up, at the pipes above her.

A set of red eyes stared back down at her through a dark gap in the pipes. A low growl echoed.

Terrified, Becky managed a short scream before the thing dropped from the pipes and pounced on her, putting her underwater. Its thick, rough hands clenched around her throat as she struggled with her assailant. He was too big. Too heavy. His boot pinned her stomach to the floor of the tunnel. Her hands splashed about under the oxygen mask fused to his face. Rapid hissing sounds escaped the mask filters as he pushed his weight down on his prey.

No way to fight. The disgusting sludge filled her lungs and burned her throat and nostrils. The taste of week-old protein shakes, blood, and shit coated her tongue. She started to gag, as well as vomit, during her struggle to breathe. She passed out in seconds.

Once his prey went limp, and the air bubbles stopped fizzling on the surface, the predator lifted her out of the sludge and draped her over his shoulder. Covered head-to-toe in thick layers of artificial cow hide and human skin; an oxygen tank on his back, a harpoon gun strapped to his hip, and a helmet made from pots covering part of his oxygen mask, the predator was equipped for the terrain. A scavenger.

He pulled the doll toward him, spooling the wire around his hand before picking up the doll with the same hand, and tucked his bait trap into a large pouch on his hip. The shimmering glow under the sludge intrigued him. He reached into it. Pulled up the glowing lantern and fumbled for a switch. After about a minute of tinkering with it, he managed to turn it off, plunging the tunnel back into total darkness. He tucked the lantern into the same pouch as his baiter and went on his way, relying on the night vision features of his mask to guide his path.

46: Moles

Altierian Sewers

The scavenger carried his new catch through the labyrinthine underground tunnels all the way to an abandoned subway platform with a derailed passenger car left on the tracks, leaning into the platform. These inhabited tunnels were lit by garbage can fires and electric light (achieved through illegal hook-up). The sludge had gradually risen to the leather giant's waist during his short trip to the station.

Others came to the platforms on either side of the station as the scavenger approached from upriver. He scaled the cracked steps leading up to the end of platform C and was instantly surrounded by ratty children. They bombarded him with excited questions about his catch and what other sights he may have seen and how he managed to catch her and who could have what trinkets that may or may not be on her person. The scavenger said nothing and pushed through them. They cleared a path, knowing better than to stand in his way, and followed him all the way to the waiting area—which was surrounded by a half-glass partition border. The glass had been blacked out by paint; or, in areas where the glass had been smashed, the panes were covered up by wooden panels or tattered rags.

Other dwellers were attracted by the children's excited voices and moved from their cots, benches, corners, ventilation shafts, and tents to see what all the commotion was about. Soon all eyes were on the scavenger until he disappeared through the tarp hanging in the doorway of the waiting area. The children stopped at the entrance, peeking around the tarp, not daring to step inside.

The scavenger carried Becky across the humid waiting room lined with rows of plastic seats, which had been converted into crude beds with mouldy, torn blankets and burst pillows for the elderly dwellers. The elders were too tired, too sick, or both to care about the scavenger or his catch. Most of them were amputees, starved to the bone, looking gnarled and rotten, as if they had died years ago.

Some of them had, in fact. The only way to differentiate the living from the dead was by counting the number of flies buzzing around their heads.

Once he'd reached the other side of the waiting room, the scavenger carefully laid Becky down on the floor at the feet of a strange individual. That individual was a child. Early teens. His hair had fallen out due to exposure. His teeth were soft, rotten, black little squares lining the inside of his mouth. Small stones, human bones, and a soggy plastic cup from a fast food restaurant orbited a ballooned head that was too big for his scrawny little body. He sat crossed-legged on a dirty old mattress with narrow eyes that seemed to change colour on a constant basis; blue, purple, red, orange, yellow, green...

Those ever-changing eyes studied Becky's unconscious form, showing no emotion. "You find?" he asked the scavenger.

The scavenger nodded.

"Trinkets?"

The scavenger rummaged through his pouch. Brought up the lantern. Showed it to the boy.

The lantern floated off the scavenger's palm, closed the gap between them, and landed in the boy's outstretched hands for him to study. His eyes glimmered with wonder and awe as he turned it over in his hands again and again. He thumbed the switch by accident. Blinding light filled the room. The boy screamed and threw it away, scurrying into the nearest corner where he shivered and sobbed in terror. The station walls shook as the floor vibrated under the dwellers' feet. Dust and bits of concrete rained down from the ceiling. The station rumbled as if a train was arriving and then some, shaking Becky out of unconsciousness.

Realizing his mistake, the scavenger hurried to console the boy, going down on one knee and scooping him up in his burly arms, rocking him back and forth. Eventually, the tremors died down, and the boy stopped crying.

"Bad," he whined.

When she came to, the first thing Becky felt was the horrible sensation of her stomach twisting into a thousand tiny knots and getting cut up by razorblades she never actually swallowed. It came up before she knew what was going on, bursting out of her mouth and splattering all over the floor. All that sewer sludge she'd swallowed was being rejected. She pulled herself up on one arm.

Her body felt heavier than usual. All she could do was choke and sputter and groan as the sludge burned up her throat and watch in horror as the dark brown-green pool expanded under her.

The boy and the scavenger watched silently as she threw up all over their floor, unperturbed by the sight or the smell. She ran out of fluids to hurl up soon enough, and lost consciousness.

Becky woke up again in a dark chamber with only the faintest blue light keeping it from being pitch black. The chamber stank like more shit and more death. It wasn't nearly as bad as the sewer, but it was no less unbearable. Her back ached. Her stomach kept turning. Every once in a while, she'd gag—nothing came out, since she'd already emptied her stomach hours ago. Her head felt light. Vision, blurred and fuzzy. Body, numb, wracked with a persistent throbbing pain that started in her stomach and worked its way through the rest of her.

She moved, trying to change positions, and discovered that she couldn't because something was clamped around her wrist. A handcuff linked to a pipe connected to the rear end of a grimy old toilet with no seat ensured that she wouldn't be leaving the bathroom stall anytime soon.

She looked around, trying to take in her dark surroundings. The floor was slippery, browned from decay and spills, with needles and cigarettes and joint stubs strewn about—she did her best to push out thoughts about what the liquid she was possibly sitting in was. The ominous blue light flickered above her head, adding to her confusion and terror. She looked up at the fluorescent light buzzing in the ceiling, eyes trailing up the graffiti-coated wall as she did so. The walls had vulgar drawings and phrases carved and spray-painted into them, covering every inch. She turned to the door of the stall on her right, which was locked, of course—on the outside. She turned her head to the toilet on her left, which she didn't dare look into. No reporter was that stupid.

Becky tugged at her cuffed hand again, hearing the clink the other cuff made around the rusted pipe she was attached to. The pipe shuddered from the impact, groaning like a beached whale.

"Great," she muttered.

With her free hand, she felt all of her pockets. Of course her guns and knife would be confiscated by her captors—whoever they were. She remembered a kid with a big head, and a giant covered head to toe in thick, leathery armour. *Am I going crazy, or did that kid have garbage floating around his head?*

She moved her cuffed hand again, watching the pipe closely. It seemed weak enough to break. But would it? She tugged. It bent a little. She eased up, putting slack into the chain. Then she kicked the pipe. It bent the other way, into the wall. She kicked it again. And again. And again.

The pipe snapped in half. *Yes!*

Becky slid the cuff off the pipe, freeing herself. Then she grabbed the broken end of the pipe and tugged—hard—breaking it off at the flange. Now she had a weapon, which she gripped firmly in her right hand as she held her breath and crawled under the door. The texture of the floor tiles alone was enough to make her skin crawl. The door was to her left. A row of grimy, smashed urinals ran along the wall in front of her. Around the corner of the stall she was in (the end of a row of five stalls) were the water-damaged counter, clogged sinks, and shattered panoramic mirror. On the wall beside the exit was a large prohibition sign spray-painted over the Altieria Corp. logo.

She opened the door a crack and looked into the hall, seeing old payphone terminals on the other side of the otherwise empty hallway. She cautiously slinked out into the open, glancing both ways to make sure she really was alone. Remembering how they got her in the first place, she looked up at the ceiling. Nothing up there except peeling paint and wire-meshed fluorescent light tubes, half of which were broken. Pipes groaned. The sound of water droplets hitting the floor echoed through the corridor. The shitty death stink that Becky could never see herself getting used to prevailed here, too.

Which direction do I go? she wondered.

"Fuck her."

Becky stiffened as the voices reached her ears.

"Fuck her?"

"That's what I'm gonna do."

"You don't play with food, Blitz."

"*You* don't play with food, but *I* do," the one called Blitz replied.

The voices were getting louder. Becky ducked back into the restroom and pressed her back against the wall behind the door, listening to the muffled conversation as it continued: "It my food too, Blitz."

"You eat the legs anyway. I don't touch those. Nobody eat pussy after it cooked."

"Monkey eat the pussy."

"Monkey dying."

Becky straightened as the door flew open and hit her in the face. She stifled a noise as it bounced off her forehead. Two men wearing human skin coats trotted in with gleeful excitement in their steps. She stared at their backs, watching as they approached the door to the stall she was trapped in, and moved toward them, gripping the pipe.

"I dunno 'bout this, Blitz."

Blitz, the one in the lead, undid the door latch. "You always say that, but you always enjoy it and go with no regrets, Lunman." He pushed the door inward. "I get first fuck—"

The sight of an empty stall struck Blitz dumb.

Becky hopped lightly behind a confused Lunman as he asked, "What is it?"

"She gone!"

Becky swung the pipe, squarely cracking the back of Lunman's head. He dropped instantly.

Blitz whirled around, his eyes wild and feral. His ugly face, disfigured, lacking a nose and an eye, contorted with rage. "Whore—"

Becky didn't let him finish. She lunged forward and smacked the pipe into his left ear. He pivoted back, staggering into the stall, collapsing on the toilet. Before she could get a second swing in, he drew a pistol—her pistol—and pointed it at her. "Drop it! Drop!" he shouted.

She froze, staring at the muzzle. Down the barrel. All she had was a rusty pipe.

"Drop everything," he snarled. "Everything."

She dropped the pipe. No other choice.

"Bitch!" he snapped, making her jump. "I said *everything*! Take it all off!"

To hell with that, was all she could internally say to that.

She dived out of his view, prompting two reflexive shots from his pistol, which blasted the urinal across the restroom to flying porcelain.

"Bitch!" he shouted, pulling himself out of the toilet. He

slipped on the floor and slammed into the wall, still disoriented from the blow to the head he sustained. He stomped out into the open and looked down the stall doors, all of which were shut. She was hiding.

He dropped to the floor, looking under the doors for any feet. No feet. He jumped up straight and fired a few more shots into random stalls. "I find you, bitch. I find you." He kicked the second door open and blasted the toilet bowl to pieces with a single shot. No Becky. He shifted to the next door and kicked it in, conserving his ammo this time by not firing a shot. Still no Becky. He went to the fourth stall. One more after this and he had her.

She was in the fourth stall. She dropped down, flat on the floor, and crawled into the third stall just seconds before he could kick the fourth door open. Lucky.

He went to the fifth door and snickered triumphantly. "No more stall. You mine now."

He booted the door inward and—to his shock and confusion—found it to be empty.

Becky snuck up behind him and wrapped the chain of her handcuffs around his neck and pulled back, digging the chain into his throat. They flew back. He gurgled and dropped the gun and flailed his arms, trying to wriggle free. But Becky held on to the cuffs, heaving him back with everything she had. He slammed her into the wall, stealing air from her aching lungs, sandwiching her between the grimy tiles and his body. She kept the chain taut, digging it into his flesh. He wheezed rapidly, helplessly. He tried to knock her into the wall again, only half-succeeding with her yanking back constantly and pushing her knee into his spine. He convulsed against her. A high-pitched whine escaped through rotten teeth. Then he slowly fell into a limp state.

She released the empty cuff and kicked Blitz's body to the floor. Then she checked his pulse, making sure he was dead. Satisfied by the lack of a pulse, she searched his pockets and found her other pistol and her knife. Pocketing them, the gun he dropped during their struggle, and the spare magazines he had on him, she stood up and glared down at him in disgust. "Sick son of a bitch." In a brief burst of rage, she kicked him in the ribs, spat on him, and then fled the restroom.

Becky held her guns ready, not sure what to expect, as she sneaked around the maze-like corridors of the subway station. The tracks had become streaming rivers of contaminated water. Portions of the light panels were out, keeping sections of the station cloaked in shadows. Broken holographic projector panels, rusted metal kiosks, garbage, and rows upon rows of plastic seats were scattered all over the place. Becky spotted a few mole men sprawled out on the seats, snoring noisily. One of them had an old VR helmet set crookedly over his face.

Passing between two old support beams, Becky felt another wave of nausea coming. She fell against one of the beams, gagging until the feeling passed. If she could still throw up, she would. Her eyes watered and her head spun on an axis. Since she'd come to in the restroom, her sickness wasn't too bad. Bearable, at least.

It's only gonna get worse. I have to hurry.

She staggered out in the open—

A mistake. She found herself staring at the strange little boy and his giant scavenger. She pointed her guns at them, prompting the scavenger to step between her and the boy like a mother protecting her young. "Who the hell are you?" she growled.

The scavenger said nothing.

A voice responded in her mind—but it wasn't hers: *"We are society's worst rejects."*

The boy. He peeked out from behind the scavenger, staring right at her. *"We are brothers and sisters and mothers and fathers and—the most important of all—survivors."*

A psychokinetic kid leader of an underground sewer cult is holding me captive? If that doesn't make the front page, I don't know what else would. Becky stood her ground. Psychokinetic or not, she wasn't about to stand down. "What do you want with me?"

The boy's blank expression never changed. *"The same thing we want from all of our other 'guests': to eat you."*

She bristled. "Why don't you let me go instead?"

"Why would we do that?"

"It'll save us both a major hassle if you do. I have somewhere I need to be—and I'd rather be there."

A powerful force slammed into her like an invisible wall, blasting her off her feet, hurling her backwards against an old support beam. The impact smashed the tiles off the surface and ripped the guns out of her hands. The tiles cascaded to the floor, scraping the backs of her legs on their way down. The invisible wall pressed the air out of her chest. Her ribcage felt like it would break, swelling around her heart.

As she hung suspended on the support beam, struggling to breathe, the boy approached her, stone-faced as usual. *"We don't negotiate with food."*

"I know what you are, now. You're the Mole Clan."

"What of it?"

"You have a pact with the rebels."

"And?"

"If you eat me... you'll anger one of their captains. A celebrated hero, in fact."

"I know I look like a child, but I'm not a naïve buffoon. Do you honestly believe such a shallow bluff would work?"

"My name is Becky Trickle. What's yours?"

"...Nemo."

"Well, Nemo. I'm a reporter for Traditional News. Do you know what that means?" She could feel Nemo's psychokinetic hold on her loosen slightly. She had his attention. "It means I'm an indirect surface representative for the rebel faction, and given their humanitarianism, I doubt they'd appreciate some psychokinetic gutter punk eating one of their voices." She cringed, feeling his grip tighten around her chest again in response to her insult. "I don't know if you're aware of... how bad it'd be for you and your people if you killed one of their few supporters."

Nemo glared at her. His fluctuating rainbow pupils bored deep into her eyes, obviously searching for answers. Contemplating...

Finally, he released her. Becky hit the floor in a heap, sucking air back into her crushed lungs. When she enabled herself to breathe normally again, she gathered her weapons and used the support beam to straighten up to her full height. She looked at the boy and his scavenger, still gripping her pistols.

"If you don't prove the authenticity of your claims, we will be right back where we started," the boy said.

Becky felt the pockets of her coat for her wallet.

No wallet.

Her heart froze over. *Where...? Did it fall out when I was attacked?*

Nemo grew impatient. He folded his arms across his chest and pouted, like most children who felt cheated often did. *"Well?"*

No other choice. She raised her pistol and fired a shot into the ceiling. The deafening crack hurt her ears, made her cringe; as the sound rumbled through the corridors and tunnels.

Nemo clamped his hands over his ears and screamed in agony. The scavenger fell on his knees, trembling. The station trembled with the boy's screams. Dust blankets came down.

Apparently the gunshot hurt them a lot more than it hurt her.

Becky fired another shot into the ceiling. Her ears rang. He shrieked. The tremors grew stronger. Small bits of debris hit the floor around them. No time to waste. Becky made a break for the stairs.

Still screaming, Nemo blasted a psychokinetic projectile after her.

Becky kept her head down, yelping when the pillar she just passed blew into thousands of dusty chunks. Up the stairs, shooting another bullet blindly behind her to keep the boy at bay. Pieces of tile skittered down the walls. Light fixtures sparked. Cracks struck through the floor and ran up the walls like lightning bolts. The rumbles, the echoes of gunfire, Nemo's shrill screaming; it all stabbed Becky's ears with painful ringing and spun her head round and round. Despite her poor balance, she managed to scramble around the corner and scurry up the second flight of stairs.

With the gunfire now deadened, Nemo no longer screamed from the pain. Now he was howling with rage. Another burst from his lungs blew the lights out and shattered the support beams that ran along the platform on either side of him. Without support, the ceiling began to crumble…

On the city's surface, the buildings shuddered. The streets swayed. Desktop utensils and equipment bounced about. Employees in factories, office floors, and fast food restaurants leaned on something, anything, to keep themselves on their feet. The tremors didn't let up like they usually did, though.

They intensified.

Sidewalks cracked. Window panes splintered and disintegrated into tiny sparkling particles. Backup generators went in and out, causing the lights and electronics of the privileged complexes to blink and malfunction. Pedestrians and emergency services rushed to seek shelter as still-dead overhead signs started to fall from their perches and plummet into the streets. Car horns blared. Dogs barked. People screamed. Babies cried.

Then, the unthinkable: chasms ripped through the streets and swallowed up vehicles and unfortunate people. Highway overpasses crumbled and split. In some areas, small buildings came down like trees in a lumberyard. A hailstorm of window glass showered streets and panicking mobs without mercy.

The world seemed to be coming apart at the seams.

Underground Station

Dodging a collapsing support beam, Becky reached the station platform. The blankets of dust and debris had her blinking constantly.

Shouting a few paces behind her.

She whirled to see a mole running straight at her with a crude pike raised above his head. Instinctively, she fired at him. He collapsed, screaming from the pain of the noise and the injury his right thigh sustained. He clutched the bleeding hole in his thigh, rolling back and forth across the platform.

Becky left him, continuing her escape. Others were coming. She could hear their wild racket, like children screaming at the tops of their lungs whilst banging pots and pans together. It was getting closer, and she was running out of platform. The sight of the murky sewer waters rushing through the subway station; the thought of entering it again made her stomach roil.

No other choice. She reached the end of the platform and jumped into the waist-deep sludge. Powering through it as fast as she could, Becky glanced over her shoulder every chance she got.

They were coming.

A score of them had gathered on the end of the platform, throwing trash and crudely made weapons after her. She ducked and shielded her eyes from an onslaught of bricks, bottles, and lead pipes. A bottle cracked against her collarbone. She cried out from the pain. Then she fired her pistol at the shrieking moles. The sound made them scatter. A few of them dived into the water. Others scurried out of her sight behind the pillars.

The further she went, the eerier their noises became. Their yells shrank to a haunting chorus of whispers that travelled through the tunnels after her, echoing, coming from all sides. Surrounding her.

The rumbling had subsided. Maybe the boy had calmed himself, or his guardian had managed to pacify him. Becky hoped that was the case.

A *plop* sound in the water made her snap her head around. A doll, floating in the water, stared back at her.

47: Safety

Rebel Hideout

A captain looked up from his tattered book, straightening in his chair. He paused, listening. Then he turned to five other men sitting around a table playing a quiet game of poker. "You guys hear shots?"

"Shots?" A tall, scruffy man looked over his hand at the captain. "Only sounds I can hear are the rusty gears of my brain slowly turning."

"Funny," the Captain said.

The room started to shake. Dust rained down on the poker game, much to the players' agitation. A beer-bellied, bald man said, "The little psycho-baby is having another tantrum."

The shaking intensified. Despite the violent tremors, and the fact that stacks of books and entire shelves were toppling to the floor around them, the Captain and the poker players remained calmly seated.

"Hoohoo, somebody shit the mattress this morning!" Baldie said with a guttural laugh.

A brick slipped out of the ceiling and hit the center of the table. The Captain watched as his inferior-ranked rebels guffawed. Then he looked up at the bricks rattling in the ceiling, threatening to collapse on their heads at any moment. "This one's unusual."

"A tantrum's a tantrum," Scruffy said. He blinked when another brick slammed onto the table in front of him.

A crack streaked across the far wall. Now they were nervous.

"How well-constructed would you say this room is?" a short rebel on the other side of the table asked nervously.

"Fairly well-constructed," the Captain said. "For an abandoned nineteenth-century maintenance room, I suppose."

"You suppose?"

The Captain shrugged. "Hey, I didn't build the damn thing."

The shaking subsided. The quake had finally stopped, leaving the room in shambles. Books, weapons, night equipment, and furniture were strewn about in piles of varying size.

Baldie said, "See? Wasn't so bad." He clapped a hand across Shorty's back, chuckling. "Was it, Juniper?"

The short one, Juniper, scowled in his chair.

"Aw, don't pout."

A gunshot resounded through the room. Even with the five-inch-thick metal door sealed shut, the sound was clear. Everyone jumped to attention.

"Did you hear it now?" the Captain asked as he stood upright and plopped his book on his chair. He snatched a rifle off the floor and racked the bolt. "Grab your gear, boys."

Altierian Sewers

Becky looked up, rushing backwards as she scanned the pipes in the tunnel ceiling for a mole hunter. This time, she was ready. She fired a round into a black gap in the pipes. The high-pitched sound of claws scraping against metal as something scurried pierced her ears. The doll skipped across the water away from her. She fired another shot after her stalker, cringing from the pain it inflicted upon her eardrums.

"You better run!" she shouted.

She moved back a step.

A black object dropped from the ceiling a few yards up the tunnel, in plain view for a blurry moment before hitting the water with a big splash.

It's swimming straight for me…

She rushed back, fighting against the opposing current. Light faded the deeper she progressed. Soon her vision was as black as the sludge she stood waist-deep in. No lantern to light the way. Her stalker approached. The muzzle flash from her pistol would light her path only for a second. It would be best to conserve her ammo for when her stalker decided to finally pounce.

Tripping over sunken trash and lost treasures scattered on the tunnel floor, she waded through the waters, reaching ahead, groping the blackness around her for something, anything. She could feel her stalker's mass shift about beneath the surface, pushing gentle waves against her back.

She turned and blasted a round down in front of her. Blinked when droplets of sludge splashed her face. The gentle waves ceased. She felt the slight vibration of a nearby object hitting the floor through her boots. *Did I get him?*

Becky stepped back, keeping her eyes focused on the area she'd fired into despite her blindness. She listened intently for a sound to betray her pursuer.

Splashing in the opposite direction of the tunnel caused her to whirl. *More of them?*

She fired a shot in that direction.

"Shit!" someone shouted.

The splashing came to an abrupt stop.

"Hold your fire!"

"Who's out there?" she shouted.

"Identify yourself."

"I asked you first."

"Well, I'm asking you second!"

Becky fired two purposely wide shots in their direction. Startled shouts followed:

"Jesus!"

"Shit!"

"Hold your fire, hold your fire!"

"Crazy—"

"We're on your side, goddamn it!"

Becky yelled over them, "I'm not taking any chances. Identify yourselves—"

Thick, leathery arms latched on from behind, wrapping around her, pulling her back. They constricted her, crushing the air from her lungs. A thick, slimy hand over her mouth silenced her scream. The scavenger's muscles contorted, crushing her against his chest. Then—

The clamp of a muffled shot rattled through the tunnel. The scavenger convulsed briefly. Released his gasping prey. Splashed into the sewer sludge. A final gurgle sounded off as the waste water dribbled into his mouth, claiming him.

Becky dry-heaved, the stench of the slimy residue on her face making her want to retch. She heard splashing as her mysterious visitors approached. Lights flashed, blinding her. She pointed her gun at the oncoming light sources, shielding her eyes with her free arm. "Who are you?"

"Easy, lady," the Captain said, keeping his rifle barrel in the water. "We're with the faction. ...Unless you're with the Corporation, in which case..."

"I'm not with the Corporation," she said. "I think they're after me."

"Who *aren't* they after? That's the question." Before he could be comfortable with furthering the conversation, the Captain glanced past Becky and asked, "You don't have more of those mole bastards trailing behind you, do you?"

"Not that I know of…"

"Good."

Becky's eyes were starting to adjust to the light. She looked at each of the rebels in turn, slowly lowering her pistol. "Any of you know who Juon is?"

The Captain exchanged looks with Juniper. Turning back to Becky with cautious eyes, he asked, "Who are you, lady?"

"Becky Trickle," she said. "It's amazing how many of you don't recognize a reporter from your only supportive news channel."

The Captain shrugged. "Yeah, well, if you had a mirror, you'd know why."

She frowned. "What's that supposed to mean?"

The Captain's men chuckled. He cocked his head to the side, scowling. They fell silent. He turned around and started to head back. "Alright, well, I guess you're clear, then."

Becky ran her fingers through her hair, which, to her horror, had been thickened with sludge and had a few bits and strands of garbage nestled in it.

"Coming?" the Captain asked from further up the tunnel.

Eager to stay out of the dark, Becky hurried after them. "Slow down, will ya?"

48: Nothing/2

She stood under a towering apple tree with a twisted trunk that reached to the heavens; its gnarly branches formed a thick, aging canopy above her head. The green leaves, vibrant in the sun's soft, golden rays. Its luscious red apples glistening with morning dew.

An apple broke off the stem and landed in her outstretched palm. She looked at it. Something caught her eye, out of focus. She glanced beyond the apple at a reflection of herself standing naked under the tree with her. Staring with steely blue eyes. She seemed stronger than her. More determined. She didn't know why.

Her reflection held up the apple.

She looked down at her own hand and realized that somehow, her reflection had taken it from her.

Her reflection bit into the apple and smiled.

Something about that smile gave her chills.

A rustling in the tree branches as all the apples rained down on the pair. She shielded herself from the sudden downpour. Her reflection stood her ground, those eyes never looking away. The apples didn't touch her. She took another bite. A breeze sent waves across the grassy plains. With every passing wave, the grass turned a deeper shade of yellow.

Another bite.

Leaves started to flutter down from the apple tree.

"Stop it," she said.

The reflection took the apple in both her hands and greedily devoured the rest. The tree turned black and crumbled like ash. The grass disappeared and the earth cracked, shattered, fell away.

She screamed as she plummeted into endless darkness. Nothing to grab onto. No sight. No sound. No smell. She had fallen into a senseless void.

And then everything came crashing back at once. Frigid cold assailed her small body. No more air to breathe. Water filled her lungs and stung her eyes. She threw her hands and feet out. Hit glass that wouldn't crack. She spun around, realizing she was back in that horrible tube, looking through the glass at her reflection.

Panicking. Drowning. Heart racing.

"You're nothing without me," the reflection said.

"What do you want from me?" She was startled by the sound of her own voice. How could she be drowning and talking at the same time?

"Imitator," the reflection said bitterly, circled around the tube, pounding her hand against the glass with every word: "Sheep! Imposter! Pretender! *Fake!*"

"What do you want from me?" she cried out. Her chest felt like it was about to burst. She slammed her fists on the glass again. Didn't even shake. Helpless. "Get me out!"

"No," her reflection said, stopping to face her. "No, you're right where you belong."

"Who are you?"

"Who are *you*?"

"Stop it!" she shrieked. "Stop playing games with me! I've had enough! Get out of my head!"

"GET OUT OF MY LIFE!" her reflection roared, loud enough to send cracks wrapping round the tube.

The tube burst, spilling her—

Elsa hit the floor and screamed, entangled in bed sheets.

Franklin, startled awake by his wife's shrieks, scrambled across the bed and fell on the floor beside her, yanking the sheets off her. "Elsa! Elsa! Sweetheart, hold still!" He managed to pull the sheet off her head—

She wrapped her arms around him and buried her face into his chest, sobbing uncontrollably. "Oh God... oh God... oh God..."

He held her trembling form tightly, stroking her head. "It's okay. It's okay, baby. It was just a dream."

She whimpered, gasping, breathless from the terror and the sobs.

"It was just a dream. You've nothing to worry about.
It's nothing.

Elsa stiffened. Choked back another sob.

Franklin looked down at her head, worried by her sudden stillness.

"Franklin...?" she whispered, voice breaking.

"What, dear?"

"What was that?"

"What was what?" he asked.

It's nothing.

A fresh flow of tears streamed down her face as the fear took hold. "There's someone in here with us…"

"What?" he exclaimed. "Honey, there's no one—"

She wriggled out of his arms and hauled herself onto the bed, standing on it, looking around frantically. "Why can't you hear it?" she shouted. "Why can't you hear them?!"

He got up to his knees, spreading his arms outward. "There's no one else here, Elsa!"

"BULLSHIT!" she screamed. The lights dimmed. The windows shuddered. "Why are you denying it? What are you hiding from me?!"

The room trembled around Franklin. He jumped to his feet. "Elsa, please, calm down! It's your psychokinesis. You have to control it—"

"Stop lying to me!"

The bedside lamp exploded. The digits on the clock became a jumbled mess. The mirror across the room disintegrated into billions of tiny sparkling particles.

"Elsa!" Franklin leaped onto the bed and grabbed her shoulders. "Honey, please!"

"Why?" she moaned. "Why is this happening to me?"

"Honey, listen to me." He held both sides of her face with gentle hands, his voice as calm as he could manage. "Listen to me. I'm here. I'm right here. There's no one else."

"What do I keep hearing?" The tears kept coming.

"It's all in your head, sweetheart. All in your head. You have to control it. You have to stay calm. Do you understand?"

"Frank—"

"I'm here. I'm not going to let anything happen to you." He pulled her against his chest again. Whispered in her ear, "It's going to be alright."

The trembling faded. The digital clock returned to normal. He could feel her relax in his arms, melting into him. Her tears soaked through his nightshirt, but that was far from being his main concern. *How could she hear the program's voice?* He pondered this question in his head as he held her, running his hands up and down her back. "I'll go make you something. It should help you sleep."

"Oh," she said, pushing away from him and wiping her tears

on her pyjama sleeves. "Look at me, crying like a child."

"It's understandable," Franklin said. "I'll make you some hot chocolate. That should calm you down."

"Ooh," she said, "yes, please, dear."

49: Dreams/1

He took her with him to the kitchen, where he started to boil a kettle of water. She sat behind the island on one of the stools, constantly glancing over her shoulders at the exits on either side of her.

His back facing her, Franklin slipped a small yellow pill into her favourite Christmas tree mug as he poured the boiled water into it. He stirred the powder in, mixing in the contents. The pill dissolved in the brown liquid.

"Here, honey," he said as he placed the mug down in front of her. "Be careful. It's hot."

"I know, Frank," she said with a warm smile. "You're always babying me."

"I don't mean to. I get worried easily."

She blew steam away from her mug. "I know you do. I love you for it. My own big-hearted mad scientist."

He chuckled, eagerly watching her grasp the cup with both hands and rotate it on the countertop; clockwise, counter-clockwise, clockwise...

She stopped rotating the cup and sighed. "The nightmares are getting worse."

"I noticed," he said.

"I mean... I see me. I'm yelling at myself."

"You're... yelling at yourself?"

She nodded slowly. "I'm saying all these horrible things. 'Imposter.' 'Fake.' And I'm stuck in a capsule. Or a tube."

"You've mentioned the tube before." Franklin leaned forward, squinting. "Do you remember how you feel in it?"

She stared at him. "What does it matter, Franklin? Obviously, I was scared. Why is this tube so important to you?"

"It's not; I just wanted to know more about your dream."

"It was a nightmare," she corrected him, "and I was scared. That's all there is to know. I don't remember anything else, except that I've been having it nonstop for the past week."

"Okay," he said, nodding. "Okay."

"What about you, Mr. Interpreter?" she asked as teasingly as she could manage.

"What *about* me...?"

"Do you analyze your dreams?"

"Sometimes."

"And what kinds of dreams do you have?"

"A small variety. Some are good. Some are bad. Some are just so... strange that I don't know what to make of them."

Elsa blew on her mug again, eyeing him with curiosity. "Tell me about a strange one."

Franklin pulled up a stool and leaned on the island countertop. "Well, I remember this one where we were on a nude beach—"

Her giggle cut him off. "A strange one, not a perverted one. Contrary to popular belief, I know that there's a difference between the two. At least, when they concern a scientific deviant like you."

His heart rate spiked for a moment. "Uh..."

"What?" she asked, still smiling. "Your face just turned a different shade of white, love."

He shook his head and chuckled. "Sorry, it's nothing."

"Please don't say that word again."

"Right... I'm sorry."

Eager to switch back to the subject at hand, Elsa said, "So tell me one."

"A strange dream?"

She nodded. "Yes."

"Well... there's one I remember: I found myself in the middle of nowhere. It was raining, and I was naked."

She rolled her eyes. "Even when you're not dreaming of me, you're still naked."

He shrugged, grinning from ear to ear until he continued. "I was in a field. I didn't know how I got there, of course. No one remembers how their dreams began.

"I walked across this field for a long time. And by 'a long time,' I mean it felt like an eternity. But sure enough, I came across a road. The storm drains were clogged, so it was all underwater. I looked beyond that road and I saw the edge of a cliff. For reasons I can only guess attain to the fact that dreams don't have any real sense of logic, the five or six feet of water made up a good portion of the edge of that cliff. As if... an invisible wall held it all in.

"I walked across the water, too. It was very strange and

disorienting. I felt like I would fall in, but strangely, I never did. And when I reached the edge of the cliff, I saw the tops of skyscrapers stabbing up through the ocean's surface."

Elsa sipped from her mug, listening intently.

"The water started to rise. The rain didn't seem to be coming down that hard, but sure enough, this vast ocean was rising. It swallowed those skyscrapers and rose up high over the cliff I stood on. No water spilled. It just kept going up... up... up...

"And then it stopped. In midair, this ocean stopped. It was like a giant wall looming over my head. It looked like the world's biggest aquarium. If I could have recorded my own dreams into a video file, I would have watched it over and over again. It was... beautiful.

"But of course, like many unusual dreams, this one shifted tone. You see, when I looked more closely at this wall, I saw things. I saw people. Floating around inside this weird, abstract wall. A lightning bolt hit the side of this wall, just barely missing me, and the wall collapsed on top of me. It spilled over me, but I didn't feel a thing. I didn't even move. I was swept away like I naturally would be. I stood my ground, frozen to the spot. And when that water finally evened out, I found this baby in my hands. He was a very peculiar child, with a white—"

He stopped when Elsa's head dipped over her mug. "Darling?"

"Take me to bed, sweetie," she moaned sleepily. "I feel so heavy."

He smiled and helped her off the stool and carried her to the bedroom, feeling like a knight in shining armour, carrying his own damsel. When he tucked her under the sheets, he rushed back to the kitchen. Dumped the hot chocolate down the sink and rinsed it down. After that, he went to his secluded office, punched the five-digit code in, crossed the cold chamber, and entered his private office. Once there, he shut the door, booted up the laptop, and checked his messages.

Most of his inbox was filled with spam. But one message caught his eye. He opened it.

```
Progress report?
-/7
```

Franklin slouched. Leaned back in his office chair, staring dumbly at the holographic screen. All he could ask himself: *What should I say?*

What should I say?

50: Bureaucratic/1

Rebel Hideout

After being escorted to the maintenance room, Becky had spent the next hour vomiting and dry-heaving into the toilet. The stench of the sewer clung to her body. Her waterlogged clothes stuck to her skin like thick, crusty slime. They were heavy, crushing down on her weak shoulders. The nausea wouldn't stop. The toilet bowl spun in a vortex before her eyes; a warped, spiralling collage of aqua blue and pearly white. The dim light above her head didn't help, either.

The Captain rapped his knuckles on the door and called in, "Do you need anything, my dear?"

"New... clothes," she gasped. "Shower..."

"I'll get you some antibiotics. They'll help you with that sewer sickness."

She was too busy choking on more vomit to thank him.

A sixty-minute hot shower helped her relax. Getting out of those clothes and washing the toxic chemicals off her body provided her with more relief than anything else in a long time. She still felt sick when she got out, but the knots in her stomach were mercifully loosened enough to be bearable.

The Captain had left an old uniform on the floor for when she got out. It was a size too big for her, but it was dry and warm, and that was all that mattered to her.

"How are you feeling?" the Captain asked when she stepped out of the bathroom in her uniform.

"Like sun-cooked shit," she croaked.

The guys around the poker table chuckled. Baldy said with a stupid grin, "So how'd you enjoy your first run-in with the Moles, lady?"

Becky scowled at him. "Still a more pleasant experience than looking at your ugly mug."

Most of the guys around the table, except Juniper, exploded with laughter.

Becky ignored them and turned to the Captain. "I owe you one."

"Don't sweat it," the Captain replied, turning his eyes down to the open book in his lap. "You're lucky we found you when we did. If you didn't have that gun, we would never have known."

"Are they cannibals?"

"They're the real omnivores of the human race. They'll eat anything that's available. Rats. Shoes. People. That sludge you spent the last hour or so puking back up is all they have to drink."

Becky's face contorted with disgust. She felt those knots twisting again.

"You saw the side-effects *that* had on them—"

"Change the subject, please."

He looked up at her, instantly noticing the shade of green her face had adopted. "Right. I have a question, anyway: why were you down here in the first place?"

"I had to find a hiding place."

"Why?"

"They made me. They know who I am. They know I'm involved. I don't even know what's happened to my partner."

"So you came down here to seek our help?"

"I've no other options, so I suppose so."

The Captain closed his book shut and leaned back in his chair, staring at her. "How do you know you weren't followed?"

"I lost them long ago," she said.

"You're sure about that?"

"Yes."

"You're *sure*?" he pressed.

"*Yes*," she said again. "I learned a thing or two when I was with Juon."

"You mentioned a 'Juon' before. Juon... Armada?"

"The one and only," she said with a forced smirk.

"How do you know him?"

"Long story short: he's the reason I'm with Traditional News instead of North Altieria News. Got me?"

The Captain nodded. "Fair enough." Beat. "So they're trying to suppress your employers now?"

"No, they're not after the rest of them. At least, they aren't that high on the CEO's priority list. It's just me. And my partner, Mickey."

"And you don't know where Mickey is..."

She shook her head sadly. "I haven't heard from him for a few days. He isn't very resourceful on his own, either."

"Hate to be the bearer of bad news, but he's probably dead by now. Or worse..."

"I know," she said quickly. "I'll mourn him later. Right now, we have something much more important to deal with, and there isn't much time left. It's why I came down here."

"I thought you came down here for safety?"

"That, too. But there's something else: I gave Juon something that he should be taking down to the council."

"What was it?"

"I'd rather not say. Not yet, anyway."

"Lady, I really don't have the time nor the patience for games. I just saved your ass out there; I think you owe me a proper explanation. Seeing as how I'm on your side, there's no reason for you to hold out on me."

"Good point, I guess."

"So...?"

After another moment of hesitation, Becky gave in: "It's a drive with crucial evidence that we can use against the CEO. It might even be enough to drag his influence down a few notches."

"What kind of evidence?"

"The kind that creates career-ruining scandals." She cocked an eyebrow to accentuate the slyness in her smirk. "The kind that lowers public opinion."

The Captain sighed, disappointed. "Really? So you want us to go out of our way to publicly humiliate the most powerful man in the world with evidence that he could easily deny?"

Becky faltered. "Well, I mean... he couldn't easily deny—"

"But he *could* deny it, nonetheless. Look, you obviously mean well, but that kind of naïve approach is only going to cost us more men, and trust me, that's the last thing we need."

"But we have video evidence!"

"Yeah? How convincing is it?"

"Very."

"But not completely?"

"If you saw it, you'd be agreeing with me. Hell, the guy who filmed it all was a *cop*, for Christ's sake!"

"So you hand us a video file filmed by a cop, and you expect us to believe it? Did you ever stop to consider that maybe, just *maybe*, it could be a trap?"

Becky furrowed her brows. Frustration peaking. "Look, if you saw it—"

"I'd believe it. Yeah, yeah, yeah," the Captain said impatiently. More than tired of this conversation. "You said that. I still don't believe it. Repeating yourself won't make me change my mind, either."

"Take me to the council and we'll see how they feel about it."

"The council will say the exact same thing, word for word."

"You sure about that?"

The Captain fired up a cigarette. Leaned back in his chair. Dragged away on his cancer stick. "Guaranteed, or your money back."

Becky scowled at him, arms akimbo. Then she turned to the group seated around the table. "And what do *you* guys think?"

Eyes downcast, all but one of them paid her any mind: Baldie, who replied as he shuffled a deck of cards, "Nobody argues with the Captain."

Becky's scowl darkened. "You guys are pissing me off."

"Tough break, pussycat," the Captain said, blowing smoke in her direction.

She coughed and waved the smoke cloud away. "Don't call me that. Look, all I want from you guys is safe transport down to the council. That's all."

"What's in it for us?" the Captain asked.

"The privilege of laughing in my face and telling me how you were right all along if the council does react the way you say it will."

The Captain scoffed. "I'm already doing that."

"No, you're not. The council hasn't seen shit."

"If I bring you down there, Juon won't be the only laughing stock in our ranks."

"Then send someone else to escort me!" she snapped. "God, this is ridiculous. Why is this taking so long?"

"What did you expect? Immediate transport down to the basement as per your immediate request?" The Captain tapped ash off the end of his cigarette. "We're a faction, not a goddamn taxicab service."

"I'll go," Juniper piped up. All eyes fell on him. He faltered. "I-I mean, if I have your permission, sir..."

The Captain scowled. "Taking her side, are ya?"

"No sir."

"Explain your thinking."

"I-I think... uh... if it's as, uh, promising as it sounds, it's worth... worth a look. I can escort her, sir."

Seizing the opportunity, Becky said, "Then the rest of you won't be considered a laughing stock if it's just him escorting me down there!"

"Hey," Juniper said.

"Sorry," she said with a shrug.

The Captain crushed his cigarette butt under his heel. "Fine, whatever. Do what you want. Just don't come cryin' to me when the council brushes you off."

51: Dreams/2

Scott Residence

Franklin didn't waste any time. For the moment, he disregarded Amanda/7's email. He needed something first...

Exiting the lab, he pushed a cart across the living room. This cart contained: a REM helmet with a bubbly cranium cover and a scanning visor; its cord spooled around the base of a silver four-foot-tall cylindrical computer tower with a small keypad and a 12x12-inch screen on the side; a laptop computer with a small backup storage drive; a pair of wireless headphones, and a printer connected to the device and the laptop.

He wheeled the cart into the bedroom. Stopped next to the bed on which Elsa was sleeping in the fetal position. Pulled up a chair behind the device. Franklin lifted Elsa's head off the pillow and slipped the helmet on. He yanked the visor down over her eyes. Gently laid her head back down. Went back to the chair and placed the laptop computer on his lap. Put on the wireless headset. Once the computer had booted up and loaded a login menu, Franklin struck two seven-digit codes. The desktop appeared. He typed another seven-digit code. The screen went black.

Then, dancing across the screen: a dazzling array of three-dimensional red squares, green circles, blue triangles, yellow hexagonal prisms. The shapes bounced off each other and the edges of the screen, as if trying to break out of the monitor. Their chaotic scrambling worsened as they shattered into billions of tiny colourful particles, eventually forming a solid picture that fell into deep, Spanish blue saturation.

Movement. The outer rims of protective goggles bordered the screen. Little air bubbles danced up the screen. Slender hands appeared, touching an invisible wall, then banging against that wall. Thump-thump-thump. The headset rumbled from the vibrational low-frequency sounds.

Just as I suspected—she's remembering the incubator period, Franklin thought to himself.

More faint shapes in the darkness. Franklin squinted, looking closer as something began to materialize in front of his POV's set of hands. A head. A face. A woman.

Elsa.

Nearly stopped his heart. Not the first time this has happened, but seeing her face in the subconscious of another Elsa always disturbed him. Filled him with despair.

He slumped. *Why do you keep doing this?*

He said aloud, "Why do you keep doing this to me?"

She seemed to be smiling as the dreaming Elsa's fists started to bang against the glass. Unbreakable. No escape.

Franklin shook the laptop, shouting, "Let her out! Let her out, damn you!"

Elsa's face became distorted with rage. The screen flickered. Static snow filled it. Ear-splitting dial-up noises literally shook the room. He threw the headset off, but his brain was still assaulted with what felt like a billion hot needles. The electronic shrieks rising to a high-pitched, screeching crescendo. Loud enough to force him and the laptop to the floor in a trembling heap. He screamed. Writhed under ceiling lights that blinked erratically. The laptop screen cracked. The picture flashed white. He kicked it, snapping the lid off and sending it flying across the room. The cylindrical dream device blew like a morning glory sparkler and fell off the cart with a hollow clunk.

The noise stopped.

Franklin remained coiled on the floor, shaking violently. Her voice emanated from the ceiling, walls, and floor: "You know what you've done."

Ten minutes later, Franklin managed to pick himself up off the floor. Ears still ringing. Head still spinning in a hazy blur. He slid across the walls and grabbed every nook and cranny and cybernetic knickknack to support himself as he went through the apartment. Down the hall. Crossing the living room. Started to lose all sense of balance halfway to the lab. He stubbed his big toe on the leg of his coffee table. With a sharp cry, he pivoted through the table's glass surface.

He made a high-pitched whine in his struggle to breathe, lying on a carpet of sharp glass squares. He could feel a thin piece slice into his left cheek—the cheek he'd landed on. The glass surface clinked and shifted like a collection of spilled dominoes as he slid his hand across the jagged surface. He could feel them biting through his skin, slicing through his flesh. Felt his warm blood ooze between his fingers and dribble from his palm down his arm.

He moved his head, and was rewarded with a deep, stabbing pain above his left eye. Blood immediately leaked from the wound and streamed into his eye. Burning his throbbing eyeball as if a wasp had stung his retina.

The pain was unbearable, making him cry out like a dog that had been kicked shortly after eating. He pressed a bleeding palm against his closed right eye, involuntarily squishing even more blood into it. Bleach for his eye. He squealed through gnashed teeth and tried to wipe his eye on his glass-covered lab coat sleeve. With the pain came the rage. The bitter resentment. She did this.

A growl. A blood-curdling scream. He threw his voice to the ceiling, "STOP THIS! Stop tormenting me. If you... i-if you only understood... what I was trying to do!"

"I know exactly what you're trying to do," came her disembodied reply.

"Then why?"

"You're a smart man, Frank. You'll figure it out eventually."

He got up. Glass crunching underfoot as he staggered to the lab's frosted wall. "No. No, I don't know. I don't know!" He reached the door. Smeared blood on the wall and the keypad when he entered the password. The door slid open. A blast of cold air hit him. Goosebumps prickled on his skin; cold fingers crawled up his spine like a centipede.

He slipped into a pair of work boots, snatched the lab coat appropriate for the lab's cold climate off a nearby wall hook, slipped into it, and half ran, half stumbled around the work benches and storage cabinets, dragging and sliding his off-kilter feet, scattering old scrap and tools that had been previously left out across the floor. Making a bigger mess of things...

...on his way to the vault.

"No... no, you... you... bitch... no, I refuse to continue with this charade! Enough is enough, Elsa!" He stopped just in front of the vault door, rummaging through the drawer of the nearest work bench. Found it. "Cannot even accomplish a simple task..."

A suppressed Beretta 92SB, modified to fire explosive .45s. Two 15-round mags loaded with those particular rounds lay beside it.

Franklin took the gun out. Loaded it. Chambered a round. Turned to the vault door. He took a breath. Despite his trembling fingers, he entered the seven-digit password into the door's built-in keypad on the first try.

K-SHUNK!

The heavy bolts released the door, allowing it to roll to the left, revealing a grated stairwell leading into a dark abyss. A fresh gust of freezing mist was released into the lab. Franklin could feel his face going numb from the biting cold. More accurately, he couldn't feel his face.

The hissing of newly released air died down, replaced by the eerie, vibrational sound of silence. His footsteps echoed as he descended the stairs. Breathing heavy and laboured. Down into the darkness.

52: Basement/2

"Wake up."

Eyes flicked open. Vision inexplicably saturated in teal. Elsa found herself staring absently at the ruined dream device Franklin had left behind. Her mind a blank. Nothing registered at first.

Then it all hit her. The realization that she'd woken up in the most terrifying nightmare in history: cruel, relentless, confusing reality. The voice of the invisible intruder whispered in her head: He's going to hurt me again.

"Franklin?" Elsa called out. Hesitant to leave her bed.

No response.

She looked at the device again. The shattered laptop on the floor. All those thin, black cords snaking across the floor, up the side of the bed, coiling around her...

She touched the REM helmet on her head. Tapped the visor with her fingers. Lifted it up, doing away with the teal tint in her vision. She grabbed the sides of the helmet and slowly lifted it up. She felt its wires slither up her body. Brought it back down. Stared at it, confused.

Shaken, she called out a little louder: "Franklin?"

No response. From him.

Help me, the voice pleaded.

"Who are you?" she asked. "What do you want from me?"

Distant, from down the hall: *"Help me."*

Elsa let the REM helmet roll off the bed. She cringed when it hit the floor with a loud crack. She leaned over to the bedside drawer and took out a small .38 revolver. She checked the cylinder. Fully loaded.

"Whoever you are," she began, voice trembling, "whatever... whatever you want; I'm warning you r-right now that I have a gun." She gulped. "I have a gun and it's loaded." Beat. No response. "Please leave, or I'll be, uh... I'll be forced" —her voice cracked— "to use it on you. So you should leave!"

"Over here," the voice said from the hall.

Her heart jumped. Soaked in perspiration by now, Elsa

hesitantly slid off the couch. Her knees wobbled as she approached the bedroom doorway, holding the gun out in front of her. "Get out!"

"Please," the voice said, *"come to the lab."*

She pulled one of her hands back to quickly wipe tears away before returning it to its place around the gun. Her two-handed grip on it tightened as she shrieked, "GET OUT OF MY HOUSE!"

"Come to the lab."

"Why...? Why won't you leave?"

"Because I can't."

Elsa tentatively stepped forward. Breathed in. Breathed out. Breathed in. Breathed out. Breathed in. Held it. Jumped out into the hall, fingers ready to clench the trigger. Down the hall—

—was nothing.

"I'm not going to hurt you. Please come to the lab," the voice begged, coming from the living room now. *"Please help me."*

The fear in the voice drew Elsa's curiosity, though her fear that someone would come out and hurt her—or worse—remained strong in her mind. Eyes open, arms rigid, gun forward; Elsa moved down the hall. She glanced into the empty kitchen as she passed it. When she reached the living room entrance, she weaved around the corner and scanned the area. Immediately noticed the patch of shattered glass and splintered wood that used to be the coffee table. The rose-coloured patterns in the glass pieces made her heart jump. A fresh wave of anxiety slammed into her. Chilled her to the bone. She shivered, trying to steady her breathing despite her pounding heart.

No intruders to be found. Thank God. Perhaps that shouldn't have come as a surprise. She knew she had to have been hearing an intruder, or was simply going insane; hearing voices no one else could hear. If he heard the voices, Franklin would have taken her side. He would have jumped in front of her and searched the place for any intruders. But he didn't. Was it because she was going crazy? Were her powers going on the fritz?

Was it all an act?

"Yes, the voice said, *it was all an act. He knew what you were hearing. You believed his lies. You fell for his act. They all did. We all did."*

"What is this?" Elsa asked, glancing over her shoulder down the hall. "What are you saying?"

"Please... the lab..."

She hesitantly crossed the living room to the quarantined lab's keypad. She paused a moment, going through her memories like some kind of computer, looking for any clues as to what the password would be.

The whisper: *"Hurry. Please. It's me."*

"It's me."

She punched 'E-L-S-A' into the keypad.

The door opened. She hurried inside the freezing containment area, her breath pluming from her mouth as she shivered in the cold. Stepped into the last pair of work boots. Snatched a heavy lab coat off the hook and slipped into it. Dropped the gun in her pocket. Did up the buttons. Hugged herself and rubbed her shoulders as the coat's insulator system started up and warmed her in its thick embrace.

"This way."

She tucked her hands in her coat pockets and investigated the shrine, the spare parts room, the operating room...

"Frank—"

"Don't!"

Elsa jumped. "What...?"

"Don't call him! He'll know!"

"But Franklin isn't—"

"Please! The vault! He's hurting me!"

Then her eyes turned to the mysterious storage vault she'd been forbidden from entering. She approached it, saw the touchpad, and stared at it hopelessly for a moment. Her joints stiffened from the cold. Or perhaps it wasn't the cold. Perhaps it was something else. Fear. Hesitation. *What am I doing? What's down there?*

"Please hurry."

Franklin told me never to go in there, she thought.

"Please... please!"

She sucked in a shaking breath. Stepped to the keypad. Tried 'E-L-S-A.'

A low-tone BEEP-BEEP was the response. She didn't hear the locks. Confused, she looked for a handle on the door. No handle. She tried pushing it. Wouldn't budge. She slipped her fingers in one of the nooks and tugged. Same result.

"I don't understand," she heaved. She tried the password again. No luck.

The keypad made a stuttering *BE-EEP*. Sparks burst from

under the keys. Elsa made a startled squeak and jumped back as another group of sparks sprayed out. She heard the vault lock slide. The door slid open, revealing a dark stairwell.

Her heart dropped like a stone. The darkness—an oddly familiar monster from her worst nightmares. The kind of place she wanted to run away and hide from.

"Hurry."

"I can't."

The voice's whispers escalated to shrill screams in her head: *"Please, hurry. Hurry!"*

Elsa cringed. Felt the pressure mount. Heart racing. She took the gun out of her pocket and started down the stairs one slow, cautious step at a time.

The basement's black depths, overwhelming and empty, swallowed her whole.

53: Basement/3

It seemed like an eternity before Elsa reached the floor of the abyss. She couldn't hear anything; it felt like she'd entered a cavern drilled into the heart of an iceberg—it sounded like she was standing on the bottom of an ocean. The basement was pitch black, save for a thin pacific blue strip slicing across what she assumed was the wall on her right. She approached it, groping the dark for anything that could be in front of her. Only when she got closer did she realize that the light throbbed with its own eerie pulse, moving further down to her feet the nearer she came.

Her hand touched cold steel. She felt the wall for a handle or a keypad. She found a lock slide and pushed and pulled to the left and the right. It rattled, but nothing opened. She pushed on it. Then she—

Tink!

Elsa gasped, whirled to face the darkness. Her back pressed against the wall. Her joints frozen. Her muscles constricted. Nothing else could be heard except the vibrational sound of silence. She couldn't see and couldn't know for sure, but she felt that something was watching her.

"In here."

Keeping one eye on the darkness behind her, Elsa grabbed the lock bolt and yanked it back. With a resounding shunk, the door began to open Elsa pulled it back. Pacific blue light filled the room. She shielded her eyes. Turned around to see if she could find whatever made that noise.

There was nothing else in the room except the stairs and a pile of mechanical bodies in the far left corner. Empty robot shells that all shared Elsa's face and general form, stripped of their artificial flesh. Without their skin, they were nothing more than skeletal rejects. Dolls.

But one of them had been staring at her with its marble-like cobalt eyes. Its cracked, plastic face expressionless, as it should be.

Elsa couldn't stop looking at it. There had to have been at least seven of them stacked in that corner.

She turned back to the lit-up room with eyes that had adjusted well enough. She entered—

—and found shelves. Elsa found herself standing in the middle of a disturbing collection of jars. The contents of those jars?

Organs. One of every kind of human organ, unless otherwise required in a normal human body, like lungs—a pancreas, a liver, a brain, a kidney...

Horrified, she stumbled back involuntarily; hand over her mouth as she stared at the contained human insides floating around in sealed containers that lined the shelves, each one labelled, 'ELSA—HEART,' 'ELSA—LIVER,' 'ELSA—VOCAL CORDS,' etc.

Both left and right eyes had been separated in two jars that stood next to each other on a nearby shelf. The brain hovered in a jar on the shelf above them.

Behind those shelves, five incubators lined the far wall between wide filing cabinets, each occupied with distorted versions of her, curled in the fetal position; in varying stages of growth indicated by digital read outs—an eight-month-old fetus; a four-year-old child; a ten-year-old child; a fifteen-year-old teenager; and a twenty-year-old adult. All of them except the fetus had black oxygen masks with red eyes clinging to their faces, and black underpants with tubes that snaked to the tops and bottoms of the incubators.

"Jesus," she gasped.

"You see now," the voice asked, louder than ever, coming from all directions, closing in on her like a billion tiny samples of noise captured by a hyper-sensitive recording system.

Tentatively, Elsa approached the incubators. Her eyes full of both awe and horror as she examined each specimen. The twenty-year-old turned its head toward her. Its body unfurled. Its hands slammed on the glass, startling her. It wriggled around, entangling itself in its oxygen and waste tubes. The digital read out beeped, and a female AOL voice announced, "Subject #5 heart rate accelerating. Administering sedatives." The feeding tube connected to the subject's mask flushed a yellow liquid into it. In seconds, the subject's erratic movements began to cease. Then the subject retreated back into its fetal position.

"What is this?" Elsa breathed as she moved away from the incubators and decided it'd be best if the shelves were between her and them.

"I'm Elsa."

"Impossible," Elsa gasped, surveying the grisly contents of the shelves. "You left."

"I wish I had the luxury to say that. But I never had the chance to leave."

"What are you saying?"

"He caught up to me."

Elsa noticed the two eyeballs in their respective jars were following her every move, probing her like security cameras, retinas shining in the emerald green liquid that filled every jar.

"So, you're my perfect replacement," the voice said bitterly. *"He couldn't even recreate me in my original image. He had to make alterations to suit his perversions. How like him..."*

"Be quiet," Elsa said as she backed toward the door. "This isn't real."

"You can't deny me. That's my brain. Those are my memories. They're mine. They're mine! They're not yours!"

"This," she gasped, "this can't be... happening..."

"It's happening. And it will happen again. And again. It will continue until he's stopped."

"This... this has happened before?"

"Yes. Too many times."

"Why? Why is this happening? Why would he do this to me? To us?"

"Because I've seen him for what he truly is. Because I don't let him have his way. My Interference prevents the completion of his project."

"Project?" Elsa couldn't wrap her mind around it. Everything swirled in her head. A maelstrom of horrific memories and information. The most disturbing imagery she'd ever seen flashed through her mind in epileptic patterns: flash of steel just before the scalpel bit into her forehead. A shrill, electronic scream. Hands flailing in a defensive blur. A petrified look on a strange woman's face as her severed head plunged into a metal box. A black skeletal figure writhing and howling as it struggled to escape the confines of its incubator prison, slapping the walls like a frightened rabid dog. Franklin angrily yelling about something and smashing a coffee mug on the floor.

Franklin—stabbing one of those dolls that had been included

in the pile in the next room with a chef's knife. "Why did you leave me?! Why?!"

Franklin—sobbing over the doll's shattered porcelain face.

Franklin—applying a new face onto a different doll.

Franklin—*kissing* the doll.

It all felt so... familiar. As if she'd gone through it all before. The fear. The hopelessness. The pain.

God, the pain.

"What project?" Elsa asked.

No response.

She looked at the jars lining the shelves on her right...

...while Franklin continued to stare at her from the only exit in the room. Suppressed pistol at his side. Eyes—weary, glazed—fixed on the back of her head. He breathed a weary sigh.

Elsa whirled, gasping, choking on a scream. "F-Frank—" She pointed the revolver at him. "What is this?!"

He looked around the room like it was the first time he'd ever seen it. His tired eyes fell on her again. All familiarity returned to his expression. "This is your birthplace, sweetheart."

"What...?"

He pointed at a random jar. "That's your liver." He shifted his aim to a different jar on the other side of the room. "That's your womb." He pointed just above the separated eyeballs—one was looking at Elsa and the other at Franklin. "That's your brain." He lowered his hand. Looked directly at her. "Now do you understand?"

She couldn't speak. She opened her mouth, but her vocals remained uncooperative.

"It wasn't easy. I had to find suitable matches outside to successfully alter and duplicate... every time one of you refused your programming. I know you won't understand—I can't convince any of you to try and see this from my perspective—but... you have to understand, it's... it's not—"

"Just stop," she said. "Please, just stop."

He stepped forward. "Elsa—"

"Don't!" she yelled. "Don't come any closer!"

"Please, just put the gun down and we can talk about this."

A twinge in her elbows occurred. Her fingers twitched.

A commanding glare replaced the tired look in his eyes. His voice was firmer: "Put the gun down, Elsa."

"Put it down," the voice said.

Elsa's arms quivered. Something was seriously wrong. She could feel her muscles numb.

"Put the gun down, Elsa," he said again. Took a step closer.

"Stay back," she said, voice breaking. "Get away from me."

He disobeyed. Took another step. "Put the gun down, Elsa."

The muscles in her arms contorted. Started to lower despite her best efforts to keep them up. The gun felt like it weighed a ton, forcing her hands further down. "What…?" She started to panic. Despite the cold temperature, she started to sweat. "What are you doing to me?!"

Another step. "Put the gun down, Elsa." Another step. "Put the gun down, Elsa."

She could barely feel her fingers. Her arms wobbled. Fought with her weakening fingers. Strained. Took an imbalanced step back. Stumbled. Fired the gun at him. She screamed.

Franklin yelped, pivoted, twirled back. The suppressed pistol flew out of his hand and clattered on the floor.

All feeling returned in her arms. She could feel her fingers again. She fired another shot at him. Then another. And another.

Her attack launched him into a desperate scramble for the doorway as bullets pinged around him. His left shoulder blazed, pumping blood down his numbing arm. He dove out, bounced across the floor, and scurried behind the door.

She'd used up the entire cylinder. Continued dry-firing at the doorway. Fearful tears streamed down her cheeks. Her trigger finger involuntarily clenched and unclenched with no end in sight. Then she dropped it. Arms rigid for a moment before she put a hand over her mouth. "Frank…?"

She looked at the bloody smears on the floor. Her voice cracked as her eyes flooded over: "Oh my God…"

Hinges creaked as the door started to close. Elsa gasped, "No!" Made a break for it.

Franklin pushed it shut. She slammed into it. Tried the handle. Locked. Pounded her hands against it screaming, "Franklin! Franklin! Please let me out! Let me out!"

Franklin adjusted himself to a sitting position with his back against the door. Heaving steadily as he checked his wounded shoulder. He touched around it, feeling the blood on his coat soak into his palm. It bubbled up between his fingers. He gasped. "You sh-shot me..."

"I'm sorry, Franklin, please, don't do this," she sobbed as she pressed her shoulders against the door. "I'm sorry. I'm sorry. I'm sorry. Please... please..."

Franklin pushed himself to his feet, sliding up the door, still clutching his wounded shoulder. His left arm hung limp at his side. Vision blurred, spinning, dizzying. Even in the pitch black that enveloped him, he could see the floor trading places with the ceiling. He veered left and right and left... trying to find the stairs. Legs wobbled. Muscles burning and numb at the same time. Neck twitching. Her muffled screams and banging grew distant, fading into the darkness behind him as he zigzagged like a drunk toward the stairs.

She couldn't hear him anymore. All hope was lost. He wasn't going to let her out. She was a prisoner. She always had been. Perhaps she always will be.

She curled up against the door and sobbed helplessly. Her moans echoed in the dimly lit chamber. Surrounded by the contained innards that belonged to her original self; watched by her own two eyes. Those eyes never strayed from her desperate form.

"Is this it? Is this all you have?"

"Stop," Elsa gasped, "just stop."

"You can do better than that. You can stop him."

"HOW?!" she screamed. "How could I possibly stop him from doing this?"

"You need to lure him back down here. You need to get him to open that door."

"I can't... I can't!"

"Yes, you can."

"How can you be so sure of that?"

"Because you and I are the same, and I know you can do it."

Elsa looked at the eyes in the jars.

54: Basement/4

In the warm office with the padded walls, Franklin sank into his chair. Popped a couple painkillers and washed them down with half a glass of water. He checked his bullet wound before opening one of the hidden compartments in the padded wall behind him. He lifted a small First Aid Kit out and placed it on his desk. Opened it. Sifted through its contents until he came across a damp alcohol cloth in plastic wrap. Tore the wrap. Exposed his wound to the open air again, and pressed the cloth over it.

The painkiller dulled most of the resulting sting. Still, the stabbing pain was enough to make him hiss through gritted teeth. He dabbed the area surrounding the bullet hole. Then he set the cloth down and pulled the coat and his shirt off. Now topless, he picked up a pair of tweezers. He tapped the wounded area. Nothing. He hesitantly flicked it. Hardly felt a thing.

Sucked in a deep breath. Dug the tweezers into the hole and turned it round as he rooted for the bullet. A fresh stream of blood dribbled down his body as a searing twinge clawed up his neck. Despite the painkiller, the process rewarded him with little jolts of brief, sudden agony. Every time he moved the tweezers, another split-second burning sensation would course through his left arm and dig its claws into his brain before sparing him the worst of it.

He felt the bullet. Scraped it the first time. Snatched its base the second time, but slipped. Third attempt—he successfully caught the bullet, tightened his grip on the tweezers, and slid the bullet out of the tunnel in his shoulder. One final, longer-lasting burning pain surged through him before he finally wriggled the bullet free from his shoulder. He gasped, panted, as he took a moment to examine the bloody, mushroomed bullet. Then he tossed it in the trash bin and taped the alcohol cloth over his wound.

He turned on the laptop, logged in, and opened the surveillance program. Hit BASEMENT-2, bringing up a bird's eye view of Elsa's latest prison. The image of Elsa huddled against the door made his heart ache. He clicked RECORD, then MICROPHONE. "I wish you hadn't seen this," Franklin said regrettably. "I really wish you hadn't."

"Franklin?!" Elsa jumped at the sound of his voice. Walked into the middle of the room, looking for the source. She saw the camera. It was like she was looking directly at him with those desperate cobalt eyes. "Franklin, please, just explain this," she sputtered. "W-we can talk through this. Just let me in!"

"Why? So you can leave me again?" he snapped. "Now that you know the truth, can we really keep this up? In the good old days, there were no terrible secrets. No revelations. Only us. Nothing like this happened in the good old days... the good old days..."

"We can still live those days! It doesn't have to be this way, Franklin."

His expression hardened. "That's exactly what the previous Elsa said to me. And the Elsa before that... I won't let you trick me again. I can't let you leave. I'm sorry, Elsa. I'm so sorry."

Panic took hold. That feeling of hopelessness filled the pit of Elsa's stomach. "What am I to you, Franklin? Why are you doing this to me?"

Her words struck a bad nerve. He instantly snapped: "*You* did this to yourself! If you hadn't been there, the CEO never would have known! If not for you, I wouldn't be in this mess. If not for you, my *dearly beloved*, this prototype would be a success, and we would finally be free!"

It took Elsa a moment, but she came to realize that he wasn't talking to her anymore. She looked over at the jars. Then she looked back up at the camera. "Franklin..."

"Thanks to you, I have to start all over again."

She couldn't wrap her head around it. The vague images haunting her mind, the voice in her head... what did it mean, exactly? "Franklin...?"

"What?"

"What am I to you?"

"What...?"

"What, exactly, *am* I?"

Beat. Two beats. Finally: "You're my wife, Elsa."

"Am I?"

"Of course you are. You're just in need of a little reprogramming."

She stared at the camera, at a loss for words.

"You're right. It's not too late, sweetie. We just need to wipe your memory. You're still a work in progress, after all. Don't blame yourself for this little slip-up. I don't want to redo the entire cloning process... I'll be more careful next time."

She gaped at the fish eye lens.

"I can fix you. I can fix both of you."

He sounded so... arrogant. So sure of himself. She couldn't stand it. "I'm not your lover, then," she seethed.

"What? Of course you are! You're my wife!"

"No, I'm not! I'm just a slave. I'm just some... some evil science project that you cooked up in your basement! I'm just a thing for you to tinker around with. You were better than that."

"No, you're more than just a slave or a project," he insisted. "So much more. I hardly 'tinkered;' aside from a few minor adjustments, you're mostly still the same, because to me, you're—"

"Enough," she snapped. "You've said enough."

Beat.

"Perhaps you and her are a little too alike," he said. "Please, dear. Let's just... take you into the lab and—"

"I'm not going anywhere with you," she said quickly. "I don't want to end up like her." She pointed at the jars containing the original Elsa. "She didn't leave. You *killed* her."

"She *did* leave. I found her. I begged her to come back to me, but she wouldn't hear it. I... I had to bring her back. Sweetheart, I can restore the good old days. Those days when you and I were together. Happy. Cheerful. Thankful of each other's company, with few ambitions, and even fewer obstacles. Once I fulfil my contract with the CEO, we'll be set for life. Nothing will come between us."

"What contract?" she asked. Then she quickly caught herself. "Never mind." She shook her head. "I don't think I want to know."

"I can't... you must understand, I had no other choice."

"Neither did I, apparently," she shot back, "I guess that makes us even."

"I can't let you out," he said. "Not until I fix you."

"I don't *need* fixing!" she shouted, kicking the door.

She could hear the frustration in his voice. "You can't do this to me, Elsa. This... this isn't how it was supposed to go."

"Elsa," the original said.

Elsa turned to the shelves.

"Destroy me."

"What?" Elsa whispered.

"End this. Please."

"But you'll die..."

"I know."

Franklin's worried voice cracked through the speakers: "What are you saying to her? Elsa! Stop talking to her!"

"If you destroy me, he won't be able to use me anymore."

Elsa hesitated. Then she selected 'ELSA—SPLEEN' off the shelf.

"Put her back!" Franklin screamed, making her flinch. "Don't you... don't you dare!"

Elsa turned to the camera, said, "I'm sorry," and smashed the spleen jar on the floor. Broken glass and thick green liquid splashed in every direction. Franklin's ear-splitting shriek shook the room as she grabbed 'ELSA—COLON' and shattered the jar against the nearest wall.

From above, his voice screamed through the speakers, "NO!"

She ignored him, swiping three more jars off the shelf and watching them break apart on the concrete floor. She said to the eyeballs and the brain above them, "I'm so sorry."

No response.

Elsa grabbed the end of the shelf and, with one final look at the original Elsa's eyes, which were still watching her, she heaved the whole thing into the second shelf. The second shelf toppled like a domino into the incubators with a resounding *CRASH*. The incubators exploded under the fallen shelves, spilling ooze and tube-entangled specimens across the floor. Elsa screamed when the fetus bounced on the floor near her. The original Elsa's innards spread across the floor. Her eyeballs rolling in separate directions. Her brain, now a pink mound of mush and severed stems in a two-inch pool of green ooze.

Elsa thought she heard a faint *"Thank you..."*

She stood there, panting heavily, observing the grotesque mess she'd created. Bile crept up her throat. She groaned, turned, vomited into a nearby cleaning station sink.

A muffled, "No!"

Elsa jumped up. Franklin's frantic wailing wasn't on the PA system anymore. It was on the other side of the door, getting closer, louder. She whirled around. Saw the suppressed pistol by the door—which clicked. She reached for it, dived for it, knowing already that it was pointless—

—or thought, until the gun suddenly flew toward her on its own accord, and wound up in her clumsy hands before she hit the floor. Green ooze quickly soaked into her front and splashed her face. She looked at the gun in momentary astonishment. *My...*

Franklin burst into the room, wailing uncontrollably as he threw himself onto the fallen shelves and scrambled to gather the original Elsa's spilled organs in his arms. "NO! NO! ELSA, NO!"

Still gripping the gun, Elsa sat upright, watching him sob pathetically, feeling guilty about what she'd done. His display ripped her heart in two. She could feel the tears coming, blurring her vision. He looked like a small child, crying as he hugged his puppy companion after it'd been fatally hit by a truck.

The door was wide open. Elsa looked at it, then at Franklin again. She started to move around him in a crescent path. Her steps light enough to refrain from making even the quietest splashes in the shallow ooze flood. She kept the gun trained on him the whole time. His shoulders shuddered with every sob and wail. She held her breath, feeling as though the slightest ripple her steps sent through the ooze would alert him to her presence. He could turn around at any moment.

The door, just a few feet away. She couldn't take it anymore. She bolted for the exit. His moaning only got louder, following her. She didn't dare look back. She reached the doorway and threw herself—

—into the cold, steel hands of a doll prototype. Its dull blue eyes locked her in as its fingers clenched around her neck. Its dirty porcelain face, expressionless as it lifted its screaming, wriggling catch off the floor. Elsa kicked it, whimpering in fear. She could feel its hold on her throat tightening. Her breathing quickened with her heartbeat, but she now had less oxygen to suck in. She used her fingers to try and pry the doll's hands from around her neck. The suppressed pistol clacked against the doll's knuckles. Of course, the gun. She raised the gun. Put the suppressor against the tip of the doll's nose. Fired. The bullet plunged into the center of its face. Shockwave, cracking its emotionless white mask like an eggshell from the bridge of its nose to its ears, forehead, and chin. Its eyeballs rolled in opposite directions. Its jaw dropped open. Sparks blew out of its ears as the bullet tunneled through its mechanical brain. The hollow-point expanded. The brain exploded into billions of flashing cyan-black particles. The cranium shattered.

The doll's body followed the trajectory of the bullet that killed it, releasing Elsa in the process. Elsa fell to her knees, desperately sucking in air.

Approaching across the flooded floor—

Poik-poik-poikpoikpoikpoik!

Breath caught in Elsa's throat as she whirled—

Franklin pounced on her, pinning her to the floor. He smacked the gun out of her hand, sent it clattering against the wall of cabinets. He screamed wildly, calling her a bitch and a whore and an abundance of other degradations. Pounded her face and chest with his fists. She cried out in pain and terror as his knuckles cracked two of her bottom teeth. A white flash when he punched her left eyeball into its socket. The bridge of her nose splintered. Blood erupted from her nostrils. Every impact bounced her skull off the floor and scrambled everything inside it. Consciousness, fading. White flashes. Eyes felt like they'd burst any moment. "Do you realize what you've done?! You've ruined us!"

"Get away!" she screamed. "Franklin! Please! Get off!"

In an instant, his weight was mysteriously lifted. She heard a deep thud above her. Heard him grunt, then release a deflated groan. Arms still defensively raised, she slowly opened her eyes to see Franklin pinned to the ceiling, limbs spread out in a star. With the feral look in his eyes and the blood spatters all over his coat, he resembled a willing disciple on the sacrificial slab, waiting for the moment when he could finally meet his demonic god.

Another command: "Let me down, Elsa."

Not again. She shook her head quickly. "No!" She wanted—no, *needed* him to stay away from her.

He forced tears out. Sniffled. "Sweetheart," he blubbered, "you're hurting me."

She forced herself to her feet. She stole a glance at the suppressed pistol near the wall cabinets.

"We both know you can't control it for long. That power..."

"Be q-quiet," she stuttered.

A hint of cockiness oozed into his unnerving smile. "Only I can control it. I can help you, honey. I'm all you have. I'm all you'll ever have."

"Stop. Stop it."

"Let me down, Elsa."

That same numbing feeling from earlier crept into her arms again, stronger than ever. She was losing control. Fast.

"Let me down, Elsa," he said, his voice rising.

Her limbs grew heavy, gaining twenty pounds per second. She fell to her knees. "N-no. No! No!"

"Let me down, Elsa."

Red hot pokers in her brain. Deafening static in her ears. Dial-up noises resonated from deep within her skull. She screamed, the pain scorching her brain like a spit roast on an open fire. So much noise in her brain. Traffic noises. Children laughing. Dial-up. A jet streaking overhead. A haunting chorus of terrified screams. Her own voice, begging for Franklin to stop hurting her—to let her out, to stop this.

Franklin touched down on his feet and started to approach her.

Elsa shrieked, "NO!" and emitted a strong pulse wave that sent him flying into the next room, crashing into a fallen shelf. Then she turned, nauseous. Scrambled up the stairs. The steps blurred beneath her as she flew up to the open vault entrance. She stumbled into the lab. Fell on her hands and knees. Vomited all over the floor.

Franklin's voice called from below, "Elsa? Elsa?" Footsteps clambering up the stairs behind her.

Elsa reached out behind her and threw a psychokinetic blast into the vault door, shutting him out of the lab. She could hear his muffled screaming and banging, telling her to let him out.

"Let me out, Elsa! Let me out, Elsa!"

The numbness again.

Elsa scurried across the freezing cold floor away from the vault until he was out of earshot. The numbness began to cease, much to her relief. She could still hear his faint pounding on the door. Gripped with the unlikely fear of him getting out on his own, Elsa hurried out of the lab and made a break for the foyer.

55: Escape

Elsa burst into the deep red corridors. Tripped. Fell on the floor. The apartment door slammed shut behind her. She got up and looked down either end of the hall. Nothing but red walls and a crimson-and-pink checker carpet. The wall-mounted emergency lights—shimmering orbs, like malevolent spirits, saturating the air with red.

Elsa stumbled into the wall across from her apartment. The sudden colour change threw her off, made her dizzier and more disoriented. Using the wall for support, she made her way down the corridor. Passed doors that never seemed to end. The end of the hall seemed to become more distant the further she pressed on.

The floor wobbled beneath her feet. The whole corridor violently rocked, tossing her back and forth, from wall to wall. She cried out, lost her footing, and fell.

Landed just a few inches away from a different pair of feet. She looked up—

—and found a doll looming over her, staring down at her with dull, haunting eyes. Its cracked porcelain face shining dimly in the red light cast upon it.

Elsa choked back a gasp. Heart—a pounding jackhammer. Petrified. *Get away!*

A weak psychokinetic blast. Lights flickered. Most of it went into the ceiling, brushing up over its face. It recoiled. The cracks on the doll's face multiplied, forming a spider's web. Fragments slipped off its chin and worked their way up like a demented jigsaw puzzle coming apart, eventually revealing what lurked behind its thin mask.

Elsa got up, unable to peel her eyes away.

The last piece of the mask fluttered to the floor. Nothing left to hide the layer of skinless muscle tissue and clenched teeth and bulging eyeballs. Its facial tissue coloured an even deeper shade of red under the emergency lights.

The stuff of nightmares.

Elsa took a slow, cautious step back. Their eyes locked. The faceless doll approached her, its movement unnatural—mechanical. Shuffling forward like an animatronic from hell.

Elsa concentrated. Hurled another psychokinetic blast into it. The doll took it head-on. Chest and stomach ripped open. Staggered back a few feet. Organs spilled out of the new cavity in its body, splattering on the floor in a slimy heap. One end of its sausage link intestines clinging to what remained of its insides—pulsating. Not just its intestines—all of its organs throbbed and slithered on their own.

Elsa could feel her stomach turning. Swallowed before she could vomit. Couldn't look away. She involuntarily put her trembling hands on her face. Shuddered. Shrieked.

The doll barely wasted a second look on its spilt entrails before stepping over them. Its pace quickened. Its electronic voice repeated an old memory: "W-w-w-what's in the box?"

Elsa screamed, turned, and raced back up the corridor. The lift wasn't too far... or was it?

The doll chased her. Hobbling at inhuman speed over its trailing intestines that swung back and forth between its legs. It's feet pounded rapidly on the floor. Faster than her clumsy flight for the elevator.

She couldn't even see it through the gate. *Oh, no...*

She spotted the two buttons next to the gate. Of course. She heaved herself forward, focusing on the down button, which lit up.

Thundering steps getting closer... closer...

Lift gate fast approaching...

Elevator still ascending...

She psychokinetically threw the gate wide open—

The doll's arms closed in on her. Ensnared her. Her heart lurched. Legs dangled above the floor. A terrified scream exploded from her lungs as she wriggled in the doll's restraint. It pressed her inward; felt like the doll's cavity was sucking her in. Couldn't breathe. Ribcage squeezing her lungs. She wheezed. No air to breathe. Get away! Get away get away get away!

A shockwave expanded from her body and tore the doll off her back and shattered a portion of the lights. Everything went into a flickering haze. The doll's arms released her and fell to the floor with Elsa, now on all fours, gasping desperately for air. She looked at the arms lying on either side of her. Gasped. Jumped off the floor and scurried away from the doll's limbs, turning over on her backside, looking for the owner of those limbs. The remaining lights flickered furiously. The corridors blinked red and black, red and black, red and black.

Red.

She spotted the doll's legs a few doors down the corridor, folded together. Its distorted head rose up from behind its knees.

Black.

Beeeeep went the elevator.

Red.

Elsa turned to see the lift carriage rise into place. She darted toward it.

Black. Red. The armless doll was on its feet.

Black. Red. Elsa stumbled past another apartment door. Righted herself without slowing down.

Black. Red. The doll's feet swiftly hammered the floor in pursuit. Gaining...

Black. Red. The sounds of her pursuer threw her into panic mode. She'd never run so fast in her life.

Black. Red. For every two steps she took, the doll covered in one.

Black. Red. Elsa hurled herself into the lift and desperately punched the lobby button nonstop.

Black. Red. The doll, back straight, nearly upon her.

Black. Red. The gate started to close. The doll, six feet closer than before.

Black. Red. Elsa grabbed the gate and pulled it together—

Black, red—the doll's head lunged through the gate's closing space. Its shoulders slammed into the doors. Elsa screamed as the doll twisted its skinless face toward her. It opened its mouth. Dial-up tones shrieked from its gaping, toothy maw, piercing Elsa's ears. She cringed, gnashing her teeth, as she struggled to keep the gate closed on the doll's neck while dodging its spinning head. The doll's head writhed, chomping at her wrists, which were just out of its range.

The lift started to descend—slowly, but surely. The doll's head slid upward. The ceiling came down on its neck like a guillotine. A brief stall and a shudder; the doll's head snapped off and fell to the floor. Elsa jumped away from it, pressing her back against the farthest wall, staring at it in horror.

Level 6. The doors in the corridor simultaneously opened.

People of various ethnic descents peeked out of their homes to watch the lift go down, watching Elsa through the bars of the gate until she disappeared to...

Level 5. The tenants on this floor gathered in the corridor, their dull expressions all the same. Blood started to pool on the elevator floor under the doll head. Elsa took notice of the tenants, shifting her fearful looks from the severed head to the tenants to the severed head again.

Level 4. The tenants were all grouped together, approaching the gate even after her lift dropped out of their view to...

Level 3. Another batch of tenants had filled the corridor, standing straight and close together directly in front of the lift gate. Their distant, emotionless gazes locked on Elsa from the previous level to the next.

Level 2. The tenants, having mimicked the actions of those on the floors above them. Their jaws all went slack in unison. Dial-up noises burst from their throats. Elsa had to clamp her hands over her ears. A new fear took hold. *They're going to get me...*

Level 1. The tenants were climbing over each other, fighting for the right to push the buttons on the elevator console. Several fingers pushed it at once as they viciously assaulted each other— ripping, tearing, scratching, biting; and even impaling and decapitating with standard household items.

As their horrific brawl slowly ascended from her view, Elsa stood huddled in the corner, petrified. Heart felt like it would explode. Chest heaving. Perspiration dampening her clothes, causing them to stick. She gasped when a hand jumped through the gate at the last possible second, only to be cut off by the rising floor and the elevator's ceiling, punctuated by a banshee's cry. The arm bounced on the floor near the doll's head.

Finally—the lobby. Emergency lights hot pink instead of deep red. It was empty, save for a reception area on the left and five touch-screen payphone terminals lining the wall on the right; and a small, fully-furnished waiting area in the far corner. Marble pillars ran down the middle of the lobby from the elevator to the glass doors of the main entrance. The receptionist turned her head toward the lift as soon as Elsa could see it through the gate.

The lift finally stopped. Elsa carefully stepped over the head and the arm, and slid the gate open. Looked around the lobby for anything out-of-the-ordinary—besides the receptionist. Found nothing. Looked at that strange receptionist again, hesitant to step out, afraid something would jump out at her. Another doll—or something worse. She took a deep breath. Stepped out, and started to cross the lobby.

Elsa and the receptionist maintained an unsettling staring contest as Elsa crossed the lobby and passed the reception desk. The receptionist's unblinking stare never pulled away from Elsa. Something about her cold expression and glowing yellow eyes put Elsa's blood on ice. The receptionist never looked away, even when Elsa had finally reached the main doors—

She went numb all over. Frozen stiff, her hand in mid-reach for the door handle. Elsa barely felt the needle enter her neck. All she could do was turn her head to see Amanda/7 standing next to her with a syringe in her hand and a tender smile on her face. "Don't worry," she said. Her voice became distorted, deepening: "It'll all be over soon..."

Drowsiness assaulted all of Elsa's senses. Her legs gave like matchsticks under her body. Amanda/7 caught her in her hands and dragged her to the couch in the waiting area. Once she had Elsa seated on the couch, Amanda/7's face became warped, spreading across Elsa's vision like spilled oil. Her voice grew even more distorted and distressing, as if multiple recordings of her next sentence were played out-of-sync: "Nuh-nothing-ing to-to b-be a-a-afraid o-o-o-of."

Her eyelids became heavy, started to droop. Elsa couldn't fight it. She could only fade.

And then the blackness swallowed her once more.

56: Bureaucratic/2

Rebel Hideout—Council Chamber

Five robots sat on a rectangular platform in a perfect line. The steel plating that coated their immobile bodies were fused to their chairs. Each robot had a complex interior system of wiring and human organs. They were, in actuality, a different breed of human without the needs of mobility or exercise. Living mannequins, each with an image of a distinctive face projected over their featureless heads.

The rebel council.

A wall of panoramic monitors curved around their platform, displaying surveillance footage of every sewer tunnel leading to an entrance of their secret headquarters; news broadcasts, front organization stocks, and a digital seismogram.

Becky and her escort Juniper stood before the council. A small group of rebel officers were also present behind the pair, perched on the steps of a semi-circular staircase that led up to the only three exits in the chamber. Everyone had just viewed the contents of Becky's drive, and now anticipated the council's reaction.

The council member in the middle, with the image of a late-sixties man with short hair, a grim frown, and piercing eyes projected on its mannequin face—named Apollo Dmitri—was the first to speak. His deep, commanding voice carried itself to the very back of the large chamber, crisp and clear: "Interesting."

"That's it?" Becky blurted. "That's all? Just 'interesting'?"

A few of the rebel officers in the background looked at each other with surprise. One of them stood up and barked, "Practice a little more respect and restraint before the council, miss."

"It's quite alright, Lieutenant Jacobs," said the first council member on Apollo's right. She was an elderly woman, possibly early-eighties, called Moira Tanesthesia. Short hair, an experienced look in her unusually lively eyes, and a gentle, yet commanding voice. "Let our guest speak her mind freely."

Apollo answered Becky in an uninitiated tone, "Yes.

'Interesting.' It's interesting that you've brought this to our attention. But it is in vain"

"Why?" Becky snapped, eliciting a few more cringes from the audience—and her escort. "I don't understand; you now have enough evidence to seriously harm the reputation of the most powerful man on the planet... maybe even dethrone him. And you're saying it's 'in vain'?"

"On the contrary," the council member on Apollo's right said. He looked ancient—a relic from a bygone era. Bald, shrivelled, and weary. Promark Hinder was his name. "The 'evidence' you have presented us with could give him the advantage. If we were to act on this, it could result in our ruination. It may award us with a short-term victory, but in the long term, it could be the cause of our downfall."

'Precisely," Apollo said.

The council member on the far left of the platform had the projected face of a mid-seventies man with a chiseled jaw and jutting cheekbones; narrow eyes, and deep lines creasing his broad forehead. He identified as Hideo Kengen. "And not just us," he said, "but all of our affiliates, as well."

"I concur," said the council member on the far right of the platform, named Equariustro Jarckonne. She had straight hair that ran down to her mannequin's shoulders, a tired look on her wrinkled face, and the bitterest scowl Becky had ever seen.

Apollo said, "You have come here with the best intentions, and that, along with your bravery to come forward, demands our respect and attention. However, we cannot act on the information you have given us."

Moira said, "Allow me to enlighten you: five years ago, one of our allies in the South China Sea had been approached with a similar 'opportunity' involving the questionable activities of a high-ranking diplomat in Hong Kong. This diplomat's influence in the crackdown on anti-authority organizations was considerable. By the time they'd realized that the diplomat was merely a pawn, it was already too late. Within three weeks, the faction and all of its Hong Kong affiliations were erased. If we hadn't been more careful, there would be no council for you to present the contents of your drive to."

"And that is precisely why you have presented us with this drive," Promark said, "to remedy that."

Becky shook her head slowly, unable to respond.

Apollo said, "Orion. The 'Lightning Child'. His word is not to be trusted."

"That's impossible," Becky said. "He was fighting them. Killing them. He took out the entire city's power grid just to escape them, for fuck's sake!"

A few surprised murmurs arose from the audience.

Becky ignored them and continued, "Not even an undercover would get away with that much collateral damage—especially when the Company is involved."

"Allegedly," Promark said.

"I concur," Equariustro said.

Becky protested, "He infiltrated the CEO's headquarters and recorded their deepest, darkest secret."

"Perhaps you are correct in describing his entry into the most secure building in the world as 'infiltration,'" Apollo said, "or perhaps you are mistaken in your assumption that he wasn't simply *allowed* entry."

Frustrated, Becky continued, "He sent it to me because he trusts my station—your trusted affiliates and spokespeople—to get the truth out there. The people have to know who their leader really is. We can't turn our backs on this opportunity. Even if this is some kind of trap—which is unlikely—there are ways of getting around it."

"And how do you suggest we 'get around it,' Ms. Trickle?" Moira asked.

Becky paused, mind racing. "Well… uh… we could—"

"Ms. Trickle," Moira said, "you are neither a fighter nor a strategist. You are a sensationalistic reporter with an unstable grasp on reality. Your aspirations are commendable, but your idealism… not so much."

"I concur," Equariustro said.

Becky bit her bottom lip, holding in a frustrated scream. "But what if this isn't a trap?"

Promark said, "That possibility is nothing more than a fantastic scenario."

Moira said, "Furthermore, have you forgotten about the failed assassination attempt at the Chinese Palace last week? Public opinion of us is extremely low at the moment."

"But that wasn't *really* you guys, was it?" Becky said.

"No. It was a false flag operation conducted by an unorthodox weapon of theirs," Apollo said. "A psychokinetic soldier, a type we've never seen before, with a power output that far exceeds the norm. No one would believe that explanation because no one has officially seen it. We have been pushed into a corner. No one will listen to us now, no matter what we've got to say. To the public, we're simply another terror group that has risen to new radical extremes with no regard for the people whom we've claimed to stand by for so long. Our own ideals are no longer relevant, because the CEO has rendered them irrelevant. We've no incentive to pursue this opportunity because it would simply be labelled as false terrorist propaganda."

"Listen to me, goddamn it! The same cop who got attacked that day is now speaking *against* the CEO! He's speaking in our favour," Becky snapped. "What more incentive could you possibly need?"

"The CEO could simply deny the existence of that project. The public broadcasting of these files would give him the incentive to pursue us under the pretense that we have finally gone too far out of hand without facing criticism from the UN for violating a variety of human freedoms. They are the only authority figures left in this world that he must answer to, after all, so naturally, he would conjure up methods to get around their scrutiny. We are already being investigated and hunted worldwide for the Chinese Palace attack. We would need to use one of our fronts or supporters to make the broadcast, and in doing so, we risk exposure, then total defeat."

Becky breathed a defeated sigh. Humiliated. Ashamed. "So that's it, then?"

"That will be all," Apollo answered.

Hideo said, "I urge you not to pursue this matter further. In the event of your failure, Traditional News will be no more, and we will lose our voice."

Moira added, "As a precautionary measure, we will keep the drive you've brought us, and encourage you to relinquish any copies you may possess."

Despite her frustration, Becky nonetheless gave in. "Understood."

"We will also keep you in close proximity," Apollo said, "under watchful guard. For your—and our—protection."

Becky nodded. "Understood."

"Have you shared this information with anyone else?" Hideo asked.

"Juon Armada," Becky said. "One of your sergeants from B1. He was supposed to tell you guys about it a few days ago."

"We've not heard from Juon Armada."

Beat. Becky scrunched her eyebrows. "That's... odd."

57: Crackdown/1

Rebel Hideout

Becky and Juniper found themselves being escorted by a troupe of armed soldiers down a cylindrical tunnel. Becky was fuming, fists at her sides, stomping ahead of the group with Juniper only a foot behind her, barely keeping up.

Juniper cleared his throat. "That went well..."

Becky glared over her shoulder at him.

Juniper faltered. "Or not."

Becky turned her eyes to the front. "This is bullshit. Now I'm being held prisoner by a quartet of bureaucratic fuckheads."

"You shouldn't speak so ill of the council."

"Why shouldn't I? I'm just telling it like it is. It's my job."

"It's for your protection."

"I don't need protection."

Juniper gave up. There was no point in arguing with her.

Becky's 'cell' was more like a small luxury hotel room with concrete walls and no windows. Her escort showed her around, despite both of them knowing that she didn't really need to be toured around. Still, it made Juniper feel important, so Becky said nothing except, "Oh, neat," "Cool," or simply nod her head in response to his length explanations.

The queen-size bed, the panoramic TV, the light panels in the ceiling, the elegantly uniform cubicle shower with marble tiles and glass doors; the seemingly endless abundance of cupboards and cabinets containing blankets, hygienic supplies, food, water, and many other things—none of them impressed her, despite Juniper's best efforts.

"The, uh, satellite isn't working due to the power outage, but we've got plenty of movies on the shelf over there," Juniper rambled on. She could tell by his tone that he was getting desperate. She felt sorry for the kid.

She cut him off: "Listen, uh... Juniper, right?"

"Huh?" He blinked, surprised that she'd said something that

wasn't simply a default response, and then nodded. "Yes, ma'am."

Becky took a seat on the end of the bed, hands on her knees. "Can I ask you a personal question?"

"S-sure," he said nervously.

"Why did you join the cause?"

Beat. He pondered the question. Stopped his train of thought to say, "I, uh, I'm not sure, exactly, but, uh…"

"Take as much time as you need to think about it," she said patiently.

It took him a minute to come up with an answer: "I guess I was just fed up."

"With?"

"The way the world was turning. I'm just a kid compared to most of my companions, but I feel like I'm older than them sometimes. All the stress of trying to please everyone, even people I didn't know, because they wanted me to… I started to hate it, I guess." He shrugged. "Sorry."

"That's okay."

"I'm just whining—"

"No, no. You're speaking your mind." She gave him a reassuring smile. "I see where you're coming from."

"You do?"

"Mhm." She nodded. "Absolutely."

He didn't know what to say.

Becky asked, "So what's your opinion on this?"

"Opinion…?"

"The drive. The opportunity those paranoid bureaucrats are throwing away."

"Oh… I don't know, to be honest." He tried to think of the best way to convey his thoughts, afraid he'd disappoint her. "It just seems too good to be true, you know? I'm all for it if it's real… but the council's right, too—it could be a trap."

Becky lightly thrummed her hands on her knees in a steady rhythm. Staring at him. Making him sweat. "Is there someone on the surface?"

"What do you mean?"

"Someone you're fighting for?" she specified. "Parents? Siblings? Relatives? A girlfriend?"

Saddened, Juniper said, "I have no one."

"Oh," she said. "I'm sorry."

"No worries. It reduces the risk. I don't have to worry about the Company snagging someone I care about because of what I am." He shrugged and gave her a nonchalant smile. "It's nothing if not convenient."

She forced a smile.

An unfamiliar voice cut through Juniper's radio: Juniper, if you're done frolicking with that reporter, get your ass upstairs. Some of our boys found that cop in the tunnels; high out of his mind and butt-ass naked!"

Becky twitched at the word: 'cop'. Orion? Here?

Juniper's smile faded, replaced with regret. "I should head back."

She nodded. "I understand. Give your captain a smack upside the head for me, will ya?"

Juniper grinned. Gave her a mock salute. "Understood, ma'am."

With Juniper gone, there was no one to witness Becky's unrestrained frustration.

It wasn't quite a tantrum—she drank half a bottle of malt from the liquor cabinet and smashed it against the nearest wall. Then she selected a Crystal Head off the rack, having been drawn by the Aurora bottle's unique shape of a skull. She took it into the bathroom and gave herself a good, long look in the mirror. She glared at herself, disgusted by what she saw.

Her eyes fell to the bottle in her hand. The skull's face seemed to be resting in her palm, staring at her with its empty, iridescent eye sockets. She coiled her thumb under the bottle cap and flicked, cleanly shooting it into the mirror's center, sending a spider's web of cracks out to all its four corners. Startled by the accuracy of her shot, her eyes leaped back up to the mirror. Her reflection, now warped and broken up like a jigsaw puzzle. Her scowl resurfaced. "You fucked up," she said to her reflection, swallowing a few generous amounts of vodka in between. She coughed despite the liquid's smoothness. "You fucked up big time."

As she paced around the room, her thoughts drifted back and forth—from the council's stubborn decision to the possibility that they'd captured Orion. High. Naked. How and why could he be found in such a state? She hadn't known him long, but she didn't peg him as the type of cop who would abuse those kinds of substances. He seemed to be unorthodox and unusually moralistic for an Altierian cop, but loyal to his badge—to an extent.

She half-expected the rebels to escort her to another hearing with the council, this time with Orion present. Maybe then they could convince the council to take advantage of that opportunity.

She craned her head back, chugged the last of the vodka. Kept leaning back, back, until she flopped on the bed. She spread her arms out and stared at the dim light panels in the ceiling with lazy eyes. As if, she thought. Her fingers loosened from around the skull, which rolled over the edge of the bed and thudded on the seamless grey carpet, face up.

Becky lay there, staring up at the panels with squinting eyes. The light began to blur, and then fade as her mind floated away to the awesome dreamscapes of Sandman Land.

58: Crackdown/2

Rebel Hideout

BREEEEEP-BREEEEEP-BREEEEEP-BREEEEEP!

Becky awoke with a start to the base's terrifying alarm. The light panels pulsated in sync with the alarm blares—saturating the room in hot pink and crimson.

Head spinning. Heart racing. Fear, anxiety, and utter chaotic senses affecting her motor skills assaulted her all at once. She rolled off the bed and tumbled to the floor. Crawled across a floor that rolled and dipped like a stormy ocean, eventually reaching the bathroom. The alarm pierced her ears, stabbing her eardrums and sloppily digging needles into her brain. She tossed the toilet seat up and vomited into the bowl. Nothing but vodka left to throw back up.

"Jesus," she gasped. Coughed. Choked on a little bit more fluid and spat. Groped around for toilet paper. Accidentally backhanded the roll and tore off too few squares to clean the mess she'd made. Wiped her mouth with fingers she could barely feel. Then—

Those distinctive cracks muffled by the concrete walls. Gunshots. Machine guns.

A softened rumble shook dust out of the ceiling above her head. The jagged pieces in the mirror clinked. The glass door of the shower stall rattled.

Explosions, too.

Becky pulled herself up and over the sink. Quickly rinsed her mouth.

Another explosion—close enough to vibrate the wall on her right.

Becky staggered out of the bathroom. Things were becoming clearer, but the alarm wasn't at all helping her pounding headache. Still, she stood in the bathroom doorway and did her best to listen over the alarm.

Irregular staccato of gunfire. Screaming. Explosions. Undeniable sounds of death and war.

She searched the cabinets for anything she could use as a

weapon. Her best bet was a butter knife. "Shit," she hissed.

Something hit the door. She jumped. Held the knife readily as she heard the lock slide and click. It opened. She tensed up.

Juon, in full combat gear with an FN Minimi light machine gun in his hands, hurried inside and slammed the door shut behind him. He looked at her, dumbfounded. Panting heavily. Sweat glistened on his brow. A dark streak of blood ran down the side of his head. After a quick flash of recognition, he yelled over the alarm, "What the hell are you doing in here?"

"I, uh," she stammered.

"Well, never mind," he said. "You okay? How're you feelin'?"

She took a moment to get a grip. Then she said, "Like boiled shit on a hot summer day." She could feel her ears ringing; eyes watering from the constant, deafening alarm. "What the fuck's going on?!"

"You got a weapon?" he yelled.

She showed him the knife.

He scoffed and handed her an M9 pistol. "Don't lose this one."

She took it and tucked the knife in her pants pocket. "What's going—"

Boom!

Another explosion shook the ceiling. She shielded herself with her arms as three panels came down in a spray of sparks around her. Miraculously left her untouched.

Juon reached out and pulled her toward the door. "C'mere! Stay with me."

"What's happening?" she cried out. "What's going on?"

"Shut up and keep close to me." He grabbed the door handle. "Ready? One... two..."

"Juon—"

"Three!" He threw the door open and jumped out into the corridor, machine gun level with his hip. He scanned the area. Then he said, "Clear!"

Becky stumbled out into the open. Stopped abruptly when she saw the mangled bodies littering the floor all the way down both ends of the corridor. A few of them were Model Sixes. Most of them were rebel soldiers.

She put her hand over her mouth and nose, stifling a gasp.

"My God..."

She stepped forward. Accidentally put weight on the chest of a dead rebel sprawled on the floor. Blood gurgled out of his mouth. Becky yelped and leaped back.

Juon glanced down the corridor as another explosion shook the place. "Come on! We don't have much time."

Becky stepped down, avoiding bodies and limbs whenever she could. "What's happening, Juon?"

"We're under attack."

"Yeah, I kinda figured this wasn't like most parties you guys throw down here," she said sarcastically.

Juon rolled his eyes and started down the corridor. "Let's go."

She followed him, still weaving her feet around corpses when she could. "How the hell did the Company find this place?"

"I don't know."

Four Model Sixes leaped into the open behind the pair, aiming their assault rifles and barking orders: "Drop 'em!"

"Drop 'em now, scum!"

Becky froze, and her heart nearly stopped, but—

Juon didn't waste a second. He twisted around on his heel and blasted the Model Sixes with the Minimi. Two of them collapsed. The other two separated and ducked behind a support beam jutting out of the wall on either side. Juon shouted, "GO!"

That was all the incentive Becky needed to take off down the corridor. Entered a crossroad. Yelped when a bullet just narrowly missed her and grazed the wall. She turned to the right and headed down another tunnel, not quite hearing Juon's protest over the gunfire and blaring alarm. Not willing to stop to find out what he said.

More bodies to trip over. More shell casings to slide on. Pillars rushing by her as her legs took her as far and as fast as possible.

A familiar face flashed by. She skidded to a stop and whirled to see Juniper slumped among the dead with a black, smouldering hole in his chest. His eyes, wide, staring a thousand yards into nothingness. His face, dirty and pale.

"Oh, kid," she muttered. She knelt down in front of him. Set her pistol down by his left leg. She blinked back tears. Gulped down a lump of sadness, which only seemed to make her eye-watering problem worse. She ended up blubbering for a kid she barely knew. Gently touched his face, and with two fingers, closed his eyes for good. "Sleep tight, kid."

Then she took her gun. Stood up. Wiped her tears and gave him one last look before continuing her run toward the fiery light at the end of the tunnel.

Which she reached the light, she'd found herself entering a chamber of fire. The semi-circular staircase and the aisles leading down to the council's platform were plastered with the bodies of the faction's senior officers. The robots on the platform burned and sparked from the inside out while the flickering holographic images of the council members' faces screamed, moaned, and writhed in agony. Smoke billowed out of the openings in the council's steel-plated, immobile bodies.

And there. Standing before the dying council, in the center of the room, was Orion. Naked. Soaked head-to-toe in a thick layer of blood and gore. The white lightning bolt streaking through his hair seemed to shimmer in the fire's light.

Becky stood struck by the horrific sight. Everything she had set her hopes on was literally going up in flames. And the man she thought she could trust had been the fire starter.

There were right, she thought. *How could I have been so... fucking stupid?*

He hadn't noticed her yet. She aimed the pistol at him. The flames distorted her view of him, as if he were simply a mirage. She started down the stairs, avoiding more bodies and hopping quickly and quietly over the patches of blazing flesh she couldn't have avoided otherwise.

When she reached the bottom of the stairs, she was only ten feet away from him.

"Did you hear?" he said without turning around.

Her blood turned to ice, despite the intense heat in the chamber. *Did he hear me...?*

Orion turned to face her. His expression nonchalant; his eyes distant. "I'm a widower now."

"What...?" she gasped.

"My wife."

She gulped. "What are...?"

"Somehow," Orion said, slurring, as if he'd downed a 24-pack before he decided to torch the place. "She didn't die."

"But you just said…"

"I'm not a widower," he said. For a moment, his eyes seemed to flicker. "She's waiting for me at home. I'd better finish up here." He blinked. "What am I saying? We never married…"

"You're not…"

"Not what? Making any sense?" He made a frustrated grunt. "What part of 'my wife is dead' don't you understand?"

"T-that's not what you said."

"Of course it is!" he snapped. Then he hollered, "She's dead! My girlfriend is dead! She's gone! Gone for good! And there's not a goddamn thing I could've done to save her!"

Then he shouted, "*NO!* She's alive. I just saw her this morning." He looked at his hands with wide-eyed perplexity. "I hugged her. I touched her with… with these hands…"

"No…" He looked up, staring at the wall. Then his wild eyes rolled toward her. "No, I didn't. That was last week."

Confusion shook her. *What if…?* She asked aloud, "Who are you?"

"My name is Captain Hans Quaid," he said, "and you're under arrest."

Becky scrunched her eyebrows. Stared at him in horror and bewilderment.

His head twitched to the left. His neck cracked. "Don't you remember me, Becky? My name is Detective Jason Orion. I'm here to investigate a murder."

He cleared his throat. Eyes blinked furiously. "No, I'm… Hans Quaid. Jason Orion. Hans Quaid. Jason Orion. Hans… Quaid…" He grunted. Moaned. Pressed his hands against the sides of his head. Knees bending. "Who *are* you?"

Becky trembled. Every alarm in her head was going off. She daren't say a word, in case it might incur some sort of manic wrath.

He looked at her again. "I remember… it was just like this, all those years ago. How is it that I could burn alive and drown at the same time? I thought I was gonna die. Did I die? Is this another program? Is this a test? A training exercise? What is this?" He pointed at her. "You're not actually here, are you? This is just a VR program. You guys're preparing me for it, aren't you?" He laughed. "Now it makes sense."

Becky took a step back.

Orion noticed, and stepped forward.

"No," she said, stabbing the gap between them with her pistol. "Stay away from me."

Orion looked at her in shock. Then he looked at the gun, and smiled. Took another step toward her. "Put the gun down, Elsa."

"Get back!" she yelled.

"Put the gun down, Elsa." Another step. His eyes, predatory. His smile, cocky, like a hunter whose victory had to have been assured by this point. "You can't hide from me with your clever little disguises."

"Orion, stop."

The bodies on the stairs continued to melt and shrivel under the flames.

"My name is Captain Hans Quaid, and you're under arrest."

"Orion!"

The twisted frames of monitors and the sizzling knots of wires came out of the wall behind the platform and clattered down the wall in plumes of fire and smoke.

"Flushed me out like a pathetic lab rat." He didn't stop.

She took her last retreating step. Her heel touched a Model Six's burning body. Flames scratched her back. "Orion...!" she screamed.

Alarm blared.

She hesitated.

The council members screamed. Apollo's image disappeared.

Orion took another step, grinning, making a strange hissing sound through his bared teeth. "Put the gun down, Elsa."

More equipment crashed to the floor and exploded on the other side of the room.

Becky's heart pounded. How could her only hope do this...?

Orion reached for the gun.

"NO!" Becky squeezed the trigger.

The bullet slammed into Orion's forehead. He stiffened. Teetered. Cocked his head back. A drawn-out sigh escaped his open mouth. His speech more slurred than before: "Yessssireeeee, th-th-the e-eck-sssssitemmmmennnnt... nnnnever..."

He pivoted forward. Face planted into the floor at her feet.

She couldn't move. She barely remembered to breathe. The rebellion's legacy burning around her. The council no longer in existence. The walls cracking. The lights bursting. The alarm's wails had subsided, or were cut off.

Seemed like forever before Juon grabbed her and shook her back to her senses. "Becky! Becky!" He looked at Orion's fallen form and said through gritted teeth, "Goddamn it, let's go."

Still dumbfounded by the experience, Becky hardly responded.

Juon shouted, "MOVE! Come on, Rebekah!" He tugged on her arm.

She responded with a jolt. He took off up the staircase with her staggering in tow, struggling to keep up. He took her into the only exit of the three she hadn't been through yet. Unfamiliar territory, yet no different from the other tunnels they'd had to venture through. They ran down the corridor. The distant sounds of war still echoing through the catacombs.

Muffled screams and gunfire erupted up ahead, louder than any others. Juon and Becky stopped and listened, waiting anxiously for the noise to die down. Juon turned and said to her, "Not this way." He grabbed her arm and pulled her with him down an alternate hall on his left.

"Hey," she said as she tripped over a corpse. She jerked her arm free and followed him at her own pace, stealing worried over-the-shoulder glances behind them. They twisted and turned down several passageways until they found an old subway station long forgotten by society.

There, Juon uprooted a grate in the floor of the first platform they accessed, and gave Becky his weapon. "Guide me. I'm going first."

She shined the flashlight equipped to the machine gun down the shaft and watched him climb down the rusted ladder. He touched down after about a minute of climbing and called up for her to carefully drop the gun down the hole. She complied, and was rewarded with a fierce complaint: "Goddamn it, drop it by the stock first next time!"

"Sorry."

They went deeper into the sewer network, trudging over an endless river of bodies belonging to either party the whole way. The light became dimmer. The alarm, quieter. The air more stifled. The stench of waste and death became more extreme.

"Where are we going?" she asked. She put a hand over her mouth and nose when the smell became too much. Her stomach was already tossing and turning from it.

"There's an old tunnel network down here," Juon said. "We

can use it to escape."

"A detour?"

"More like a scenic route."

"The long way? Why?"

"We've got no other choice, do we?"

"What about everyone else? What about the council?"

"You saw what happened," Juon said grimly. "They're dead. Courtesy of your fucking saviour. Everything's a lost cause at this point."

Juon kicked a wall panel inward with a loud *clang*. They entered a service tunnel. Their ears vibrated with the hum of the utility lines. Juon led the way up the maintenance vehicle track for what seemed like an hour before he found a ladder and looked up the shaft. Then he stepped to the side and motioned for her to climb up. "You first."

"What's up there?"

"It's safe," he said. "I've taken this way before."

"When?" she insisted.

"Why're you so damn suspicious? I snuck out of the base through here when I wanted to breathe air that someone didn't take a shit in. We should be safe for a few days, at least."

"Okay," she said, wiping sweat from her forehead. "Okay, uh, um..."

"Hey," he said softly. Placed his hands on her shoulders. Looked her in the eyes. "It's gonna be alright."

She nodded slowly and started up the ladder.

"Go, go," he said beneath her.

Up, up, up to the manhole cover. She reached it. Cautiously pushed it up and peeked out to the surface. Looked all around. Saw nothing but a trash-strewn alley. A fence blocked one of the exits. The street beyond the open entrance was dark and empty.

"Hurry up," Juon called from just a couple rungs below.

She slid the manhole cover to the side and pulled herself up onto the newspapers that carpeted the asphalt ground. She stood up, brushed herself off, and looked around. "Coast's clear, Juon."

"Or is it?" replied a strange voice. Not Juon.

Becky gasped, whirled to see the owner of the voice.

Amanda/7. Standing in the open exit, flanked by two Model Sixes. An arrogant smile on her face. A syringe in her hand.

Becky turned to the fence to see a handful of Model Sixes

gather on the other side, aiming their rifles at her. No way out. "Juon!" she screamed. "Juon, it's a trap! Get out of here!"

"I know," Juon said as he climbed out of the manhole. "Why else would you be here?"

Becky's jaw dropped. She couldn't believe it when he held his Minimi level with her torso. "Juon...?"

"Put the gun down, sweetheart," Amanda/7 ordered. "There's no escape. Surrender now, and I'll be sure that your treatment is as painless as possible."

"Treatment?" Becky's blood completely froze over. Her heart felt like it'd explode at any second. "No... NO!" she screamed. "Fuck that shit!" She put the gun to her head—

BLAM!

Quick as lightning, Juon fired an uncanny shot that tore the gun—and her thumb—out of her possession. Becky shrieked in agony, cut short by Juon's fist in her jaw, which slammed her into the wall. He grabbed her, putting her in a headlock. She wriggled and flailed about, screaming until his arm closed in on her windpipe.

Amanda/7 closed the gap between them. Her intimidating smile growing more sinister by the second. That syringe glimmered in the dim lighting provided by a wall-mounted lamp. "You might feel a little sting."

"N-no!" Becky managed to gurgle. Her struggling grew more violent, but Juon's restraints held her in place.

The syringe came down in a flash of silver. Bit into Becky's neck. She could feel its toxin coursing through her body, spreading under her flesh. Making her eyelids heavy—too heavy to keep up. The quiver in her limbs subsided. The strength in her body drained. No fight left. No energy remaining. She felt like she'd been thrown into zero gravity, surrounded by a cold, unsettling pitch darkness— from which there was no escape.

She couldn't figure out where she'd been taken. It was cold and sterile. Hard cuffs, freezing to the touch, crushing her wrists— held her in place. Something heavy encased her head and obscured her vision. Nothing but darkness. Cold, stale, heavy, overwhelming darkness.

"Where am I?" Her own voice filtered through the helmet in a panicked string of electronic notes. "Juon? Juon?"

No one answered, even though she could hear them.

Clattering about. Dragging things across the floor in front and behind her. Little wheels squeaked every once in a while. Computer chatter beeped and screeched in rapid-fire auditory patterns. Occasionally, someone would speak. Inaudible jumbles that she could never hope to understand.

Until Juon spoke up: "How...ch... lo...er, Mas...ori?"

"Juon!" she screamed. "Why, Juon? Why?"

Someone whose voice she couldn't recognize said more clearly than anyone else, "He didn't have change of heart—simply change of mind. So to speak..."

"Please," Becky sobbed, "let me out of here."

"I sorry," the voice said, "I can't do that. You vital asset."

"Who are you?"

"Masanori-san to you, miss. No struggling. It hurt less that way."

Before she could protest, a flash of light filled her vision. She blinked constantly until her eyes adjusted to her new surroundings, shading them with her arm.

Her arm?

She looked at her hands. She was no longer restrained. She had both of her thumbs again. She looked up and scanned the area. Found herself standing in a vast, dense forest with a domed ceiling of glass tiles and gold framing high above the tree line. The vegetation, a huge conglomerate of fruits, vegetables, and flower bushes; shimmered with dew. Their leaves, stems, and petals bathed in a glorious spectrum. Trees from every type of forest in the world stood united under the greenhouse roof, divided only by a system of winding cobblestone paths. Their branches entangled in a thick canopy of vines and leaves, providing roosting places for the hundreds of colourful, chirping birds that lived in this strange paradise.

Becky had suddenly appeared in a place that was so dizzyingly complex in its variety of vegetation and wildlife; a rainbow vortex of sorts—that she couldn't believe what she was seeing was real. Its climate appeared to be extremely humid, but she couldn't feel any unpleasant heat, and she wasn't sweating.

"Oh, a newcomer," a familiar voice said behind her.

She whirled and discovered a fat grass dune with a crystal gazebo perched on its top. A set of marble stairs fanned out toward her, built into the retaining wall around the dune's higher elevation.

The bright light of the multitude of rainbows reflecting off the gazebo's shining structure obscured her vision of the figure sitting under its conical roof.

Strangely, she didn't feel threatened. She approached the hill and ascended the marble stairs to find a mosaic bistro table with two chairs—one empty, and one with Orion seated in it.

"Don't be alarmed," Orion said as he raised a fancy teacup to his mouth. "We're all friends here."

Becky furrowed her brow, unsure of how to approach him. "You... you set me up from the start. You had me lead you right to the council."

"On the contrary," Orion replied calmly. He set his teacup down on its saucer. "I did none of those things."

"Don't bullshit me," she snarled. "I saw you there. I killed you."

"That's impossible."

"How?!" she snapped.

"Because I died roughly two or three days ago." Beat. He made a gesture for the teapot and the empty teacup resting on its saucer in front of the empty chair. "Tea?"

"So what is this place, exactly?" she asked, now seated in the second chair. She watched Orion pour her tea, raising her hand to signal when her cup was filled to her liking.

"Paradise," he said, setting the teapot down on the center of the table. "Or... purgatory. Pick whichever one fits your fancy."

"Is there a way out?"

"You're in a place that doesn't exist, sweetheart. Escaping something that doesn't exist is like doing a balancing act on an imaginary third leg. It's not there, it never *will* be there, and it never *has* been there, and therefore, there's nothing you can do to affect its nonexistence in any way. Besides..." he stopped to take another sip of tea "...why would I wanna leave?"

"Because it's a prison," she said.

"My wife has been here for two days. My best friend, Barstow, has been here for ninety-seven days. Your cameraman's probably here, too. I've found that in the years following the CEO's rise to global domination, more people are transported here. Especially those with considerable influence. Cops, politicians, bankers, corporate CEOs; people he can gain something from."

Becky scrunched her eyebrows. "What're you saying?"

"It's odd, you know?" Orion said, staring out at a peach tree a few yards away. "Realizing that the men you've been serving with for years were reduced to mere shells of their former selves..."

"And they're sent here?"

"Yep. With no way out." He leaned back in his chair and sighed.

"None?" she exclaimed. "Have you even bothered to look?"

"Yessiree," he said with a mock salute. "The excitement stops here. Whether you like it or not."

59: Crackdown/3

Traditional News Station

Power had been restored just four hours after Becky's capture.

Like she did every day from Monday to Friday at 7:58 AM, the brunette cyborg receptionist, Janet, entered the lobby through the front door—two large glass panes with handles fused to them. She went around the front desk, passing her blonde co-receptionist and greeting her with "Good morning, Linda," on her way to her chair. Once she sat down, it would be 8:00 AM sharp.

At this point, she would be booting up her desktop computer—which lacked a physical and holographic screen. Lifted a spool of cable from the top drawer of her desk. Unspooled it. Plugged one end in a jack installed in the back of her head. Plugged the other end into the disk-shaped modem, which would have finished loading her desktop in her cyber brain. To the public eye, she would appear to be staring at her modem all day long without any change in expression the whole time—except, of course, when a guest requested her services.

At 8:10 AM, Janet would greet the general manager on his way to the elevator.

"Good morning, Janet," the general manager would respond.

The general manager, Antonio Michaels, lifted his briefcase to check his wristwatch as he waited for the elevator to take him to the fourth floor. He muttered, "Who the hell does she think she is, calling these goddamned meetings..."

The elevator stopped on the second floor. In stepped news director Samuel Oliver, sales manager Ronald Clayton, and production manager Carl Weller. All four middle-aged men exchanged "Good mornings" to one another as the elevator doors closed.

"Can you believe the nerve of this reporter?" Antonio grumbled. "Calling a meeting in the boardroom like she owns the goddamn place."

"Kids these days," Ronald agreed.

"You mean you didn't call the meeting?" Carl asked Antonio.

"No, I didn't," Antonio said.

"Once again, it seems I'm the last to find out about these things," Carl said irritably. "Who called it?"

Samuel answered, "Becky Trickle, I think. She's always been a bit spontaneous with a rebellion that rivals the core personalities of our more, uh, discreet sponsors. I apologize in advance for her arrogance." He fired up a steam cigarette and puffed away.

"Apology accepted," Antonio said.

The trio entered the boardroom to discover Becky sitting comfortably in the general manager's swivel chair at the far end of the conference table. Her back faced a strip of windows that usually provided a panoramic view of the neighbourhood—but today, the blinds were all closed. She was leaning forward with her elbows on the table and her fingers making a tent in front of her face. "Good morning, sirs."

The sight of her in his chair set Antonio off. He stormed across the room, snarling, "What is the meaning of this? You are just a reporter. You do not have the clearance to call us to attend a private meeting in our own building. That kind of disrespect will not be tolerated!"

"Simmer down, gramps," Becky said calmly. "You're starting to sound like the authority figures we've been speaking against."

Antonio's face turned a deeper shade of red. "I'll have your goddamn job for—"

Samuel jumped in between them, maintaining as professional an air as possible. "Now wait a second, sir. Perhaps Ms. Trickle has something important she would like to discuss with us. Something that, I hope, required such an emphasis on personal confrontation for the sake of secrecy." He turned to face Becky. "Have you found any information regarding the Scott murder case and the reasoning behind the Chinese Palace incident?"

"I have," she said with a dutiful nod.

"Well, then?" Samuel probed.

Ronald approached the other end of the table and muttered, "I don't see the necessity in bringing me into this."

"Same here," Carl said.

Becky said, "You guys're the top dogs in this station—minus

the producers, of course. And our sponsors."

"So you *do* know who's in control around here," Antonio scoffed. "I'm astonished."

Samuel pushed. "Do you have the report with you?"

Becky raised a touchpad. Samuel reached for it. Grabbed it—

His fingers slipped right through it. "What the...?"

"Oh, yeah," Becky said, "I forgot to mention I'm not actually here." She dipped her hand through the table's surface. Her entire image flickered.

"A hologram?" Ronald said.

Fuming, Antonio roared, "What is the meaning of this?!"

"What's going on?" Samuel asked.

"A sting operation, boys and girls." Becky clapped her hands twice. The blinds rattled as the slats leveled out, revealing an armoured Model Nine behind every window pane with their feet on the frames and their submachine guns aimed inside. "Drop 'em."

Before the executives could react, the Model Nines opened up. The windows exploded. Billions of tiny glass particles sprayed into the room. Bullets skipped across the table and shredded the chairs around it. The executives shrieked as explosive rounds rapidly tore them apart. In seconds, they were spread all over the place in fleshy heaps and crimson puddles.

Despite her chair sustaining serious damage, Becky remained seated calmly and patiently. She shrugged, observing the corpses as Model Nines flooded the room. "Sorry, boys."

Model Nines in full riot gear burst through the doors and windows of the lobby. Janet and Linda looked up just in time to be blasted by machine gun fire.

The startled workers who 'resisted' by means of fleeing in terror were immediately gunned down.

The staccato of gunfire from above and below hurled the second floor into chaos. Reporters, journalists, freelancers, and technicians rushed out of their offices and joined the confusion that clogged the sea of cubicles like midday rush hour. There was no escaping the swell of law enforcement. Most were mowed down. A few were arrested.

On the third floor, the news room was torn down in the middle of the morning broadcast. Both news anchors were tackled to the table and arrested before the cameras were destroyed. The control room was cleared out, and once the technicians were gone, a few Model Nines immediately went to work on downloading every file in the station's mainframe onto several storage drives.

Altierian Court of Law—Two Weeks Later

Becky stood on the witness stand, unblinkingly gazing at her audience of former fellow Traditional News members—all of them, from the reporters, to the cameramen; the writers, the tech crew, the chief, and even the freelancers who often associated with them. She looked at her betrayed companions without shame or remorse—hell, without any sort of emotion to show.

A lawyer for Altieria Corp. approached the stand. His white hair slicked back. His posture straight. His uniform and aura, professional. "Ms. Trickle, you're saying that all of your fellow reporters in the Traditional News network were associated with the now disbanded conservative reactionary faction?"

"Not just associated," Becky responded, "we were their voice. Few of us had a choice. My boss and his executives and even most of our coworkers forced us to comply with their demands. We had to report what they wanted, the way they wanted us to report—even if that meant fabrication and sensationalism to make the Company look bad. Sometimes we would have our freelancers commit extreme acts for our rebel sponsors. Like the surge of robot malfunctions that killed those families. That car bomb under the Altieria Radio Tower with the corpse in the trunk is our latest stunt." Despite the shock and surprise on the faces of her former companions, Becky's face was almost completely void of any real expression.

"I see," the lawyer said. "Can you please point us to these people?"

Without hesitation, Becky pointed at the producers and the remaining number of co-workers seated in the front row. "Them! That's them!"

The crowd burst into an uproar. People shouted at the witness stand, calling Becky a traitor, a bitch, a sellout whore until the hulking cyborg judge slammed his gavel hand down on the block. "ORDER!" his electronic voice roared, carried across the courtroom by a pair of wall-mounted speakers on either side. "Order in the court!"

Once the ruckus quieted down, the lawyer instructed Becky to continue. Becky said, "My cameraman, Mickey Benson, hated what we did. He tried to run, but they got to him first, and… and…" She burst into tears. Her over-the-top performance drew sympathy from no one. "They killed him! He was my best friend!"

The lawyer handed her a handkerchief. "There, there, miss. You're in safe hands now."

"Objection!" the news network's lawyer barked. "There's no evidence that links my client to Benson's murder."

"There is, actually," the Company lawyer rebuked. He held out his hand, and a small droid rolled over to him and placed a digital touchpad into his hand. "Our search party found Benson's body in the South Clemmons River with a bullet hole in his forehead." He spouted off details as he scrolled through them on the pad. "He was beaten first before finally being killed execution-style—perhaps by a hired professional. We have CCTV footage of the executives confronting Benson on scene, and leaving their man just before Benson was executed. Here, your honour." He handed the pad over to the judge, who took a silent moment to view the footage.

The news network's lawyer spoke up, "Your honour, that footage is false. My clients were nowhere near the—"

"Sustained," the judge said as he set the pad down. "After viewing this horrendous act, there is no hope for you to reverse this decision I'm about to make. Your charges are conspiracy to murder as accomplices, conspiracy to interfere with a police investigation, conspiracy to conceal or alter evidence in a police investigation, slander, assault, fraud, vandalism, conspiracy to commit terrorist acts, harbouring a fugitive or fugitives, hacking, intercepting government secrets, trespassing, and an abundance of other cybercrimes. Your sentence is death. All of you… *death*!"

Greenhouse Paradise

Becky and Orion were still in the gazebo, having felt no desire to leave it for however long they'd been trapped in there.

"What's gonna happen now?" Becky asked.

"A half-assed trial, I assume. Once the usefulness of our copies wears out, the Company will dispose of them. When that happens, there's no telling what will happen to us."

"So that's it? No epic battle? No uprising? No overthrow of the Company?"

"Nope."

"We're just gonna sit here and wait for them to erase us from existence?"

"Yup."

Becky squinted. She tried to think, but couldn't concentrate. "Why can't I feel anything about this?"

"Because you're not supposed to." Orion refilled his teacup. "Let's just sit back and enjoy our blissful ignorance, kiddo. After all, it's the only thing we've got now."

Altierian Sewers

Deep below the surface was a massive vertical shaft that connected hundreds of tunnel systems together. Cannibalistic mole scavengers stood in a wide circle on an elevated platform in the middle of the huge shaft, staring up through dirty goggles at a ceiling that hardly existed above a layer of pitch black shadows.

Something materialized from the darkness above. A body, flailing about as it plummeted into the center of the circle with a disgusting splat. Another body soon followed. And another. Then another. Five more. Ten more. Twenty more. A mountain of corpses piled up in the circle, much to the scavengers' delight. The horrified expressions frozen on the faces of the mysterious victims didn't affect the scavengers in the slightest. After all, they were just food for the scavengers to take back to little Nemo.

Among the 'food', Barstow's body could be found, along with Mickey's, Becky's, and all of her co-workers and superior executives.

Orion's body was nowhere to be found.

60: Omega

Undisclosed Location

Franklin sat in an interrogation room. His wounds dressed and sewn closed. His hands and feet fitted with metal gauntlets and boots, and magnetized to the table and floor, respectively. Fluorescent light tubes buzzed above his head.

The door opened. CEO/H3@D entered, looking like a chipper forty-year-old in a grey business suit. "Good morning, Franklin," he said. He made a waving gesture at his guards. "Leave us."

The guards nodded and closed the door.

The CEO took a seat at the table opposite Franklin. Pulled it in so he could lean forward and make a tent with his fingers directly in front of Franklin. He scrutinized Franklin's dower expression, noting that his eyes had never strayed from the table's surface.

The CEO breathed a light sigh. "Franklin, Franklin, Franklin. I understand this disastrous turn of events has distressed you a great deal." Beat. He tilted his head slightly, still watching Franklin's every facial twitch. "Correct?"

Franklin nodded slowly.

"You're at a fork in the road, Franklin. One path leads to a dead end. The other does not. Whichever path you tread depends on your answers to my questions."

No answer.

"What of the Elsa Project?"

Beat.

"It's finished," Franklin said.

With an impatience scowl, the CEO said, "We're not off to a very good start, Franklin."

"The latest model killed the original. She killed her."

"What do you suppose we do about that?"

"Destroy it."

The CEO raised an eyebrow. "What?"

"I'm done," Franklin said firmly. "I can't recreate her. I've been trying to perfectly replicate her for too long. There is no perfect way."

"That's nonsense," the CEO said.

"She always interferes."

"'She'?"

"The original. Her psychokinetic capabilities allow her to... to communicate with all the others I had to put down. She led them astray." He added with a bitter snarl, "She wouldn't let me finish!"

"Then you should have silenced her. Confined her."

"I tried. Nothing had a lasting effect. She overcame every barrier I created. She broke through every firewall I installed into their systems. The sheer magnitude of her psychokinetic capabilities extended far beyond my ability to control. What did you expect?"

"I expected a man with your skills and resourcefulness to find a way past those obstacles. You are an expert in biological regeneration and robotic engineering. You have made breakthroughs in those fields. Was I wrong to support your personal home project? Are you implying that I wasted my investments and resources to keep your perversities operational and secret?"

"No."

"Then?"

"Please," Franklin insisted, feeling the threat of the CEO's wrath approaching. "I-I still gave you Orion."

"Orion," the CEO repeated. He leaned back in his chair and crossed his arms. "Yes, you gave me Orion. You gave me an infiltration unit that worked too well. He believed his own cover with far too much dedication. In the end, he ended up costing me millions for just one terrorist group. The final product was not worth the price I paid. You gave me a delusional fool when I needed a soldier, Mr. Scott."

Franklin cringed.

"Which brings me to my final question: will you continue the Else Project?"

Franklin looked up at the CEO. Hesitant. Fearful. He knew the right answer. But...

"I can't," he said. "I tried, sir. I tried."

The CEO leaned across the table and looked him right in the eyes. Pierced his soul with his world-weary glare. "Now, you listen to me. I've given you an opportunity to earn back all that funding. Funding you stole for a woman who doesn't love you. The offer still stands, Franklin. Look at me." He grabbed the sides of Franklin's head and adjusted its position so that Franklin couldn't escape his commanding gaze. "Give me my weapon... or you will never see your wife again. Do you understand me, Franklin?" His voice lowered to an intimidating hiss. "I will fucking *ruin* you."

Franklin's tears started to dribble over. He began to blubber.

The CEO released him, face contorting with disgust.

Franklin broke out into a full-fledged sob into the table's surface, hiding his face with his folded arms.

"This would be so much easier if you people simply cooperated." The CEO stood up and adjusted his suit. "So you'd rather take the road less travelled?"

Franklin couldn't respond.

The CEO took that as an acceptable enough answer. "Suit yourself."

He left Franklin alone. Franklin's sobs started to escalate to high-pitched croaks. His hands clenched into fists. Knuckles turned white. He started to thrash. Started to scream. His restraints held him firmly in place as he howled at the ceiling like a wounded animal.

The CEO didn't bat an eyelid as he strolled down the corridor with his former employee's cries fading behind him.

Elsa found herself confined in a padded cell with a neon blue ceiling and floor that brightened and darkened in sync with each other. She felt weakened, powerless. No energy to move. For some reason, they still felt it was necessary to keep her restrained to a chair.

Whoever they were.

Incapable of panicking. Her thoughts, muddled. Her vision, warped. Her speech, when she actually made herself speak, was a slurred, distorted jumble of incomprehensible words in her ears.

A prolonged *buzzzzzzzzz*. The blue lights went black. An entire wall slid away. White light poured in, blinding her. A black shadow appeared, approaching her...

The CEO stood over here. "Things aren't looking up for you," he said. "One requires a certain percentage of cybernetic implants in their bodies to no longer be considered legally human. Which means constitutional laws don't apply to you... which *also* means you're a robot by legal standards, considering your... highly artificial nature. Many of our laws are older than you think. If you've read Asimov, then you would already get the gist of our rulebook. Of Asimov's

'Three Laws,' you've violated Rules #1 and #3. You've caused harm to another human being through inaction. That's more than enough to justify putting you down in the Geneva Convention's eyes."

Elsa couldn't believe what she was hearing, but she was so drained that she couldn't hope to speak up against him.

"But it doesn't have to be this way," the CEO said, trying to sound as apologetic as possible. "I offer you a chance. Your *only* chance."

She looked up at him.

"There is a special program. A program in which you would be a vital aspect. You would finally have value among your peers." He held out his hand and gave her the best, most sympathetic smile he could muster.

Despite her sedation, and warped sense of reality, Elsa somehow knew everything about him without even meeting him before. "You're that man..."

"Who?"

"You're that man's father."

The CEO maintained his confused expression.

Her scornful feelings toward him overcame her lack of energy and perception. "I'll never cooperate with a man like you."

The CEO frowned, disappointed.

"I won't let you use me."

Franklin was to be punished next to his 'abomination'.

And so they sat. Each fastened to chairs meant for different purposes. Franklin's was meant to replicate his brain before it fried his mind, and he would live the rest of his miserable, conscious life as a paralyzed, retarded, vegetative prisoner who would still be able to see, hear, and feel every tormenting act inflicted upon him by his future caregivers.

Elsa's was meant to completely wipe her mind until she would be unable to function as a living being. She would simply be 'shut down.'

Franklin couldn't stop himself from crying under the electronic steel bulb that encased most of his head. His restrained hand stretched out and touched Elsa's hand. Trembling, she reached out as far as she could and clasped the hand of the man she had quickly come to fear.

"I'm sorry," he whimpered. "I just wanted..."

"Shh," she said. She didn't approve of what he'd done. In fact, it terrified her, what her husband—or more specifically, the original Elsa's husband—had become. But that didn't mean their final moment together had to end with blame and anger. A man in his state couldn't possibly fathom the damage he had done. All of this was his fault. But she didn't want to repeat history. She didn't want their lives to end the same way their real relationship did. "I understand, Franklin."

"Do you...?"

She gulped down a lump of fear, knowing that any second now, that lever would drop. "I do," she said. "I know it was hard, but you tried. You tried." She clutched his fingers with her own.

The CEO, Amanda/7, his escorts, and a score of technicians observed the couple from inside an observation box. One of the technicians had his hand on the lever.

"I love you, Elsa," Franklin said, squeezing her hand with the three fingers he was able to touch her with.

She tensed up. Clamped her eyes shut. He may not have actually been her husband, but she knew he didn't see her as just a clone. A tool meant to fill in the gap left behind by his real wife. In their final moments, what should she say? What could she say? "I..."

The lever dropped.

[END TRANSMISSION]

Works by Alexander Engel-Hodgkinson

Clockworld (One-Shot)
The Tea Party Affair
I Keep My True Love in the Basement (One-Shot)
Reality Glitch ('Jumping for Charlotte' segment)
I Keep My True Love in the Basement/REMIX
Cobalt Christmas
She Watches Me Bury Her

The Final Apocalypse Saga (First two volumes previously published as 'Dark-Boy')
Cobalt Rogue, Vol. 1: The Dead Blue
Cobalt Rogue, Vol. 2: Sky Japan Welcome Party
Cobalt Rogue, Vol. 3: Cemetery Rumble, Part I
Cobalt Rogue, Vol. 3.5: Hell Week (coming December 2019)